those people

Also by Louise Candlish

Our House
The Swimming Pool
The Sudden Departure of the Frasers
The Disappearance of Emily Marr
The Island Hideaway
The Day You Saved My Life
Other People's Secrets
Before We Say Goodbye
I'll Be There For You
The Second Husband
Since I Don't Have You
The Double Life of Anna Day

those people

LOUISE CANDLISH

SIMON & SCHUSTER

London · New York · Sydney · Toronto · New Delhi

A CBS COMPANY

First published in Great Britain by Simon & Schuster UK Ltd, 2019
A CBS COMPANY

1 3 5 7 9 10 8 6 4 2

Simon & Schuster UK Ltd
1st Floor
222 Gray's Inn Road
London WC1X 8HB

Simon & Schuster Australia, Sydney
Simon & Schuster India, New Delhi

www.simonandschuster.co.uk
www.simonandschuster.com.au
www.simonandschuster.co.in

A CIP catalogue record for this book
is available from the British Library

Hardback ISBN: 978-1-4711-6807-9
Trade Paperback ISBN: 978-1-4711-6808-6
eBook ISBN: 978-1-4711-6809-3

Typeset in Sabon by M Rules
Printed and bound by CPI Group (UK) Ltd, Croydon, CR0 4YY

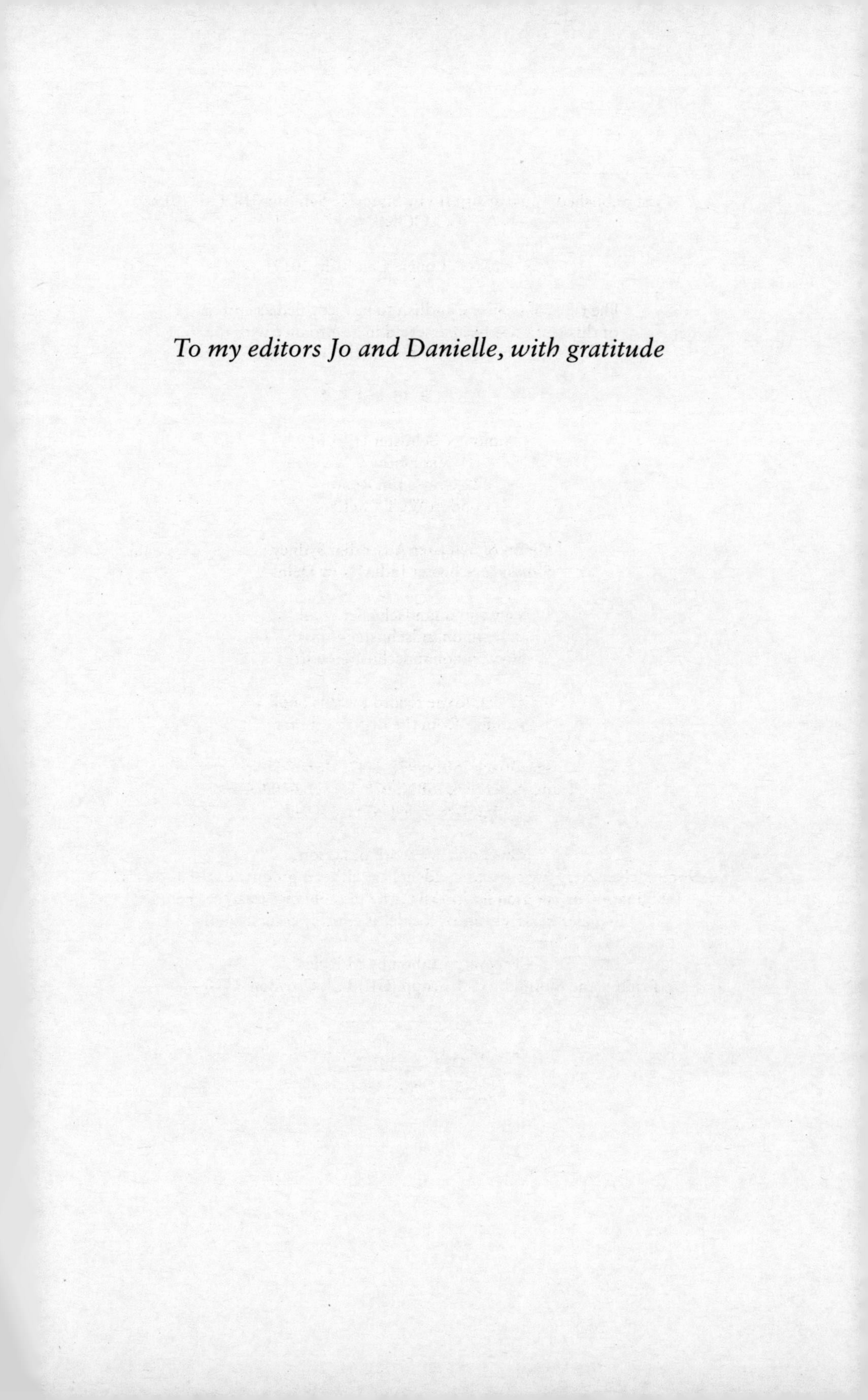

To my editors Jo and Danielle, with gratitude

1

Ralph

—Yes, we're aware that someone's been killed, of course we are. What a terrible way to die, absolutely horrific. My wife was one of the first on the scene. She's over the road right now at number two, Sissy Watkins' house – Naomi Morgan, she's called, you've probably spoken to her already?

—I personally wasn't here, no, I was playing tennis at the club on the other side of the high street. I must've left here at about eight.

—Yeah, it all looked normal on the corner when I left. The usual scrapheap. Piles of rubble everywhere, cars wedged in like some crazy 3D jigsaw. A total disaster zone. Listen, I don't mean to do your job for you, but you'll save yourself a whole lot of legwork if you forget the rest of us and go and ask him how this happened.

—Darren Booth, of course, who do you think I mean? The man responsible for this tragedy! And

while you're at it, maybe you should find out from the council where they've been while all of this has been going on, eh? If you ask me, they've been completely negligent these last few months. These budget cuts have gone way too far and all it takes is one character like him and suddenly we're living in the Wild West.

—My relationship with him? Mutual hatred, I would say. I recognized his type straightaway. Doesn't give a shit what anyone else thinks. Uncivilized, basically. I remember the first conversation we had – if you can call it that – the weekend he moved in. He almost came at me with a hammer . . .

Mr Ralph Morgan, 7 Lowland Way, house-to-house inquiries by the Metropolitan Police, 11 August 2018

Eight weeks earlier

The first clue that something was amiss that Friday evening was that the parking space outside his house was occupied by a filthy white Toyota so decrepit it was bordering on scrap. Certainly not the vehicle of choice of anyone *he* knew on Lowland Way.

If you entered the street from the park end, as Ralph generally did when he drove home from his warehouse in Bermondsey, you proceeded along a sliding scale of house sizes – and prices – from pretty workmen's cottages through narrow three-storey terraces to the large detached Victorians at the Portsmouth Avenue end. These were indisputably the prize properties, their old brick glowing furnace-red in spectacular contrast to the green of the elms that lined the road.

Ralph and his family had occupied number 7 for over fifteen years, while, right next door at number 5, his brother Finn and his family had been in residence for twelve. It was as good as it got, the brothers agreed, and for half the price you'd pay in some parts of London.

Parking was the big compromise. The front gardens were too shallow for off-street parking and the street bays were unrestricted by the council, which effectively meant a free-for-all. Hence the occasional intruder.

Nosing past the Toyota, he became aware of his windscreen blurring. It took him a second or two to register that the wall of number 1 was being smashed to smithereens by some barbarian workman, a dust cloud drifting into the road. Nearby, a white-panelled van hogged the spaces of two cars, which explained the parking disruption.

'What the hell . . . ?' Ralph pulled over, wound down his window, and called to the builder: 'Excuse me, what's going on here?'

The guy didn't hear him. Under his grey overalls, his physique was unexpectedly slight given the dirt tornado he'd produced single-handedly.

Ralph raised his voice: 'Hey! Can you please stop!'

This time, the worker halted, remaining for a second or two with his back to the street, to Ralph's car, with a stillness that struck Ralph as a little sinister. Then he turned and approached, lump hammer in hand. His face was smeared with dirt, his expression casually defiant.

'Can I ask who hired you to knock down this wall?' Ralph said.

'You can *ask* what you like, mate.' The accent was standard South London, not Eastern European as Ralph had naturally expected, and the mild tone made Ralph's own sound peremptory, officious.

'Was it the council? Because they've got no right to demolish it. This wall is one hundred per cent the property of number one, I've seen the documents with my own eyes.'

Occupying a generous plot next to Finn's house, semi-detached numbers 1 and 3 were the only pair of post-war houses on the street and, set back far enough to allow a short, shared drive, the only ones with private parking. The high wall on the corner, all that remained of the original Victorian villa that had been flattened in the Blitz, had in recent years been under threat by the council, who wanted to widen the left turn from Portsmouth Avenue – basically turning Lowland Way into a rat run. Supported by the owner of number 1, Old Jean, the Morgans had led the campaign against – and won.

Since late December, when Jean had passed away, the house had stood empty, the wall forgotten. Ralph had taken his eye off the ball, evidently.

A new thought struck him. 'Unless . . . wait, is there a new owner? Is that who hired you?'

'There *is* a new owner, yeah.' There was a malevolent swagger to the way this guy gripped his hammer, Ralph's open window just swinging distance away. How easily he could bludgeon Ralph's skull if he chose!

Ralph's fingers hovered over the window controls. He was

experiencing a primitive antipathy towards this person, as if encountering a member of a rival tribe who'd entered his settlement without permission. He jerked his gaze back to the man's face, tried to size him up. He must be, how old? Mid-fifties? He had a large bald patch, pink from sun or exertion, and deep facial lines mortared with dirt: older than Ralph, certainly.

Ralph coughed, the dust catching in his throat. 'Can I have his number? I'll fill him in on the situation.'

'Another time, mate,' the builder said. 'I'm in the middle of something here.' And returning to the wall, hammer raised, he smashed it with an unrestrained violence that made Ralph brace in his seat.

Plucking lines from his anger-management toolkit – *Breathe out more than in . . . Repeat to yourself: you are perceiving a threat that may not be there* – he sealed the window shut and reversed down Lowland Way and into the first available space, all the way back at number 19. He was normally very skilled at parallel parking, but this evening it was necessary to make several adjustments before he finally turned off the ignition.

Checking his phone, he saw, too late, a missed call from Naomi, followed by a text:

New neighbour at No. 1, looks tricky! Come straight home and let's discuss.

Oh, fuck.

Letting himself in, Ralph struggled to reconcile his horror at the wall demolition with the nervous exhilaration of renewed battle.

'You seen what's going on out there, Nay?'

'I certainly have.' Naomi was in the kitchen at the back of the house. The co-founder of a website for mums of pre-schoolers – 'curator, not editor,' she would correct Ralph – she was based at her partner's live-work unit a twenty-minute power-walk away and usually had dinner underway by the time he arrived home (Ralph prided himself on taking over the cooking at weekends). Lean in grey activewear and tall even in black ballet pumps, she looked like a wife and mother in a commercial as she stood at the marble-topped island, tossing the glistening leaves of a salad; as usual, she scooped the cherry tomatoes to the top in the hope of hoodwinking the family's lettuce-haters.

At his approach, she turned, tongs raised. A strand of dark hair – long and smooth, policed regularly for grey – drifted into her eye and she used an elegantly bent wrist to dislodge it. 'I'm as appalled as you are, darling, believe me. But it's too late to save the wall, so there's no point getting into a row with the new owner tonight. I thought we'd go and introduce ourselves to him in the morning when the dust's settled – literally. Find out his plans, stop him from doing anything else crazy.'

As if by his master's voice, Ralph was soothed. There was a lifetime of confidence in Naomi's well-formed vowels, the conviction that she would not just meet your expectations but blow them out of the water. 'What makes you think this bloke is the owner? I thought he was just the builder.'

'I checked the Land Registry website and it's showing someone called Darren Booth. I googled him and found a photo. It's definitely the guy who's smashing the wall.' Finished with the salad, Naomi opened the fridge and handed

Ralph a beer. Friday was one of their four permitted drinking nights, with the declared long-term aim of shrinking it to two. Though the kitchen doors were fully open to the garden, there were enough appliances humming to obscure any building noise three doors down.

He took his first swallow. Okay, so he'd made a mistake, that was not the way he should have handled interaction with a new neighbour. No need to bore Naomi with the details. 'There isn't any preservation order, so I suppose there's nothing to stop him replacing it if he doesn't like the style,' he conceded.

This they knew only too well. As a community, the residents took great pride in their street and had gained modest celebrity with Play Out Sunday, their initiative to clear the street of traffic so the kids could play outdoors the old-fashioned way (Naomi's brainchild; she'd been given an award by the mayor). Aesthetically, however, each household was free to make its own decisions, thanks to the council's irritating tolerance on building permissions.

'Do we know anything about him?' he asked. 'Where he's come from?'

Naomi began laying out plates and pairing cutlery. 'He's not on Facebook or Twitter, so I don't know anything personal, but he came up in recommendations for car repairs in Forest Hill – that's how I identified him. Sissy's doing some digging. She doesn't recognize him, but he must be a relative of Jean's to have inherited the place.'

'I think you're right,' said Ralph. The house had not been listed for sale and when the neighbours at number 3, Ant and Em Kendall, had rung the solicitor to enquire, they'd been told probate was proceeding at a standard pace –

butt out, in other words. 'Even in the state it's in it must be worth seven hundred thousand. There's no way someone like him could've found the money to buy it.'

Someone like him: this was rich coming from a self-made man like Ralph, who grew up on a council estate in Kent, but perhaps it was also the reason he was qualified to generalize. He understood first-hand the limited routes available for success.

In his case, it was raw talent that had propelled him to his status as sole proprietor of a wholesale business specializing in small leather goods. Manager of a staff of twenty. Owner of a riverside warehouse now worth ten times what he'd paid for it, thanks to the gentrification of Bermondsey in the noughties that made the rise of Lowland Gardens look sluggish.

He was making short work of the beer. 'It's bad news for the Kendalls. The dust is terrible.'

'They're on holiday, so hopefully they'll miss the worst of it.' Naomi put on oven gloves and transferred a large Le Creuset casserole from oven to table, calling for the kids, who were upstairs in their individual chambers, doubtless getting post-school fixes of their chosen digital poison. Ralph imagined them with their heads tipped back and eyes half-closed, like the junkies in *Trainspotting*. (There was no Play Out Friday, evidently.)

'Where're the dogs?' he asked.

'Tess is walking them for me. I must remember to return the favour sometime.' Naomi pulled a face. 'God knows when.'

The kids arrived, lethargic at first but soon out-bellowing each other with their news; Libby was twelve, Charlie seven, but the age gap did nothing to temper their rivalry. The subject of Darren Booth was dropped. Naomi didn't agree with slagging people off in front of the kids; it set the wrong tone. Never underestimate appearances, her mother had taught her.

Fuck what anyone else thinks, Ralph's father had taught *him*.

Oh yeah, and also, *Defend your turf.*

As usual, his wife's instincts were impeccable, Ralph noted with satisfaction. Declaring it tactically smarter to welcome the newcomer as a group, she summoned Sissy and Finn and Tess to join them for the meet-and-greet.

Finn arrived while Naomi was out delivering the kids to their Saturday morning activities, entering through the bespoke steel-framed glass kitchen doors that had cost an arm and a leg ('Return on investment, babe,' Naomi had argued, quoting house prices; she knew exactly how to sweet-talk him). The brothers' houses had free access to each other's at the rear, the fence between the two gardens having been removed when the kids were very young – which was, in case anyone wanted to know, *completely* different from this new guy's butchery. They'd returfed the communal garden to create a space wide enough for a game of football or badminton and now their kids were growing up with the equivalent of a small park for a garden eight miles from the centre of London – who wouldn't feel like a smug bastard about that?

'I've come to join up,' Finn said, helping himself to coffee with the strong, oversized hands that reminded Ralph of his brother's spell labouring on a building site one summer in his twenties. Two years younger than Ralph and arguably more handsome (thicker hair, bluer eyes, whatever), Finn was, however, neither as rich, which everyone said was the most important thing, nor as tall, which everyone *knew* was the most important thing.

'Good man,' Ralph said. 'I've got a bad feeling about this Booth character.'

'Is that what the invader's called?'

'According to Nay. She'll be here in a minute. Where's Tess?'

'Doing the swimming run. She said to go without her.'

No matter. Tess was no pushover, but she didn't have her sister-in-law's talent for first impressions, a fact demonstrated when Naomi sailed back in, dynamic in blood-red ribbed top and vintage jean skirt, legs still tanned from their Easter holiday in Dubai. Her hair swung free the way Ralph liked it.

'Hi, Finn, ready for the charm offensive? Sissy says she'll join us over there.' She swept up the tin of biscotti she intended to give the newcomer. 'I'm guessing he'll invite us in for a coffee?'

I wouldn't count on it, Ralph thought. This guy wouldn't know biscotti if it pounded him from the sky in a blizzard.

The child-free window being narrow, the three set off at once. Since the Kendalls had revived number 3 with fresh paintwork and palm-print roller blinds, number 1 had been a drab counterpart to its twin, but the contrast this morning was more pronounced than ever. The wall was completely eviscerated, or rather, redistributed into a mountain of bricks and rubble on the lawn, and the effect on the house was to make it look far more desolate than when it had been unoccupied. The white van had been moved into the drive, parallel with a ten-year-old Ford Focus parked partially on the grass, and bumper to bumper with a Honda, which hung off the bottom of the drive and blocked the pavement. The Honda was raised by a professional-looking hydraulic jack and under its chassis lay Booth, his face just visible.

'Hello again,' said Ralph. 'I think we got off on the wrong foot yesterday.' Perhaps it was his choice of words, perhaps the shattered remains of the wall in his peripheral vision, but he had the sudden hooligan impulse to step forwards and stamp on the man's head.

Don't be a nutter. Breathe more out than in.

'Any chance you could come out from under there for a minute?' Naomi called, pitch-perfect breezy, and Booth duly slid out and sprang to his feet, unsettlingly agile.

Devoid this time of dust and dirt, his features were clearer to see – a bulging forehead and flat boxer's nose; a relaxed, almost gentle mouth that was at odds with the insolence of his pale-eyed gaze.

Was it insolence or was that Ralph's own projection? He wasn't so egocentric as to not suspect that the others' instincts might differ from his. *They* might like him.

'We wanted to welcome you to the street,' Naomi said, warmly. 'I'm Naomi Morgan and this is my husband Ralph and his brother Finn.'

Booth glanced from Ralph to Finn, settling on Ralph. 'What is this, the return of the Kray twins?'

Naomi smiled gamely. 'They're not twins, no, but they are next-door neighbours. We're at numbers five and seven.'

Booth screwed up his eyes like this was hard to process. 'You're *brothers*, living *next door* to each other?'

'Yes,' Naomi said. 'We're lucky, it's a very happy arrangement. You're probably wondering who lives next door to you?' She gestured to number 3 and Booth glanced over his shoulder as if only now noticing his new house had another one attached to it. 'Ant and Em Kendall, a lovely couple with a gorgeous baby boy. They're on holiday at the moment, back next weekend, I think.'

Poor buggers, Ralph thought. 'I didn't catch your name yesterday?' he said. He knew it, of course, but he didn't want the guy to know they'd been checking up on him like the secret police.

'Darren.'

'Well, full disclosure, Darren,' Naomi said, her voice conspiratorial. 'It's disappointing for us to see the wall taken down because we campaigned to save it three years ago, when the council wanted to widen the road. It was blatant land grabbing, completely illegal.'

'You need to make sure you rebuild on exactly the same boundary, otherwise they'll be straight back in there,' Finn advised.

'He's right,' Ralph said. 'That's why I was so shocked yesterday. I'm sorry if I was a bit abrupt.' He was aware that the apology didn't sound sincere – it wasn't – but the sight of Sissy crossing to join them inspired fresh bonhomie: 'Ah, Sissy, come and meet our new neighbour, Darren!'

'Morning, everyone,' said Sissy, in her pleasant, unassuming way. She held a bunch of crocuses, hand-tied with green ribbon. 'I'm very pleased to meet you, Darren. I see you've already been busy . . .'

Destroying a historic part of our street, Ralph finished,

silently. To him – to all of them – Sissy was a touchstone of old-school decency. Solidly built and direct of gaze, she always kept her silver-streaked hair pinned from her face as if to display the full force of her integrity. Today she was dressed in a well-pressed skirt and blouse, which probably meant she had B&B guests, as she often did at weekends. Breakfast must have been served by now. Lowland Way was wide, wide as an avenue, but Ralph didn't envy her the direct view she had of the tip Booth had created in less than twenty-four hours.

'Are you related to Jean?' she asked Darren.

'She was my mum's half-sister. We weren't close.' Even though it was Sissy who'd asked the question, Ralph noticed that Darren eyed *him* when he answered.

'She was a lovely lady,' Sissy said. 'I'm sorry for your loss. Are you new to the area? Where did you live before?'

Again, he directed his response at Ralph. 'Loughborough Estate.'

Quite an upgrade then: the Loughborough Estate was a few miles north and not without its share of crime and deprivation.

'Is it just you or do you have a family?' Naomi asked.

'Just me and my other half.'

'Is she in? Busy unpacking, I expect. I'd love to give her these.' Sissy raised the flowers. 'They're from my garden.'

'She's still in bed, I think,' Darren said.

Ralph didn't need to look to know that both Sissy and Naomi would be suppressing raised eyebrows at this. It was ten thirty; the families on the street had been up since seven.

'This house has got so much potential, hasn't it?' Naomi

said. 'Seventies houses are really in vogue right now. Have you had an architect in?'

'An architect?' Darren sniggered, scornful, as if she'd suggested getting the Historic Royal Palaces people in to advise on his moat. 'I'm doing all the work myself, love.'

All the work?

'That sounds ambitious.' Naomi cocked her head. 'Have you applied for permission to extend, then? I don't think I've seen the notice up.'

Ralph smirked. Nobody did it better than Naomi, that easy reminder that there were rules (even in this council) and they'd all get along just fine if Darren remembered to follow them.

Darren shrugged. 'Need to have a proper look at the place first. New bathroom for starters and the roof needs fixing.'

Neither of which required permission, Ralph knew.

'What d'you do for a living?' Finn asked.

Darren gestured to the tools at his feet. 'I'm a mechanic, aren't I.' As if it were a totally moronic question.

Ralph remembered what Naomi had said about the repairs recommendation and his gaze swept past the three vehicles in the drive to a Peugeot parked in the street, its bonnet open: if that was Booth's as well, that made five including the van. And maybe the dirty Toyota too. The van was presumably a repository of tools, though Ralph stopped short of opening the doors and inspecting its contents. 'Where's your garage based?' he asked, then, when there was no response: 'You're not thinking of working from *here*, are you?'

Darren looked from brother to brother with the same mocking expression as before. 'What is this, the Spanish

Inquisition?' But Ralph knew a deflection when he heard one. You needed a licence to run a business from residential premises and he had a strong hunch this guy didn't have one.

He met Darren's eye. 'So these vehicles are all for your personal use, are they? All taxed and insured?'

'Ralph,' Naomi said, mildly, 'we don't want to jump to—'

'Keep your fucking nose out, mate,' Darren snapped at Ralph, interrupting her, and there was a collective intake of breath.

'I'm really not sure that's how you want to be speaking to your new neighbours,' Ralph began, and he felt his wife's fingers on his arm, steering him backwards. As if in counterbalance, Finn took a pace forwards to stand shoulder to shoulder with his brother.

'Well, I'm sure you'll love it here,' Naomi told Darren, as if the scene had not taken an unpleasant turn. 'We'd love you and your wife to come over for a drink sometime, wouldn't we, boys?'

'Yeah,' Ralph said, though to his knowledge no man of Booth's charmless ilk had ever crossed the threshold of number 7, not unless he'd come to read the meter.

Having presented the biscotti and flowers, Naomi and Sissy turned to leave. Finn, fixing Darren with an unimpressed last stare, followed them. Only Ralph lingered, he and Darren regarding each other in silent dialogue.

You've been warned, Ralph's stare said.

And Darren's responded: *I see who you think you are, but I know you're no better than me.*

Suppressing a shudder, Ralph retreated. Some of the rubble from the wall had spilled across the shared drive to Ant and

Em's side and he spent a moment or two toeing the stones back across before joining Finn and Naomi on the pavement. Sissy was already through her own gate at number 2, rows of bays in tall pots like staff lined up to greet her.

'I have two words,' Naomi told the brothers as they walked back.

'What?' Ralph said. 'Complete Twat?'

Loud enough, maybe, for Booth to hear.

'No,' Naomi said. 'Open Mind. And don't even *think* about going near those cars. I know what you two used to get up to back in the day.'

The brothers had done their share of keying cars and letting down tyres as kids, edited highlights of which Ralph had shared with his wife. She was happy to joke about juvenile delinquency, sure, but he was under no illusion that she'd have been repelled if she'd known him growing up. If she'd looked at him at all it would have been with pity, perhaps while helping in the community as part of her Duke of Edinburgh's Award or whatever. Lucky they'd met in their twenties, then, when Ralph was a reformed specimen, already twice promoted by a big importer based in Battersea and researching start-up costs for his own business. He'd flat-shared in Clapham with a young colleague and barfly, and Naomi had been among the many attractive female graduates who'd gravitated to the area's drinking holes in the late 1990s.

Back then, they wouldn't have cared about someone like Darren Booth. They wouldn't have cared about old walls or cars being repaired in neighbours' front gardens.

Well, they cared now.

2

Ant

—No, no one saw it happen, as far as I'm aware, but we heard it. Well, I was upstairs in the shower, so I didn't hear it so much as feel it. My wife Em was downstairs and she rushed straight out. She's told you she was the one who called the ambulance? She had to run back in for her phone and she shouted upstairs to me to take over with Sam – that's our baby. I could tell from her voice something awful had happened, but I had no idea it was this awful! By the time I came out the emergency services had already arrived and the whole street was in chaos. The cordons went up and all the cars coming up from the park end were having to turn and go back down. There was a big crowd of gawkers.

—I'd say we are close, yes. Friends as well as neighbours.

—Darren Booth? No, I wouldn't trust him as far as I could throw him. He's made our lives a misery

from day one, he's the proverbial neighbour from hell – and I say that as someone who's genuinely tried to give him the benefit of the doubt. I mean, who wants to fall out with the guy next door? It destroys your life.

—Come on, you can see for yourself the state of the place. Those officers I've seen taking bits away, are they Forensics or something?

—Health and Safety Exec, right. Well, they'll tell you the same: the place was a total deathtrap. I'm amazed something like this didn't happen sooner.

Mr Anthony Kendall, 3 Lowland Way, house-to-house inquiries by the Metropolitan Police, 11 August 2018

Seven weeks earlier

The flight into Gatwick was late, the traffic on the A23 the usual nightmare, and so tiredness at the wheel must surely have been a factor in Ant failing to recognize his own street. He missed the turn off Portsmouth Avenue and had to take the next right, coming back up Lowland Way from the park end.

Already, about half of the residents' cars had been removed for Play Out Sunday.

'Looks like someone's bought next door,' Em said, peering in horror at what looked like a landfill site where the neighbouring garden used to be, right down to the bathroom sink angled atop, almost jaunty, like a cake decoration. 'What a state! I can't believe no one warned us.'

'Didn't want to ruin our holiday, probably. They're obviously putting in a new bathroom. How many cars have they got?' Ant had grown used to having the shared drive to themselves, but now he had to reverse the car into their side with care.

'Our windows are going to be caked with dust,' Em grumbled. 'I hope we didn't leave any open.' There was a faint edge to this remark. Ant knew she considered locking windows and doors men's work – some throwback perhaps to when primitive females lacked the muscular strength to roll the boulder into the mouth of the cave. Crazy.

'We should go and say hello to them,' he said, but once inside and swept up by the unpacking and getting the laundry on and feeding Sam and the whole bath and bedtime routine that bisected every evening, he forgot all about the new neighbours, the apocalyptic new landscape next door. Then, at about eight, when Em was still settling Sam to sleep, his Winnie the Pooh music box tinkling its lullaby, there was the sudden ear-splitting stop-start of drilling.

He dashed up in time to see Em appear from Sam's room, pulling the door behind her. 'What the hell was that?'

'It came from next door.' Em led the way into the spare bedroom, a stud partition from where Sam slept. 'They must be putting up shelves or something on the other side. At this time!'

'To be fair, they don't know we've got a baby here,' Ant said. 'They probably haven't even noticed we're back.'

'Then we need to tell them.' Em sighed. Thanks to the best sleep of Sam's young life on holiday, she looked more like the old Em, which was to say young and attractive and smiling freely. Though fair-skinned, she'd even tanned a little. 'We knew someone would move in sooner or later.'

This was true, but what they'd possibly taken for granted was that the new neighbours would be, if not older and peace-loving like Jean, then certainly self-aware and considerate like Finn and Tess Morgan on the other side.

Even before Sam was born, the Morgans had been solicitous about their children's noise, which could be considerable, what with their communal garden arrangement with Finn's brother, Ralph, who had two kids of his own – Ant was still not sure who belonged to whom. Often there were friends over, creating an unholy chorus of screams and bossy voices, plus a pack of dogs in the mix, one of which was a bit of a yapper. But the moment levels rose intolerably, an apologetic face would appear over the wall, usually Tess's: 'Oh God, is it a nightmare? I'm *so* sorry. It's Isla's birthday and we've got the whole class here, plus all the parents. You'll see, when the time comes, you can't leave anyone out! Why don't you come over and have a glass of prosecco?'

On this basis, Ant and Em had been invited to half a dozen gatherings, once even offered a lightweight stepladder to climb over the wall, though Em, pregnant at the time, had opted for the traditional method of front doors. She and Tess had struck up a friendship – they were both stay-at-home mums (if you were allowed to use that term anymore), temporarily in Em's case, as she'd be returning to work at the end of the year.

Privately, Ant preferred Naomi Morgan, who was standout charismatic, and sexy, too, for a woman in her forties. 'It's against the rules to fall out on this street,' she'd told Ant the first time they met, borderline flirtatious with her wide ink-black eyes and smile that curved naughtily at the corners. In a culture of highlighted blondes, her drape of raven hair was exotic. 'We're practically a hippie commune,' she declared.

Hardly. The two families' gardens were shared but Ralph and Naomi's house was manifestly their own, with Elton John levels of floristry and a profusion of original art that Em said Finn and Tess had no hope of replicating. (There was one particular sculpture, some sort of copper spiky cactus-man, that Ant had mentally noted as a hazard for when Sam started toddling.)

'They obviously haven't got young kids or there's no way they'd be being so noisy,' Em said now and, on cue, voices rumbled behind the wall, a man's and a woman's, the words not quite distinct. Then, half a minute later, there was rock music. Very heavy rock.

'They've put that on to drown out the drilling,' Ant said. 'Sounds like thrash metal or something. What were those old bands called? Was Megadeth one? Wow, that's brutal. What's wrong with a bit of Ed Sheeran?'

Em peeked around Sam's door and made a face that meant, *We're all right for now.*

'I imagine they're perfectly nice,' Ant added, hopefully.

Em's brows twitched. 'That's like a line from a movie before you find the Boston Strangler adjusting his balaclava on the doorstep next door. Oh, *come on*,' she said, as the churn of the drill began again and the music was turned up a notch. 'He's not going to sleep for much longer if this goes on.'

When the drilling sounded a third time, they stared at the wall as if expecting to see a hole open up in front of their eyes.

The air tasted different, Ant thought, its atmospheric properties altered. It was surreal to think that there was someone standing a couple of feet away on the other side of the wall, almost as close to them as they were to each other. Was this person aware they were here? Could he hear their voices? And what kind of an architect designed semi-detached houses like this, anyhow, with the front doors and stairs on the outer sides? Wouldn't they be better side by side in the centre, twin pockets of hallway and stairwell providing insulation between living rooms? The two households might as well have been a single barn with a screen down the middle.

'You need to go and say something,' Em told him. *We* had become *you* with emphatic speed. More man's work, clearly.

'It's only been going five minutes,' he reasoned. 'Sam's shattered after travelling, he might sleep through it. Let's go down and have another go at the Great Aim.'

The Great Aim was to finish an episode of something on Netflix without being interrupted by Sam crying. In the old days, they'd binged on TV drama with the rest of society, a season of *House of Cards* in a working week, like a second job. Now, they were living in a house of cards. One false move, like not reaching the front door before the delivery guy rang the doorbell or cracking open a window just as one of the Morgans' dogs barked at a fox, and the whole thing collapsed.

Sam's cries came thirty-four minutes and a large glass of red in. It was only when they paused the TV that they realized just how loud the music was. You could easily make out the lyrics – something by Metallica that Ant vaguely recognized.

A slightly slower tempo than the earlier thrash, but equally as pounding. Here came the chorus: 'Sad but True'.

You could say that again.

Em went upstairs and reappeared with Sam in her arms. He was pressing his head into her neck, burrowing for re-entry into the sleep he was being so violently denied. 'Ant, can you *please* go and ask them to break up this Monsters of Rock tribute night!'

Her uncompromising streak was in evidence, which made Ant feel as if *he* were the child. As a boy, he'd frequently been berated for acting too much on impulse – 'Just stop and think for a minute,' teachers would say; 'Act in haste, repent at leisure, Anthony' (that one was from his grandfather) – and in an adult effort to override this fault he'd become, perhaps, a little too passive.

'You're right,' he said, jumping to his feet.

Outside, there was an unpleasant post-demolition odour, as if ancient sewers had been disturbed. Across the road, Sissy's pristine garden, the golden glow from her sitting-room window, felt like another country. He passed the new neighbours' living room window to get to the door, but could make out little through the crack between the curtains that had remained hanging since Old Jean's departure: packing boxes spilling open, bin liners swollen with possessions. At the door, he rapped the knocker, but nobody came, which made sense since the music was almost loud enough to burst the walls. Then, abruptly, the song ended and he was able to take advantage of the seconds before the next track started to knock again.

This time the door opened. Facing him was a short, bony blonde woman of about forty-five, her clothing in the grey area between sportswear and pyjamas and her demeanour that of someone easily angered – or perhaps simply drunk. She gestured rather than spoke her hello, can of Heineken in hand, face set in irritation. 'Yes?'

'Are you the new owner?' Ant raised his voice over the music, which tore past him into the night. If the other neighbours hadn't heard it before, they would now.

'What?'

'I said, are you the new owner?'

Inexplicably, she laughed, a brittle, humourless sound. 'You want Darren.'

'Okay, well, it's about the music—'

But she was already turning away, yelling at the top of her voice: 'Darren! *Darren!*'

The man who came forward was the DIY enthusiast, judging by his filthy overalls. He was in his fifties, his face weathered to an extent that suggested either committed drinking or a passion for coastal hikes. He too gripped a can, as well as a cigarette, the burning tip close to his knuckles.

'Yeah?' he said to the woman, as if there wasn't an open door in front of him and a stranger standing a few feet away.

'He wants a word with "the new owner",' the woman said. 'Get you.'

'Fuck off,' Darren told her.

His pulse stuttering, Ant struggled to produce a convincing smile. 'I'm Ant Kendall. I live next door with my wife, Em. This house right here.' He pointed to the wall with his index finger, emphasizing the intimate proximity between the two households. 'So you are Darren and . . . ?'

'Jodie.' Her face clenched in fresh distrust. 'Wait, this isn't about the wall again, is it? We've had a load of busybodies on our case about it all week. How were we meant to know there'd been some barney with the council?'

Startled by her hostility, Ant was nonetheless heartened by that 'load of busybodies': someone had been here to complain before him, Sissy or one of the Morgans, presumably. 'No, not that, it's just, we've got a baby next door and his bedroom is right here, on this side of the house . . .'

As Ant gestured to Sam's window, Darren tossed his burning cigarette end at Ant's feet and, mindful of the nearby cars, Ant ground it out. Em had joked about serial killers, but he could think only of those movies when a frat house moved in next door to upstanding suburbanites and proceeded to party. Comedy gold – for everyone else.

'I'm not sure if you can hear, but he's getting very distressed,' Ant added. There was an unravelling sensation inside him, the knowledge that he was handling this poorly.

But at last the woman seemed to get it. 'Not a problem,' she shrugged.

'Thank you. I appreciate your understanding.'

But in between watching the door close in front of him and stepping back over the threshold of his own house, he became aware first through his feet – in the form of powerful rising vibrations – and then through his ears that the music had in fact been turned *up*. He hurried back to the new neighbours' door, but his hammering was either inaudible to them or ignored.

At home, Em still had Sam downstairs. He was screaming now, as if in physical pain. Babies had that supersensitive hearing, didn't they? Was this decibel level even more unbearable for him than for them?

'What happened?' Em asked – yelled. It was as if there was a live band on the other side of the wall.

'I don't know.' He perched on the arm of the sofa. 'They said they'd turn it down, but if anything they've turned it up.'

They looked at each other in bewilderment.

'When I said we had a baby, they couldn't . . . They couldn't have thought I was talking about *our* noise? Apologizing for the crying?'

'Only if they're complete morons.' Em became suspicious: 'Why? Did you sound like you were apologizing? How much of that bottle of wine did you drink, Ant?' She shook her head. 'We can't put up with this. I'll take Sam out in the car and drive him around till he falls back asleep.'

'What, this late?'

'It's only nine thirty. It's either that or call the police.'

'We can't do that. We've only been neighbours for a few hours.'

He followed her out and helped her get Sam into his car seat, screaming guitars in one ear, wailing baby in the other, before watching the car pull forwards into the street. Back inside, he poured a new glass of wine and took it into the darkened rear garden. Next door, the song had changed, the intro accelerating and exiting the neighbours' open kitchen window like a series of controlled explosions.

Without thinking, Ant picked up the nearest loose object, a scrap of broken terracotta plant pot, and hurled it over the wall.

He was taken aback by his own fury.

In the morning, Em and Sam slept late, but Ant, having been unable to sink any deeper than an agitated semi-consciousness, dressed and went out to the bakery on the high street for coffee and pains au chocolat. Next door was mercifully silent, but outside, the buzz of Play Out Sunday was already building. As usual, Ant was grateful that his off-road parking meant he didn't have to relocate his car as the other residents did, creating a tarmac runway on which kids swarmed and shrieked. The scheme had been a draw when they were house-hunting, the agents having shared a link to a feature in the *South London Press* that Ant had since seen framed in Ralph and Naomi's kitchen. He revisited it as he waited in the queue at the bakery, reminding himself of the solid, unassailable respectability of his neighbourhood:

South London Street Wins Urban Spaces Award

The residents of a street in Lowland Gardens, South London, have won an award for their community initiative that gives children a taste of the kind of safe outdoor play older residents took for granted years ago.

Every Sunday, Lowland Way is cleared of vehicles, closed to traffic, and turned over to the kids for 'Play Out Sunday'. From skateboarding to stilt-walking, hopscotch to hula hooping, anything goes – except for one thing: screens.

'For a long time, I'd felt uneasy about how much time my kids were spending indoors on their screens,' says website curator and mother-of-two Naomi Morgan, forty-three, who came up with the idea. 'Now we don't have to persuade them to turn their devices off – they do it themselves!'

Attending a reception at City Hall with her sister-in-law and next-door neighbour Tess Morgan, thirty-eight, Naomi Morgan received the Urban Spaces Award from the London mayor, who commented: 'Play Out Sunday is a wonderful example of a community coming together to improve its own quality of life.'

Lowland Gardens, a leafy enclave west of Crystal Palace, has long prided itself on its low profile, but with house prices rising by almost five per cent higher than the capital's average in the last six months, it seems its discreet charms are set to be discovered by a stampede of new house-hunters.

There was a photo of Naomi and Tess with the mayor, Naomi towering in her heels, her open-mouthed smile elongating her face and giving her the look of a glossy racehorse. (Tess, unfortunately, had been caught mid-blink.)

No, he wouldn't dwell on last night, an unfortunate episode that had happened to coincide with their return from holiday. Busy with renovations over the last week, the newcomers must have had a few drinks to let off steam and only a killjoy would begrudge them that. Today, Lowland Way would be back to its community-spirited, rising-house-prices best.

His mood vastly improved by the locally roasted black Americano in his hand, he retraced his steps, at first registering only the usual buoyant, high-pitched volumes of children playing. Then, walking alongside the Portsmouth Avenue boundary of number 1, he picked out lyrics that had no place in kids' ears:

Gonna get you . . .

Fucking whack you . . .

What on earth . . . ? Turning into Lowland Way, he expected to see parents gathered in objection, but all was just as he'd left it, the throngs slightly thicker, the voices a little more excitable: some of the kids were on their bikes and racing a slalom course between bollards. At the bottom of his drive, he judged that the music was probably not of the volume to trouble anyone other than those near the corner and he experienced a sudden tremor of disquiet. They were a little isolated here, out on a limb with number 1; if this turned into *something*, would they be able to count on the support of the other neighbours?

It was a moment before he spotted Darren, who was at the open doors of his van, and a shock to see he was bare-chested. His chest hair was a faintly repulsive light fuzz of grey.

Ant approached before he could get cold feet. 'Hi again, Darren.'

'Huh?' Darren looked as if he'd never seen Ant before in his life.

'We met last night.' Though Ant was technically on his own side of the drive, it felt like an invasion of Darren's privacy to speak to him when he was not fully clothed. Though fifteen or twenty years older than Ant, his new neighbour was in better shape and not in the slightest self-conscious. A deep red-brown tan suggested his half-nudity might be a habitual state. 'I live next door?'

'Oh, yeah. Y'all right?' Neither polite nor rude, but simply preoccupied with something else.

'I'm fine. I mean, well, except . . . Would it be possible to turn the music down? You might get complaints that the lyrics aren't exactly family-friendly.' *Might get complaints*? How cowardly he was. Thank God Em wasn't out here to hear him.

'Family-friendly?' Darren's expression changed – to one of deep suspicion. 'Hang about, was that you that woke us up?'

'What?'

'Half an hour ago? Someone banging on the door like a fucking bailiff.'

'No.' Ant recoiled at the casual profanity. 'Perhaps it was someone asking if that Peugeot is yours? Or the white Toyota outside number seven? We close the road to traffic every Sunday. Play Out Sunday? It's quite famous in the area, I'm surprised you weren't told about it when you bought the house.'

'Every Sunday?' Booth gave a short laugh. 'No chance, mate. If these kids're out screaming like this every weekend, that's gonna do my head in.' He shut the van door with a crunch in obvious dismissal of Ant, who stood uncertainly, bag of croissants hanging limply by his side.

The adrenaline was making him shake slightly; he felt ashamed to be so unfit for confrontation.

No sleep left for you

Bitch, got plans for you . . .

Before he could get his key in the lock, the door swung open and Em came springing out. She'd clearly dressed in a hurry, her top misbuttoned, feet in flip flops, one of Sam's soft building blocks in her hand. She passed Ant with a quick look of disbelief – not that this was happening, he understood, but that he had failed to stop it.

'Excuse me?' she called out to Darren, tone strident. 'I said, *excuse me*? Can you please turn this music down? It's far too loud!'

Ant understood her exasperation, of course he did, but it

was the wrong thing to do, to get upset and combative off the bat, before having even introduced herself, and inevitably, the guy reacted with a defensive scowl.

'Says who?'

'Says *me*. The mother of a six-month-old baby!'

Now Jodie appeared to even up the numbers, standing closer to Ant and Darren, which gave the impression it was the three of them against Em. Fresh from the shower, Jodie's hair was damp and stringy, face shiny. Her nose sharpened at the tip, Ant noticed, and as she turned her attention from one person to another, it was as if she were led by her sense of smell. 'What's the problem?'

'Your music is the problem,' Em snapped. 'Can you *please* turn it down?'

'There's no need to be so aggressive,' Jodie told her, squaring up. There was a small tattoo on the side of her neck, Chinese characters of some sort.

Em flushed. '*I'm* aggressive? What about the fact that you've been playing heavy metal all night and now *this* on a Sunday morning? Is that not aggressive, then?'

'Em, let's not argue,' Ant said, hoping he didn't sound as disloyal as he felt. He was aware of glances from the street; if this went on, they'd attract a crowd.

'Can you believe this place?' Darren said to Jodie, as the sound of Sam's screams came pouring through the open door. 'Their kids are going mental, but they can't handle a bit of music.'

'There's a difference!' Em cried, and Ant was relieved when she abandoned the argument to return indoors and tend to Sam.

'Perhaps we could talk sometime when you're not so busy?' he suggested. 'Just let me know when you're free.'

Em had closed the front door behind her and he felt foolish having to open up separately. 'Not much of a laugh, are they?' he heard Jodie say to Darren as he finally got in.

He waited in the doorway of the kitchen while Em quietened Sam's cries. He could see her shoulders heaving with anger.

'Who the hell *are* these people?' she demanded.

'They're the people we have to live next door to, so I'm not sure how wise it is to fall out with them on day one.' At the sight of her furious scowl, Ant wasn't sure how wise it had been to make this comment.

'Might have known you wouldn't back me up,' she huffed.

'What are you talking about?' he protested. 'Of course I'm backing you up!'

'Well, it didn't sound like that to me. "Let's not argue": typical Ant, sitting on the fence.'

Typical Ant? The escalation took his breath away.

'Except we haven't got a fence, have we, not out front? And if we did, they'd probaby tear that down as well.' She glared at Ant as if he were directly responsible for this catastrophized misdeed. 'Well, things'd better not carry on like this, because there is nothing separating us from them, is there? *Literally* nothing.'

3

TESS

—I was here this morning, yes. I was in the back garden playing with the kids, when we heard this boom, like a car being blown up – hush, Dex, the nice officer is talking about something very serious. You go and finish watching Spider-Man *with your sister.*

—Yes, so I'm sure I heard screaming as well, but I might be imagining that. My husband came out and we just looked at each other and said, 'What on earth . . .?' Then our sister-in-law Naomi told her daughter to mind the younger ones for a couple of minutes and we ran out front and saw a huge cloud of dust in front of number one. Em Kendall was already there and she said Booth was on the ground somewhere in the rubble. We could hear him moaning and coughing. He was the only one we saw at first, we didn't realize there was someone else under there. Then we saw this foot sticking out. It was so awful, I'll never forget it.

—I have to say that even though it's the most shocking thing, in a way it feels totally inevitable. None of us has been safe from them. Sooner or later someone was going to get hurt.

—Who do I mean by 'them'? Darren Booth and his horrible wife, of course. Jodie, she's called. You know, this morning, she didn't even come out, not at first. Did anyone tell you that? The whole street was there, desperately trying to help, and she was still inside, asleep! Someone had to go in through the back door and get her. She's on medication, apparently, but if you ask me she was in a drunken coma from the night before. They're big binge drinkers, they like to party.

—Well, I'd describe them as chippy. No interest in co-operating with the people around them. They're a law unto themselves. It's a form of sociopathy, I suppose, or narcissism.

—No, I'm not a psychiatrist, I'm a stay-at-home mum. There are more parallels between the two than you might think, let me tell you.

MRS TESS MORGAN, 5 LOWLAND WAY, HOUSE-TO-HOUSE INQUIRIES BY THE METROPOLITAN POLICE, 11 AUGUST 2018

Six weeks earlier

Oh, but the cygnets were beautiful. Still so tiny and soft and trusting. What a joy that their elegant parents had chosen the pond in Lowland Gardens to raise their family, the first time here in living memory. Birds had built their nests on the little island before, there'd been goslings and ducklings, baby coots (did they have a special name? She'd look it up later), but never cygnets.

Tess was on her way to Isla's school for morning drop-off, a short stroll down Lowland Way and south through the park. Once considered too close for comfort to the Rushmoor Estate to the north, the lung of green that gave their suburb its name now had the best landscaping gentrification could afford and a vintage beach hut for a snack bar, a pair of posh girls dispensing artisanal flat whites for £3 a pop. God knew, there were probably kids on the estate who didn't know what cygnets were (let alone an artisanal flat white) or, if they did, then they thought it a good idea to feed them crisps. Only a minute ago, Tess had politely cautioned a mum and her preschoolers against this very crime.

Six cygnets had hatched in the third week of May and made their first watery forays – following Mum with a synchronicity worthy of Busby Berkeley – with a phalanx of iPhones filming from behind the railings. Since then, Tess, Naomi and some of the other neighbours had been conducting Cygnetwatch, sharing pictures with the street on the residents' Facebook page.

Tess took a quick head count: four, five, six. Good. Everyone present and correct. Dad was patrolling nearby, seeing off the crows. She took her daily picture and then gathered her own dependents, nine-year-old Isla, four-year-old Dex and her golden retriever, Tuppy, plus Naomi's two dogs, Kit and Cleo, who Tess had somehow committed herself to walking every morning. The dogs, comically anxious that they'd been abandoned for ever, had been tied a safe distance away to avoid their being hissed at by the swans.

Once, she'd told Finn she loved Tuppy as much as she did their two human children and he'd reacted as if she'd told a hilarious joke. Then, seeing her earnest expression, he'd said, 'I know what you mean. *Almost* as much. But a dog dying isn't as bad as a child dying, is it? When push comes to shove?'

Depends what the pushes and shoves were, Tess had thought. A cruel death was worse than a kind one no matter what the species.

'Mummy, can we have an ice cream?' Dex asked.

'No. It's eight thirty in the morning, you've just had breakfast. Anyway, they're not open yet.'

'I would have chosen salted caramel,' he said, sadly.

'Libby says salted caramel gives her a headache,' Isla said. Libby, Naomi's eldest, was Naomi with hypochondria, basically, but Naomi had duly banned salted caramel from her kitchen, saying it had reached critical mass anyway and there would surely be a backlash soon. This made Tess picture a slow-moving but deadly golden-brown tsunami rising over London and heading where? Wales?

When Tess had had Isla, Naomi had urged her to keep working, even if only part time, in order to protect the future employability she didn't then know she would later want or need, but Tess had not listened. Had she thought it through properly or had she subconsciously sought to defy Naomi? As soon as Dex started school in September, she'd start looking for a job. Okay, so she'd been led by the media to believe that all jobs were now being done by automatons or unpaid millennials, but that was surely an exaggeration, and Naomi said she *might* be all right while she was still in her thirties (she was thirty-nine).

Why was it that Naomi's words powered her thoughts like this? As if she had none of her own.

'Come on, let's get Isla to school.' But Dex was clinging to the railings near the swan family, snivelling. 'Oh, darling, you heard what I said, you're not having an ice cream.'

'He's worried about leaving the cygnets,' Isla explained. 'He's scared the new man will get them. He doesn't like animals like us.'

'Like we do. What new man? You mean the new neighbour on the corner?'

Having missed introductions on the Booths' arrival (Naomi had of course picked a time conducive to her family's schedules, not Tess's), she'd intended to pop by alone, but Finn had said not to bother because the guy was an arsehole. Em's complaints of a hell-raising couple with no awareness of other people's feelings – or hearing – seemed to support this.

'Are they going to be a problem?' she asked Finn.

He shrugged. 'If they are, Ralph and Naomi'll handle it.'

Indeed, Naomi had been quick off the mark to post on the residents' Facebook page:

Naomi Morgan: Does anyone else have an issue with what's going on at number 1?

Sissy Watkins: What is going on? Isn't it just renovations?

Em Kendall: I have a BIG issue. Loud music. We've complained SEVERAL times, but they won't listen.

Em had spent the whole of their first get-together since the Kendalls' holiday ranting about the newcomers. 'Can *you* hear their music?' she'd demanded repeatedly. 'Did I tell you I rang the police and they say it's a council issue? Unless we feel threatened, they won't do anything. *And* you can be charged for misusing the nine-nine-nine number. Unbelievable.'

Tess had made the decision not to get personally involved, so long as they didn't come anywhere near the kids – or the dogs. 'Well, it's good that you don't feel threatened,' she said.

'Not yet,' Em said, in the sort of tone people used when determined to be proved right even at their own expense.

'There's really no need to be scared of him,' Tess told Dex now. It was a dry, airless summer and the now-familiar heat was rising already. 'Sometimes people seem a bit gruff, but are really nice underneath.'

'He *isn't* nice,' Isla insisted. 'He was very rude to us.'

'You've spoken to him?' Tess said, startled. 'When?'

'When I was with Libby.' She said this with pride, Libby being three years older and an idol to her. 'We were walking the dogs and we saw all this rubbish in his garden and Libby said litter should go in the bin, not on the ground, or else he'll get rats. He got really cross and then he tried to kick Tuppy!'

Tess tightened Tuppy's lead and bent to ruffle his chest. 'What? He didn't actually touch him?'

'No, he only *pretended*,' Isla explained. 'He said, *Get that dog off my property!* And he *swore*. He said the "f" word.'

This last detail at least distracted Dex from his tears and

allowed Tess to move the party on. The park's glories seemed a little less vibrant suddenly. 'I think the best thing for now is to not walk past his garden unless you're with an adult. Walk on the other side instead, okay?'

'Okay.' Nearing school, Isla's thoughts had raced on, but once Tess had bid her farewell for the day and returned with Dex and the dogs to Lowland Way, hers remained fixed on the kids' remarks about the new neighbours – and her own previous reluctance to ally with Em. What was that famous quote, 'to remain neutral is to choose the side of the oppressor' (who said that? Nelson Mandela? Gandhi? Not Naomi, anyway)? Suddenly it made perfect sense that on arrival home she should park the dogs in her front garden and make directly for number 1.

The drive and much of the garden were filled with the apparently growing collection of old cars and discarded pieces of kitchen and bathroom. Though there were no signs of activity, the front door was slightly ajar and Tess pushed the door and poked her head into the hallway.

'Hello? Did you know your front door is open?'

There was no reply. She stepped inside, Dex's hand in hers, and peered into the living room. She knew from visiting Jean that the downstairs layout comprised a narrow hallway leading to a downstairs loo, with the living room through a door on the immediate right. Glass-panelled double doors divided the living room from the kitchen. These had been removed, an alteration Tess knew was permitted by the council so long as the frame and load-bearing wall remained in place.

'It smells horrible,' Dex said, trying to pull her back as she inched further into the living room. The sofa, a flammable-looking chunk of brown nylon, was strewn with empty lager cans, the floor around it a flotilla of food plates and bowls of cigarette ends – she thought of little Sam on the other side of the wall: was he at risk of passive smoking? There was a huge TV screen against the centre wall, an old-style stereo with speakers – presumably, this was the delivery system of the music that tortured Em – and a tangle of cables and gaming consoles. The window sills were grainy with building dust. While hardly full-blown squalor, it was certainly in squalid contrast to other properties she'd been into on Lowland Way, even those not in Naomi's league of engineered oak flooring and Christian Lacroix cushions.

In the kitchen, a portion of the left-hand wall was bare and scarred where units had been torn away and she was disturbed to see a flame on one of the hob rings. That couldn't have been left on all night, could it? With the front door ajar, it might easily have blown out. She turned it off.

'We'd better come back later,' she told Dex, returning to the hallway. But at the bottom of the stairs, she paused, compulsively drawn up Jean's old blue stair runner, now grey with trodden dust. 'You sit here on the stairs, sweetie, I'll be half a minute. Don't touch anything, okay?'

As she tiptoed up, past the dark rectangles on the wall where Jean's pictures had been removed, and the bathroom, where renovations appeared still to be at the demolition stage, a sickening instinct began to swell inside her. Something was not right here. Was domestic violence a factor? Drug abuse? And that open door: might an intruder have come in and murdered these people in their bed?

Don't be ridiculous.

She sneaked along the landing towards the open door of the bedroom at the front, smelling sweat and exhaled beer breath before she actually saw Booth. He was lying on his back on a double bed, alone and fully clothed. Asleep, not murdered. By the door stood his boots, the same ones most likely that had lashed out at a defenceless animal. Having arrived in a spirit of indignation, Tess suddenly felt irrational hate. *I could kill him*, she thought, unexpectedly. *No one saw me come in.*

'Mummy! *Mummy!*'

Startled, she dashed to the top of the stairs. Below, a middle-aged woman in frayed black jeans and the sort of clinging white top Tess had stopped wearing in her mid-twenties was looming over Dex, her expression understandably disgruntled as she spun to face her intruder.

'Who the fuck are you?'

This, evidently, was Jodie. She had a blue plastic bag in her hand, indicating an outing to the corner shop on Portsmouth Avenue and Crofton Road, which would have taken at least ten minutes from Lowland Way. What kind of a person left the front door open while they went shopping? And a gas ring alight?

'What are you doing up there?' she demanded. 'Why are you in my house?'

Descending at speed, Tess reached for Dex and drew him towards her, instinctively covering his ears. Though he seemed more confused than scared, she was horrified: what had she been thinking, leaving him by an open door like that? 'I'm so sorry, I was looking for you – if you're Jodie? I'm Tess, from a few doors down. I thought something was wrong, because the door was open.'

'Don't mean you just walk in and start nosing around,' the woman snapped, and she had a point. She was not unattractive, Tess saw, under the smudges of her hangover, and her eyes had a quickness to them. Not stupid either, then.

'You're right. I thought I smelled gas,' she lied. 'I turned your hob off, I hope you don't mind. You'd left it on. You *are* Jodie?' she tried again.

'For my sins.' Jodie half-bared her teeth. The upper ones were perfectly straight but the lower excessively crooked, as if they belonged to two different mouths.

Tess remembered her original mission. 'Well, look, the reason I came round is I wanted to have a word with your husband about my dog. I heard he tried to kick him? I didn't see it myself, but my kids were quite upset about it, so if you wouldn't mind passing on the message . . .'

'What message?' Jodie tore open her cigarettes and plucked one out with sharp fingernails painted petrol blue. Tess hoped Dex would not see the photo on the pack of diseased lung tissue.

'That Tuppy's completely harmless and it's not acceptable to lash out at an animal.'

'Tuppy? Is that a name?'

'After the P. G. Wodehouse character,' Tess said. 'While I'm here, can I ask how long renovations are going to take? I know these things are hard to estimate, but . . .'

But at least she could go to Em with some useful information.

Jodie shrugged. 'A few months, I expect.'

'I heard you're doing the work yourselves?' In Tess's experience that meant years, not months.

'Darren is, yeah.' Jodie turned from Tess into the living room, evidently finished with her visitor. Next thing, her phone was ringing and her manner when she answered it was quite altered, friendly and forthcoming: 'That's right, do you want to book in for a test drive? Any time this afternoon. Darren's out of action this morning. Let me grab my diary.'

'Okay,' Tess murmured, 'well, I'll leave you to it.' But when she tried the front door she found she couldn't work out the locking mechanism, a fitting recently installed judging by the gashes around it.

Dex picked up on her panic. 'Mummy? Are we prisoners?'

'Of course we're not prisoners, sweetie. Excuse me?' Tess called to Jodie, and she could hear the overreaction in her own voice. 'The door's stuck. Could you let us out please?'

Her jailer ambled forwards, the phone call – or cigarette – evidently having improved her mood. 'No need to panic, darlin', just a new lock. Not planning to kidnap you. The sex dungeon's not up and running yet, know what I mean?'

Tess frowned. 'I don't think that's appropriate language to use in front of a child.'

'You're the one sneaking around other people's bedrooms,' Jodie said, with a laugh. She unlocked the door and ushered them through. 'Why *were* you upstairs? Don't think you said, did you? Bye, then.'

Back on the doorstep, Tess heard Jodie's phone ring once more and she lingered, straining to hear. 'That's right, Lowland Way, just setting up. Thanks, yeah, it came a bit out of the blue and Darren wanted to sell it straight off, but then we saw what a nice bit of land it was, and we were both sick of our old jobs, so we thought, yeah, let's give it a go, start up on our own, you know?'

Start what up? Tess thought. Hang on, what had Jodie said a minute ago about a test drive? On the far side of the plot, two cars were set apart from the rest and half-covered, the exposed portions of their bodywork gleaming, as good as new. Since the great pile of bricks and torn-out bathroom fittings prevented access from the drive, Darren must have driven across the pavement to park them there. Kids and dogs came hurtling around that corner all the time.

At home, she joined the Facebook discussion about number 1 she'd previously eschewed:

Are they running a second-hand car business?

It was a while before the reply came from Naomi, who was at work and very strict about separating business and personal social media during office hours:

Fairly sure they are, yes. Ralph is investigating.

*

'I just hope this tension with the new neighbours is sorted out in time,' Tess said to Finn that evening, closing the feature on the *Guardian* website that listed bad neighbours as the second biggest obstacle to selling a house (after flood risk). She'd of course recounted to him the unsettling incident involving Jodie and the unattended gas flame, choosing not to include the detail of her inexplicable decision to creep upstairs and stand over the woman's sleeping husband. (*I could kill him.*)

'In time for what?' Finn asked.

'For when we put the house on the market.'

Finn reacted with the kind of non-reactive expression that took real effort. Sometimes, when she looked at her husband, Tess couldn't see beyond the resemblance to Ralph – both brothers had cropped dark hair, a square jaw and a strong Roman nose – but only when he was feeling confident. Not, like now, when he was unsure. 'We haven't a hundred per cent decided we're going to move, have we?'

She cocked her head, brow creased. 'Well, *I've* a hundred per cent decided.'

'Right.'

But there was only one of her – the non-breadwinner at that. He didn't say this, of course, only motioned to the scene in the communal garden: children and dogs, barks and squeals, balls flying everywhere. 'I'm not so sure. Look how happy they are with their cousins.'

Dex was in fact in bed and only Isla involved, but Tess didn't split hairs. 'We'd still visit, we'd still be close.'

'Not like this.'

No, she thought, *not like this. That's the point.*

It wasn't that Tess disliked Ralph and Naomi, because she liked them very much – most of the time. It was that she worried about being subsumed by them. She worried that Ralph would never stop asking Finn to leave his job as a logistics manager for a corporate events specialist and join him at Morgan Leather Goods and that one day Finn would lose heart in turning him down and agree that his skills *were* eminently transferable and it *would* be nice to earn more money, yes. We can't live next door *and* work together, was the line, but how long could it hold?

It wouldn't be so bad if it were Finn's business and Ralph the one being recruited, but the fact was that Ralph and Naomi were always the ones with something better to offer, always the ones who did things first. They did things first and then they briefed Finn and Tess on how best to do them next, expansively, generously, including which pitfalls to avoid. Well, Tess wanted to experience the pioneer's exhilaration for herself. She wanted to make her own mistakes.

Though the feeling of claustrophobia must have been percolating for years, it had presented itself abruptly, over the issue of secondary schools. With no decent state option within range, Naomi had intended to switch Libby to a private school, but Finn and Tess couldn't possibly afford for Isla to follow: they had neither the same income as Ralph and Naomi nor Naomi's wealthy parents to help out. They would have to move out of the area.

But it hadn't happened like that. Naomi had discovered the train link between Lowland Gardens and the nearest of the Kent grammars, Libby had been duly tutored to ace the eleven-plus, and soon Naomi was passing on the tutor's phone number to Tess with the furtiveness of a drug dealer. 'You need to start now to be safe,' she advised.

Finn, for one, had assumed that this was the end of the matter. Thanks to Naomi's tutor, Isla would follow where Libby led, followed by Charlie, followed by Dex. Job done. 'I don't know how people deal with school applications without this insider information,' he'd crowed.

'Maybe they enjoy finding out for themselves,' Tess had said.

He looked astonished. 'You want Isla to be rejected?'

'Of course not! I just want to decide for myself which school she'll go to. Can't you see it's not *us* who thinks she should get on a train to a school miles away, it's *them*. She's not *their* child, Finn.'

'No, but we'd be mad not to learn from their expertise. Ralph says you have to start with the tutor two years in advance.'

'You're not listening to me,' Tess said, and there'd been, for a while, a stalemate. How would Naomi manage a stalemate with Ralph, she wondered? She had an instinct it might be through sexual negotiation of some sort. Well, Tess relied on patience in *her* marriage.

After the press coverage of Play Out Sunday, she'd had the house valued by an estate agent, careful to arrange a day and time when Naomi would be at work. Explained how easily the fence between their place and number 7 could be rebuilt and traditional boundaries restored. Finn had been amazed when she'd told him the valuation; he'd flushed with the pleasure of all that free money.

'That's four times what we paid for it!'

'I know. If we moved further out, maybe closer to my brother, we could buy the new house outright. Imagine being mortgage-free.' Ralph-and-Naomi-free was what Tess meant and Finn was not stupid; he read between the lines.

Inevitably, his interpretation was totally reductive. 'She does use you, I know that.'

'She doesn't *use* me.' Tess was careful not to get emotional.

'I'm happy to help her out. But I'd also like to help my side of the family.'

And *be* helped once in a while, she thought.

'I feel like we're plotting,' Finn said, looking morose.

'That's exactly the problem,' Tess said. 'We're *not* plotting, we're just deciding what's best for our family, like families do up and down the country. I don't want to be made to feel like Lady Macbeth for suggesting something completely sane and reasonable.'

'You're right,' he said. 'Just let me get my head around it.'

'Remember, not a word,' she warned him.

To Ralph, she meant. If Ralph got wind of this, he'd stop it. Naomi was a busybody, but she was also a pragmatist. She could recruit a new deputy with ease; she could pay a professional for the services Tess supplied as a family member and next-door neighbour. But Ralph was different. Having lost their mother in their late teens and with contact with the extended family sporadic at best, having risen from bunk beds in a 400-square-foot council flat to master bedrooms in a pair of 3,000-square-foot piles in Lowland Gardens, having basically reinvented themselves, the two brothers had only each other as any claim to their original identity. Most Fridays, they went for a drink together, men only, calling it a tribute to their father, who had died before Tess had met Finn and was by the brothers' own admission an unreconstructed chauvinist and bully. The arrangement peeved Tess more than it did Naomi, the only woman Tess knew who continued the tradition of Saturday date night with her husband fifteen years into her marriage. Booking proper restaurants and hogging Daisy, their shared babysitter. Dressing to seduce.

That last conversation had been two months ago. But Tess hadn't allowed for new neighbours two doors down who had the potential to make their house unsellable – at least at a price high enough to turn Finn's head.

'Well, whatever we decide, we definitely can't do anything this summer,' she said now and this placated Finn. He survived displeasing Ralph another day. 'That's actually pretty loud,' she added, as music drifted through the open doors. Not an assault, but an intrusion, certainly.

'Black Sabbath, "War Pigs". Great song,' Finn said. 'Not loud enough to wake Dex, is it?'

'His window's closed. But think how loud that must be for Em and Ant.' Tess frowned, thinking once more of cars being driven across pavements, of dogs being sworn at and threatened. How soon before one of them was under the wheels? 'I wonder if we should suggest to Ralph and Naomi we have a meeting about those people? Before it starts to get silly.'

Those people. The phrase was snobbish, the tone contemptuous, but Finn didn't correct her. Instead, he agreed it was high time the couple Tess resented for their kingpin ways – to the extent that she sought to sell up and escape them – stepped up and challenged the invaders.

4

Sissy

—No, I'm really not sure I'm up to this . . . But if it's just one or two questions . . .

—Yes, I was at home this morning.
I was upstairs in one of the bedrooms at the back when I heard the noise outside. I thought maybe it was a lorry delivering gravel across the road. So I went to the bedroom at the front to check . . .

—Sorry. Please, just give me a minute.

—No, it's fine, I can carry on. The set-up over there? Well, it was a building site, an amateur one, completely unsafe, with cars everywhere, doors and bonnets open – he'd leave them with the engines running while he went inside. It was an accident waiting to happen and now it's happened.

—No, I didn't get on with him before this. I know some of the other neighbours saw him as just selfish, oblivious, and maybe I did as well at first. But I soon realized the truth.

—That he was plain nasty. A bad person.

Ms Sissy Watkins, 2 Lowland Way, inquiries by the Metropolitan Police, 11 August 2018

Five weeks earlier

You have a new customer review on CitytoSuburb!

The alert came with the sort of urgency that used to be reserved for surgeons on call, but now meant someone of no importance had made a passing remark about someone else of no importance with no thought whatsoever as to the consequences. Sissy had read in the *Telegraph* how Silicon Valley designed everything with scores and notifications to keep you hooked on dopamine; they were modern-day Pablo Escobars. She'd seen a television drama about a community in which the services available to you were dictated by your popularity: your own opinion of yourself was irrelevant, it was only other people's that counted. Terrifying! (It was set in the 'near future', whenever *that* was.)

She duly logged into the CitytoSuburb members' area. Ratings were out of five like on Amazon, except they used little window-box icons, not stars. This one was her first ever two:

Beautiful old property in Lowland Gardens. Lovely host, huge room, delicious breakfast. Why the two-star rating, then? The problem was that in the morning the neighbour across the road got up at the crack of dawn and was revving engines in his drive. It sounded like a Hell's Angels rally. Talk about a rude awakening – on a Sunday! And he pulled out of his drive so dangerously when we were leaving, we felt lucky to escape with our lives! There were children playing a few feet away! So with the best will in the world, we just can't recommend others stay here. Sorry.

Harry and Elaine Cogan, near Plymouth, Devon

Sissy could only sigh. Every word was true.

The incident had occurred the previous weekend. What with the constant and unfathomable reordering of cars between driveway, garden scrubland and street, it was inevitable that Play Out Sunday would be a sticking point with Darren Booth and so it transpired. Her guests were leaving after a late breakfast and, Lowland Way being closed to traffic, Sissy accompanied them to the corner of Portsmouth Avenue to wait for their taxi. There were four cars in the street: two outside number 1, one in front of Ralph and Naomi's, and one outside Sissy's, almost certainly all Booth's. As they crossed, he was standing at the bottom of his drive with a car key in his hand – about to start moving the vehicles, she assumed (how naïve she was!).

'Oh, look at the little ones,' the Cogans exclaimed, as Sissy called hello to Naomi and the other parents out with their kids. Even though the whole point of the exercise was that the street had been cleared of potential hazards, parents would hover at their gates because, well, you never knew when a paedophile was going to stroll by and take his pick, did you? *I couldn't live with myself if anything happened*, the mums would say, hypervigilance legitimized into a sort of catchphrase. They made parenting sound so superstitious, Sissy thought. Almost medieval.

Paedophiles had not really been a thing when her son Pete was a boy, at least not that she could remember.

To give Booth the benefit of the doubt (again, naïve), he might not have read the notices Naomi and Tess distributed every Saturday afternoon and that Sissy knew by heart:

Dear Grown-up,

Thank you for moving your car off the street in good time for Play Out Sunday. This small favour has big benefits for all of us!

Love from the children of Lowland Way x

A cute hand-drawn font had been used and at the top of the flyer there was an endorsement from no less than the London mayor himself.

'I haven't seen kids playing hopscotch for years,' Mrs Cogan said.

'Yes, they're free to draw on the road in chalk,' Sissy told her. She had grown used to praising activities that had been completely unremarkable in her own childhood as exceptional, because, without fail, her guests were charmed by them and tended to go on to mention them in their reviews.

She was dismayed to see that Booth was now at the wheel of one of the cars on his drive: surely he wasn't moving another *into* the street? That really would be bloody-minded. The sudden roar of revving caused nearby children to startle and shift away. Under the wipers, the Morgans' flyer flapped unread.

'Just hang on a moment,' she told the Cogans, emboldened by their presence, their respectable expectations. She stepped onto Booth's drive and peered at him through the half-open car window. Though he did not unwind it fully or turn off the engine, he did acknowledge her, which was more than he'd done on any previous occasion. Then again, at her age, it was a common experience to be regarded on unequal terms. The fact that Booth was probably only a few years younger than her was by the by: all signs pointed to his being the kind of chauvinist who considered a woman with grey hair and a comfortable bra unworthy of attention.

'Did you not see the note on your cars about Play Out Sunday?' She took the liberty of fishing the flyer from behind the wiper and thrusting it through the window.

'Huh?'

When he didn't take it, she let it drop onto his lap. 'Have you not noticed these last few weekends? It looks like you haven't got room to squeeze them all on your drive, but there are plenty of spaces on Portsmouth Avenue.'

His head still angled towards her, Booth's gaze hardened. 'I've already said, they're staying where they are.'

Already said: he must have been approached by other neighbours and opted not to comply. Had Naomi tried? If she couldn't persuade him, no one could.

'I see. Well, thank you.' *For nothing*. What an unpleasant character he was, she thought. Jean would be turning in her grave to see this craven lack of community spirit. Sissy had known Jean as well as anyone on the street and while having been aware of a nephew living in South London, she could not recall a single reference to any familial act on his part. Perhaps Jean had thought he'd sell the place without setting foot in it, imagined another couple like the Kendalls moving in – the poor Kendalls, as Sissy thought of them now. Instead, according to Tess, these people had judged the premises perfect for their car business and moved in themselves.

At least they hadn't touched the old maple, which created a beautiful architectural shape across the side gate and left-hand edge of the house. (She remembered Libby Morgan doing a lovely painting of it when she was little and giving it to Jean for Christmas.)

She turned away from Booth and steered the Cogans beyond the bollards to the corner of Portsmouth Avenue, where traffic rolled by, indicator lights ticking off as drivers registered the red ROAD CLOSED sign. Half-listening to Mrs Cogan explain the complications of their onward journey, she became aware of the sound of a vehicle approaching, felt a flare of panic as she realized it was coming from behind her, on Lowland Way – and accelerating, not braking. She swung round to see Booth swerving to avoid the sign and knocking aside one of the bollards before, briefly, mounting the kerb. She and the Cogans scattered, barely in time, and without so much as a raised hand of apology Booth took the corner and sped down Portsmouth Avenue. He braked at the next lights, almost rear-ending a Range Rover.

'Hey!' yelled Mr Cogan, striding a few steps after the receding vehicle before giving up and returning to check on his wife, who looked breathless and confused.

'My goodness,' Sissy said, her breath ragged. 'Are you both all right?' A vehicle approaching from the right – the taxi – pulled up sharply, the driver's face as startled as Sissy's own.

'We're fine,' Mrs Cogan insisted, with effort. 'Are you? Did you see it was that rude neighbour of yours? What's he playing at, driving like that?'

The bollard had rolled into the gutter on Portsmouth Avenue and Sissy tried not to think how different the scene would look had it been human flesh and not plastic the car had struck.

'Do you know his registration?' Mr Cogan asked. 'We should report him.'

'I'll deal with it,' Sissy said. 'Please don't give it another thought.'

As the cab pulled away, Naomi hurried over. 'I saw that from down the street! Are you okay?'

'I think so.' Sissy watched her retrieve the bollard, hugging it to her as if to protect it from further assault. Even in the exercise clothes she wore at weekends Naomi always looked so groomed and sexy, like Hollywood's idea of a wife and mother.

'Honestly, there's absolutely no need for him to be a refusenik like this,' Naomi grumbled.

'Can we get the council to help?' Sissy asked.

'No, the scheme is completely based on goodwill. No one is legally obliged to move their car. Normally, if someone's resistant, I try to get their other half on side, but in this case she's a prickly character herself.'

Sissy tried not to resent the casual assumption that everyone had an 'other half'. This sort of oversensitivity, she'd found, was the most lingering symptom of grief for her divorce, just over three years ago. How would Colin have tackled Booth? He could be quite officious about local matters. But it was already clear that Booth gave short shrift to such interference. In any case, Colin wasn't here; he was living in Blackheath with his new partner, enjoying, as he'd put it with staggering indelicacy, 'my last chance'.

'I'll think of something, I expect,' Naomi said. 'Meanwhile,

I can't risk him speeding in and out like that again.' She set about repositioning the bollard and the ROAD CLOSED sign in line with the Kendalls' house, in effect cutting Sissy's house off and reopening the corner stretch to parking. 'Kids?' she called out in a posh, confident foghorn. 'Stay on this side of the sign, okay? It's dangerous the other side.'

The whole thing made Sissy cross. Not only had Darren Booth endangered the safety of her guests, but he'd caused her to be excluded from the lovely festive atmosphere. She could not let him get away with this. When he returned, an hour later, she took a deep breath and crossed the road, waiting for him to emerge from his car.

'Mr Booth?' She no longer felt inclined to use his Christian name. 'Would it be possible to have a word?' With some insistence, she managed to force eye contact. His face was pink and irritable, a smear of oil on his brow. 'The way you drove earlier was really dangerous. You came very close to hitting us, do you realize that?'

Booth slammed shut the car door, muttering his response.

'What did you say?' Sissy demanded. 'Did you call me a fucking busybody?'

'Think you're imagining it, love,' Booth said, his mouth curling. 'Never called nobody nothing.'

Ignoring his abysmal grammar, Sissy frowned at him. 'Good. Because that would be the last thing you'd want to say to someone you'd almost just run over. They might decide to report you to the police. That's exactly what my B&B guests wanted to do!'

Even as she spoke, she regretted mentioning the B&B, understanding instinctively that the less he knew about her arrangements the better. But he'd already turned to go inside.

Almost immediately, the door to number 3 opened and Em Kendall reversed out with the baby in his buggy – Sissy sensed she'd been waiting for Booth to go in before she came out, which if it were the case meant relations between the two households had already deteriorated badly. Em was a slight, pale-skinned woman, whose mood could be discerned by the set of her mouth: a pained smile today, chased by a sullen pout. She didn't remark on Sissy's agitation as they met at the end of the drive, but fussed over the baby, preoccupied.

'How are you, Em?' Sissy said, smiling herself into better spirits. 'And how is little Sam?'

Em sent a wary glance over her shoulder. 'We'd both be a lot better if we got a decent night's sleep once in a while. It's a complete nightmare. The wall between us is so thin. Sam isn't sleeping, which means we're not sleeping.'

Sissy made sympathetic noises. 'Tough for Ant, going off to work every morning without proper rest.'

'Tough for me,' Em said, not quite snapping. 'If anything, work is a break.'

Sissy knew better than to dispute this; she'd been a new mother herself and it didn't feel very long ago to her, even if Em's generation imagined it to have been centuries. *It's so much harder now* was the attitude, which was completely illogical given the countless advances since, but Sissy accepted that every new parent was convinced of his or her own unique martyrdom.

'It's early days. I'm sure things will settle down with our new neighbours.'

'I'm not holding my breath. We've said we'll give it till the end of the month and then . . .' Em tailed off, glancing at her phone. It was in her hand, as everyone's was these days, as if phones were dialysis machines that could not be out of reach without life-threatening consequences.

'And then what?' Sissy prompted.

Em looked up. 'Then we kill them.' The deadpan tone deceived Sissy, if only for a split second, and her startled expression made the younger woman laugh. 'No, complain to the authorities. Not to him, obviously. He couldn't care less.'

Later, when Sissy looked back, she thought how confident they'd all been in the notion of The Authorities.

Yes, even Em.

*

> Sissy, I believe we have a common cause. Not sure if you've seen FB, but we're meeting here on Thursday at 8 p.m. to discuss the situation. Ralph

Sissy did not respond to Ralph's text, not at once, but instead put Booth, with his dangerous driving and his churlishness, from her mind. There was, after all, the width of two pavements and a road between their properties; if she sat in the kitchen at the back of the house with Radio 4 on and the dishwasher or washing machine whirring, life was exactly as it had been before, untroubled by any external noise. As for the eyesore the new neighbours had made of their plot, she decided she'd let her hedge grow at the front, sacrificing a little light to create a screen: out of sight would be out of mind. One by one, her favourite items – a cushion knitted by her mother, a photograph of Pete on his first day at school – migrated from the sitting room at the front to the kitchen, where she now did most of her sitting.

Of course, anyone who came to her house could hardly avoid noticing *theirs* and so it was invariably the opening topic of conversation.

'What's with the place across the road?' Pete asked on his first visit since the Booths' arrival. 'It's chaos.'

'I thought you were safe from bad neighbours here,' his girlfriend Amy said, when Sissy explained. She and Pete rented in a block of flats in North London and had a neighbour upstairs who held parties on the roof, advertising them on social media. On such occasions, they lived in fear of seeing someone plummet past their window (so far, only bottles had made the trip, alarming in itself). It was different when you were renting, though: the nuisance could move – or, if all else failed, *you* could. Sissy wondered if the reign of peace she'd enjoyed on Lowland Way for almost three decades owed as much to pure luck as active cultivation. Both she and Naomi Morgan liked to believe that in their own ways they set the tone, led their neighbours by example, but maybe the truth was they'd simply not encountered any opposition.

'When did he get rid of that old tree?' Pete asked, scandalized.

'Yesterday,' Sissy said, sadly. 'He just got up and went at it with a chainsaw.'

'Why?'

'Presumably to create more space for the cars.' Sissy had checked online to see if the maple had had a Tree Preservation Order, but it had not, which was a shame, not least for the poor tree itself. Council guidelines required that measures be taken to remove trees safely and there was no evidence that Booth had not done this, no reports of injury or damage.

'Don't people normally have hoardings up to keep building work a bit more contained?' Amy said.

'I'm not sure he does things "normally",' Sissy said, but seeing Pete grow concerned, she shrugged off further questions. He had taken the divorce badly and helped campaign against the sale of his childhood home when Sissy and his father set about getting it valued. Colin had been bought out only with the aid of an uncomfortably steep new mortgage – the first she'd had in her name alone, at her age! – and a plan produced for a B&B business.

'Well, make sure you phone Amy if you need any help,' Pete said. The two worked for the same consultancy firm, but whereas his current client was based in Aberdeen, requiring him to stay there Monday to Friday, Amy was in London all week. Sometimes she visited Sissy on her own, which was lovely. *She* was lovely. Sissy hoped the two would marry and start a family, but knew better than to suggest such dull, conventional notions.

It was still light when they left and she walked them to the gate. They lingered for a moment, eyes drawn, inevitably, to number 1.

'You know, I don't think I'd ever even noticed that house before,' Amy said.

'There wasn't really anything to notice,' Sissy said. There was the usual dust cloud caused by the day's labours: it was as if the house and its overspill had been produced by some evil spell.

'Who's the woman coming out the door?' Pete asked.

'Oh, that's Jodie.'

Retrieving something from the car at the foot of the drive,

Jodie was evidently in a spiky mood, slamming the door shut with unnecessary force. Sissy had had little contact with her since her arrival and was not encouraged to seek more. The woman couldn't muster a smile, and had such a mean-spirited look in her eyes, a look not so much of a hard life lived but of a hard attitude towards that life. A good match for Darren, she supposed.

Seeing them watching, Jodie stalked to the edge of the pavement and yelled across, 'Take a picture, yeah? It lasts longer.'

'Maybe we will,' Amy replied, loudly.

'Don't,' Sissy said, both mortified and thrilled by her boldness.

Jodie gave them the finger and turned to go back in.

'Wow,' Pete said. 'You really weren't exaggerating.' He kissed her goodbye. 'Remember what we said about you ever needing help.'

After they left, Sissy found a new notification on her phone – another bad review:

> Everything was great except the position of the house on the street – I suggest CitytoSuburb adds the Google Street View function so you can see. Even these nice streets have a dodgy end. (Two window boxes.)

She opened her text messages and selected Ralph's. *A meeting is an excellent idea*, she texted. *Count me in.*

5

Ralph

—A 'specific grievance'? How long have you got?

—Well, from my point of view it hasn't been the building work so much as the cars. He sells them from the premises without a permit and has at least six parked in the street at any given time. It's completely disrupted the parking situation. You see that clapped-out monstrosity right there? That's his. I swear he keeps it there just to wind me up. Deliberately lowering the tone, you know?

—Wait, I can see what you're thinking and I'll tell you something for nothing: Lowland Way isn't one of those middle-class bubbles where people act all entitled. No, we count our blessings here. The Rushmoor Estate's just on the other side of the park, as I'm sure you're aware. I cut through there sometimes, remind myself how different life could be. What I'm trying to say is, it's ironic. We live right next to a high crime zone like that, but the criminal

is here on Lowland Way. Right where we thought we were safe.

MR RALPH MORGAN, 7 LOWLAND WAY, HOUSE-TO-HOUSE INQUIRIES BY THE METROPOLITAN POLICE, 11 AUGUST 2018

Three and a half weeks earlier

On the evening of the residents' meeting, Ralph was driving through the Rushmoor Estate, which housed, among others, two teenagers recently remanded in custody for stabbing a third to death, when Finn called with his early evening update on the parking situation. It was their new thing.

'Sorry, mate, but it's still there.'

'Surprise, surprise,' Ralph said. For the last week, a decaying Ford Focus belonging to Booth had been parked outside his house and he'd had to leave the Beamer right down the other end of the street under a plane tree, which meant there was now birdshit all over the roof.

'Why the fuck doesn't he just put the house on the market and take the cash?' This was a sentiment Ralph had expressed repeatedly since Tess had heard the terrible truth from the horse's mouth (well, Jodie's): the unusually large corner plot was ideal for Booth's Motors – or whatever he called his tawdry little business. 'He obviously doesn't belong here,' he added.

As a rule Ralph liked it to be known that he wasn't one for pulling up the ladder; he wasn't like those first-wave incomers who voted against the second. Darren Booth would be as welcome on Lowland Way as he had been himself – were he to respect the prevailing culture. Assimilate. But running a repairs workshop and/or used car showroom from his wasteland of a front garden was not respecting the prevailing culture. It was not assimilating.

'No arguments there,' Finn said. 'Where are you, anyway? You haven't forgotten about the meeting?'

'Course not. Ten minutes away.' Ralph ended the call, preferring not to specify his location or explain why he often detoured through the bleaker pockets of south-east London when returning home from Bermondsey. With the right song playing – nineties guitar rock, attitude trumping melody, though by no means replacing it – he would experience a rush of sensory memory that was almost erotic as he cruised past the featureless flats of, first, the Loughborough Estate and then the Rushmoor. By the time he reached Rushmoor, with its obstacle course of speed bumps to deter the joyriders, he'd be going slowly enough to absorb the mood of the pedestrians he passed, the dismal-looking underage mothers who he'd never, ever seen interact with their babies; the old blokes with their collapsed posture and collapsed dreams (if they'd ever had any dreams in the first place). People who were light years from him and yet almost close enough to touch.

He'd heard a phrase to describe this kind of activity: poverty porn. Which made him uncomfortable but at least suggested he was not the only sick fuck in town.

'Hey!' He braked sharply, causing the seatbelt to lock across his chest. A teenage girl with a beat-up buggy was in the street in front of his car, walking down the middle of the road as if there wasn't a fucking pavement for just this purpose! She was mesmerized by her phone, surprise, surprise, probably spent more money on it than she did on the child's upkeep.

Since the sound of two tons of deadly machinery braking didn't register, he swung the car alongside her and rolled down the window: 'Hey, do you want to use the pavement? That's what it's for, y'know.'

She had earphones in, so he reached to pull the wire, dislodging the buds. Straightaway she began screaming at him, abandoning the buggy to march after his car and smack a hand against the roof, spitting words he didn't recognize but was fairly sure were no official language. Urban invective of some sort.

'Get off my car, you crazy witch,' Ralph yelled, hitting the switch to close the window. 'Go and get your baby out of the road before he's run over! People like you shouldn't be allowed to have kids!'

He couldn't hear her response through the glass, but he could see the damp black hole of her bellowing mouth and the hatred that had gripped her face.

Jesus.

He put his foot down and she slid from view. The landscape changed abruptly, the way it did in South London, square footage too overvalued to allow for subtle transition, and the concrete of the Rushmoor Estate was soon replaced by old brick and new spring leaf. Family cars and dug-out basements. Teenagers with GCSE revision, not babies.

On Lowland Way, after he parked – the closest spot to his house was on the corner outside Sissy's place – he scanned Booth's plot for new atrocities. For all his agitation, it was astonishing how quickly the situation had become, in its way, sport and on the rare days that there was nothing new he felt not so much relief as anticlimax, the flatness of a tie.

But this evening, there *was* something: an ancient camper van parked in the drive, dirty and ugly and square, with hideous copper orange paintwork.

Plucking his phone from his pocket, he googled the council's policy on parking camper vans in a residential area, groaning when he read the results. Glancing up, he was startled to find Booth at the end of the drive, smoking, watching, infuriatingly casual. He was in his overalls, as usual, face and hands stained grey.

'I see you've got another classy set of wheels to add to your collection,' Ralph said, mock-friendly.

'Mind your own business, mate,' Booth said, hardly audible. For all his crashing and banging, he had never been heard to raise his voice.

Ralph strode forwards, ready for his second confrontation in the space of ten minutes. 'I don't *have* a business, not on the street, that's the point. These are homes, not workshops.' He tried – and failed – to disguise the rage in his voice. 'Enough is enough, all right? This is a residential neighbourhood and you can't use your front garden as a showroom. I suggest you look into alternative premises for all these vehicles as a matter of urgency, before we get the whole lot towed away.'

Booth grinned. 'Think you'll find it's a free world, mate.'

Much too free for Ralph's liking. As he turned to leave, an involuntary sound escaped him, a kind of suppressed war cry. It was as if he'd been walking away from Darren Booth his whole life, thwarted and provoked, their sparring a biological imperative, almost what he had been born to do.

This meeting with the neighbours couldn't come soon enough.

Given the Kendalls' uncomfortable proximity to the source of the aggravation, it was not surprising to Ralph that they arrived in a microclimate of marital high pressure.

'*I'll* find somewhere for Sam, shall I?' Em said to Ant, with a harpy sharpness that Ralph had never heard from Naomi, not even in the heat of early parenting.

'Come upstairs with me, we'll find a quiet place,' Naomi told her, while Ant, looking harried, joined Ralph, Finn and Sissy in the living room.

'Wine?' Ralph offered. He and Naomi had agreed to serve modest measures in order to keep the discussion focused. It was all too easy to degenerate into drunken ranting, Naomi said, with not the slightest suggestion that he might be one of the more susceptible of those assembled.

When she and Em reappeared, they were talking about Em's return to the workplace.

'If things continue as they are, it would be better for Sam's welfare if he spent the day at nursery, in which case I'll go back sooner rather than later,' Em said, and Ralph noticed Ant's look of confusion at this.

'That's why we're here now, Em,' Naomi told her, with conviction. 'We're not going to *let* things continue. Ah, here's Tess, finally!'

Tess arrived via the kitchen, preoccupied as she took a spot next to Em on the smaller sofa under the window.

'Tuppy's a bit unsettled,' she explained. 'It's the noise from the corner, he hates the sound of machinery. He's on red alert the whole time.'

'Aren't we all,' Ralph said. If you asked him, she cared more about pets than people. 'Anyone else coming, Nay?'

'No, but I'm reporting back to Sara Boulter at number six and a couple of others. They'd like to get things sorted, but they're not as badly affected as we all are. So . . .' Naomi sharpened her manner, keen to open proceedings. 'Thank you all for coming. We're here to share information about what's going on at number one and to have a think about how we can restore the street to the safe, peaceful place we know and love. First of all, I think we can all agree that Darren and Jodie are not remotely troubled by informal complaints. I've approached them together and individually and while I wouldn't say they've been overtly antagonistic' – here she glanced pre-emptively at Ralph – 'they certainly haven't been interested in sharing plans or listening to reasonable objections.'

'Sorry to contradict you, Naomi,' Em said unapologetically, the moment Naomi drew breath, 'but I would say they *have* been antagonistic.'

Sissy nodded her agreement. 'You might find that complaints actually spur them on. He, in particular, sees himself as a bit of a rebel.'

'Which is why we need to start some official processes,' Naomi said. 'We don't need rebels on Lowland Way. Now, what we found with the Rat Run and Play Out Sunday campaigns was that it was most effective to centralize the effort because it's very easy to duplicate and overlap and you end up splitting the vote. We need to be systematic. Let's start with the cars.'

Ralph was already beside himself. 'Has everyone seen the camper van?' He described its hideousness to those who had not with a relish that made his heart pump faster.

'Isn't there a law against parking something of that size in your garden?' Tess asked.

Ralph shook his head, grimly. 'I've just checked and you'll be delighted to hear that our council is one of a handful in London that has no restrictions whatsoever. He can park it in the street if he likes. He can park a whole bunch of them.'

'Do we know exactly how many vehicles he's got in total?' Naomi asked.

'It's hard to keep track,' Ant said, 'but maybe twelve? He rotates them, so it's musical cars out there most evenings, and now this camper van is taking up the space of two he'll be looking for even more spaces on the street.'

'Have we established that he's actually selling cars?' Sissy asked.

'He definitely is,' Ralph said. 'I put a couple of the registrations into the Auto Trader website and they were listed for sale.'

As the others murmured in horror at this, Ralph reflected on the fact that he'd stored the phone number from the listing in his contacts.

'So to update you all,' Naomi continued, 'Ralph and I have reported him to the Trading Standards Department at the council and it's confirmed that he doesn't have a permit to sell cars either from his premises or the street. Needless to say, they're suffering from staff cuts, and before they can get an enforcement officer on the case, they want us to provide evidence of money changing hands. A photo or video would be ideal. Could you look out for that, Ant and Em? You're probably best situated.'

'Of course,' Ant said.

'Can I just ask,' Tess said, 'what's the best-case scenario with all of this? Even if you do get the evidence? Is it just him getting a rap on the knuckles and agreeing to pay a fine and fill in the right forms? Wouldn't he then just be doing legally what he's currently doing illegally?'

Trust Tess to trot out this sort of defeatism, Ralph thought. 'My expectation is that the council will deem his premises completely unsuitable for a business of that kind,' he told her. 'They'll shut the whole thing down.'

'You really think that will happen, Ralph?' Sissy said. 'Maybe we should prepare ourselves for living with him running the car business in some modified form. Perhaps it wouldn't be so terrible if he landscaped the premises properly? He could even create an entrance on the Portsmouth Avenue side. It's a main road, after all, with quite a few shops and businesses.'

'No way!' Ralph was astounded that Sissy of all people should contemplate compromise of any description. Did she want to live opposite a car showroom? 'We don't want him doing anything that establishes the premises as commercial. This is a residential street, always has been, and it's our job to protect that.'

'He doesn't mean your B&B business, Sissy,' Naomi added, hastily.

'Sure,' Ralph said, 'goes without saying. His changes the

whole character of the street. Plus, give this guy an inch and he'll take a mile. Give him permission to sell cars and what's next? A scrap yard? A go-karting track? If the council strikes a deal with him to widen the road, he might rent out some sort of bay for lorries to pull over in? A gypsy encampment, maybe?'

'Ralph.' Naomi arched an eyebrow. *Enough.* 'Shall we move on to the noise issue? Ant and Em, this is very much your department, I think.'

'Yes, it's pretty bad for us. Not like *this*, that's for sure.' Ant gestured to the open window, through which drifted birdsong and the sound of trees stirring in the evening breeze. You could catch the beat of music, but not to the point of distraction. 'We've complained repeatedly. We've rung the police, who say they don't have powers to prosecute domestic noise nuisance. It's the council's responsibility. But *they* say they no longer have the budget to send out noise pollution officers, so they only respond to written complaints after the event. We need three people to complain before they'll proceed to the next level.'

'Which is?' Naomi prompted.

'Issuing me with diary sheets. After I submit those, they'll investigate and hopefully issue a noise abatement order. Then it's a question of how the perpetrator decides to respond to that order.'

'By ignoring it,' Em chipped in, rudely. She seemed determined to undermine Ant's efforts, Ralph thought. What a shrew.

'Maybe you should get one of those apps that measures decibels?' Finn suggested.

'Great idea,' Ralph said. 'Then you could get a paediatrician or a social worker to say how damaging that could be to Sam's development?'

'A social worker?' Em looked stricken.

'Just to strengthen your case if this goes to court?'

'Well, possibly,' Ant said. 'But we don't want to risk getting blamed ourselves. The stories you hear about children being removed from their homes . . .'

'We have no reason to fear that,' Naomi reassured him. 'And I think it's premature to talk about court appearances, Ralph. Now, failing all this, we can appeal directly to the councillor. It's a bit long-winded, you have to allow twelve weeks for a response, then if you're unhappy with the way the issue is being handled, you can go to the Local Authority Ombudsman. That's another twelve weeks.'

'*Twenty-four weeks?*' Em burst out. 'We can't wait that long!'

'These things can go on a lot longer than that, I'm afraid,' Sissy told her. 'When I set up my B&B business, it took an age for all the applications and paperwork to go through. Maybe seven or eight months from start to finish.'

'Eight months!' Em echoed, her voice a near-screech. 'No way. No bloody way!'

Ant's shoulders sagged. He regarded his empty wine glass with such dismay that Ralph relented and offered him a refill.

'And it's not just the music,' Em continued, tearful now, 'there's also the building noise. All the dirt and dust.'

'Renovations are always a pain,' Naomi said, passing her a tissue, and Ralph remembered his wife's regular visits to neighbours with wine and updates when they'd had their kitchen done. 'We can't do anything about their new kitchen and bathroom, but they'll need planning permission and Building Regs for an extension or any structure he decides to build for his cars. Again, it takes time, but a multi-pronged attack will wear them down eventually. Now, the downside of all this is that when they start to get official visits and letters, they'll guess who made the complaints and may become verbally abusive.' She pre-empted Em: 'I mean, more than they are already. We need to avoid petty feuding and take the moral high ground, focus on the issues we can get investigated. Keep each other informed and supported. That reminds me, can I ask . . .' Through the open windows came the sound of a car engine in the street and she had to raise her voice to make her final request: 'Can I ask that from now on we only update each other on WhatsApp and not on text, email or the residents' Facebook page?'

'Why not?' Tess said.

'WhatsApp messages are end-to-end encrypted,' Finn explained. 'That's what terrorists use.'

'Terrorists?' Sissy repeated, startled.

Naomi hastened to reassure her. 'The point is, Sissy, we don't want anything in writing that can be twisted to make *us* look bad.'

'We certainly don't,' Ralph said. 'Let's not forget that we're not the ones breaking the law here.' He winked at Finn. 'Not until I burn his house down, that is – with him in it.'

'He'd still own the plot,' Finn said, with a bleak grin. 'He'd just move into his lovely new camper van.'

Naomi's eyes flared. 'Don't joke.'

The Kendalls left first, Em barking at Ant to carry the nappy bag, and Ant cutting short his goodbyes to follow his wife meekly from the house. Stressful neighbours or not, the man was pussy-whipped, Ralph thought, idly wondering if he ought not to get him out for a drink soon. Then, with sudden horror, his brain released a thought it had previously suspended: that engine they'd heard a minute ago, it had been unusually loud, more abrasive than modern ones sounded. It couldn't have been . . .

He dashed to the door, a pre-emptive rage swelling.

Unbelievable. The orange behemoth was right outside their gate, glowing grotesquely in the evening sun, blocking any view of the fine houses across the road. 'I don't believe this! Nay! *Nay!*'

Naomi joined him, shushing: 'You'll wake Charlie! What is it?'

'The bastard's switched the clapped-out Ford Focus for *that.* He did it just now, right in front of our noses, while we were inside discussing him!'

Though her mouth was pinched with distaste, Naomi maintained the professional, pragmatic tone she'd used throughout the meeting. 'Keep this in perspective, babe. It's not a deliberate provocation.'

Ralph was halfway to the gate, careless of who heard his bad temper. 'An hour after I had a go at him about it? Of course it's a deliberate provocation!'

Naomi overtook him, her hand on the closed gate. 'It's *not.* He's probably swapped it with the car so he can work on it on his drive. You know that's how he does it.'

'Bollocks. He could have swapped the car for any of the others. He's put this here because he knows I'll want to torch it.'

'*Torch* it?' Naomi flicked him a cautious look. 'You mean like you're going to burn his house down? Don't be an idiot.' She led him back to the door, though they didn't go inside. As she stood on the doorstep, with Ralph below on the path, her face was level with his and he wondered for a moment if she was going to kiss him out of his fury.

'Tess was a bit down, I thought,' she said finally, in an undertone. 'Has Finn said anything else about her wanting to move?'

Ralph recognized a tactical change of subject when he heard one. 'It's on hold. She thinks what's going on at number one would put buyers off.'

'It'd definitely do that. Well, that's something, I suppose.'

He raised his eyebrows. 'Don't tell me I've actually got something to thank the bastard for?'

Naomi chuckled, enjoying the irony of it. But Ralph, glimpsing the reflection of burnt orange in her eyes, was incapable of laughing with her.

6

Ant

—For us, it's the noise. He's either out front with his cars or out back with his saws and tile cutters or he's inside with all the doors and windows open and music blaring. They don't care what day of the week it is or how late in the evening. You never know when it will start or when it will finish.

—It's our son I'm worried about. Who knows how he's been affected by this, growing up with constant noise. He's probably suffered the same stress as some kid in a shantytown in South Africa or India or wherever – no exaggeration. This is supposed to be a good area! Not while Darren Booth's living in it, it's not.

—Sure, the council are sympathetic enough, but they just tell you to follow the correct procedure. Well, no offence, Officer, but look where correct procedure's got us. Is that a police guard, that guy there? Making sure no one tampers with the

scene over the rest of the weekend? Is it a crime scene then?

—Don't worry, I've got no intention of stepping over the tape. And I hope that works both ways, yeah?

MR ANTHONY KENDALL, 3 LOWLAND WAY, HOUSE-TO-HOUSE INQUIRIES BY THE METROPOLITAN POLICE, 11 AUGUST 2018

Three weeks earlier

If your neighbour is making a noise that is causing you distress, we strongly recommend you DO NOT RETALIATE . . .

Ant had looked at the Anti-social Behaviour Help website so many times its icon now appeared on his Frequently Visited screen.

'Is the music every night?' his assistant manager Paul asked, craning over his shoulder at the conference table, and Em's voice resounded in Ant's ears from that morning: '*Five nights out of the last seven, Ant!*' Accusing him, imploring him, as if he could bend time, alter the physics.

Ever since becoming a father, he had regarded the weekly Monday-afternoon stock control meeting at White Willow Foods & Drinks as something to be endured and, within his powers as procurement manager, cut short so he could dash to catch his train home to see Sam. But since the arrival of Darren and Jodie, he felt differently. With its well-insulated walls and absence of any threat of thrash metal, the meeting room had become a safe space for him to relax – and to field the opinions of his colleagues on his domestic predicament. It had made him, in an odd way, more interesting to them.

'Weekends are worst,' he said. 'But even on a quiet night their TV is at cinema levels.'

'What kind of thing do they watch?'

'Motor racing. Sometimes *Sons of Anarchy*. Sometimes porn.'

'Nice.'

'But like I say, we're plotting with the neighbours to put a stop to it. The council has sent me these diary sheets to fill in.'

'Diary sheets won't help a baby,' said Marie, a stock controller with a heart harder than most. 'This kind of stress could affect his development.'

'I know.' The adverse effects listed on the World Health Organization website for excessive noise made him shudder: chronic tinnitus; permanent hearing loss; blood pressure problems; muscle spasms; and, of course, cognitive effects. Any damage would be cumulative and likely irreversible. Ant had ordered the best, safest ear defenders for babies on the market, plus a selection of earplugs for Em and him.

Something else he'd discovered: music torture was banned under the United Nations Convention against Torture as a violation of basic human rights. Banned for use against terrorists, but not peaceful neighbours! This was the society they lived in now.

Increasingly, Em cited Ant's 'escape' to the office as an unfair advantage. As for that comment she'd made to Naomi before the meeting about returning to work as soon as she could . . . Previously she'd spoken of a desire to prolong time with Sam, finances allowing.

Thank you for the update, he'd thought. Had they become one of those couples who needed the presence of others to announce important personal decisions to their spouse? Like a government hiding news of poor performance in the clamour of a crisis.

There was a sudden excitement in Marie's manner as she promised Ant a tip he had not heard before: 'You know what? My friend complained dozens of times about the student house next to her place, but nothing ever came of it. She kept a record of everything – she had video, all sorts, but the process was ridiculously slow. The whole thing dragged on for well over a year. Warnings and letters and abatement orders, the full works, but these students just ignored them. She cracked it, though. You know what she did?'

'What?' Ant said, eagerly.

'Rang the police with a drugs tip-off. Anything to do with drugs, they take super seriously.'

'Is that true?'

'Apparently. In her case, the neighbours backed off. No more parties. A visit from the drugs squad feels like shit got real, huh?'

As the others laughed at her terrible gangsta accent, Paul took Ant's phone and fiddled about on YouTube. 'Listen to this. A mate played it to me the other night and I promise you it's worse than anything your neighbour can subject you to . . .'

He was right, the sound was bone-chilling, grotesque,

like the death throes of some terrifying mutant beast, and all present cried for him to turn it off.

'What the hell *was* that?' Ant asked.

'It's called a death whistle.' Paul read the caption aloud: 'A deeply disturbing noise produced by a carved skull-shaped instrument . . . The earliest use of sound torture, favoured by the ancient Aztecs . . . Used to accompany human sacrifices or to unsettle the enemy before battle.'

'Human sacrifice,' Ant said. 'Don't tempt me.'

When Ralph had asked him at the residents' meeting to look out for cash changing hands next door, Ant had been unsure how he might help, since he was out at work all day and Em was either busy with Sam or doing what she could to avoid being at home.

Then he had an idea. 'I'm going to set up video monitoring from Sam's room,' he told her. 'Using my old iPhone. We should get a good view of his drive from there.'

'Motion-triggered surveillance,' Em read from the app product description. 'Would it be permissible in court?'

'Probably not,' Ant said, 'but we'll let Ralph deal with that.' The thought of a courtroom showdown unsettled him. You gave your testimony and then afterwards you and the accused returned to your next-door residences. How would that work?

He checked the footage daily, training his eye to find the sporadic glimpses of the man himself. Trundling back and forth to his van for tools or strolling down to the street to take delivery of building materials and then lug them up the drive. Then there were the breaks for coffee and a cigarette or snacks wolfed on the go, the wrappers and crusts dropped as if in active encouragement of vermin. Since there was no audio, it meant none of the accompanying crashing and slamming and pumping of music was recorded: it all appeared mundane and harmless.

Once, Booth was standing in his drive smoking, when he went rigid and his mouth opened to roar at something he'd seen at the bottom of his drive. A quick rewind revealed the object of his displeasure to be a dog – Ant couldn't tell which one from the head poking into range, but most likely Finn and Tess's retriever Tuppy, who had a reputation for scavenging litter.

The range included a background section of the pavement beyond Booth's boundary and it was a bit creepy at first to see their neighbours strolling by – Sara Boulter, sweeping past the mess with a look of horror discernible even in miniature; Tess out with her kids – and often Naomi's younger one too.

Ant hadn't realized quite how much Tess did for Naomi, though Em had said Naomi liked to make little digs about her sister-in-law not working. Tess moved languidly, with a kindly, dreamy air, an earth mother figure never without a child or animal by her side, unlike Naomi, who was a force of nature, often seen striding – alone – from house to house. In the aforementioned court battle, he knew who he'd send into the witness box.

Also picked up in the footage were Sissy's occasional evening forays, which sometimes involved her stalling on the pavement to stare, arms hugged across her chest, feet locked in place, as if to take a step over Booth's boundary ran the risk of detonating a landmine.

There was little to see once darkness fell for the app had a limited night-vision function and there was no security light on either side of the drive. Sometimes, the outline of a figure against car headlights revealed Ralph or Finn walking Daisy home after babysitting.

'We have to agree this is purely to get Booth,' Ant told Em. 'If we happen to catch one of the Morgans snogging that babysitter, we don't tell anyone.'

Em scowled. 'Daisy is seventeen. I think we would be morally obliged to report it to her parents.'

'I was only joking,' Ant said, groaning.

He didn't have to wait long for success. Within ten days, there was clear footage of a visitor handing Jodie an envelope in return for a set of car keys and a package of what Ant presumed were vehicle registration documents. As Darren and Jodie watched, the man then got into a polished-up Renault on the drive and slid from range. He did not return.

'That'll be cash in that envelope,' Ant crowed, replaying Em the segment. But she wasn't nearly as thrilled as he was, paying more attention to Sam, who'd been grizzling all day. It was Saturday and next door the TV played an extended stand-up comedy routine, complete with roaring audience. 'Isn't it great? You all right, Em?'

She flashed him a disbelieving look. 'In case you haven't noticed, Sam's teething and in agony and I'm trying to comfort him while you play with your toys.'

'It's not a toy,' Ant protested. 'It's equipment to capture the documentary proof we've been waiting for. What's the problem? Anyone would think you didn't want to catch them in the act!'

'Anyone would think *you're* getting some stupid macho satisfaction out of buddying up with Ralph over this. Like this is anything to him but a pissing contest.'

'What do you mean?'

'I mean, he lives two doors down in a detached house with state-of-the-art double glazing! His children aren't a thousandth as badly affected as your own son.'

'Sam's the reason I'm helping Ralph,' Ant protested, his patience thinning.

'Are you sure?'

'Of course I'm fucking sure.'

Em's shoulders went rigid, her jaw jutting as she spoke: 'Please don't swear at me.'

'I'm sorry.' He regained his composure. 'I'm just disappointed you're not more excited about this breakthrough.'

'"Breakthrough"?' Her scorn had an awful ferocity to it. 'Proof of something that was already obvious to anyone with a pair of eyes?'

'Yes. Because what's obvious to anyone with a pair of eyes doesn't count, believe it or not! So can you please stop being so obstructive!' He could feel himself flushing, his blood surging.

'Why are you having a go at *me*?' Em cried. 'I'm not the one wrecking people's lives!' As Sam began wailing, she handed him to Ant and dropped into the nearest chair, face in hands.

Ant squatted next to her, trying to comfort both mother and child. He was frustrated to feel his own tears rising as laughter erupted on the other side of the wall.

'We have to work as a team, Em. There's literally no other way. We can't beat them alone.'

'We can't beat them at all,' Em said, her voice thick with misery.

'Don't say that,' Ant said.

The exchange left him feeling wounded – and confused. Even as the four walls closed in, he didn't know where he was with Em anymore.

At least Ralph was thrilled. His head appeared on the other side of the garden wall when Ant was in the garden later that afternoon. 'That footage you sent me is fantastic, mate, well done! If that's not proof he's running a business from the premises, then I don't know what is.' He spoke in a low, intense voice, like a producer briefing his star reporter.

'Can you believe they're so brazen?' Ant agreed.

'I know. Shame it's not coke or E or something. Then he'd be banged up all right.' Though, technically, it had been Jodie caught committing the misdemeanour, Ralph spoke exclusively in terms of Darren.

'Fancy a beer? Hop on over. Hey, maybe we should think about pulling down this wall, as well? The bigger the better.' Ralph passed over the stepladder and Ant climbed into the Morgans' garden as if he'd been doing it all his life. Whatever the cause of Em's scepticism, he considered the Morgans a godsend. They knew the street inside out. They would correct this dire momentum towards anarchy before the Kendall marriage imploded.

A flicker in his upper peripheral vision told him they were being watched, he presumed by a needlessly disapproving Em. He tried to recall when it had begun, her tendency to deride his efforts. The slide on his part into the kind of man who might swear at his wife. Was it with Booth's arrival, as cut and dried as that? Or had it been earlier? Exacerbated by neighbourhood unrest, not born of it.

But when he looked again, he saw that the figure was not in his own window but in the one beyond. Booth.

'Freak,' Ralph said, following Ant's gaze. 'Wouldn't be surprised if on top of everything else he was a paedo, would you?'

7

Tess

—Yes, we've complained, we all have, some of us repeatedly. But none of it has had any effect. He either ignores you completely or smirks and walks away. She's a bit more willing to engage, but then she is front-of-house, isn't she? Running the business side of things while he does the labour. Quite the dream team, eh?

—The most difficult issue for us? I suppose what I hate the most is how it alters your relationships with your neighbours. You get caught up in other people's dramas as well as your own. Basically, this one couple has destroyed the whole atmosphere of the neighbourhood. Even before this awful tragedy, they'd destroyed it.

Mrs Tessa Morgan, 5 Lowland Way, house-to-house inquiries by the Metropolitan Police, 11 August 2018

Two weeks earlier

'Do Ralph and Naomi *really* care what's going on?' Em asked, her oversized sunglasses masking the now-habitual blaze of indignation in her eyes. 'They can't be *that* bothered by it, with their amazing double glazing. Is this campaign just some vanity project?'

They were in the Morgans' garden with Dex and Sam. Thanks to Finn's sprinkler system, the lawn had survived the July heatwave to resemble a vivid, shimmering paradise in a blanched and thirsty land. A shuttlecock lay savaged on the terrace, Kit's handiwork, if Tess had to guess (or maybe Charlie's). Ralph and Naomi had paid for the deep natural stone terrace they shared, chosen to suit their own extension and laid in place of the existing red-brick herringbone design Tess had been fond of. Two hundred and fifty thousand pounds that extension had cost, Ralph had told Finn, and sometimes, when Tess caught a glimpse of Naomi at her central island, white marble gleaming in the mid-morning sun like a source of light in its own right, she thought of a spaceship – and of how pleased Naomi was to be the earthling entrusted with its controls.

She took a moment to consider Em's question. 'They do care, yes, but for different reasons. Ralph's on a mission about the cars, but Naomi's real concern is Play Out Sunday. I said to her the other day, should we cancel it, you know, because he won't clear his cars? And she said' – here, Tess mimicked Naomi's gravelly, well-spoken tones – '"Over my dead body, my friend."'

Em laughed. Tess noticed she laughed in that way people

under stress did, as if their signalling might at any time malfunction and turn laughter into sobbing.

'When will he wake up?' Dex asked, prodding baby Sam in his buggy. 'He's *always* asleep.'

Poor, poor little Sam, Tess thought. They'd just been to the park to see the cygnets, but he'd slept through the whole outing. Like his parents, he'd had no choice but to turn semi-nocturnal. Em had shown Tess the special noise-cancelling earmuffs they had bought for him to wear at night, but he sometimes pushed them off in his sleep and woke up.

'Soon,' she promised Dex, 'but we need to leave now to pick up your sister from school.'

'You'll be off to school in September, won't you?' Em said to Dex. 'It'll be nice to escape, won't it?'

An odd verb to choose, Tess thought. Dex said nothing, just nodded, solemn-eyed. It was almost as if he sensed Em's fragility, the need to handle her with care

But when the mothers and sons, plus Tuppy, emerged into the street together, he was more typically boyish. 'Another truck!' he yelled, excitedly.

Sure enough, at the bottom of Em's drive there idled a lorry laden with scaffolding. Whatever cheer Em had gained from the hour in Tess's garden now drained, her whole countenance slumping. She removed her sunglasses. 'Oh, God, what's going on now?'

'He must be starting on the roof repairs,' Tess said. 'Finn said he mentioned those when they first met.'

'Great.' Em began pushing the buggy, her stride brisk, and Tess had to scurry to keep pace. 'He hasn't finished the inside yet. Why can't he do one thing at a time?'

Reaching Em's drive, they had to navigate with care as scaffolding boards were carried to Booth's house by two builders. Booth and another man were already assembling the poles for the lower level.

'Is that a proper scaffolding company?' Em said. 'Those boards look a hundred years old.'

'Off the back of a lorry in both senses of the word,' Tess murmured.

'And the workers don't look like professionals, do they? Shouldn't they be wearing hard hats and those fluorescent jackets? Wait a minute!' Em stiffened. 'Those poles are sticking out over my window!'

It was true: the horizontal poles poked a good foot across the obvious dividing line between the two houses and slightly over the Kendalls' living room window.

Em checked the brake on Sam's buggy and strode forwards. 'Excuse me? Hello! Don't pretend you don't know who I am! You need to take this down – it's extending right across my property!'

Though the scaffolders paused to look at her, Booth barely glanced up, absorbed in his task. He was bare-chested, as he often was in the hot weather, and it made Tess uncomfortable to see his skin greasy with sweat. She had a horrible image of him being impaled on one of his rusting poles.

'Did you hear me? I said you're extending across our property and you haven't asked my permission!' Em stepped under the poles and rapped Booth on the shoulder.

Tess caught her breath: it was the first time she'd seen any of the neighbours make physical contact with him.

'What's the big deal?' He grimaced, impatient of the interruption.

'The big deal is you should have asked! Like everything else you do, you do it without any warning or explanation, nothing. It's completely unacceptable – *we live here too*!'

It was unfortunate that she sounded so emotional, almost wild, and Booth exchanged a look with one of the workers, who failed to suppress his laughter.

'Don't make fun of me!' Em screamed, but they ignored her and carried on with what they were doing.

Hearing her distress, Sam woke and began whimpering, and Tess knelt to comfort him. Both Dex and Tuppy were riveted by the argument, Tuppy rigid with attention.

'Just you wait,' Em continued, shouting now. 'We're on to you, you know. We've got proof!'

'Proof of what, love?' Booth was unruffled. 'D'you want to get out the way or you might lose an eye.'

'Is that a threat?'

'It's safety advice.' He shouldered past her, not violently, but with enough momentum to cause her to overbalance slightly and stagger towards the near side of the scrapheap.

Tess checked the brake was on Sam's buggy. She wouldn't have handled this as Em was doing but she was damned if she was going to watch him ride roughshod over another woman like this. Assigning Dex Tuppy's lead, she marched up to Darren. 'Can't you stop for half a minute and have a civilized conversation about this? You've hardly started putting the scaffolding up, it won't cost you anything to start again and move the poles along a few inches.' Then, when he disregarded her plea as easily as he had Em's: 'Is your wife in?' Dodging the passing workers, she beat on the open front door with her palms. 'Jodie!'

Jodie emerged, phone in hand, mid-call and harried. 'What's going on? I'm trying to talk on the phone here.'

'Would it be possible to ask your husband to re-start this scaffolding?' Tess said. 'He's got it right over Em and Ant's window.'

Jodie sighed before speaking sharply to Darren. 'Move it along a bit, all right? Makes no difference to you.'

'Thank you.'

For two or three seconds, it felt like a significant compromise in relations, until Dex shrieked from the pavement, 'Mummy, Tuppy's run away!' and suddenly Tuppy was at Tess's feet, barking and rearing up, and Booth was snarling at him, 'Get that fucking mutt off my drive!' And he raised the tool in his hand as if to hurl it at the dog.

'You need to leave,' Jodie told Tess, putting herself between her husband and Tuppy. 'We can't have kids and dogs running wild on a building site.'

As if she were the rational one, not Tess! As if her husband were not the one putting up dodgy scaffolding half-naked!

Capturing Tuppy's lead, Tess retreated. 'I'll be ringing the council about this,' she called. '*And* Health and Safety. Then I'll come and watch you take it down again, piece by piece. Are you okay?' she asked Em, who was now with Sam, her face and neck streaked with high colour. Sam was bawling at full volume.

'I'm fine.' Em fumbled with the brake, not meeting Tess's eye. 'Thanks for helping, but I need to go in and feed Sam. Oh, God, he's really upset.'

'She's deranged, that one,' Tess heard Booth say to the scaffolders in his odd, mild voice, as Em thumped the door shut behind her. 'Am I meant to be moving this or what?' he asked his wife.

'Don't bother,' Jodie said, puffing her cheeks as she sighed.

Hurrying away, Dex trailing, Tess googled the council's website and found the relevant page:

> You do not need a permit to put up scaffolding on your own property. You must, however, use a builder or scaffolding contractor who is trained and competent.

Trained and competent according to whom?

'Mummy, no!'

'Sorry, Dex.' Tess put away her phone before she committed the very sin she warned her son daily as being the deadliest: crossing the road without waiting for the green man.

It was easy to blame Booth categorically for what happened on that week's Play Out Sunday, but in Tess's opinion it was partly the parents' fault. *All* of the parents, herself included. After all, they'd known they couldn't continue to trust the safety of the arrangement the way they always had, not until they secured his co-operation and stopped him from moving his cars in and out. There was now the camper van outside Ralph and Naomi's, an obstruction by anyone's standards, as well as four other vehicles left in the street.

The heat was brutal. Even the shade, in the form of the paper-dry canopy of elms, felt exposing.

A group of kids, led by the Boulter twins, who, at

thirteen, rarely partook these days and whose presence was something of a draw, were skateboarding on the stretch outside their house. Dex and Charlie were attracted by the energy of it, though they didn't have boards of their own, and Charlie clamoured non-stop to be allowed a turn until eventually Naomi went out and tasked the older boys with giving him a few tips. It was after Naomi had returned indoors to fetch sunscreen and Tess had redirected Dex's attention to Isla and her friends' skipping game that the incident occurred.

The first thing was a yell from Ethan Boulter, followed by an eruption of younger voices. Charlie was lying motionless on the ground by the rear bumper of Darren Booth's white van. Booth had evidently reversed out of his drive into the street, turning downstream into the boarders' path and hitting the first moving target he'd met. He remained in the vehicle, with the engine still running.

'Where was he hit?' Tess cried, dashing over, Dex in her wake, and was assaulted by a cacophony of panicked children's voices:

'Is he dead?'

'His eyes are open!'

'He needs the kiss of life!'

'Turn the engine off!' she screamed to Booth, who, for once, complied without a word. Kneeling next to Charlie, she could tell he was breathing, but it was still the most ghastly sight, a little boy – her nephew – inert and open-eyed, as if hovering between one state of being and another. He was conscious, but unbending, perhaps from the shock. She called over her shoulder to the thickening crowd: 'Someone get

Naomi! Isla, you go! Charlie, Charlie darling, can you hear me? You're going to be okay . . .'

There were no obvious wounds to his head, arms or legs and, when she lifted his T-shirt, nothing visible on his chest either. His clothes were intact, other than his left trainer, which had come off and lay nearby. Though the van's engine was now off, she could still feel its low heat as Booth emerged from the driver's seat – leaving the door open as if he intended to get back in and continue his journey!

Em and Sara had appeared at the frontline: 'Why the hell were you reversing like that?'

'He came out of nowhere,' Booth said, tonelessly.

'You shouldn't have been driving in the first place,' Em cried. 'The road is closed today! For God's sake, why won't you follow the rules, like everyone else?'

'Couldn't you see the kids playing?' Sara demanded.

Booth made no comment. Was he *shrugging*?

'Did anyone actually see it happen?' Tess said, then, over a barrage of children's accounts, 'I mean an adult?'

'I saw it.' It was Karen, a mum from further down the street who had a daughter Charlie's age. 'I came up to get Lola for lunch and I had a clear view. The little boy was on his skateboard and he wasn't in control of it. He went scooting off into the path of the van and collided with the side, just near the back.'

'Where was the impact?' Tess asked.

'His chest, I think. He must have been winded.'

'How fast was the van going?'

'Now hang on a minute!' Booth protested, but Karen was already explaining:

'Really slowly, just a couple of miles an hour. The boy was going much faster – I doubt he'd have been visible in the wing mirror.' She gave Tess and Em a look of apology. Though from the far end of the street and not exposed to the full force of Booth's nuisance, she appeared to know who he was and was a reluctant defence witness.

It was then that Jodie appeared from Portsmouth Avenue, shopping bags in either hand, and Naomi and Ralph came sprinting up from number 7, Libby a step behind. Seeing her brother prone in the road, Libby let out a cry and clutched her father, while a tear-stained Isla hovered near Dex, who was sobbing.

'Oh, my God,' Naomi cried. 'Oh, my God, Charlie!'

At the sound of her voice, Charlie's eyes moved and, sick with relief at the first signs of his emerging from his stupor, Tess relinquished her spot to Naomi and pulled her own children close. At the gate of number 7, Kit and Cleo barked frantically, sensing that an emergency had gripped their pack.

'You fucking ran him over?' Without waiting for an answer, Ralph lunged at Booth, but Libby was still clinging to him, which weighed him down and prevented his outstretched fingers from grabbing the other man's throat. At the sight of this, Jodie dropped her shopping and tried to swat Ralph away, catching poor Libby in the process and making her wail in pain.

'The kid ran out!' Booth protested. 'I didn't see him.' Neither he nor Jodie went near Charlie or asked how he was, Tess noticed. He was, in fact, rallying, moving his arms and legs and crying in Naomi's lap.

Enlisting Finn's help, she tried to pull Ralph away. 'You

should back off, seriously. Karen saw the whole thing and it might not be what it seems.'

'There,' Jodie exclaimed. 'I knew it weren't his fault!'

'He shouldn't have been in his car!' Ralph hissed.

'I said that! No one listens to me,' Em said. She was making things worse and Tess wished Ant, who was standing some distance away with Sam in his arms, would do something to calm her.

'Do we need to call an ambulance?' Tess asked Naomi. 'He was hit in the chest, apparently. He might have broken a rib.'

'There's a forty-five minute wait on Sundays,' Naomi said, 'I was just reading about it yesterday. NHS cuts. Quicker to take him ourselves, if it's safe to move him.' At this, Charlie began to struggle into a sitting position. 'We'll take a chance. Go and get the car, Ralph. *Ralph!* Finn, can you make sure the road's clear for him to pull in?'

'Yes, of course.'

As the brothers mobilized, Ralph haring off to Portsmouth Avenue for his BMW and Finn moving bollards and clearing onlookers, Em and Jodie continued arguing, neither listening to the other and both flushed with heat and anger. Booth stood in the street as if uncertain of his next move. He reached for the van door handle.

'Leave it exactly where it is,' Naomi snapped. 'The police will want to check it out. Has someone called them? Tess?'

'Not yet,' Tess said.

'Well, can you do it, please!'

Moments later, Ralph's BMW began crawling into the street and turning in the most painstaking way. When it came to a halt, Naomi and Finn lifted Charlie and positioned him, prone, in the back seat, then Naomi slid in next to him.

'Want me to drive so you can sit with him?' Finn offered.

Ralph passed him the keys. 'Can you, mate? Then I can call ahead to A&E. Let's go.'

Before Tess could protest, Naomi called across to her: 'Can you look after Libby and the dogs?'

'Of course.'

'And call the police,' Ralph reminded her. 'He's not getting away with this.'

When they'd gone, a subdued shock reigned. Those families not directly involved in the drama departed, play resuming for the younger kids at the lower end of the street, and Booth and Jodie retreated inside.

The van remained in the same spot, at the same angle, as on impact. It was obvious to Tess that Karen's account was true and Booth had reversed in a standard shallow arc; the police would find no skid marks from speeding. But there'd been that incident with Sissy, hadn't there? When he'd almost hit *her*: he'd been driving dangerously then, Naomi said.

'Just come and get me when the police arrive. I'm at number fifty-three,' Karen told Tess.

One of the cottages at the other end of the street, far from the war zone.

Having put Libby in charge of her cousins and told them to wait inside with the dogs, Tess rang 999. There was some confusion as to the extent of the emergency, given the victim's removal from the scene, but eventually a squad car arrived and Tess directed officers to numbers 1 and 53.

'Do you need any background?' she offered, when they reappeared, and she explained the rules of the Play Out Sunday scheme. 'He almost ran over the lady at number two a few weeks ago – Sissy Watkins, she's called, if you'd like to speak to her? And look at the scaffolding! If that's not dangerous, I don't know what is.'

But she could tell by the way the officers thanked her that they considered this outpouring semi-hysterical, and she could only watch helplessly as they exited the scene for a more urgent call. She'd just reached her own gate when Jodie came stomping towards her, as livid as before.

'What's your problem, huh?'

'Are you talking to me?' Tess said.

'I don't see anyone else crawling to the cops, do you? Why d'you have to get them in, anyway?' Aggression radiated from her; it almost had its own scent. Tess had a vision of herself being shoved to the ground or belted with one of those freak blows you read about in reports of violent altercations that ended in terrible handicaps or even death.

'If you can't see why your husband is in the wrong in this situation, then I'm not going to be the one to explain it to you.'

'Don't need you to explain nothing,' Jodie sneered. 'It's obvious what's going on here.'

Tess lost her patience. '*What?* Other than the fact that you two are putting the welfare of this community at risk?'

'Don't give me that,' Jodie said. 'You've had it in for us from the second we arrived on this street. You were all over the scaffolding the other day.'

'Because it wasn't being put up right!'

'Don't think I haven't forgotten you broke in, neither. Maybe I should tell the police about that, yeah?'

'I did not break in,' Tess said.

'Had a good look around, did you? Decided we're not good enough for you? You're a bunch of snobs, the lot of you, and I reckon you're the worst.'

'I am not,' Tess protested, though her response implied a certain agreement with Jodie's broader accusation. 'None of us are snobs,' she clarified.

Jodie glowered. 'I'm watching you,' she said, no less disturbing for being a cliché and, as she walked away, she turned twice to look back at Tess in illustration of her warning.

It wasn't till seven in the evening that Ralph and Naomi returned from the hospital. Tess was with the kids in the den at number 7 when she heard them let themselves in, call hello, and take Charlie straight upstairs to his bedroom. Finn, she assumed, must be parking the car. Libby tore off upstairs, leaving Tess to hover until someone appeared.

'How is he?' she asked, when Ralph came down. She had to hand it to him, he looked fired up, forceful, the exact opposite of how she felt.

'He's sleeping. We had to wait an age for him to be seen. The NHS is in a shocking state.'

'Did they do a chest X-ray?'

'Yeah, nothing's broken, thank God. He's going to have bruising down his side, that's all. But if he'd hit his head, it'd have been a different story. As it is, he's going to be terrified to play out again.'

'Children should be able to feel safe in their own street,'

Tess agreed. There was no way she was going to say that a helmet was a good idea when learning to skateboard. At the sight of Naomi descending to join them, she repeated, brightly, 'Great news about Charlie! What a horrible scare. I made the kids carbonara for tea, Libby helped me cook. She's been very brave. And we took the dogs out together.'

'Oh, good.' Naomi sank onto the stairs, as if she couldn't trust herself to make it all the way down, her eyes shiny with tears. 'So what happened with the police? They haven't phoned us yet. Did you give them my number?'

'Nothing happened really,' Tess admitted. 'I mean, I explained he'd been knocked over – well, Karen from number fifty-three did. She was the only adult witness. Booth was questioned, as well.'

'Did they arrest him?'

'No, he's still at home, I think. It does sound as if it was a genuine accident. He's moved the van back onto his drive.'

'Not the camper van, though,' Ralph said, coldly, as if that were Tess's fault as well.

Naomi gazed down at her in disbelief. 'Did he at least get some sort of verbal warning?'

'I don't know.' Under their joint scrutiny, Tess felt totally inadequate. 'I couldn't really tail the police into his house, but I hope so.'

'You *hope* so?' Ralph echoed. 'This is unbelievable. I'm going round there, Nay. If the police won't sort him out, I will.'

'No, Ralph.' Naomi spoke to him sharply, a vein pulsing by her left eye. This was the most stressed Tess had ever seen her, not helped by the fact that Libby had appeared on the stairs, complaining of a migraine. Naomi rose to go back up, at least remembering to say goodbye to Tess, which was more than Ralph managed as he began competing with Libby for his wife's attention. Not a word of thanks from either of them, Tess noted. But this wasn't about her, she reminded herself, it was about poor Charlie.

Next door, Finn took Dex from her and put him to bed while Isla went to change into her pyjamas. It seemed incredible to think there'd be work and family life the next morning, business as usual. Tess began hunting for something for Finn and her to eat for dinner. She couldn't tell if the ache in her stomach was nerves or hunger, but the stinging red blotches on her skin were from anxiety, she knew. She opened the kitchen window, tried to cool herself. There was music coming from the garden of number 1, fainter than Booth's usual levels, and Ralph's voice was suddenly audible over it.

'Don't look at me like that, babe. I need it.'

He must be having a cigarette, Tess thought. No sooner had she made this deduction than she smelled the smoke.

Naomi sounded like her composed self again. 'Charlie's decided to sleep in our bed. Libby's lying next to him. They're both maxed out on paracetamol. I can't believe Tess didn't notice Libs had a headache.'

'I can't believe she didn't handle the police better. One of us should have stayed here to deal with them,' Ralph said.

Wait, this was completely unfair! And, as usual, *they* were the most important people in the world, theirs the only perspective to be considered. *The rest of us are only here to serve them*, she thought. *They're egomaniacs, not so different from the Booths—*

She caught the thought, ashamed of herself.

'I'll phone them tomorrow and make the situation clear,' Naomi said. 'I suppose when you think of all the stuff they're called out to day in, day out, this was one with a happy ending.'

'You're right. Charlie's okay, that's the main thing. But it's not an ending.' Ralph paused, presumably to smoke, and Tess imagined the toxins entering his lungs and streaming through a network of tiny tubes in search of his heart.

'As far as I'm concerned, it's the beginning,' he said.

When Tess and Finn were finally alone, at the kitchen table with soup and bread and cheese, she hardly knew where to begin.

'Don't start about moving again,' he said, forestalling the onslaught. 'I'm exhausted. Children's A&E has got to be one of the worst places in the world. All that screaming and they keep it so hot, even in summer.'

'I wasn't going to say that,' Tess said. 'And you didn't have to go to A&E. It didn't need three of you.'

Finn began tearing the bread as if he'd never been fed in his life before. 'I'm sorry. I just offered on the spur of the moment. I did the coffee runs.'

Tess raised her eyebrows. 'Oh well, in that case.'

He grinned, dropping his bread to reach for her arm and give it a squeeze. 'What *were* you going to say, then?'

Tess exhaled. 'I want to bring our holiday forwards. Tomorrow or the next day, I want to get out of here. I don't care what it costs to reschedule, I've got to have a break from this street.'

It seemed to her that a week on the Atlantic Coast of Portugal was all that stood between her and a breakdown. She wanted the roaring ocean in her ears, not the neighbours' sniping, not children's cries.

'I might not be able to rearrange my leave at such short notice,' Finn pointed out. 'I've had it booked in for months.'

'But will you try? Or just call in sick?'

He nodded, spooning the last of the soup into his mouth. Tess had not begun hers.

'I meant to ask you,' she said, the sudden, mid-distant thunder of a Motörhead bassline reminding her. 'Em said you made one of the official complaints to the council Ant needed to get his diary sheets? I thought we agreed we wouldn't go on record in case we decide to sell? You know you have to disclose any disputes to the buyer.'

'It's too late for that, Tess.' Finn gazed at her, jaw thrust uncannily like his brother's. 'Haven't you just called the police yourself about the man? We're all on record now.'

8

Sissy

—Have I had any previous reason to complain? Are you really asking me that now? After what's just happened?

—All right, the main point. The main point is he's run me out of business. Will that do? He's run me out of business and there's not a thing I can do about it!

Ms Sissy Watkins, 2 Lowland Way, inquiries by the Metropolitan Police, 11 August 2018

One week earlier

'Thank you, these are lovely,' Naomi said, raising the roses to her nose, and Sissy watched her inhale their scent with a kind of born-again appreciation. Her skin shimmered as if it had gold in it. The shock of Charlie's accident, the intimation of tragedy, suited her beauty.

Sissy remembered the last time she'd given flowers to a neighbour: crocuses for Darren Booth, that first Saturday – a far less poetic experience. He'd probably dropped them on his rubbish tip the moment her back was turned.

'I'm sorry I didn't catch you earlier in the week. I've tried a couple of times, but no one's been in.'

'You know what August's like,' Naomi said. 'The usual school-holiday complications. Tess and Finn went to Portugal early and I took the kids and dogs to my parents', so I've been working late while I've got the chance.' As Naomi updated her on the victim's bill of health and on her and Ralph's follow-up phone calls to the police and the council, Sissy felt, to her horror, a yawn stretching her mouth.

'I assume that's thanks to the eighties metal last night?' Naomi said. 'I didn't realize the music was such a problem across the road. You know, you could always go down the double-glazing route? I can give you the details of the company that did ours?'

'I don't really have the budget,' Sissy said, sighing. 'I can barely afford to clean the windows I've got.'

'Has business really been so affected?'

'Yes, I'm still getting bookings, but all the recent feedback is the same: they wouldn't come back because of the shambles over the road. Soon, my rating will be too low to attract anyone but desperate last-minute bookers.'

Noisy neighbours, said one recent review. *Fine for a night or two but you wouldn't want to live there*.

There was another property in Lowland Gardens, previously more available than hers, but now more booked up.

'What time did you finally get to sleep?' Naomi asked.

'Oh, I don't remember. Too late.' Sissy's heart thudded as she pictured Naomi's face if she told her the truth about last night. First, she probably didn't think women in their sixties had sex. (She probably didn't think she would ever get old enough to find out, imagining herself immune to anything grisly and menopausal that lay in wait for other women.) Second, might she think it borderline sordid to run a B&B and sleep with one of your guests? For this was what Sissy had done. Darren Booth could have had the entire chorus line of the Folies Bergère cancanning outside his house last night and for once she wouldn't have so much as tweaked the blind.

Actually, that wasn't quite true. The conversation with her erstwhile paramour had been struck up, the offer of the first drink, precisely *because* of Booth. Everything was because of Booth now – if it wasn't in spite of him.

Graham Reddy, her booking from Solihull, had come down to the kitchen at 9.30 p.m. with a bottle of wine and asked if he could use one of Sissy's wine glasses. She was about to point out that there were glasses in his room when he offered her a drink. Asked if business was booming.

'It *was*,' she told him, exactly as she had Naomi just now. It was definitely her feelings of helplessness regarding Booth that led her to open the second bottle of wine, but there was obviously an attraction in the first place. He was her age, twice divorced, ready for retirement but financially unable to. 'Not ever,' he said. 'It is what it is.' And the statement seemed to summarize his incautious air. It had been her only sex since divorcing Colin and standing here now on Naomi's doorstep, in the sane and sober reality of the day, it seemed fantastical, like some sort of delusion. Oh! Might it have been illegal to take money from him? Did it make her the keeper of a brothel? Guests paid in advance via the website, but had it been done the traditional way, writing a cheque or handing over cash on departure, she couldn't possibly have gone through with charging him.

She'd noticed Booth's music when they were lying in bed in the bedroom at the front. It must have been one in the morning by then.

'Is that your bogeyman?' Graham asked, going to the window. He didn't cover himself and when he pushed aside the curtain and the streetlight exposed his pale body, Sissy felt heat suffuse her face. 'He and the missus are having a fag out the bedroom window. Looks like a wimp to me.'

'He's stronger than he looks,' Sissy said. Wrapping herself in the bedsheet, she joined him. Partially backlit, the scaffolding at number 1 was a stark exoskeleton, Darren and Jodie's joint silhouette a shooting target at their window. It was impossible to tell if *they* had seen Sissy and Graham or not. Perhaps it was the wine or the post-coital boost of self-belief, but Sissy felt more confident of taking them on than at any time before. 'I'm sure we'll resolve it one way or another,' she said. 'For now, all I can do is move into this room myself when I have guests, so they can stay in the back.'

'Except when they join you,' Graham chuckled. He returned to the bed. Would he expect to stay all night in here, she wondered, or would he return to the room he had paid for? 'My sister had a problem a bit like this, years ago.'

'Many people do, I'm learning. What did she do?'

'Oh, a couple of us scared him off.'

'How?' Sissy asked.

'Not sure you need to know that, Sissy.'

Nor did she need to know the sister's name or any other detail about his life, his and Sissy's connection being so transitory. It struck her that he might have lied about being single. Or did people bother lying at their age? She certainly didn't. If you couldn't tell the truth by your seventh decade, you probably weren't ever going to.

The next morning, she said goodbye at the door, determined to recapture the air of professionalism she'd possessed when she'd checked him in. Graham masked any awkwardness by turning to the street as they talked.

'Now I see it in the light, that scaffolding looks a bit dodgy.'

'He put it up himself, apparently,' Sissy said. 'I went out one day and when I came back it was up.'

'Always the way,' he said, as if he encountered Booths every day of the week.

There were no plans to keep in touch. It wasn't that sort of thing.

Returning from Naomi's house, Sissy's mind turned to what she needed to get done before a two-day visit to her old friend Anthea in Wiltshire (she'd sleep well there, that was for sure: Anthea and her husband lived on the edge of their village and had no neighbours). Strolling past Tess's house before turning to cross, she became aware that the object of the street's displeasure was watching her from the first level of his scaffolding. She avoided his eye and stepped into the road, which was when, for the first time in their acquaintance, he initiated dialogue with her.

'Good night last night?'

She hesitated a few steps into the road. What did *that* mean?

'Get along okay with your paying guest, did you?' he added.

He *had* seen them. Jolted though she was, Sissy stepped back onto the kerb and faced him with a steady gaze. Bearing down on her from behind the waist-height railing, he had a peculiar menace about him. Baiting was a brand new dynamic between them; previously, he'd dismissed her, swatted her complaints aside like stunned wasps.

Well, if he wanted to talk, she would talk. 'To answer your first question, I think everyone's night would have been a lot better without the heavy metal soundtrack, thank you. But we do our best, given the limitations. You won't get away with it for ever, though. This is anti-social behaviour, whether you're capable of seeing it that way or not.'

Booth regarded her with mild contempt. 'Should've called the police if you were so bothered.'

Was he really so unaware that he didn't guess his neighbours had tried the police, that they had the council on speed dial? Surely he'd begun to receive formal letters by now? Then she remembered Naomi's warning: *They'll guess who made the complaints and become verbally abusive.* Something must have happened, which was a good thing, even if this particular interaction was unwelcome.

'Sooner him than me, that's all I can say,' he added.

'I beg your pardon?'

'Your bloke last night. An old cunt like you.'

Sissy gasped and a flush spread upwards from her chest like bushfire: had he *really* just said that? No, he couldn't possibly have. And yet, he had. Speechless with fury and humiliation, she picked up a chunk of brick from his scrapheap and hurled it at him, yelping in frustration when it hit the wall instead and clattered back to the ground. As Booth laughed at her incompetence, she backed away, stumbling across the road, her legs trembling and eyes brimming.

'What? What did I say?' he called, taunting her. He wanted her to repeat the word back to him, turn it into her crime, not his. How could he be so cruel?

How had he survived this long saying things like that and not been murdered in his own bed?

9

Ralph

—To be honest, I'd say the noise has been worse for other people than for us. Like my brother and his wife, they're only two houses away from Booth and they don't have double glazing. Plus their dog's very nervous, barks a lot. But everyone has their own pain threshold, don't they?

Mr Ralph Morgan, 7 Lowland Way, house-to-house inquiries by the Metropolitan Police, 11 August 2018

One day earlier

Lately, Ralph had been suggesting the Star on the Rushmoor Estate for his Friday drink with Finn over their traditional drinking hole the Fox and Hounds, a gastro pub on the high street that was frequented by people like them. 'Pigs in blankets and dogs in jackets' kind of people, as Finn put it, and

Kit, a lurcher, had a particularly extensive collection of cosy coats chosen by Naomi and Libby.

Why he was attracted to the Star, with its dilapidated fittings and edgy clientele, he wasn't altogether sure, but it may have been an extension of those diversions on the way home from work – deprivations revisited. What would a psychiatrist have to say about that? That he felt under threat in Lowland Way and needed to reassure himself that his grass was greener than everyone else's? Or that the conflict with Booth had moved him to study further members of his tribe, the better to understand (and defeat) Booth himself?

Either way, Finn had resisted the idea of the Star until this evening, saying he fancied the longer walk after a shit week at work. As usual, when Finn made a passing complaint about work, Ralph discerned a reflex of regret, as if Finn feared yet another poaching attempt, which would have been hurtful if Ralph didn't know exactly what was behind his fear of joining Morgan Leather Goods. Or, rather, *who*.

It was nine by the time they got there and the bar was crammed with Friday drinkers, a fair few of whom wore an air of boozing as a primary career.

'Jesus,' Finn said, as they waited to be served, 'is it me or can you still smell the smoke from before the ban? When was that?'

'Two thousand and seven,' Ralph remembered. It was when he'd given up. Or 'given up', perhaps, considering his occasional weakness. 'It doesn't look that different from the Bell, does it? Remember when Dad used to take us with him? We must have been Libby's age. Well underage.'

'Different time,' Finn said. 'Different world. I don't remember anyone saying, "Shouldn't those kids be in bed?"'

'Or, "Shouldn't their young lungs be protected from the fog of cigarette smoke?" Our clothes must have reeked.'

When they settled at a table near the door, Ralph resisted the temptation to mop up the previous occupants' spills with the Pret napkin in his pocket. There was a man at the next table who his eye kept returning to. Though he was physically the same type as the other middle-aged, beer-bellied punters, there was something about his expression, his body language, that connected with Ralph in an unwelcome way. It made him see who *he* might have become had he not had the right drive at the right time (the right place, you could always find). Bitterness was the closest word, but it was subtler than that, more like the final scrabble for an escape route before surrender. 'You know how people say, "There but for the grace of God go I"?'

'Yeah,' Finn said.

'Well, I hate that saying. Why is everyone supposed to be so *humble*? Why can't people say, "I got where I am because I worked fucking hard. I didn't want second best."' Ralph glanced out of the window to the concrete 'garden' forecourt, to the grey expanse of road with drifts of litter in the gutter and, beyond, a caged sapling, a pathetic attempt by the council to inject green. The caging was torn; it was only a matter of time before the tree was bent flat.

There was an explosion of male laughter from the neighbouring table, followed by a chorus of heckling as a bony, pink-faced lad was ejected from the group in the direction of the bar. Never keep the blokes waiting when it's your round,

Ralph's father had taught them and they never had. His gaze moved to another of the group, a man in his thirties who was powerfully built and charged with violent energy.

'You know what I reckon?' he said to Finn. 'We wouldn't need to look very far if we needed help. You know, with *him*. If it comes to that.'

'You think it will?'

'It might.'

While Finn went to the bar for another round, Ralph checked his work mails. A notification for an earlier Facebook post by Naomi popped up: *Play Out Sunday will go ahead as usual.* Following Charlie's accident, they would close the road lower down, outside the Morgans', using extra bollards and a rotation of adults to guard the sign. Like fucking riot police, Ralph thought, newly enraged. Whatever it was Booth thought he was doing on Lowland Way – building a business, renovating a house – he was, in fact, jeopardizing a community. *Their* community. Ralph and Naomi had been a big part of raising their street to the heights it had reached and he was damned if he was going to let one man bring it back down.

Yes, he would get help, if it came to it. He would not let him win.

Finn returned with their drinks. 'Guess who I've just seen sitting with his mates on the far side of the bar?'

'You're kidding me? He's been here this whole time?'

'Both of them. Date night.'

Ralph took a look on his way to the gents. It was a jolt to see Darren and Jodie out of context, Darren in civilian clothes and Jodie half-decent in a short black dress, makeup and heels, two of a group of six. Pints and cigarettes and phones on the table. Darren was silent – he was never going to be loquacious – but he was grinning, relaxing. Ralph thought of Charlie on a gurney, of the oppressive heat and ancient, faintly aromatic upholstery of Children's A&E, and glowered. This was the man who put him there, who could easily have *killed* him.

He fished for his phone and tapped out a text:

This is your final warning: move that heap of crap from outside my house by 8 a.m. tomorrow.

Was Booth the kind of person to respond to a text the moment it arrived? Evidently not.

'Shall we head back after this one?' Ralph said to Finn. 'Have one at home with the girls?' The evening had soured for him, the dubious-at-best pleasure taken in the Star evaporated. He'd told Finn they wouldn't need to look far for help, but Booth had got here long before they had. He belonged.

They trudged home, Finn teasing him about his devotion to his wife. Yeah, yeah. It was only as they approached their end of Lowland Way that he felt his phone vibrate in his pocket and he drew up next to the camper van. It was a mild, moonlit evening, the kind where you'd appreciate seeing a vintage Jag outside your door, not this hulking, malodorous piece of wreckage.

'You go in,' he told Finn. 'I won't be a minute.'

'Okay. Don't go slashing those tyres now,' Finn warned, joking. 'Then he really *would* have an excuse not to move it.'

'I won't. At least not with you as a witness,' Ralph returned.

The message was from Booth:

Or else?

Ralph placed a hand on the side of the camper van for support. It was the first time he had touched the vehicle and the metal was warm after a long day in sunlight. When he removed his hand, you could see his palm print in the dirt on the paintwork, fingers and thumb perfectly captured, like evidence.

He tapped out his reply:

Or else you'll regret it.

10

Ant

—Worst off? Well, we are, of course, we're right next door! I have to say, Sissy Watkins has had it pretty bad, as well. The poor woman's aged visibly, we've been really worried about her, even before this.

—Mind you, people would probably say the same about us.

Mr Anthony Kendall, 3 Lowland Way, house-to-house inquiries by the Metropolitan Police, 11 August 2018

One day earlier

For the first Friday since Darren and Jodie had moved in, they were out when Ant came home from work. Out! It caused a powerful kick of nostalgia right to his gut: this was how a weekend was supposed to feel, especially in August. Sun-baked and frisky, the air sweet with freedom.

Except for the stink of next door's scaffolding. It was revolting, as if the boards had been dredged from the bottom of the Thames. The lower platform was loaded with materials: Booth appeared to be using it as a semi-permanent storage facility, with a security alarm box so flimsy-looking it might have been one of those fake ones, the wires not actually attached to the power.

Following Em's reports of cowboy builders, Ant had watched a YouTube video to check if the scaffolding had been put up properly and had concluded there was a longitudinal brace missing between the two platforms. 'Keep Sam away from it, in case something falls from above,' he'd told Em.

She'd reacted defensively: 'I'm not stupid, I'm keeping his head protected every time we go in and out.' She'd complained this week of the peace-shattering sanding of exterior features between the upper floor windows and roof line, of the sudden wince-inducing scrapes and crunches of materials being dragged along the boards, but the fact was that all of it was perfectly legal during the hours of 8 a.m. and 6 p.m. Monday to Friday and 8 a.m. to 1 p.m. on Saturdays. The law paid no heed to stay-at-home parents, home workers or anyone hoping for a lie-in after a back-breaking week at work.

'All quiet on the Western—' he began, closing the door behind him, but faltered at the sight of a large suitcase standing in the hallway. 'Em?'

In the kitchen, Sam was in his high chair, face smeared with pureed carrot, while Em collected items from the fridge and decanted them into Tupperware. The radio was on, as it always was, a permanent low-level defence against what might advance through the walls and windows.

'Why is there luggage in the hall?' he asked, stooping to kiss Sam hello.

Em turned, efficient, determined. 'Because I'm going to go to my mum and dad's. Just for a week or so.'

Ant blinked repeatedly, as if his vision had suddenly blurred. 'You mean with Sam?'

'Of course with Sam.'

Without discussing it with Ant, who had not yet been parted from his son for longer than a night or two. 'What, right now?'

'No, I can't face the Friday night traffic. We'll go in the morning. I've had a horrific day, non-stop noise. I can't take any more.'

Ant gestured in the direction of the common wall. 'I thought we were in the clear for once.'

'Yes, they just went out. But, rest assured, they'll be back later and it will start again.'

Rest assured? As if he *wanted* the torture to resume. 'Unless they've gone on holiday?' he said, hopefully.

Em shook her head. 'No, he wouldn't have left all that stuff on the scaffolding. Plus, I heard *her* on the phone this morning saying, "It'll be ready this time tomorrow," which must mean one of the cars.' Em no longer used Darren and Jodie's names. They were *him* and *her*, interchangeably abhorrent.

'Okay.' Ant wiped Sam's mouth and extracted him from his chair. He was getting heavy, wriggling to be lowered to the floor and have another try at crawling. 'Ralph mailed me today with some good news. He chased up the council over the car trading and they say the clip we sent was exactly what they needed. They've done some preliminary investigation and found matches between the cars advertised and those parked on the street.' He paused for a show of enthusiasm on Em's part that did not arrive.

'Wow, quite the Sherlocks, aren't they?' she drawled. 'Why don't they do something about it then?'

'They have. They've written to Booth, but he's so far failed to respond.'

'Surprise, surprise.'

'They allow twenty-eight days for a response.'

'Of course they do.' Her sarcasm felt pointed, as if she blamed Ant personally. 'Why not twenty-eight weeks? No need to rush him into anything he's not comfortable with.'

Ant sighed. 'I know it's frustrating, Em. Everything you feel, I feel the same.'

'No, you don't.' She stopped what she was doing with the Tupperware and locked her left hand onto her right wrist. 'You're at work most of the time. I'm here all day long, touching distance from those lowlifes!'

Ant took a bottle of wine from the rack and last night's glass from the draining board and sat down at the table. 'I know and I wish you weren't. But I, for one, feel better knowing that we're tackling it as a group.'

'Well, I, for one, feel better getting as far away from the whole lot of them as is physically possible,' Em said. 'And since a desert island isn't an option, Gloucestershire is going to have to do.'

Ant began drinking, but the effect was not as instantaneous as he would have liked. 'Fine. I'll come with you for the weekend and get an early train in on Monday.'

Em was unyielding. 'No. You don't get it: I want to go on my own. I need some headspace from this. I have to have a break from discussing *them*.'

He felt his heart rate pick up, his skin redden. 'You're asking me not to spend the weekend with my wife and son because I might comment on an issue affecting our welfare?'

'Yes. Or *I* might. It's what we talk about now, isn't it? The *only* thing.'

He had to admit she was right. It had happened insidiously and yet startlingly quickly. New parents were famously one-track in their conversation, but in this family, Sam shared his parents' attention with their neighbours. *How's he been today?* When Ant came home and asked Em this question, it applied as easily to Darren Booth as it did to Sam.

Em returned to her task, stacking pots in the fridge. 'Please don't make a big deal of this, Ant.'

He did his best to co-operate with this request. The idea of a weekend alone need not be a desolate one. He could go to a museum or a food market, maybe the theatre, one of those mythologized pursuits lost to new parents that he wasn't sure they'd done much of in the first place.

He became aware of how hungry he was. 'What are we eating?'

'I haven't had a chance to think about dinner.'

Too busy plotting her getaway.

'We'll order a pizza. I'll do Sam's bath first,' he said and Sam, at least, co-operated, not tensing in objection as he sometimes did when separated from Em.

'I love you,' Ant told him as he carried him upstairs to the bathroom, and there was a choke in his voice, as if these were the only words left in the family – the only emotion – untarnished by external forces.

Without any disturbance from next door, Sam's bedtime routine was textbook smooth and, after sharing a pizza in front of the TV, Em took advantage of the silence and went up for an early night. Left alone, a second bottle of wine open, Ant felt his mood plunge. Why was he sitting here on his own? He and Em should have been wallowing in the peace, catching up and having a laugh (maybe, God forbid, having sex). Instead, it was just him and his familiar new companion, self-pity.

Until Darren and Jodie returned at about midnight, voices raucous with drink, and turned on the music. There'd be ten minutes, maybe fifteen before Sam woke and either Em brought him down or Ant went up to join them for the latest hissed conference.

He opened the front door and stepped into the night air. Across the road, in Sissy's front garden, foot-level uplights led the eye to the bay trees in their tall pots, the dark mapping of wisteria under the first-floor windows. When they'd first looked around their house, he and Em had stood together at the bedroom window and joked about the view from here being a lot better than the one from there.

'I'd rather live there, obviously,' Em had said, 'if I had the choice.'

'Me too,' he'd replied. 'All in good time.' As if anything were possible. As if they'd found their place in the world and it was simply a matter of increasing their share of it.

His eye rested on the van on the Booths' side of the driveway. Maybe he and Em could dig up their half and put in a hedge of cypresses to block their view, create some separation. Then again, if they did that, where would they park? The nearest six or so street spaces were filled with Darren's vehicles and competition for the remaining ones had become fractious. The camper van outside Ralph and Naomi's had been there for weeks now, the battery probably dead.

The music faded out. In the second or two between songs, there was a cry from inside. Sam.

You bastard, Ant thought, *you've reduced my life to the gaps between songs. You've made my home intolerable to live in, you've stolen my son's right to proper sleep, and you're well on your way to wrecking my marriage.*

Because Em's departure in the morning was the beginning of the end, he was sure of it. Not a week, but a week *or so*. While Booth reigned, while Jodie supported and enabled him, Em would not return. How long before she found a lovely nursery near her parents' place? A flexible local job for a returning new mother?

The door to number 1 opened and Jodie emerged. She set off down the drive, staggering slightly in her heels.

Expelling the breath from his lungs in a bid to calm himself, Ant had a very strong sense of how it must feel to face your enemy with nothing left to lose.

11

Tess

—Yes, I would agree the Kendalls have had it worst. Em has been particularly distraught, close to the edge, I'd say. There's been no escape for her. Still isn't.

Mrs Tessa Morgan, 5 Lowland Way, house-to-house inquiries by the Metropolitan Police, 11 August 2018

One day earlier

In the taxi back from the West End, Tess closed her eyes, partly out of exhaustion and partly to avoid having to engage with Naomi. Their mother-daughter theatre trip had been Naomi's idea, with the aim of making it a school-holiday tradition (on her website, there was a whole section devoted to 'making memories', a phrase Tess hated). She didn't want to be ungrateful, but if this outing was anything to go by, she preferred not to subscribe long-term. Isla's view of the stage had been restricted by a tall woman with exorbitant hair in the seat in front, Libby had come over dizzy and overheated, and the entire interval had been taken up with queuing for the loo. The tickets alone had cost more than most people earned in a week and Tess, of course, earned nothing.

They'd only been back from Portugal three days and already the thought of their holiday – silver sands and cuddles with the kids in their damp beach robes – had a profound sense of loss to it, leaving her with an overwhelming desire to stave off her London life for as long as other people allowed. To her shame, following a bumping into with Em that had brought her up to speed on the very Lowland Way antagonisms she'd sought to flee, she'd avoided suggestions that they have a coffee so she could hear more of the same. Today, Em had messaged: *Not going to be around next week. You can guess why.*

Booth, of course.

'Just here,' Naomi commanded the driver, as they turned into Lowland Way. 'Can you sort this, Tess? I'll get Libs in before she's sick.'

'Sure.' Petty to note that she'd never get the money back. Naomi was cavalier about shared expenses, especially when it came to making memories.

By the time they were all inside and the kids in bed, Finn and Ralph had come back from the pub and proposed the four of them have a bottle of wine in the garden, since there was no music booming from number 1.

'Ralph, you open the wine,' Naomi ordered. 'I'm going to sit with Libs for a couple of minutes, she's still a bit queasy. Finn, just walk Daisy home, will you?'

Tired and scratchy, Tess finally lost her cool. 'Can you please not tell my husband what to do, Naomi! He's not staff!'

'I beg your pardon?' There was an odd gleam in Naomi's eye as she halted in front of her five-grand fridge (or whatever it cost), a rare meanness, and Tess saw it was too soon after the scare with Charlie to cross her, especially now Libby was worrying her as well. 'Oh, for God's sake, Tess, just because you've been out of the workplace so long you've forgotten the art of delegation, it doesn't mean the rest of us have to. We're not all martyrs, you know, insisting on doing everything ourselves.'

Tess gasped. 'What do you mean by that?'

'Exactly what I say.'

Tess's heart banged in anger. 'Has it crossed your mind that if you didn't have me to delegate to all the time, *you* wouldn't be practicing this "art" either? And your workplace is hardly the prime minister's office, is it? Posh mums dispensing advice to other posh mums from one of their posh garden offices!'

Naomi's expression turned thunderous. 'I wonder if that's how the families of the founders of Mumsnet spoke to *them*. Really, Tess, you might want to update your attitudes to working women, for Isla's sake, if not your own.'

Tess wheeled round to Finn, her voice wild: 'Are you hearing this? And you wonder why I want to sell up!'

There was a moment of frozen silence at this first public reference to her desires, followed by an exchange of covert looks between the other three. It took an excruciating ten seconds for Tess to understand that this was not because her declaration was a shock to Ralph and Naomi, but because they knew it would be a shock to her to realize that they already knew. What was going on in this family? Next they'd be planting a chip in her head and stealing her dreams.

'Finn?'

He struggled to speak, obviously hoping the crisis would depart as quickly as it had arrived. Ralph, meanwhile, took his time reaching in the cupboard for wine glasses, his back to the room. Naomi had told Tess once that he had a strict policy with cat-fighting (as he termed women's disagreements): to intervene was to risk being clawed yourself.

'Come on, you're not going to sell up,' Naomi said, at last, and Tess knew her well enough to recognize that she was steering them away from that ugly trading of slurs, in itself an acknowledgment of regret on her part. 'It's honestly not worth trying, Tess, not while this thing with Booth is going on. The Boulters were considering getting a valuation, but they've postponed for now. To be honest, I think we have to accept we're in for the long haul with this guy.'

Did Tess detect *relish* in her tone? Was it paranoia to imagine that calling meetings and co-ordinating complaints was Naomi and Ralph's way of keeping Finn and Tess on the street, under their control?

'Anyone can sell anything,' she said, stonily. 'It's all just a matter of price.'

'Of course.' Naomi shrugged, as if anything less than the best price was of no interest to her.

'I ought to head off,' said a young voice from the kitchen door. Daisy. In their rancour, they'd forgotten the babysitter was still there.

Ralph re-entered the earth's atmosphere then, satisfied

presumably that Naomi was, as ever, victorious, queen of all women. He produced his wallet. 'Has someone paid you?' he asked the poor girl. 'Come on, I'll walk you home.'

She knew she wouldn't sleep, even before the music started. Finn wanted to have sex, but Tess wanted to get a few things straight.

'How does Naomi know we're thinking about moving?'

He groaned. 'Do we have to talk about this? Anyway, we're not moving yet, so let's not make it into something it's not.'

'I'm just asking, because it would be quite useful to know: is it no longer a subject we're keeping private? Is any subject?'

Finn resigned himself to the debrief. 'It's never private when it comes to property. People speculate all the time, even when they haven't got a madman driving them out.'

The worst part of it was that Naomi was right. It was crazy to imagine anyone would pay the market rate, let alone a premium, for a house two along from one that couldn't be plainer in advertising itself as toxic if it had a sign on the door saying CONDEMNED. They were hostages to these people, it was as simple as that.

We're not all martyrs ... Her mind spun with the indignity of it, of Naomi's clear wish to degrade her in front of the men, of Finn's conspicuous lack of intervention, and she cut the conversation short, unable to look at him. His conscience evidently clear, he fell quickly asleep, with the soft nasal snore of a cat.

Downstairs, Tuppy was howling. On his own behalf or on hers, she wondered? And why was she suddenly icy cold? Was she ill? The chill went through her arms and chest and settled deep within.

She got out of bed and slipped on sheepskin slippers, the ones that looked like moccasins and that she sometimes wore outside. Then, closing the bedroom door behind her, she crept downstairs.

12

Sissy

—None of this would have happened if you'd responded to complaints – you and the council. That's right, you shake your head, deny everything. You don't like hearing you've failed us, do you? Well, it's too late now. Are you even aware that two lives were lost this morning, not one?

Ms Sissy Watkins, 2 Lowland Way, inquiries by the Metropolitan Police, 11 August 2018

One day earlier

When Amy phoned to say she had some news for Sissy, news she wanted to tell her in person, Sissy suggested she come for dinner and stay over. Pete had been delayed and wasn't due to return from Aberdeen till the Saturday afternoon, so there was no reason to rush back to North London.

Sissy had a horrible feeling the news was not going to be

welcome. Aberdeen was to be replaced by Dubai, perhaps, or Jakarta, any future wedding vows exchanged before strangers on a far-flung beach.

She didn't think she could remember ever having been so exhausted and it wasn't simply the fact of having spent the day cleaning and preparing all three guest bedrooms, one for Amy and two for the following day's B&B guests. No, it was also the weight of the warning she'd received from CitytoSuburb that morning, which had come in the form of an automated email:

> Dear Property Owner,
>
> You may be aware that your property at 2 Lowland Way, Lowland Gardens, has received less than positive reviewer feedback recently. Poor ratings can lead to a drop in bookings.
>
> Be aware that CitytoSuburb sets a minimum requirement of 100 nights' bookings a year and you are falling short of this target.
>
> The following are ideas to boost your business …

The ideas included offering a gift with every booking made at least four weeks in advance. Food went down a treat: local honey or some homemade biscuits. She could then opt to pay CitytoSuburb to promote this on its site. Of course she could.

A shame she couldn't pay them to pour local honey down Darren Booth's throat until he choked. Then she wouldn't need a special offer.

Nice house, nice host, shame about the place opposite, one guest had commented, succinctly. Three window boxes, which was as many as she could hope for these days.

She'd approached Jodie that morning, a last-ditch attempt to make her consider a point of view beyond her own.

'What're we meant to do?' Jodie had asked, and her eyes clouded, the line between her eyebrows deepening. Sissy saw she was insulted, even hurt. 'We're only making a living, same as you.'

'But my business doesn't disrupt the street the way yours does,' Sissy said.

'You don't call chucking a brick at someone disrupting the street?' Jodie's phone rang, ending the exchange before Sissy could decide whether or not to disclose the reason for her violence. Did Jodie know her husband spoke to neighbours the way he had Sissy?

She could no longer put off ringing her mortgage lender. 'I wanted to talk about pausing my repayments for six months,' she told her appraiser. 'Pause' was a verb Sissy used a lot these days; it was important to keep the faith that this dispute with the Booths had only suspended normality and not replaced it.

'Let me just bring up your file, Mrs Watkins, and check the conditions of your contract.'

As if she were a convict out on parole.

'*Ms* Watkins,' she corrected him.

He asked her to confirm her date of birth, saying, when she told him, 'Not a problem,' the implication being that it *was* a problem, the more years lived the more severe one's disadvantage in such negotiations; especially threatening when you considered the lender had the right to repossess her house were she to renege on the terms of the loan.

'Your product doesn't qualify, I'm afraid. It's not a flexi product. The payments are fixed for the term of the loan.'

'All right, but I'm asking you to allow this on a discretionary basis. Just while I smooth out a few bumps.'

And so on, until finally she was authorized a short 'holiday' (as if she planned to spend it in the Seychelles): three months. Her next payment would be the first of December. That task done, the spreadsheet of expenses remained frighteningly replete: the non-negotiable utilities of gas, electricity, water; council tax and various insurances; cable and phone. She had to eat, even if luxuries like the hairdresser must be put on hold. Thank God she had no car. A small charitable contribution – that would be the next to go, which broke her heart. She knew of equity release schemes, but considered that a last resort, if she became very ill, for instance.

Of course, there was no question of complaining about this to anyone. People thought that because you owned a big house you were rich, but in reality you were rich only if you sold the big house. Until then, you were as wealthy as your income allowed and Sissy's income allowed very little.

At least she had two bookings for the following night: for Saturdays in August, people would take what they could get.

Meanwhile, across the street, deliveries abounded. She'd watched them from the bedroom window all week: a mountain of bricks and tiles and sacks of what looked like sand was piled on the lower level of the scaffolding and Booth was rigging up some sort of pulley, presumably to hoist them to the upper level, where he was working on the roof. Renovations were costing him, but – unlike Sissy – he had the money to pay.

*

She vowed not to raise the subject with Amy. It was one thing to agonize with the neighbours, but she was damned if she was going to let Darren Booth infect her family relationships.

'What beautiful flowers! You didn't need to buy me those, Amy.'

Amy had brought sunflowers, a huge bunch, their stems stiff and muscular, the petals soft and half-closed, as if disturbed in their sleep. As Sissy fixed drinks, she arranged them in a tall glass vase and updated Sissy on her latest project at work. Though she spoke cheerfully, it seemed to Sissy the girl was tense with withheld information.

'So . . .' As they met at the table, each taking her seat, Sissy felt her own expression turn stupid, coaxing. 'Are you going to tell me your news?'

Amy beamed, her face pink. 'Pete really wanted to be here. He's going to phone later, but he said I could tell you on my own. We're going to have a baby!'

Sissy felt a wild, leaping elation. 'Oh, that's wonderful, Amy!' Almost immediately, she began weeping and Amy made pleased and sympathetic noises, saying she felt like crying too, she was so overcome with it all. Then, when Sissy plainly should have stopped, she continued, the sobs growing stronger not weaker, until she was heaving with a deep, primitive sorrow. Amy began to look worried. She must already have told her own mother, Sissy thought, and Faye would not have reacted like this. *Stop crying.*

'What is it, Sissy?' Amy cried. 'Oh, God, you're not unwell or anything like that?' The poor girl feared a confession of some terminal illness, a life expectancy short of the baby's due date.

At last Sissy managed to calm herself and speak sensibly. 'No, no, I'm really happy for you both. It just seems to have opened the floodgates. It's been the most stressful time. But tell me more, how many weeks?'

'Ten.' Amy frowned. 'But why is it stressful at the moment? Is it to do with the business? The noisy neighbours? It seemed quiet over there when I arrived.'

'They're out tonight, I think, but my customer rating has gone right down and I had an email from the website, a warning that I'm not getting enough bookings. I checked the terms and conditions and they can remove my listing whenever they like.' She wiped her nose with a tissue. 'I honestly don't know how to deal with it. I don't see a way.'

'I thought you'd got together with the other neighbours to complain?' Amy said.

'We have, but it's a long-winded process.' *Twenty-four weeks*, Em had screeched at the meeting and Sissy had thought her uncontrolled, hysterical. But she hadn't bargained for the cumulative strain. Where Em had been then, she had reached now. 'I'm just having a weak moment,' she told Amy. 'Really, let's forget it.'

'If you're sure,' Amy said, doubtfully.

At bedtime, the street was still quiet and Sissy put her guest in the master bedroom at the front, an act of faith these days if not downright defiance. In her preferred room at the back, she fell asleep easily. Woke again easily, too, aware of Amy moving around downstairs – and, inevitably, the faint pulse of bass from across the road. Booth and Jodie must have come home steaming drunk, put the music on, and had one for the road, or however many they liked to consume.

She cursed herself for having taken the risk of putting Amy at the front.

'When did it start?' she asked, finding her in the kitchen by the kettle, peppermint teabag in hand.

'About an hour ago.'

The wall clock said 1.20 a.m. 'You've got your shoes on?' Sissy noticed.

Amy smoothed her rumpled hair. 'Yes, I was going to go over and say something, but I changed my mind.'

'Good, because it's not worth it. Let's swap rooms. You won't be able to hear the music from the back.'

Amy looked unsure, mindful no doubt of Sissy's earlier distress, but tiredness got the better of her and she followed Sissy up, tea in hand.

At the front, Sissy lay awake for some time, unable to marshal the maelstrom of new emotions. A grandchild, how joyous! But how could she have broken down like that? How dare Booth drive her to such shows of despair?

Inevitably, she found herself at the window without having noticed she'd got up and moved there. She thought briefly of Graham, the sensation of his body against hers, humid breath on her neck. It was dark finally at number 1, but there was still a light on upstairs at the Kendalls'. Another broken night for them. How could they continue like this? Was the poor baby awake too?

After Pete and Amy's baby was born, the natural thing would be for Sissy to invite the young family to live with her in her huge house, while they saved for a place of their own. But would they consider it, knowing that the child in the house opposite had been equipped with ear defenders and a protective helmet? Would they come even for the night? Avoid Sissy's house altogether in favour of Amy's mother's?

Imagining herself alone, alienated, she sat on the abandoned bed, stirring the covers angrily at the sound of Booth's voice, as clear as if he held his mouth to her ear:

An old cunt like you . . .

At last, knowing she wouldn't sleep, she dressed for a day that was still hours from dawning.

13

Amy

11 August 2018

As she stepped onto the drive of number 1, she felt a shudder of unease, a trace of bile in her throat. She'd never been one to dwell on the vibe of a place, but in recent weeks she'd grown more sensitive to mood – and the mood here was sordid. More like that of a decaying tower block on the nearby Rushmoor Estate than a house undergoing renovations on tree-lined Lowland Way.

No wonder Sissy was so distressed by the situation.

Part of it was the stink of the scaffolding – as if you could smell the skin shed by the thousands of builders who'd handled the boards and poles over the decades. The dirt they'd sweated, the cigarettes they'd smoked: all of it soaked into the wood and rusted onto the metal. It didn't help that right by the front door there was a huge smear of dog shit. Urgh.

The man crouching on the upper level, loudly tapping the

frame of an open bedroom window with a tool of some sort, was presumably *him*. The nuisance. Disturber of the peace. Realizing she didn't know his name, she called up to him with a general air of confidence: 'Excuse me? Hello there! Could I have a quick word?'

Given what she'd been told, she expected to be challenged or, more likely, ignored, but instead he replied promptly, 'Give me a minute, love, all right?', and there was the thud of his tool dropping onto the boards. She imagined it skidding off the edge and hurtling down towards her – a broken nose or collarbone, her vision spinning – and she moved under the shelter of the lower platform, just in case. Avoiding the dog mess, she waited with her back to the front door, looking out to the street. It was actually a gorgeous day, somehow both rich and fresh, a rarity in the heatwave. She'd enjoy escaping the foul air of this particular spot and spending the rest of the morning on Hampstead Heath, filling her lungs with particles of sunshine.

There was movement overhead: she'd thought he would step through the open window and come down through the house, but instead he was descending the scaffolding via the ladders between platforms. The one between the lower platform and ground level was on her side, so he'd be standing right beside her in a matter of seconds. She still didn't know what she was going to say to him, not exactly. Since pleas and negotiations were reportedly futile, she would need to make some sort of threat and the only thing that mattered with a threat – especially one from a woman to a man – was how credible it was.

Let's just say I know some people you really *don't want to fall out with . . .*

Could she pull it off?

She'd call Pete straight after, let him know she had not left Sissy to suffer alone. If this didn't work, she'd talk to her senior partner at work, who was married to a housing lawyer. This detail had occurred to her earlier, though she hadn't said anything about it to Sissy at breakfast, the subject of the neighbour having been best avoided after last night's upset. She'd discuss that – and what transpired here – with Pete.

There were footsteps above her head on the lower platform. Should she move out into the light, where he could see her? No, she'd stay where she was and take the initiative the moment he hit the ground. Wouldn't say who she was, just let him know that—

'Hey!'

But his voice – and her answering cry – was lost in a diabolical thunderclap of metal and wood and stone. As flat ground flew up to meet her, the last sound of her life was that of her own skull smacking the concrete.

14

Ralph

—For what it's worth, I've always thought the scaffolding looked completely unsafe. Told my kids not to go anywhere near it. Seemed to me like you only needed a windy day and the whole thing would come crashing down. Looked at the positioning of the sole plates, have you? That can destabilize scaffolding, can't it?

—I know about it because I googled it! A shame he didn't, eh?

Mr Ralph Morgan, 7 Lowland Way, house-to-house inquiries by the Metropolitan Police, 11 August 2018

The same day

He was on the tennis court when he got the summons to return to Lowland Way. The session was a drop-in singles ladder (Ralph preferred singles, the simplicity of living and dying by your own sword) and between thrashing Richard Masterson from Cranbrook Lane and preparing to dispatch Jamie Something-or-other from Oldfield Road, he took a water break and checked his phone. There were voicemails from Naomi and Finn.

Naomi's panic poured into his ear: 'Ralph, it's me, you need to come home.' There was, in the background, the most terrible wailing. It sounded female: Libby, who hadn't been well after the theatre? Another trip to Children's A&E? As if anticipating his terror, Naomi added, in a rush: 'Not the kids, don't worry. It's bad, though, really bad.'

Finn's message was starker: 'Mate, you at tennis? Come back. Armageddon here.'

Which made Ralph think something might have kicked off again between Naomi and Tess after last night's row. Jesus, had Tess physically attacked Naomi? He'd always thought her more volatile than she allowed people – or herself – to believe. Then again, the wailing had been in the background while Naomi was speaking, which suggested . . . No, Nay wouldn't use violence, not ever.

A text popped up from her – *At Sissy's* – which left him none the wiser.

He'd walked to the club and now retraced his route at a jog. Reaching the parkside junction of Lowland Way, he paused, his breath tight. At the far end, their end, a crowd had formed, reminding him of two weekends ago, the terrible moment he'd seen past the forest of children's legs to Charlie lying on the ground. Not known if he was alive or dead. There were two squad cars, the unmistakable blocks of yellow and blue on their sides, hazards blinking, while lengths of blue-and-white tape caught the late-morning sun in a series of spangles.

Ralph broke into a sprint, his racket held to his chest, the handle banging against his right hip. As he approached, he saw that number 1 had been cordoned off: DO NOT CROSS.

Booth. Of course Booth. Nothing to do with Naomi or Tess.

Arriving, he saw the issue: the lower level of scaffolding had collapsed on the left side, directly over the front door, which was inaccessible. One of the boards had split clean in half, Ralph assumed under the weight of the bricks and breeze blocks and tiles, now massed below; a huge sack of sand had split open, its contents mixed with fragments of stone. Access to the house appeared to be via the side passage.

Watching from her doorstep was a visibly distressed Em, her hands, face and clothing white with dust, while Ant stood in the window with a child's toy in his hands and an appalled look on his face. Unable to reach them through the mob, Ralph turned to a nearby woman, not a face he knew from the street.

'What the hell happened?'

She squinted at him, the sun in her eyes. 'The scaffolding came down. There was a girl underneath.'

He inhaled sharply. Not Libby, he reminded himself. Naomi had said it wasn't the kids. 'Who? You mean Jodie?' Could Jodie be described as a girl? 'The woman who lives here?'

'No, someone said she wasn't from around here?'

The squinting woman made a question of this, as if Ralph might know more than she did. Hopeless. Where were Finn and Naomi? At home with the kids? He began retracing his steps to his own gate, before remembering his wife had said she was at Sissy's and he dodged the bystanders in the road to cross to number 2.

'Ralph, thank God!' Naomi came out onto the step and, before he could even return the greeting, cried out like a confession: 'Amy is dead!'

Ralph took her in his arms. He was sweaty from tennis and her body heat was uncomfortable, but she clung tightly. Too terrible to admit he couldn't think off the top of his head who Amy was. Best to wait for the detail to trickle into place. 'Sissy's son's girlfriend, right?' he recalled, with decent enough speed.

Naomi drew back, her eyes wet. 'Yes, we met her at Christmas, remember? And at Sissy's sixtieth last year. She was only twenty-nine, Ralph. Oh, it's just horrific.'

The girl's face was coming into focus – pretty in a natural way, soft brown hair, freckles. 'What a dreadful thing. Why was she over there?'

'Complaining on Sissy's behalf, I would guess. Unlikely she was buying a car. She must have been at the front door, right under the scaffolding, when it happened. She didn't stand a chance. They pronounced her dead at the scene.'

'Bloody hell.'

'Oh, Ralph, it's even more awful: the poor girl was pregnant! I heard Sissy say it to the paramedic when they were trying to revive her, but there was nothing they could do. Sissy was hysterical. It was the worst thing I've ever seen.'

Ralph said nothing, just held her as she cried. Her tears were sticky on his neck. It was hard to absorb narratives like this: too brutal, too final, with nothing redemptive, nothing to console. At last, he said, 'Where is Sissy now? Here, inside?'

'No, she went with the ... with Amy in the ambulance. To the hospital; I suppose they must have taken her to the morgue?'

'Yes.' Was there any more appalling word than 'morgue'? He'd never heard Naomi use it, they'd never had need of it. A shoot of hope pushed itself into his mind. 'What about Booth? Have they arrested him?'

'Did I not say? He was on the boards that collapsed. He's been injured, but not badly. He was conscious, could probably have walked to the ambulance, with support. Oh! I hope Sissy doesn't have to go anywhere near him at the hospital. He'll be in A&E or on a ward, won't he? She won't bump into him, will she, Ralph?'

'I'm sure she won't.' Ralph recognized the stream of consciousness that denoted shock. 'Come home, Nay, you don't need to stay here.'

Naomi shook her head, composed herself. Behind the glaze of tears, there was determination in her eyes. Duty. 'I do. I said I'd wait for Sissy's B&B guests. Two couples are checking in this afternoon and there are still jobs that need doing.'

'Can't they be cancelled?'

'I don't think so, it's too late and you have to pay a penalty. She was getting really upset about it, said she wouldn't be able to cover her direct debits, so I said I'd hold the fort. She'll probably want to stay with Pete tonight, or Amy's parents. And the police will need to talk to her. To all of us, I imagine.'

As Naomi recovered her organizational vigour, Ralph saw that he had been summoned for moral support as much as for anything practical he could contribute and he had the momentary self-congratulatory thought that his was an excellent marriage. His wife was the powerhouse others relied on and yet she needed him. He remembered his first instinct. 'So you and Tess, you're okay after last night?' Silly question. That was just a petty family squabble, while this was . . . God, this was horrific. What a grotesque way to die, to be *crushed*. 'The kids didn't see what happened, did they?'

'No, Tess and Finn have taken them all to the high street to distract them while the police are here. Can you go and find them? Make sure Libs and Charlie don't hear any upsetting details?'

'Of course.'

Naomi blew her nose, blinked damp eyelids. 'I keep thinking, this could have been any one of us.'

'I know,' Ralph said, grimly. Was she thinking yet what he already was? What a tragedy it was that innocent, undeserving Amy had been crushed by the scaffolding and not guilty-as-sin, deserving-of-the-absolute-worst Darren Booth. What a shame it was not him in the morgue, their neighbourhood enemy eliminated by his own hand.

Not appropriate to voice, obviously. And not appropriate even to *think* that since Booth was now in hospital, unable to work, then there was less chance than ever of that bloody camper van being moved from Ralph's parking space.

Sunday dawned bright and cheerful, oblivious to the fatal wounds of its predecessor, and in the time it took Ralph to grind the beans for his first coffee the kids were in the garden with their cousins filming a video reconstruction of the accident on Libby's phone.

'No, you lie on your front and I'll turn you over!'

'But I don't want to be the dead one, I'm not a girl!'

'Isla can be dead, then. You be the one who phones for the ambulance. Quick, do it, she's *literally* just been *flattened*!'

'Is this in good taste, guys?' Ralph asked, and the way the four looked at him made him wonder if they'd ever heard of the concept. So much for protecting them from events: Charlie, his own scare at Booth's hands forgotten, was indecently bloodthirsty; Libby, enjoying rare interaction with the younger ones as their creative overlord, now ailment-free. The dogs swarmed, nosing the 'victim'.

Ralph took refuge in caffeine and read the first report of the accident to appear online:

Woman Crushed in Scaffolding Collapse

A woman has died after being crushed by falling scaffolding at a residential property in Lowland Gardens, South London, the Metropolitan Police have said. The victim was standing beneath the scaffolding at the front door of the house when the structure collapsed on top of her. Fire fighters and paramedics freed the buried woman and fought to revive her at the scene, but her injuries were found to have been fatal.

'Health and Safety Executive inspectors have attended the site and we are making ongoing inquiries in conjunction with them to investigate the circumstances of the incident,' a police spokesman confirmed. 'We are unable to comment further at this time.'

Ralph wondered when Naomi was coming home. In the end, she'd stayed at Sissy's overnight with her guests, Sissy having been with Pete at his flat. Heartbroken though Ralph was for Sissy, he wasn't altogether comfortable with his wife being in the house with two sets of complete strangers. He supposed if Sissy found it a safe enough arrangement, then Naomi would be fine. She'd been up early: there was a message from her on the residents' Facebook page posted at 7.30 a.m.:

> IMPORTANT NOTICE: Play Out Sunday is cancelled 12/08 following an accident. Police still need access to the upper part of the road.

He phoned her mobile. 'Breakfast service done and dusted?'

'Yes, I only had to make coffee and warm up some pastries. They've just left.' She spoke in the same sombre tones as yesterday. 'It was surreal, Ralph. I mean, I didn't say anything about Amy, but what must they have thought? Okay, the ambulances had gone by the time they arrived, but they still saw the police and all the debris. One of them asked me if there'd been a gas explosion and they got all anxious about that.'

'Not exactly what you imagine when you book a B&B room,' Ralph said.

Naomi sighed with rare weariness. 'I'm honestly not sure Sissy's business is going to survive much longer. Before, she was opposite a repairs garage, but now she's opposite a crime scene. That's what it is, isn't it?'

'I should bloody well hope so – and *he's* the criminal. Have you spoken to Sissy this morning?'

'Yes, just now. She's still at Pete's, with Amy's parents, dealing with everything. The death certificate, the police. They have to open an inquest when the death is like this – you know, sudden, unnatural. Then they can issue a burial order. It sounds complicated, I can't imagine coping with that on top of the horror of losing her.'

Leaving the kids with Tess, Ralph and Finn took the dogs out, detouring past number 1, where the police cordon remained in place. Yesterday afternoon and well into the evening, the place had been swarming with personnel, including officers from the Health and Safety Exec, who'd removed pieces of scaffolding and taken photos and video of the scene. Meanwhile, uniformed police had called house to house, looking for witnesses, noting local opinion (Ralph hadn't pulled any punches there, oh no). But now the site was quiet, a solitary police guard the only official still present. Looking at him – he was expressionless, resistant of eye contact – Ralph had the most dizzying sensation of disbelief: six months ago, *three* months ago, they couldn't have conceived that they'd be standing here in August discussing a death on the street. They'd been so content, so harmonious.

'Well, that's one way to get the bastard to turn the music down,' he said to Finn. 'Put him in hospital. Heard anything about how he is? Naomi said it wasn't life-threatening.'

'That's right,' Finn said, glumly. 'They kept him in overnight, apparently. Ant heard one of the police say last night. Jodie came back to pick up some things, but they're not allowed to move back in for a few days. Staying with mates. Health and Safety have already reported to the police, Ant says.'

'Really? That was quick.'

'I know. Then again, it must have been pretty obvious what happened. The scaffolding was unsafe. With a bit of luck, Booth'll go straight from the hospital to a prison cell.'

'If there's any justice,' Ralph agreed.

When he left for work on Monday morning, there was a car double-parked near the corner with its hazards on and, even though his BMW was parked in the other direction, he turned right for a closer look. In the driver's seat, a man Ralph didn't recognize sat with his eyes on his phone. Police? Press? It was impossible to tell.

There was a different guard today, this one standing at the end of the drive, and friendly enough to nod hello.

Ralph did the same. 'I was wondering, where's the officer who came to our door on Saturday? I wanted to ask him how you're getting on. PC Harold or something.'

'He won't be here again. The case has been passed to CID now.'

Ralph knew his police TV dramas well enough to know this meant the real business was now underway: they were going after a prosecution, just as he and Finn had speculated. 'I'm assuming they've arrested the owner by now? He wasn't that badly hurt, I heard. I told your PC they should get on with it.'

'Did you.' The officer, stripping the words of any suggestion of a question, looked at Ralph differently then, though Ralph couldn't tell if it was with greater interest or less. He'd taken Ralph for a concerned neighbour, perhaps, easily moved on, not a man of action.

Well, he *was* concerned, concerned that Booth should be put behind bars.

As he was about to leave, a figure emerged from the house, startling Ralph, who hadn't realized there was anyone else on site. She was a short, curly-haired woman, mid-thirties, in black trousers and a grey blazer, her eyewear on-trend a couple of seasons ago. She called out to the man in the car – 'Jason, do you have a minute?' – ignoring Ralph, who disliked being made to feel invisible on his own street. But he was running late for a meeting and he couldn't spare the time for a charm offensive.

Heading for his car, however, he felt the unmistakable heat of their gaze on his back. Not invisible, after all.

15

TESS

—I wouldn't be surprised if the whole house caves in next, no one really knows what he's been doing in there. He's been operating completely off grid.

—It's a disgrace, a complete disgrace.

MRS TESSA MORGAN, 5 LOWLAND WAY, HOUSE-TO-HOUSE INQUIRIES BY THE METROPOLITAN POLICE, 11 AUGUST 2018

Five days later

'Close the gate,' Tess instructed Isla and Dex, 'and try to be quiet while I speak to poor Sissy.'

If she spoke to her. As far as Tess was aware, no one, including Naomi, had been able to break Sissy's defences since Amy's death, though they knew she had been back in residence since Sunday evening. Each day, deliveries of flowers were left on her doorstep, only to have vanished by morning; Tess sincerely hoped this was because Sissy had gathered them in the privacy of the night and not because thieves had taken them.

As she rang the bell, she glanced across at number 1. The removal of the scaffolding had served to unveil the half-measures Booth had taken with the exterior of his house: plaster chipped off here and there; one of the upper windows removed and boarded up; a length of tarpaulin over a section of the roof. If he were jailed, would any of it ever get finished?

For goodness' sake, when were the police going to let them know what was going on? They'd all phoned and been fobbed off – again, even Naomi! – and so far, the only news in relation to the investigation was that Em had been asked to 'reconsider travel plans' and stay in town.

'It was a polite request rather than an order,' she'd told Tess.

There was no answer to Sissy's bell and so Tess pushed open the letterbox and put her mouth to the narrow gap: 'Sissy! Sissy, it's Tess again!'

As well as calling at her door twice daily, she'd taken to texting little messages, pictures of the cygnets, anything to keep her connected to her community (the cygnets were almost full size now, but still grey-feathered, not yet ready to leave their parents).

'Sissy? Are you okay in there?' She turned her head to put her ear to the gap and caught the distant sound of sobbing.

'She's too sad,' Isla said, at Tess's side, and Tess's heart caught at the simplicity of it.

'Can we go on our adventure now?' Dex asked, from

the path, as if he thought he'd been patient long enough. When she'd sat him down to explain Amy's death, he'd been unmoved. Amy was not a real person to him.

Tess let the flap fall back. It was then, as she straightened and reached to take Dex's hand, that she heard it. Above the low churn of traffic on Portsmouth Avenue and the whine of a strimmer from the Boulters' garden: the melodic sound of whistling. The hairs on her arms stood on end as she followed the noise to its source: Darren Booth, standing on his drive. Where had he appeared from? He'd not been there when she'd glanced across two minutes ago.

It was the first time she'd seen him since the accident and he appeared to be moving quite normally, the only signs of injury a sling for his left arm and a bruise on his left cheekbone. He was inspecting one of the cars, wiping off the dust with his free hand, and whistling.

Whistling! The prerogative of the carefree if ever there was one! A reckless courage took possession of her and, telling the kids to wait by Sissy's gate, she stalked across the road, calling out to Booth in a sharp, menacing voice she hardly recognized as her own: 'Are you allowed on the premises? Isn't this still a crime scene?'

There was no reply, of course; in any case, the absence of the guard and removal of tape gave her her answer. Booth only stared at her, his demeanour sullenly undiminished. Unrepentant.

'You can look at me how you like,' Tess snapped, 'but it doesn't change the fact that you killed that girl. What you did was no different from cold-blooded murder.'

He took a step from behind the car to face her. The sling

containing his bandaged arm was dirty, his fingers grey. 'You don't know what you're talking about, love.'

'Don't call me "love"! You can't be stupid enough not to know I hate you. We all do!'

His mouth fell open and, to her astonishment, he laughed. Not bitterly or dismissively, but freely, with gusto, as if she'd said something brilliantly absurd. As if a life had not been lost less than a week ago in this very place.

Loathsome behaviour. Sickening. And with Sissy sobbing in the house across the road.

'Screw you,' she said, under her breath, and re-crossed to retrieve Isla and Dex. She'd promised them a day out, and that was what she'd give them. 'Come on, guys, let's get in the car. We're going somewhere you've never been before!'

Ralph had messaged the WhatsApp group that CID had taken over from the uniformed officers who'd conducted initial inquiries, so she googled the address – in a larger police station a few miles south – and plugged it into the satnav. Twenty minutes later, pacified with KitKats, Isla and Dex sat on scuffed royal-blue chairs and watched the door for criminals in handcuffs as their mother approached the staff at the enquiries counter.

'I'm a neighbour of Sissy Watkins, a relative of Amy's . . .' She faltered, realizing she didn't know Amy's surname. 'The woman who died at One Lowland Way last Saturday. I need to tell you that someone is at the house right now. They're contaminating the crime scene!'

The person summoned to deal with her looked about eighteen. Had his voice even broken? 'There's no need to be concerned, Mrs Morgan. The residents have just been cleared to return to the house.'

'Already?' Tess was astounded. 'So if you've got all the evidence you need, why haven't you arrested the only suspect?'

'Who do you mean by "the only suspect"?' the man-child asked.

'Darren Booth, of course! He's the one I've seen back at the house. Who else could I possibly be talking about? The Scarlet Pimpernel?'

With exaggerated patience, the junior repeated that the detectives working on the case were presently out of the office. 'Do you have a personal involvement in the case, Mrs Morgan?'

'I've just told you, I'm a friend and neighbour of the victim's boyfriend's mother.' Which suddenly sounded a flimsy, even fabricated, connection, as if she could only be here out of prurience. 'Isn't there *anything* new you can tell me?'

But the conversation was only ever going to end one way: 'I'm sure you understand that we can't share the details of our investigation.'

'You didn't say goodbye,' Dex reproached her, mournfully.

'That's not good manners,' Isla agreed.

'I didn't say goodbye because they wouldn't help me,' Tess said, feeling more childish than her children. How was she to explain this to them if she couldn't understand it herself?

But how quickly stormy skies could clear! As they returned to the car, parked in a street behind the station, her eye was caught by a figure remarkably like Darren Booth in her wing mirror. He was being ushered out of the back of an unmarked car, his plainclothes escorts steering him into the building through a back gate, exactly the way it happened on TV. His face was impassive, mouth shut tight.

They must have collected him – apprehended him – from the house minutes after Tess left. Had the young officer known that? He could have thrown her a bone, stopped her ranting on as she had.

You're not whistling now, she thought.

'He's been arrested,' she reported to Naomi, as soon as her sister-in-law arrived home from work. Tess was euphoric, though unsure how many more mood swings she could experience in a day without being sick. 'I saw it with my own eyes. He's out of hospital and he's at the police station on Milkwood Lane.'

'Are you sure?' Naomi asked. 'Did they put handcuffs on him?'

There was no mistaking the level of distrust that remained on Naomi's part when it came to Tess's interpretation of police procedure. The memory of Charlie's accident had, if anything, intensified in importance since Amy's death, as if it had been some sort of dress rehearsal. Though their row the night of the theatre trip had of course paled into insignificance next to the horror of what came after, contact had been far less frequent, updates exchanged between the men, not the women. Naomi had, without any explanation, engaged a local dogwalker to take Kit and Cleo out on work days; Tess didn't know if the change was intended to lighten her load or punish her.

'I didn't see any handcuffs,' she admitted, 'but his arm is in a sling, so maybe they don't use cuffs when someone has an injury? But he was being escorted by two people who looked like they knew their way around a police station. Detectives, I think. And they didn't use the main entrance.'

'That does sound like progress,' Naomi said. 'Jodie's back in the house, did you know? Sara just told me. She arrived earlier this afternoon, but I haven't seen her.'

'She must have followed him to the station – if she's even allowed to see him. They'll have charged him by now, he'll be in a cell.'

'Right place for him,' Naomi agreed, satisfied.

'Should we tell Sissy?' Tess asked. 'I tried her again this morning, but she wouldn't come to the door.' Tess paused. Naomi was closer to Sissy than she was, but it felt like a betrayal to mention the sobbing. 'I'm not suggesting we break in, but I do keep a spare key for her . . .'

'Let's go over together this evening, the four of us?' Naomi suggested, with more of her old warmth. 'If she won't answer, we can always let ourselves in and call from the hallway. My mum's here, so I'll see if she can mind the kids for an hour or two.'

'Good plan,' Tess said, and the relief she felt that she and Naomi might be back on friendly terms was dismayingly acute.

On the other hand – and obviously it was petty even to think it – she hoped Naomi didn't intend on presenting the news about Booth's arrest as her own.

16

Ant

—If you're looking for witnesses, it must be because you don't think it was a straightforward accident, is that right? What kind of a charge are we looking at here? Okay, maybe not murder, it's not like he planned it. Manslaughter, then? You should have him for something, seriously. Come on, it's basic stuff. A child could solve this case.

Mr Anthony Kendall, 3 Lowland Way, house-to-house inquiries by Metropolitan Police, 11 August 2018

Five days later

Sissy looked worse than Ant had seen anyone look *ever*. He had expected grief, of course, but in a form that had recognizable colour and texture. The raw, raised skin of day-long sobbing, the red of eyes cried dry. What he saw was profound, a human being stripped to the soul. When he hugged her, he could feel the break in her, the imminent bodily collapse. 'I'm so sorry, Sissy. Really. Is there anything we can do?'

Sissy choked a few words that he was unable to make sense of.

'Nobody can do anything,' Naomi interpreted. 'Not yet. But thank you, Ant. Try to breathe, Sissy, deep and slow.'

It was Naomi who had answered the door when the Kendalls arrived. Though Ant had rung several times since the accident, it was only when he and Em were able to piggy-back on a visit from the Morgans that he actually set eyes on Sissy. Naomi had kindly suggested they leave Sam with her mother and the other children ('Libby *adores* little ones') and follow them across, the unspoken message being Sissy should not be reminded of babies. Because Amy had been pregnant – Ralph had told Ant that. Horrific.

'I should have stopped her from going over there,' Sissy told Naomi, suddenly lucid. 'She didn't tell me she was doing that, I thought she was going home.'

'You couldn't possibly have known, darling,' Naomi said. 'We can't control the decisions other people make. I've been thinking, thank God it wasn't the two of them, her *and* Pete.'

Sissy bowed her head, unable to answer, and Ant ached for her, wordless himself.

While Ralph organized drinks, Finn opened the kitchen door to let in fresh air, and between them they managed to steer Sissy a few steps onto the terrace. As if natural light was all that was needed to reanimate an annihilated soul! In any case, it threatened drizzle, the sky low and morose. Ant couldn't be certain he was remembering correctly, but he had a sense that the good weather had ended last Sunday, overnight. Like a mark of respect, a flag flown at half-mast.

'How are the formalities going?' Tess asked Sissy. 'Have you got a date for the funeral yet?'

With a ghostly detachment that unnerved Ant, Sissy explained that Amy's funeral would be taking place the following Monday, a private affair in her home town of Chichester. Pete was staying with Amy's parents until afterwards.

There were degrees of grief, Ant supposed, a natural order or even entitlement, and Amy's parents' was the deepest, the most abominable. Imagine if it were Sam who'd died! A terrible shiver passed over him. He became aware of the smell of rotting vegetation, soon identifying the source as a vase of dying sunflowers on the window sill, the water slimy and opaque. 'Shall I throw these away?' he suggested, hoping to be useful, but Sissy protested with an abrupt keening and once more Naomi acted as her interpreter.

'Not those ones, Ant. But would you let us change the water, Sissy?'

As the weird, sucked-dry version of Sissy gave her assent, Naomi murmured the explanation: 'Amy gave these to her. When she was here last Friday.'

'Oh, God. I'm sorry.' Ant flushed deeply at his blunder.

'I'm going to look up how to dry and preserve them. These things are symbols, you know. Links.'

'Yes, thank you.' Ant looked gratefully at her as if she were a goddess bestowing a blessing on him.

'I've got bookings for early September,' Sissy was telling Tess, in response to a question about her business. 'I can't afford to turn them down.'

'I can help you,' Tess said, squeezing the other woman's hand. 'I've got more time than Naomi.' She sent a glance Naomi's way that Ant could not decipher; he had never been able to tell if the sisters-in-law were accomplices or rivals. 'Maybe it will be good to have the structure? You know, while things are still going on.'

Now she and Naomi traded a different sort of look, something more buoyant.

'Sissy, we have some news,' Naomi said, and her raised voice caught the others' attention. 'I don't know if you've heard, either, Ant and Em, but Darren Booth was arrested this morning. Tess was there when it happened.'

'What?' As Ant's spirits soared, Sissy visibly stiffened. For the first time, she looked square at the faces in front of her, fully concentrating as Tess described an expedition to the police station on Milkwood Lane that had ended with her witnessing the event they'd all been anticipating since Saturday morning.

'What did they look like, the detectives he was with?' Ralph asked her.

Tess narrowed her eyes. 'A tall Asian guy, late twenties, maybe, and a woman about my age, quite short, brown curly hair and glasses.'

'They're the ones I saw at the house the other day.' Ralph nodded, satisfied. 'Good work, Tess.'

'Well, we'd have found out soon enough, anyway,' she said, going pink.

'Every second of peace of mind is a gift, though, isn't it?' Naomi said, including Sissy in her remark. How tactful she was, Ant thought, how subtle, warning the others not to display too much glee. This was justice, not victory.

But it was too late for Em, who had let out a cry of triumph. 'That's *fantastic* news,' she gasped, joyfully. 'Why didn't you tell me as soon as it happened, Tess? I'd have—'

'Em,' Ant interrupted, frowning. 'Sissy's the only one directly connected.'

As Em gave him a piqued look, Sissy turned helplessly from Ant to Naomi. 'I can't bear it,' she whispered, suddenly.

'Oh, Sissy.' Naomi looked horrified. 'Perhaps we shouldn't have told you, but we thought it might be of some comfort.'

Ralph moved forwards then, almost theatrically grave as he drew Sissy into his embrace, and Ant withdrew, feeling both drained by the exposure to grief and sick with excitement at the good news. Yes, there would still be Jodie, but without her mechanic she would surely have to wind down the car business. As for the building work, unless she had hidden DIY skills of her own, she'd need to hire other workmen, preferably professionals, or abandon the renovations entirely.

Slipping upstairs to use the bathroom, he strayed afterwards into the bedroom at the front to look out the window. Taking in the pocked exterior of number 1 and the heap of junk before it, the confusion of cars and vans, he had a very clear sense of how momentous this occasion was. An end to a short, intense period that had obliterated all memory of the good times that went before.

An appalling tragedy for the bereaved families, but a miraculous reprieve for the Kendalls.

They stayed at Sissy's only an hour or so, not wishing to exhaust her, and left as they'd arrived, en masse. Ant was at the rear, still on the doorstep, when the quiet evening air was torn abruptly by an ugly mechanical sound. A tile cutter or something similar, a screaming noise that must have been terrifying for the street's pets. There was a collective seizure. It was almost eight o'clock: who but number 1 would be so anti-social as to start noisy work two hours beyond the 6 p.m. permitted hour?

'That isn't *him*?' Naomi said, finally.

'No.' Ralph spoke with authority, as if on behalf of all of them: 'Can't be, can it?'

As they shuffled on, the screaming noise stopped and the side gate to number 1 sprang open. Pieces of tile were hurled out, landing on the edge of the slagheap. Then the noise began again.

'It *was* him,' Finn said. 'I saw his grey overalls.'

'Tess?' Em said, moving from Ant's side to her friend's, eyes bright with fear.

'I don't understand,' Tess said, stammering slightly.

'You said he was in a police cell,' Naomi hissed at her, 'and now we've told Sissy that!'

'Look, I only told you what I saw,' Tess protested.

'Which must have been him going into the station for some other reason, because they obviously haven't charged him,' Ralph said, glaring at her as if she were a complete idiot.

'Hang on, mate,' Finn said. 'He might've been bailed.'

'Not after everything we said when they went door to door. How can they not see him as a risk to others? To *us*?' Naomi shook her head with vigour, as if to make the statement true. Her hair glistened with damp. It had begun drizzling, but no one mentioned it or made any attempt to seek shelter.

'I'm going over there,' Ralph said, 'find out what's going on.'

'We'll all come,' Finn said, falling into step with him.

With a soldier's posture, Ralph strode past the cars on the drive and picked his way through the debris to the side passage, cluttered with materials. The rest of them tailed behind in single file, arriving in the rear garden as the rain grew heavier. A work station had been set up on the concrete patio, which was littered with tools, and the rain was turning the dust to dirty smears. Booth could be seen through the kitchen window, moving about in the living room beyond.

'Booth?' Ralph yelled. 'Get out here, will you!'

He emerged, his expression as disobliging as ever. His wrist had been freed from the sling, though it was still bandaged almost to the elbow. Ant felt weighed down with dejection: Ralph was right, Tess had misunderstood what she'd witnessed that morning. This was not an end to the horror but a resumption of it, business as usual.

Booth addressed them with a gruff shout: 'Get off my property, the lot of you!'

Ralph folded his arms, his stance broad, every inch the immovable defender. 'Not until you tell us what's going on. Are you out on bail or something?'

Booth stepped forwards, a shard of tile in his hand at his side, like a switchblade. 'You're the one who should be out on bail, mate. You could've fucking killed me!'

Ralph glowered at him. 'What the hell are you talking about?'

'You're responsible for your own injuries. That must be obvious even to you,' Naomi told him, undaunted by his aggression.

'It's fucking well not,' Booth said, nostrils flaring.

Now they were faced with his anger, the animal strength of it, Ant saw that it had never before been fully roused. Feeling the bleak, hardwired fear of prey in the path of predator, he took a shameful step back.

Startling them, Jodie now called down from the upper window, leaning out above their heads. Even at this angle, Ant could see that her face was swollen from crying. 'Right. Let's get this sorted: which one of you was it?'

'Which one of us *what*?' Ralph said.

'Messed with the scaffolding. They've told us all about it.'

Ant got it first: she was saying that the police were considering the possibility that this had been a crime committed not *by* Darren but *against* him. That Amy's fate had been intended for him. For a long moment, he couldn't breathe. The rain on his face felt sticky, as if coating him in solvent. Behind him, Em began to whimper.

Now Ralph made the same deduction. 'You've told the police someone deliberately made the scaffolding collapse? In order to injure *you*?'

'That's ridiculous!' Naomi cried.

'Total bollocks,' Finn said.

Jodie scowled at them from on high. 'That's not what the police think. So if any of you trespass on our property again, we'll apply for a restraining order!'

Em started sobbing then, noisily, unable to control herself, and Ant moved across to comfort her, grateful Sam was not here to witness his mother's distress. 'Let's head off,' he said, 'get you inside.'

'I'm not going in there,' she railed. 'No way, never again!'

'Em, it's our home.'

'It's not, not while *they're* here. Get me the car keys, I'm going to my parents.'

'You can't drive,' Ant protested, 'you're too upset.' He was struggling to hide his annoyance with this scene. Why couldn't she keep her cool? She wasn't the only one overwrought by events, and yet she behaved as if she were. And God knew how it must look to the others as she resisted his attempts to steer her back towards the side gate: like some grisly scene of domestic abuse, though in this case it was the man who was getting the worst of it, Em's open palms smacking down on him as she yelled, 'Don't tell me what to do! I hate you!'

Ralph moved towards them, frowning. 'Stop this, guys. Don't give them the satisfaction.'

'That's right, fuck off!' Jodie screamed, furiously. 'Did the rest of you not hear me?'

Behind Ant, Ralph gestured to the others that they should follow. 'Don't worry, we're going. We're not going to stand here and listen to your insane persecution fantasies.'

The last Ant saw was Booth standing in the rain in his soaked overalls, gaze tracking Ralph as he moved away. 'It's no fucking fantasy, Kray boy. Ask the cops yourselves. They're coming after you.'

17

Darren

—I'm loads better, thanks, yeah. Concussion, pretty bad bruising, a bit of a twisted wrist, you know. Whatever the medics call it. I was lucky, turns out.

—Happy to go over it again, sure. Like I told your guy in the hospital, I just felt the boards give way under my feet, didn't I? Not right away after I stepped off the ladder, no, but when I was about halfway along.

—No, I'd only been out a couple of minutes. Came out the upstairs window, just been to the loo, hadn't I? I was checking what I needed up top when I heard the girl calling.

—Didn't have a clue, mate. Didn't know her from Adam. Wouldn't have bothered answering, but I could tell she weren't gonna go away and Jodie weren't feeling well, I didn't want her hammering on the door and waking her up.

—Course I know who Sissy is, yeah. Sissy Spacek,

we call her. Not someone I'm looking to spend any time with, to be honest with you. Same goes for all of them on this street.

—Because they're all fucking mental, that's why. Take my word for it, mate, they're on my case morning, noon and night, the lot of them. Obsessed with parking and clearing the street all the time like it's a fucking jubilee street party, you know what I'm saying? Like they haven't got massive gardens for the kids to mess around in. Always whining about noise and dust, like they've never seen anyone do up a house before.

—Huh? Yeah, so she went out of sight. Under the scaffolding, by the front door. She was only there a minute, not even that. As long as it took me to come down the top ladder. Then, like I say, I was on the lower level and when I was about halfway along I felt it move and then the whole bloody thing went down and I was trapped on my side. Thought there'd been a fucking earthquake.

—You tell me, you're the detectives! If I'd walked on it earlier, then it would've collapsed earlier, wouldn't it? Simple as that. All I know is it was all right the day before. Solid as a rock. I was on it off and on all day, didn't have any kind of problem.

—Someone messed with the nuts on the couplings, didn't they? No other explanation. There's no way vibrations could've made them come loose in that time.

—Do me harm? Jodie? No way, mate, you're

barking up the wrong tree there. One hundred per cent no way. Anyone could've had a go at loosening them, it's basic stuff.

—The neighbours? They have been violent, yeah, since you ask. Chucked a brick at me, old Sissy Spacek did, I was lucky to get out of the way in time. And one of them tried to strangle me. That was the Morgan bloke. He got all arsey when his kid ran into my van on his skateboard. I had to touch up the paintwork, not a word of apology.

—Jodie reckons the bird with all the dogs is up to something. Dunno her name but she's with the other Morgan bloke, the brother. If you ask me, the one that's really deranged is her next door. She is totally out of control. Someone needs to keep her in line and I don't think the husband's up to the job, if you know what I'm saying. Hey, maybe they're all in it together?

—Yeah, I know a girl died. I'm not laughing. I'm just saying, if it was them and they cooked it up between them, then they got the wrong person, didn't they? Cos look at me: I'm still standing.

Mr Darren Booth, 1 Lowland Way,
interviewed by DC Shah and DC Forrester at
Milkwood Lane Police Station, 16 August 2018

18

Ralph

'Deliberate Sabotage' in Scaffolding Collapse Horror

The death of a twenty-nine-year-old woman in a horrific scaffolding collapse is being treated as suspicious, police said today. The tragedy occurred on 11 August, when marketing executive Amy Pope from North London was visiting the property on Lowland Way, Lowland Gardens.

According to police, it is now thought that the scaffolding had been tampered with in the hours before the tragedy. Forensic experts found that the bolts used to secure the poles had been loosened and concluded that this was the direct cause of the event that led to the woman's death. Today, the Metropolitan Police described the crime as an act of 'deliberate sabotage'.

'We believe that someone intentionally weakened the structure, which ultimately resulted in Ms Pope's death,' a police spokesman said. 'There is no evidence yet that she was specifically targeted and it is possible she was the accidental victim of this appalling act.'

SOUTH LONDON PRESS

'Seriously, are you really doing this?' Ralph asked at the door. He hated opening it now, thanks to the taunt of the camper van, unavoidable in his eyeline and, apparently, semi-permanent. 'Asking us for alibis! We thought you'd arrested him? Why did you take him to the station yesterday if it wasn't for that?'

DC Eithne Forrester – he had an excellent memory for names, had no need for badges or cards – betrayed no surprise at his instantly confrontational style. She couldn't know that he still throbbed with fury from the altercation with Booth the previous evening, that he was still considering – privately, not even with Naomi's or Finn's input – whether what he'd experienced had amounted to a declaration of war. And now, that morning, a news item had appeared online confirming the bastard's hare-brained notions!

'Are you saying you would prefer to go to the station for *our* conversation, Mr Morgan?' the detective said, with perfect humourlessness. She at least did not insult him by asking who he meant by *him*.

'Here's fine, come in.' This was plainly more serious than the doorstep informalities of the PC's visit. And if the residents' group chat was up to date, CID had chosen to call on *him* first. 'You're lucky I'm working from home this morning. We go on holiday this weekend and I've got a lot to sort out before then.'

Details of his business were noted: did the police need that? How much of their work was plain old nosiness?

On the other hand, this woman was the first person ever to enter the Morgan kitchen without commenting on its epic dimensions or glamorous fittings, so she wasn't *that* nosy.

Without asking if she wanted one, Ralph poured two glasses of iced water from the fridge dispenser and selected spots for them at the table, his at the head, hers to his left. 'So someone sabotaged the scaffolding, did they?' He chuckled. 'Jesus Christ, I can think of easier ways to get rid of him than that.'

Behind faintly cat-eyed frames, DC Forrester's eyes were unblinking as she considered this: 'Such as, Mr Morgan?'

'Such as *anything*!' He threw out his arms. 'Come on, loosening scaffolding bolts? Who on earth would think of that? It's far more likely he didn't secure them properly in the first place, or he went over the legal weight limit with all those materials and they came loose and gave way.' But, as he relaxed into a familiar rant about slapdash practices and escalating hazards, his visitor looked less than fascinated. The clue was in the lack of note taking, though an A4 pad lay splayed in front of her.

'So, your own movements, on the night of the tenth?'

Ralph provided the required information in flat, inattentive tones.

'You say you saw Darren and Jodie in the Star. Did you say hello to them?'

He pulled a face – *are you crazy?* – but she continued to regard him with an intent, expectant gaze. Clearly, she was not like detectives on TV, with their demons and their combustible moods. She had one temperature: bloody cold.

'No,' he said, finally.

'So you were home by eleven. Did you get up in the night?'

Ralph raised his eyebrows. 'You mean because of his music? No, we've got great double glazing, so we slept through whatever nonsense was going on. Then I was up and out in the morning to play tennis, well before anything happened.'

'What time did you leave?'

'About eight. The session starts at eight thirty, but I usually pick up a coffee on the way. And before you ask, yes, there were plenty of people at the club that morning who can vouch for me.'

'That's useful to know,' DC Forrester said. 'It sounds to me as if there might be quite a few people who'd have a reason to want to harm Mr Booth.'

This was interesting: her manner had altered very subtly to bring a hint of welcome, as if she'd considered him a fool but had now decided they might be able to collaborate. Clever.

It worked, but not in the way she was probably hoping: it made Ralph understand this was no time for irreverence. 'No,' he said. 'We don't like him, ideally we'd like him to leave the street, but we don't want to harm him. Not under any circumstances.'

If she was disappointed, she didn't show it. 'You're not missing a spanner, are you, Mr Morgan?'

'I'd have to look,' Ralph said, calmly, 'but I don't think so.'

'You said you picked up a coffee on the way to tennis. Where from? Which café?'

'I don't remember.'

'There's only one café open from eight a.m. on the route

and that's Bean2Cup at the station.' She didn't consult her notes, she just trotted it out.

Hold your nerve, Ralph thought.

'I beg your pardon?'

God, had he said that aloud? 'I said, it must've been there, then.'

The meeting was over, a card presented. 'If you think of anything else . . .'

Sure, the moment I notice my spanner's missing and remember what I got up to in that fugue state, you'll be the first to know.

He saw her out. On the doorstep, she ruffled the hair at the nape of her neck with her fingertips as if relieved to be back in the fresh air. Then she gave her first half-smile of the encounter. 'You mentioned a holiday, Mr Morgan. It would be useful to know where you'll be and when you expect to be back.'

Ralph frowned. Breathing was suddenly painful. 'Do I *have* to tell you?'

'Absolutely not, it's just a polite request.'

'But why? What's going on here, am I some sort of suspect?' Then, thinking it best not to wait for an answer: 'We're going to Devon for a week. I'll have my mobile, so you can phone me if you need me.'

'Thank you,' said DC Forrester. 'I'm very grateful.'

Naomi said they should read nothing into it. She would phone the police herself with the address of their hotel and all their contact numbers, so they'd be seen to be co-operating fully. 'Fine, so they've found these loosened bolts and they're investigating more widely, but they can't discount negligence on his part, can they? I know it isn't as exciting as the sabotage angle, so it doesn't get the press headlines, but surely he should have secured the site? And he definitely shouldn't have been storing materials so close to the front door.'

Ralph nodded. 'You're right. It's not such a good headline: "South London Twat Decides Not to Bother with Health and Safety".'

Naomi smiled and continued brushing makeup into the curved hollows of her eyelids. They were in their shell-pink en suite, getting ready to go out for dinner. Finn had cried off the brothers' Friday-night drink with a work crisis (unlike the employees of Morgan Leather Goods, who were all home with their families – just saying) and Naomi had promptly booked Daisy. It was a conscious stab at civilized behaviour in uncertain times.

'When Sissy's got her mojo back, we need to encourage her to sue him – or get Amy's family to. If she did, and he was ordered to pay out, he might have to sell the house to raise the cash.' Just voicing this idea ignited an emotion in Ralph remarkably close to hope. Then he noticed his wife had put down her makeup and was dabbing her eyes with the corner of a tissue. 'You okay, Nay?'

'I'm fine, it's nothing.'

She was still more shaken by Amy's death than by any police interference, had wept daily since the accident. Was that normal? Yes, of course it was horrendous to have had a death virtually on their doorstep, especially a violent one, but they had not known the girl well. Likely, the tears were for Sissy – it had been hard for them all to see her so *haunted*, roused only by the threat of dead flowers being thrown away.

Plus there was the demise of the Play Out Sunday scheme, though Naomi had used the word 'pause' on Facebook and in a text sent to the street's parents, '*until we can be confident of the full co-operation of all neighbours*'.

'Bloody police,' Ralph grumbled, and he stared glumly at his reflection in the mirror. He could have sworn he'd aged in the last few months – or was it simply the erasure of all previous marks of complacency? 'I wonder what he's going to do next.'

'Who?' Naomi asked.

Ralph turned, frowning: *you need to ask*?

'Oh. Well, with any luck, he'll take a long, hard look at his business practices and lifestyle choices and keep a very low profile indeed.' Her eyes were dry again, the eyeshadow turning them huge and persuasive, but Ralph was not persuaded.

In his opinion it was totally unrealistic to believe that Booth would adjust his behaviour, unless it was to make himself even more disagreeable.

And more dangerous.

The next morning, Ralph watched from the living-room window as his nemesis approached the camper van, a bottle of white spirit and cloth in hand. Since parking it there all those weeks ago, he'd never so much as glanced in its direction, much less made any attempt to work on it, but now, suddenly, he was here, bandaged wrist and all, setting up the longest cable extension Ralph had ever seen to power a piece of machinery that would doubtless give a pneumatic drill a run for its money. The reason for the white spirit was that overnight someone had painted the word KILLER in bright white on the side of the vehicle, which was all very well if it didn't look like the camper van belonged to the house where it was parked.

The kids had gone swimming with Finn and their cousins, an attempt to exhaust them before the long drive to Devon that afternoon, and Naomi, already packed for the trip, had popped over to Sissy's with enough home-cooked food to cover their week-long absence (she worried Sissy wasn't cooking for herself). There was no one else on the street, cars parked bumper to bumper, a very different beast from Sunday mornings of old.

If he'd been asked to predict, he'd have said Booth wouldn't care about the graffiti, but evidently he did, taking pictures of it – to show the police, perhaps, and get even more misjudged sympathy from them than he already had. It was only when he turned his phone towards the Morgan house that Ralph burst out of the front door to confront him.

'What d'you think you're doing? You can't take a photo of my house!'

Booth pocketed his phone. 'Reckon the police might like to know whose place I was parked outside when the latest damage to my property went down.'

'You mean the paint job? That could have been anyone who knows you,' Ralph said. 'Knows what you've done.' He should have left it there, gone back inside, but he could not control his anger and let rip: 'Why don't you do us all a favour and move this rancid eyesore back to your own property. And while you're at it, board the whole dump up so no one else is tempted to set foot in there and get themselves killed.'

'Go fuck yourself.' As Booth began scrubbing at the paint

with his rag, Ralph paced towards him into the street. His heart smashed against his ribcage.

'I said, *move it*.'

Booth held up his strapped wrist, his face a picture of false contrition. 'Sorry, can't drive yet, mate.'

'But you can use sanders and saws, can you? Where're the keys? I'll move it for you!'

Booth landed the first punch – from his good hand – on Ralph's right cheekbone and the pain caused an eruption of energy inside him, weeks' worth of frustration at *not* being free to smack the guy. Striking back, he almost expected to see Booth fly through the air, though he simply reeled slightly before they reconnected and grappled unceremoniously. Booth was muscular and compact, but his grip suffered from the wrist injury and Ralph was getting the better of him, until, with much grunting and a final shove from his good arm, Booth backed off. The greatest pain came from that shove, landing Ralph against the edge of the open camper-van door, the edge catching his spine.

All at once, at the sound of his howl, Kit and Cleo bolted into the street – he must have left the front door slightly ajar – springing up at both men, Cleo barking like a demented thing.

'Get away from me!' Booth roared, and reached for his white spirit – to spray at the dogs! – and Ralph recovered his balance and grabbed them by their collars, pulling them into the front garden and closing the gate on them. His right hand smarted badly. The dogs stood watching him, tails pumping, ready to rejoin the fray at the first opportunity.

'One of 'em fucking bit me,' Booth hissed, bandaged hand

gripping the bare one. The bottle of white spirit and rag had fallen to the ground.

'That's a lie,' Ralph said. 'Show me the mark.'

Sod's law, Naomi returned from Sissy's while the humans were still panting and growling at each other and the dogs going berserk. From Finn's place came the sound of Tuppy joining in and a couple of doors had now opened, neighbours drawn by the commotion.

'What's going on?' Naomi demanded. 'Why are the dogs so worked up?' Ignoring Booth, she waved cheerily to Sara Boulter, who had appeared at her gate opposite, and pulled Ralph indoors. He and the dogs followed her into the kitchen, but it was only Kit and Cleo who got fed treats and had their ears scratched. Ralph, she eyed with disdain.

'What?' He took a bag of frozen beans from the freezer and held it to his face before using his free hand to pet the dogs himself. 'Well done, guys. You know the enemy when you smell him, don't you?'

'Why were they so excited?' Naomi demanded. 'Please tell me you didn't hit him?'

Ralph shrugged. 'He started it.'

'But you launched in?'

'I protected myself. Nothing wrong with that.'

She groaned. 'How do you think this looks, Ralph?'

He raised his free hand in protest: 'No one else was there, it didn't look like anything.'

She paced the costly sandblasted floor tiles in rare agitation. 'Don't you realize this will have consequences? And they won't be what you think they'll be. It won't be that he's scared of you and won't come near you again. No, he'll report you, show them the bruises, and you'll get a police caution. You'll go up their list of suspects for the suspicious death. Which, by the way, is another way of saying murder.'

'I told you, *he* started it. He's a lunatic, he would have blinded the dogs with turps if I hadn't got them out of his way.'

'They wouldn't have been there in the first place if *you* weren't! He's the victim here, Ralph, at least according to the police. How could you have been so stupid?'

Ralph stared at her, less appalled by what she was saying than by the way she was saying it, with something close to contempt, for *him*. 'Whose side are you on here?' he cried, losing his temper. 'He's a complete cunt, you know that!'

There was silence. Naomi stopped pacing. 'You're sure no one saw you fighting? Sara wasn't watching?'

'No, she only came out after you arrived.' He stared at her, disorientated by her opposition. They always stood united and, until now, that unconditional loyalty had smoothed the instinctive differences in their responses to Booth, which had been there from the beginning. The diplomat and the warrior, that was how he thought of them, but the self-aggrandisement only worked if they were both in on it.

'What next, Ralph?' she said, and for a horrible moment he thought she was talking about them, their marriage. His unvoiced response was shameful: *I can't be the one whose marriage falls apart, that's other people, people like Ant or even Finn. But not me. Mine is the good marriage, the great one.*

'Seriously, you're going to arrive at a five-star hotel this evening with a beat-up face? Is that the plan? To look like some two-bit thug? How does this help us?'

'Who cares what a few hotel waiters think?' He adjusted the icepack on his face, brought it over his closed eye. 'Come on, Nay, no one else is going to take him on, are they?'

'No one else *should* take him on, at least only through the proper channels. Leave it to the police.'

'The proper channels are meaningless now. The police are idiots.'

Naomi sighed. She reached for the car keys to start loading for the trip, but not before adding, very quietly, as if there were a third person in the room she'd prefer not to overhear her: 'I thought we said we'd co-operate with them? It's not like we've got something to hide, is it?'

Ralph removed the ice, screwed up his eye and reopened it, testing the pain. Stars exploded. British weather or not, he'd be in sunglasses all week.

'Is it?' Naomi repeated.

'Of course not,' he said.

19

Ant

He had scarcely picked up the WhatsApp message from Ralph – *Cops asking for alibis for night before accident, can you believe it?* – when a detective had arrived at his door. Bruised and dispirited from Em's departure, Ant had phoned into the office to say he'd remembered a doctor's appointment and would be working from home for the day, so DC Shah was lucky to have caught him in. Would he have turned up at Ant's office if he hadn't? How serious *was* this?

A skinny, long-limbed guy in a suit and tie, Shah was disarmingly well prepared, referring to Ant's doorstep chat with the uniformed officer on the afternoon of the 11th without once looking at his notes. His pad was large, with a blue softcover. Did he expect to fill it with details of Ant's suspicious habits?

'In light of developments, I'm interested in the period between Friday evening at about six thirty and Saturday morning at about eight thirty,' he explained, unsmilingly.

Between Booth and Jodie leaving for the pub and Amy

Pope knocking at the door, Ant thought. So it was just as Booth had threatened and Ralph had warned: they, the victims, were now suspects in Amy's death. The world had gone mad!

'I was here, helping my wife get ready for a visit to her parents with our baby son. She postponed it because of what happened and headed off last night, instead. I can give you her number, if you need her to confirm.' He suppressed a shudder at the memory of his public clash with Em the previous evening. *I hate you!* Though she had been the more obviously hostile, he had not been as caring as he might. Chastising her in front of the others the way he had. He'd felt ashamed of her, too conscious of what the Morgans might think of them. In their impotence, they'd been able to turn on each other far more easily than on the true cause. 'Yes, so she went to bed first. I was just going up myself when Darren and Jodie came back and I heard the usual booming music.'

'Did you go round and ask them to turn it down?'

'No, I didn't. As I told your colleague, there's no point. And before you ask, no, I didn't sneak out and unscrew his scaffolding bolts or whatever you say happened. I wouldn't have a clue how to do that even if I wanted to. You're welcome to check my internet search history.' He regretted the suggestion the moment he made it, rushing to continue. 'No, no one left the house, until we heard the scaffolding come down the next morning. I'm positive about that, yes, positive.'

God, he was sounding nervous. It was self-fulfilling, though, wasn't it? Trained detectives must know that. You imagined them thinking, *He's acting guilty*, and that made you act guilty. 'Just let me know if I can help you with anything else,' he said, as DC Shah prepared to leave.

'Thank you. Just your wife's number,' the detective said, gently, as if prompting an elderly relative with early signs of dementia.

Having convinced himself that Em might never return, he almost felt like weeping when he came home from work on the Tuesday evening to find her back. Sam, already bathed and dressed for bed, let out a yelp of delight at the sight of his father, which really did bring tears to Ant's eyes. He carried his son around the kitchen as he unpacked the shopping he'd picked up on his way home, naming every item ('wine', 'curry', 'crisps') and trying to get Sam to make sounds of his own. Em passed no comment on his dietary habits in her absence.

'Feeling rested?' he asked her, immediately rueing the choice of words, since no parent of a small child was ever going to answer yes to that. 'I thought you might be away longer.'

'The police called,' she said. 'They want to see me in person. Besides, I do live here.'

'Sure. I just meant that things haven't exactly improved with Darren and Jodie.' He'd come face to face with them just once while Em was away. They'd been in the front garden inspecting an old Polo that had sustained bad scratches in the scaffolding collapse and, as Ant passed, they stopped what they were doing and stared at him with a forceful sense of menace. Only now did he appreciate the lukewarm glances of old.

'What?' Jodie challenged. 'If you've got any complaints, I suggest you talk to the police.'

'I already have,' Ant said, with bravado, but a roll of fear made his hand spasm as he tried to turn his key in the door.

'To be honest, they've just carried on where they left off,' he told Em.

She shrugged. 'Of course they have. But I refuse to be driven out of my own home by bullies.'

Well, this was welcome news.

'Plus, you have to admit we're a lot safer now the scaffolding's gone. It was far, far more likely to have been one of us than Amy.'

Ant wrested a block of cheese from Sam's grip and put it in the fridge. 'Let's not say that in front of Sissy.' But she was right, it was a truth that bore repetition: a terrible tragedy had taken place on their doorstep and, regardless of any misguided theories the police had chosen to pursue, the neighbours were the lucky ones.

'I notice he's installed a camera over his front door, so he's obviously stepping up his security,' Em said. 'The police must've told him to watch his back, in case one of us sneaks in with our next murder weapon: a vial of cyanide maybe? I'll order some online.' Her snigger caused Sam to laugh too and Ant wondered if his young brain was absorbing any of this dark talk, the vocabulary of death and hate. When they looked at photos from this period when he was older, would they be able to see that he was troubled?

Easy to forget that Sam – specifically, his education – was the reason they were in Lowland Way in the first place, neighbours and all: the road was safely in the catchment area of the outstanding Lowland Primary. Nothing was guaranteed, of course, but the Morgans had explained the form: get him into the kindergarten attached to the school, which helped in the event of a tie, then pray every night for a low intake of siblings.

That was before they prayed every night for silence. For their lives.

'Should we be worried the police are on our case?' Em asked. 'Are we suspects?'

'Top of the list, I would imagine,' Ant said.

'I assume someone's reminded them Booth almost ran over Charlie Morgan not long before?'

Ant paused in his task. 'What are you saying?'

'Just that we're not the only ones with a motive, if they're thinking in those terms. And it won't take them long to discover there's been a group campaign against his business.'

'No one's trying to hide that. It'll all be on file at the council.' But the remark caused his mind to rewind and alight, abruptly, on Em's observation: *I notice he's installed a camera* . . . A significant detail now surfaced that had somehow remained submerged: his camera app on the old iPhone, abandoned since he'd secured evidence of Booth's trading for Ralph: how much – or little – time had there been between then and 11 August? Weeks certainly. A long time for a phone battery. And yet, hadn't it been set up to work on standby? It might just have staggered on.

Thank God he hadn't mentioned it to the detective. DC Shah would have seen for himself the lack of any exterior camera or alarm system at number 3, but if he'd asked, 'You don't happen to have any concealed home security equipment, do you?', Ant would probably have said, without thinking, 'Yes, as a matter of fact I've been using a nifty little surveillance app . . .'

Unbelievable – he'd had all this time to remember the phone and, if needed, dispose of it, including several days in the house alone. He could have checked and double-checked the video to his heart's content. (And why the hell hadn't he set it up in the first place so he could access it remotely from his own phone? Fuckwit.)

'Talking of cameras,' Em said, 'if the police are right, then we should have a look at our own visuals, in case we caught the mystery saboteur on film.'

Ant pretended to focus on Sam, who was straining to be returned to Em. 'Oh, I stopped using the app after I got my money shot – literally.'

She frowned. 'I'm sure the phone was still sitting in the window when I left.'

'Yeah, but I haven't recharged the battery. It'll have died ages ago.' He was aware that he was trembling slightly.

'But it might still have had a few per cent left that night. Or there might be old footage of the scaffolding going up?' Em began to look animated.

'True, let's check it out. I think it's time for bed,' Ant told his son, then passing him to Em. 'You do that and I'll go and look.'

'No,' Em said, refusing to take him. '*You* do bedtime and *I'll* go and look.'

'Okay.' Next door, the TV was on, the lesser of two evils as far as Sam's sleeping went. Ant tried to concentrate on lulling him to sleep, all the while imagining his wife downstairs viewing grainy night film of Friday the 10th. Would she see a prowler, just like the one the police were on the hunt for? A killer?

When he rejoined her, twenty minutes later, she was bent over the phone screen. 'There *is* something. Right at the end, just before it goes dead.'

An unfortunate choice of phrase, but neither commented.

There were six short sequences from the night of the 10th–11th:

19:01: Darren and Jodie leaving the house together.
19:16: Ant arriving home from work.
20:33: Pizza delivery guy arriving at number 3 and, seconds later, leaving.
00:20: Darren and Jodie arriving home.
00:29: Jodie leaving the house again.
00:48: Jodie returning.

'I think she went to get cigarettes,' Em said. 'Look, when she comes back, she's got one in her mouth. Must've gone to the petrol station on Portsmouth Avenue, that's the only place open that late.'

'He's a real gent letting her go out on her own so late at night,' Ant said.

'Maybe that's why she fiddled with his scaffolding on her way back in,' Em said, with heavy emphasis.

Ant stared at her, amazed. 'Are you serious? Where's that bit? Show me.'

'Well, it doesn't show it on here, exactly. She's under the scaffolding and that's not within the range of the camera.

But, look, there's also this. It's the last thing the camera caught before it died.'

It was a single second of footage: Jodie backing out a few steps from under the scaffolding, before vanishing under it once more.

'That's twelve fifty,' Em said. 'Two minutes after she comes home. Two minutes is long enough to loosen a few bolts.'

'I don't know,' Ant said. 'She might have been doing anything: looking for her keys, checking her phone . . .'

Em dismissed this, intent on her theory. 'The point is, she's the only person caught on camera outside their house that night, other than you coming home and the delivery guy bringing our pizza. So if the sabotage took place during that period, then this is proof that no one else had the opportunity. *We* think he's hateful,' she went on, 'maybe *she* does, as well?'

Well, it wasn't the worst idea, Ant thought. Anything to redirect the police from *them*. 'I'll clip it and send it to the police now. The detective left me his details.'

Em went to shower and unpack, leaving him to thumb through the footage an additional time. As Em had said, the battery had failed soon after Jodie's return, the very last motion captured being the dash of a fox at 12:59. What a bizarre – and frustrating – coincidence. How much better it would have been to be able to present the police with the exact timings of Amy's arrival at the house in the morning, even if it would have felt horribly ghoulish to view the girl in her final moments. But there might have been some clue, perhaps a few words addressed to Booth that could have been lip-read by the experts.

He dug in his wallet for the card left by DC Shah and

attached the clips to an email message. There was a tense moment when he saw that the phone's edit tool was already activated, but he reminded himself that he'd used it the last time he'd checked the app. That triumphant delivery to Ralph of the clip of Jodie handling cash from a customer.

Glory days, indeed.

Though it felt like an agonizingly long time before he heard from DC Shah, it was in reality just twenty-four hours. 'Is there other security film from the morning of the eleventh?'

Ant explained that the battery had died at 1 a.m.

'That's inconvenient timing.' Was there doubt in his tone, even disbelief? 'Did you have a specific purpose for setting it up?'

Ant explained the neighbours' concerns about Booth's illicit trading activities: no harm in reminding the police who the criminal was here.

'You didn't say anything about a home security camera on the weekend of the incident or in our interview last week.'

Ant didn't like that phrase, *you didn't say anything* – it sounded horribly similar to *anything you do say*. Nor did he care for the idea of an 'interview', as if the questioning had been more formal than he'd understood. 'We assumed the battery was long dead, but we happened to check and discovered something we thought might be relevant.'

DC Shah, likely hardened to garrulous accounts of people happening to check and assuming this and that, moved on. 'Any particular reason why your neighbour would have taken her shoes off?' he asked.

Ant was startled. 'What? I didn't notice that.'

'She arrives with shoes on, then when she steps back into view for a moment, her shoes have been removed. Any thoughts?'

He had not done this when they'd met face to face: discussed the case, considered Ant's theories. It felt like an opportunity, an invitation.

'Maybe she used them to hammer the scaffolding? To loosen the bolts?'

'Loosen bolts with a pair of high-heeled shoes?'

Ant felt foolish. He imagined the detective thinking he shouldn't give up his day job.

'I'd appreciate it if you could bring the mobile in,' DC Shah said, finally. 'Leave it with one of our phone downloaders for a couple of days.'

'Anything to help,' Ant said.

20

Tess

There was something about the detective that reminded Tess of Naomi. A withheld disapproval, perhaps because Tess had not been in on the two previous occasions she'd called; the only person to give the police the runaround and yet the one with the least excuse to do so.

Imagined criticism or not, she found herself reacting to it by being really quite rude. 'This is a complete waste of taxpayers' money, if you ask me. Booth didn't have a clue what he was doing with the scaffolding, it's as simple as that. Did my husband tell you they didn't have the right number of braces? You know, the diagonal poles?'

'He knows something about scaffolding construction, does he?' DC Forrester asked. From a distance, Tess had thought her about her own age, but close up she was younger. Oddly, given what she must see in her job, her eyes had an optimistic sparkle.

'The basics, yes. Enough for us to contact the Health and Safety people about it. I meant to chase it up, but it hadn't been that long and ... well, I suppose I never imagined anyone would be injured, other than Booth himself.' Tess flushed. 'That sounds bad. I don't mean I *hoped* he'd be injured, obviously.'

As the detective scratched her throat with a fingernail, the sound seemed to amplify. The house was unnaturally silent, Isla and Dex at a sports camp all week at the local leisure centre and Tuppy sleeping in the garden. Tess imagined herself roaming the rooms of their huge house when Dex started school. *Find a job, earn some money.* And yet, she'd done nothing to get the process underway.

'Shall we talk about what you were doing the night before the collapse?'

'If you really think it's relevant.' She supplied her timeline, its events distant now, even unreal, given all that had happened since. 'When we got home from the theatre, we put the kids to bed, paid the babysitter, then had a quick drink. Can I just ask, if you're right and someone deliberately unscrewed the bolts that night, then why didn't the alarm go off? I'm sure he had one rigged up there, I saw the wires.'

DC Forrester's examination of her felt suddenly more acute. 'Do you own any wire cutters, Mrs Morgan?'

'Wire cutters? Not that I'm aware of, but I'd have to ask Finn. Why? Oh!' Tess faltered, understanding. 'You mean the alarm wires were cut? Well, that *is* dodgy.'

'Yes, we think so.'

Again, Tess thought she detected a trace of distaste. Who is this woman in her posh house, describing murder as 'dodgy'? Was that what the detective was thinking? *That's not me at all*, she protested silently. *People say I'm earnest, a martyr.*

She was just being paranoid.

'Have you considered the possibility that he sabotaged his own scaffolding for some sort of insurance scam? Have you investigated his finances?'

But the inquisition was strictly one-way, just as it had been when she'd gone to the station. She had a regrettable memory of her children sitting waiting in a building stuffed with criminals, having expected a trip to the zoo.

'You mentioned a babysitter,' said DC Forrester. 'Could I have a name and contact number, please?'

There was a new report online about the accident, the first Tess had seen with a neighbour quoted directly:

Neighbours Blame Owner for Scaffolding Death

A resident living near the site of a fatal scaffolding crush in Lowland Gardens has accused the property owner of causing the death of Amy Pope.

The neighbour, who preferred not to be named, said the police were 'barking up the wrong tree' in their investigation. 'I don't buy this idea that someone sabotaged the scaffolding. Wouldn't it be too much of a risk that it would fall on them? You'd need technical knowledge, practical experience. Surely it's the person who built such a dangerous structure on his premises who needs to be held accountable for this death?'

The same neighbour claimed that the street was in 'total agreement' on the issue, adding that residents had noticed heavy building materials being loaded onto the lower platform just days before the tragic collapse: 'I don't know if that contributed to Amy's death, but I wish now I'd pursued the issue at the time.'

SOUTH LONDON PRESS

'I said something similar to the police myself,' she told Finn, 'about pursuing the issue. Who d'you think gave this interview?'

He shrugged. 'I have no idea, but whoever it is sounds very confident.'

'Could be Ralph? He could have spoken to them on the phone from Devon. Or even Naomi? They don't say if it's a man or a woman.'

Finn's gaze narrowed. 'That phrase, "practical experience". It's almost like they're hinting to the reporter to dig in that direction.'

Following the hot words exchanged after Booth's release, relations between Tess and her sister-in-law were strained once more. Even Naomi's suspension of Play Out Sunday had bothered Tess. It had been so unilateral, as if she'd forgotten that Tess was her co-founder and equal (they'd met the mayor together, for goodness' sake!).

'Maybe not Naomi,' she told Finn. 'She's the one who's been warning us about the press, unless that's some sort of double bluff.'

Before leaving for Devon, Naomi had posted a new caution on the residents' Facebook page (she was enviably adept at running separate comms for the wider group of residents on Facebook and for their select group on WhatsApp):

Naomi Morgan: Please be aware that there are reporters on the street. The police have advised residents against giving media interviews and want to remind us that this is a live investigation.

Sara Boulter: Thanks, Naomi, good advice. We are definitely not the kind of people who want to be splashed all over MailOnline.

The police, you could not dodge for long, but Tess had so far managed to avoid any face-to-face contact with reporters. A couple of business cards had been waiting on the doormat when she'd come home from errands or picking the kids up from camp. *I'd be so interested in hearing your story!* one had scrawled on the back in biro.

'You need to be extra careful today,' Finn advised her. 'Booth's sure to be looking at the news as well and he won't like this. Ralph thinks it's only a matter of time before he retaliates properly.'

'Properly?' Tess said. 'What does that mean?'

'That's the point. We'll have no idea until he does it.'

It was only when she opened her door later that day and saw Jodie standing there that Tess realized the other woman had never before walked down the front path, never been invited in. In light of that exchange with Finn, her arrival felt like an act of threat. It felt as if the rules were changing.

'Jodie. Is this about the report in the *South London Press*?'

'What report?'

Bugger. Tess couldn't believe her own schoolgirl error. She eyed her visitor with caution, noting the clenched jaw, the eyes glowing with outrage. 'How can I help?'

'I've just been talking to the police.'

'Oh yes.' Somehow, in this unholy tangle that was neighbourly relations at their end of the street, she had been knotted with Jodie. Why was that? Had Jodie targeted her or did she somehow believe *Tess* had targeted *her*?

'Just wanted you to know that I know it was you who left that dog shit by our door that night.'

'What? What night? What dog shit?'

'Don't make out like you don't know. I stepped in it, as well. I should of made you clean my fucking shoes.'

Tess felt faint shame for noticing and disliking that 'should of'. 'If you've been finding dog shit on your doorstep, then maybe it's because the local dogs think it's an appropriate place to relieve themselves? I can't think why.'

Jodie's fists closed, the bones of her knuckles sharp under the skin. 'You mess with the scaffolding while you were at it?'

'What?'

'I reckon it was the same person. I reckon it was you – I've told the police that, an' all. Almost forgot, didn't I, what with everything going on. But when I spoke to them again, I remembered it was the same night.'

'I assume you mean the same night before an innocent woman was killed thanks to your husband's criminal negligence?' Tess said, coldly. What kind of a twisted mind dredged up some grievance about dog mess when a woman had been crushed to death on the same spot?

Jodie's face lit with inspiration. 'We could get it

tested, yeah? It's still on my shoe. I could get the forensic people onto it.'

'Oh, for God's sake.' Tess couldn't believe she was engaging in this nonsense. She had the most awful impulse to step forwards and grab a fistful of Jodie's hair, twist it hard. 'Look, good luck to you and your forensics people, but I really don't have the time to get involved. I've got things to do.'

Jodie took a pace forwards and craned her neck, as if peering into Tess's life. 'Like what? Scrounging off your husband? What d'you do all day, eh?'

As if she were a cabinet minister herself! She set up test drives for an illegal used-car business! Something was wrong with the world when mothers were considered wastrels, while known nuisances enjoyed the protection of the police.

'I spend my time caring for my children. I walk my dog, I feed the swans in the park – do you even know we have cygnets at the end of the road?' Attuned to her rising emotions, Tuppy arrived at Tess's feet and she placed a hand on his collar. 'No, I don't suppose you do. You don't care about anything but yourself. You moved to a nice happy street and behave as if no one exists but yourselves. A woman is dead, Jodie – do you and your husband really not care about that? If not, that would make you sociopaths. A great match with each other, but not with us. Not with us *at all*.' Tess stopped. She'd grown more vindictive than she'd intended – than she ever did, frankly – and inkblots of pink had crept across Jodie's face.

Her visitor's voice rose in anger: 'Who the fuck do you think you are, talking to me like that?'

'I think I'm someone who's on her way out.' Tight-chested

with the need to escape, Tess dipped inside for Tuppy's lead and dodged past Jodie to her gate. 'Do *not* follow me,' she hissed. 'I have *nothing* to say to you.'

'Fuck you,' Jodie shouted after her, as if the whole street needed to hear.

Tess wished she'd brought a jacket, because the air was cool as she walked down Lowland Way towards the park, the summer smog thinning. Overhead, trees stirred and swayed, released from the heat of July and the first half of August. That skirmish with Jodie was a very troubling redrafting of battle lines, especially in light of the fight Ralph had had with Booth. Why had she mentioned the kids? Dex was about to start school, would he be safe away from Tess?

She would make sure she arrived early to collect Isla and him from sports camp that day, make sure there was no way a 'friendly neighbour' could get there first and whisk them into a waiting van. Jodie had been seen on occasion to clean up pretty well and she certainly had the wherewithal to pass herself off as a civilized, middle-class mother.

Listen to yourself, Tess thought, appalled. *What a horrible snob.* Catching the eye of a mum from the estate who she'd seen a few times before, she beamed, overcompensating for her thoughts. Why did she even feel the need to label this woman an 'estate mum'? Was it her brood of kids? She might be a childminder or, like Tess herself, frequently saddled with extras. Perhaps it was no bad thing that the police knew better than to automatically believe the well-heeled neighbour over the downmarket one. Perhaps their default was in fact the other way around.

She dug out her phone. It was days since she'd shared any

photos of the cygnets on Facebook. They were too independent now for her to be able to get all six together in a single shot, so she took some individual portraits: one with his head plunged underwater, another with his neck elegantly twisted to groom tail feathers with his beak.

As they drifted away, attracted by someone on the opposite side scattering a bag of the specially formulated food sold at the coffee hut, Tess had a weird sensation she was being watched. But when she spun around, there was no one there.

Determined not to allow the neighbourhood troubles to defeat her, she had by the following morning shunted Jodie from her mind. Finn said goodbye amid the breakfast chaos of Dex still struggling into his sports kit while Tuppy pulled off his socks in a tug-of-war and Isla complained repeatedly that her toast was too 'untoasted' and the jam had 'bits' in it.

'Tess?' Finn was summoning her from the front door in a tone she knew meant *alone*.

'What?' She shut Tuppy in with the kids and joined her husband.

'Look. On the path.'

She followed his gaze, struggling at first to comprehend what she saw. Just inside the gate lay a shallow cardboard box with a bird in it. A very large dead bird.

'It's a cygnet,' she cried. One of the park ones, surely. She stumbled forwards and fell to her knees next to it, sliding the box out of sight of any passers-by. How heavy it was! There was no visible mutilation, it was whole and beautiful, its neck curled, as if it had died there quite peacefully. She touched the feathers, juvenile grey but flecked with adult white, her tears already flowing. The pen and the cob must know they'd lost him, they must be frantic. 'Oh, you poor baby, I'm so sorry. How did you get here?' Then she saw the red circle at the base of the neck, the bullet hole of an execution.

'Is that a bite wound?' Finn asked, squatting next to her.

'A gunshot wound, I think,' Tess said, gulping.

'You mean some kind of illegal hunting? Why's it here? I don't understand.'

'Nor do I.' But the way it had been left in the middle of her path, as though *displayed*, was not just puzzling but perverse.

'What should we do with it?' Finn said.

'We need to call the swan protection people. They work with the police. Swan Rescue, they're called. There's a number in my phone contacts.'

'I'll do it.'

She did not protest when he emerged a few minutes later to cover the box with a blanket, but remained on the doorstep as if guarding it. Time hovered: she wasn't sure how long she stayed there, only half-aware of Isla and Dex passing by with their kit bags and lunch boxes, of Finn telling her he'd drop them at their camp and go into work late. It was only when the gate squeaked and a police officer arrived that she at last struggled to her feet.

'Thank you so much for coming,' she told them.

'Swan Rescue had a report last night of someone trying to shoot the cygnets in Lowland Gardens. Any idea what it's doing here?'

'None at all.' An image flickered in Tess's mind then, too fragile to catch. 'But I am part of Cygnetwatch. We're a local

Facebook group, we post photos and share news about them. Maybe someone knew me from that.'

Would she need to post about this? She didn't think she could face it. She thought of the poor officers who had to break terrible news every day, like the ones who'd gone to Amy's parents' house.

That was when the image returned to her, sharpened into something distinct: Jodie standing where this man now stood, Tess haranguing her.

Do you even know we have cygnets at the end of the road?

And what had Ralph said? *It's only a matter of time before he retaliates properly . . .*

No, it was too fantastic, too macabre, surely? And yet, a woman had died by the Booths' hand, so why not a bird too?

'Actually, I do have an idea who might have done this,' she said, feeling the blood return to her skin. 'You might want to share your report with CID, because it's relevant to a suspicious death investigation going on here at the moment. Do you want to come in and I'll find the name of the detective I'm in touch with?'

And for the second time in a matter of days, she led a police officer into her house.

21

Sissy

Though the police's Family Liaison Unit had phoned to let her know detectives would be calling, Sissy had already heard about their presence on the street from the neighbours. Travelling to and from Amy's funeral by train, she'd followed their messages on WhatsApp as news was traded:

Naomi: Not just us, also Dan and Sara Boulter and their neighbours on the other side. They're going right down the street.

Ralph: Asked me where we were going on holiday – WTF, is that allowed?

Tess: They asked me if I own any wire cutters!

Ant: They can ask what they like, it doesn't change the fact that he's guilty.

She'd turned away when she read that one.

Now that the funeral had taken place and she was back home, she couldn't really refuse the police a proper interview, even if she feared that the grief would explode from her mouth semi-solid, like vomit.

'Thank you for seeing us,' they said in low, respectful voices. 'We know it must be very hard for you.'

There was a pair of them, she didn't absorb the names. The woman was white, in her thirties, the man Asian, late twenties, and both had smooth, enquiring faces, like children. The neighbours had reported just one questioner each; did it mean something that she had two?

Did anything mean anything now?

'I would prefer not to go back over it, to be honest, but if you think I can help.' She made them tea, laboriously, her hands beset by tremors. She thought she'd made Assam, but the man's grimace when he took a sip made her think she may have given them camomile by mistake. It was a side effect of her grief, and not a good one, that she could not taste or smell properly.

The first questions were about timings, easily answered if she thought of Amy and herself as actors who she was watching on screen. The female detective led, the male silent to the point of deference.

'You and Amy were alone in the house, were you? No visitors that evening?'

'No, my B&B guests weren't arriving till the Saturday, so it was just the two of us.'

They glanced at one another in surprise and then back at Sissy. 'I'm not sure our colleagues passed on any information about a B&B business,' they said, and Sissy blinked at them in despair. How was she supposed to account for what they did and didn't know? *They* were the detectives.

'It might not have come up,' she said.

'Would you be able to supply records of your recent bookings? Since Mr Booth moved to the street.'

Sissy frowned. 'Why so far back?'

'We're interested in establishing any links with the intended victim.'

The intended victim? A swell of nausea engulfed her. They cared more about protecting *him* than they did honouring Amy. Pete was going to be appalled when he was next brought up to date. Except for one brief visit soon after the accident, when Booth and Jodie were staying elsewhere, he had refused to come back to Lowland Way and Sissy didn't blame him. There'd been no arrest, neither last Thursday, when Tess had seen Booth at the station, nor any time since. He was back, alive and at liberty, and there was absolutely nothing to stop him building some other unsafe structure on his property.

Just get through this, she told herself. *Get through this and they'll go.* 'I'll give you the password to the members' area of the website I use. You can check bookings as far back as you like.'

'I understand Ralph and Naomi Morgan held a meeting at their house on the nineteenth of July?' the woman said. 'To discuss the issue of Darren Booth and his business?'

'Yes, we agreed which official channels to follow with our complaints.' Futile, the whole thing. It was so obvious now: the only people who cared about official complaints were the kind who didn't incur them in the first place.

The man spoke now. Compared to the woman, whose questioning style was conversational, he was more formal. 'Did Amy bring anything with her, other than the overnight bag?'

This, Sissy knew, had been found with her in the rubble and, after some delay, had been released to Pete. 'She didn't, no.'

'You're sure about that?'

'Yes, I'm sure. Why, what are you suggesting? That she brought along scaffolder's tools? That a happy, newly pregnant woman would stop by a stranger's house and half-dismantle his scaffolding, then go over in the morning in the hope that it would crush her to death?'

Fractured skull leading to acute epidural haematoma, that had been the official cause of death and, remembering Pete's devastated expression as he recited the phrases to her, Sissy began sobbing.

The male detective looked about the room for tissues and, finding a box, brought it to her. The female moved a hand in Sissy's direction but stopped short of making contact. 'Would you like to take a break?'

She mopped her eyes and nose. 'I'm fine. Let's carry on.'

'So Amy didn't say anything to you when she left about calling on Mr Booth?'

'No, but he'd been playing music in the early hours and we'd both had a bad night because of it, so I'm certain that's why she went over there. To try to help.' The words caught in her throat and she gulped the tea. Of all the thoughts to haunt her, the one that dominated was the conviction that she should never have mentioned Booth to Amy that night, should never have become hysterical the way she had.

She didn't think she would ever emerge from under the weight of her regret. As a heaving sensation began to build once more, she struggled to her feet, her hands full of crumpled tissue. 'Look, we'll have to do this another time, after all. It's just . . . it's too upsetting.'

The detectives rose obediently. 'Of course. That's fine. Perhaps we can phone you if we have anything further.'

Anything further: the phrasing of the courtroom. In a sudden desire to be useful, she said, 'Amy did bring something else: *those*.' She indicated the sunflowers, laid out on newspaper on the worktop, as Naomi had instructed. To be preserved in Amy's memory.

The visitors did not comment. Only as they left did the man remind her, 'The website details for your B&B bookings? Only when you have a moment.'

In a very kind email, Amy's mother Faye had told Sissy that her bereavement counsellor had recommended a daily local errand, no matter how painful it was, to keep her connected to the outside world, and Sissy had adopted the advice herself.

Today, Thursday, the day after the police came, it had been a walk to the high street to buy fruit. Returning to Lowland Way, she felt the sucking sensation of loss as she watched Em Kendall backing out of her drive, little Sam in his car seat in the rear. That should have been Amy, in a year's time, driving her baby around, singing to him, eager for his first words, his first steps.

Instead, no baby. No Amy.

As Sissy put her key in her lock and pushed the door, she was startled to feel resistance – complete resistance, the impact of which ricocheted into her wrist and arm as the momentum carried her body forwards. It took a moment to understand that the security chain was engaged and she froze, her body incapacitated with shock. You could only do that from the inside.

At exactly the same moment, there was a sense of another movement halted – above her head. *Someone was in her house. Upstairs.*

Overcoming the paralysis, she took a few steps back and gazed up at the bay windows of the master bedroom: there was nothing visible through the glass beyond the top of the drawers and the edges of the curtains.

Think. She had no B&B guest today and no cleaner or other worker (she couldn't afford the luxury of outside help anymore); she knew better than to leave spare keys under flowerpots. Who had a key? Pete. Also, Tess Morgan. But it definitely wasn't Pete and she could think of no good reason why Tess would enter her home without permission, much less bar the front door once inside. Someone had broken in – presumably at the back, where they were less likely to be seen – and Sissy had caught them in the act. The safety chain had bought them time to escape.

She fumbled for her phone, thinking briefly of the business card the detectives had left, before dialling 999.

'Go and wait somewhere safe,' she was advised. 'With a neighbour or in a nearby public place. Do not try to gain access and confront this person.'

'I won't.' By now she knew it was him. Booth. She had developed an animal sense for him and that sense was flaring, stirring the hairs on her arms. Disobeying orders, she approached the side gate, which opened without her needing the key. She couldn't remember the last time she'd used it – before Amy's death, certainly – and there was no evidence of the lock having been forced, so it was possible it had been left unlocked this whole time. The kitchen door was closed, as she'd left it, but also unlatched. She was only half-sure she'd locked this either: her mind was fractured these days, sequences lost to blind spots, like pigment on the retina. Had Booth arrived prepared to force locks and smash glass and found he had no need?

She stepped into her kitchen and edged through the hallway. Nothing looked different. Upstairs, she toed open each door in turn, scanning the rooms from their threshold. She knew he could be in any hiding place, in a wardrobe, under a bed, even behind the door – he could be mere feet from her at any time, their breath mingling. *If he kills me, I don't care. I'll sacrifice myself to guarantee his conviction, his imprisonment.*

Then came the sound of a car braking in the street. Rushing down to the door, she saw dark silhouettes through the glass. The police. So fast! He'd be trapped and rooted out, arrested, once and for all!

But, as she went to open the door, she found the chain was no longer on. It made no sense. Unless ... unless he'd left as she was creeping around the side – or even when she was inside herself, sliding silently past her as she moved from room to room. Could he really have been so brazen? What would he have done, what would he have *said*, if they'd come face to face on the landing? She imagined her hands on his throat, pressing until they felt something snap.

The police introduced themselves as Safer Neighbourhood Officers, different from those who'd been there on the morning of Amy's accident. They dutifully checked the house, confirmed the absence of an intruder, and listened to her account of the event.

'So you don't remember locking the gate or kitchen door?'

'No, but I *definitely* didn't leave the chain on the front door. I only use that at night.'

It wasn't hard to tell what they were thinking: if she'd left the house by the side gate, her first outing of the day, then the chain could easily have remained untouched from the previous night.

'So you re-entered through the kitchen and the intruder left through the front door? Did you see or hear them exit?'

'No. I know how it sounds.' Like a choreographed farce. Two people missing each other by a whisker. Revolving doors.

Addressing his colleague, not Sissy, one of the officers asked, 'Why would they put the chain on if they knew the occupier could re-enter through an unlocked side gate?'

'Maybe to make me doubt myself, like you are?' Sissy cried. 'To make me feel like I'm going mad?' Her rising emotion was not helping correct this illusion. 'He might have been watching me, worked out how long I'd be out. He only lives across the road.'

That got their interest. 'So you *did* see the intruder?'

'No, but I know it was him. Darren Booth. He was recently involved in an accident at his house. My son's girlfriend was killed.'

Though this prompted kind words, there was a sense that she'd just confirmed herself as unreliable. She remembered now, on the leaflet about loss she'd been given by the police liaison lady, a line about becoming forgetful, mislaying your keys and so on.

'Can't you bring Forensics in? He hasn't been here ever before, so you'll be able to find out straightaway if it was him. There'd be fibres from his clothes, wouldn't there?'

The officers did a good job of concealing their disbelief, it seemed to her. Deploy an expensive forensics operation on the basis of a hunch by a woman in the throes of grief?

She tried again. 'He's just put up a security camera, so why don't you at least check that?' But of course he'd remember his own camera. He'd probably watched her leave, turned it off, and strolled over.

'Okay, Ms Watkins, while we're here, do you want to double-check nothing's been stolen?'

They were humouring her now. Showing due respect. It was as much as she could expect, evidently. Nothing was missing, of course, not even in the master bedroom, where she spent some minutes searching. Where in the large space would a bloodhound find his strongest scent, she thought, in despair. Why had he come in here and what had he looked at? What had he *touched*?

In the absence of a single sign of disturbance, the officers suggested she get her locks changed 'to be on the safe side' and she listened with resignation to tips about window locks and extra door bolts. At least they went over to Booth's afterwards. She watched them stand at his door, talking with him for five minutes or so. When they returned to the car, she intercepted them.

'What did he say? Did you check his camera footage?'

'The camera isn't operational yet.'

As she'd thought. He wasn't stupid.

'We're satisfied Mr Booth was not involved in your break-in.'

They as good as put 'break-in' in inverted commas. They thought she was a confused old bird who'd imagined – or at best misconstrued – this whole episode. They probably had a code for call-outs to old dears.

'Sixty is not old,' she told them, a non sequitur that as a parting shot only attracted further kind looks.

When they'd left, their car no longer visible from her window, she wept, as she had every day and every night since Amy died.

22

Ant

Ant took a wary breath as he approached his house on Friday evening. Though Booth, working on the camper van outside Ralph's place, was mercifully out of range and unable to treat him to one of his new death stares, Ant had learned to fix his gaze on his own door, to avoid looking directly at the spot where Amy had died. It seemed to him there lingered a sense not only of tragedy but also of betrayal, a soundless scream of protest.

Em was in the garden with Sam, a rare sight in recent months. They had the sandpit out, which made Ant think of the huge sacks of sand loaded onto Booth's scaffolding, their lethal weight splitting the weave when they fell to the ground.

'The police just called me about the phone,' he told her, keeping his voice low in case of eavesdroppers over the wall. 'They said you hadn't dropped it off yet?'

'Oh,' said Em and her gaze turned opaque.

'I said I'd drive down with it now. They're there till late.'

Her hands over Sam's, Em helped him put spadefuls of

sand into his plastic pot. 'You can't do that, I'm afraid. I've deleted the app and the rest of the footage.'

'What?' Ant was taken aback. 'Why did you do that?'

'I didn't think we needed it.'

Her tone did not convince and unease began to creep through Ant. 'Okay, well, it wasn't backed up to the cloud, but maybe they can retrieve it from the hard drive or whatever. Where did you put the phone?'

Em's jaw muscles tensed. 'It's in the bin.'

'The main bin?'

'Yes.'

The weekly rubbish collection had been that morning.

'Why?' he repeated. 'I don't understand?'

'To be honest, Ant, I think it was a big mistake for you to have told them you used this app at all.'

He frowned, exasperated. 'What are you talking about? You knew I was sending them the clip – you were the one who suggested it!'

'The clip, yes,' she repeated, like a prosecution barrister seizing on a slip by a poor witness. 'Not the whole thing. You don't think it might look a bit voyeuristic, you having a camera trained permanently on our neighbours?'

You, not *us*, he couldn't help noticing.

'No more so than Booth's camera now.'

'His is in plain sight for everyone to see. Yours was concealed.' She tipped the pot of sand upside down and smacked its base with the spade, which Sam enjoyed. 'I've been doing some reading and just being in possession of that film could have got us in deep shit.'

Ant listened in disbelief as she detailed her research into

the law on domestic surveillance usage. Evidently, data protection issues meant they should have notified Booth that his property was within range of their camera; additionally, he had a right to demand to see any material they had recorded involving him and his property.

'Okay, so then we could have shown him. We could have shown everyone who happened to be on it. They all knew we were watching Booth.'

'*You* were,' Em corrected him.

Here she went again, separating them in language, in spirit. He gazed at her in vexation. He could see her reaction was not normal and yet he could hardly blame her. The last few days had been truly frightening: Tess's dead cygnet, Sissy's break-in . . . She had to be wondering what was in store for *her*.

He left them to their sandcastles and phoned the police with his unwelcome news. DC Forrester took the call.

'Thank you for letting us know,' she said and her lack of probing felt far more sinister than any telling-off might have. 'While I've got you on the phone, Mr Kendall . . .'

'Yes?'

'You said you didn't leave the house on the night of Friday the tenth?'

'That's right.'

'And yet we've had a report that you *were* outside that night at about midnight. Is there a possibility you stepped out and forgot to tell us? This person is absolutely certain it was you.'

Ant paused, his vision darkening slightly at the edges. 'Oh. Well, if they're a hundred per cent sure they saw me, then I suppose I must have.'

'Can you tell me what you were doing?'

'Do I need a reason to go into the front garden of my own home? To put something in the bin, maybe? To check I locked the car? I honestly don't remember.'

Forgetfulness was no excuse in the witness box, though, was it?

'Do you remember if you went near next door's scaffolding?'

'Definitely not. I mean, it was right on the centre point, slightly overhanging our side, actually, so I might have taken a few steps under it. But I didn't touch it. I was only outside for a minute or two.'

'So after you did what you can't remember doing for a minute or two, you went back inside?'

'Yes.' Ant swallowed. Was she recording this exchange? No, that wasn't legal, was it? 'Can I ask who it was who said they saw me?'

'I'm not able to give you that information.'

Of course she wasn't. But it had to have been a neighbour.

As his brain made a sudden connection, he felt his stomach collapse. The edit tool on the app: it had been activated, hadn't it? What if Em had seen the footage of him and deleted it? Never mentioned it to him, never mentioned it to the police. The tearing sensation inside his ribcage took a moment to characterize: relief. Relief that she still cared enough to protect him.

When the call ended, Ant pictured DC Forrester circling his name in red, if not on an actual list pinned to a real board, then mentally. Moving his metaphorical mugshot to the top of the pile.

'What was that all about?' Em asked, when he rejoined them in the garden.

Ant knelt on the lawn next to her, his voice almost a whisper: 'You cut some video before you came to show me, didn't you?'

Her face gave nothing away. 'I didn't cut anything.'

'You knew it wasn't backed up to the cloud, because I told you, but you chucked the phone away because you were worried it might be stored on the phone itself?'

She said nothing, just shook her head, eyes averted.

'I did go outside that Friday night, but I didn't touch his bloody scaffolding, I swear.'

Em bit her bottom lip. 'I don't want to know what you did or didn't do.'

'I didn't do anything, that's—'

'No, stop!' She raised a palm, which caught the attention of Sam, who opened his mouth as if to contribute. No sound came out. 'Seriously, Ant, don't. Then if the police do ask me, I won't have anything to tell them.'

'There's nothing *to* tell,' Ant said, fiercely.

'Good. Then let's just get through the weekend, shall we? Without anything bad happening.'

Well, he could have told her *that* was tempting fate. Unencumbered, evidently, by the police inquiries causing anxiety among their neighbours, Darren and Jodie were in the mood to celebrate. On Saturday afternoon, several disposable barbecues were brought out and lit, and a full-sized paint-spattered bin crammed with ice and beers. The music – for once, not metal but techno – began early. Both hosts had dressed for the occasion, Booth in clean jeans and an actual shirt, Jodie in an exposing red dress, her thin blonde hair fanned over bare shoulders.

'What kind of a person holds a party two weeks after someone's been killed on their property?' Em said, as they watched from the rear bedroom window.

'I think we know what kind,' Ant said. 'Who are all these people? What's the occasion? I've never known them invite anyone over before.'

'They probably advertised it on Facebook. And I don't think there *is* an occasion, I think this is a message. Like the dead cygnet.' Em sucked her teeth, her expression darkening. 'They want to show us what noise really is. You know, "you ain't heard nothing yet".'

For all her overreaction regarding the camera, Ant sensed she was totally on the money about this. If Darren and Jodie had learned anything about their next-door neighbours' disgruntlement it was that their focus was on noise.

Well, now they *really* knew what noise was. It was a sound system that made the air shudder and the human brain bounce. It made the pictures on the walls shake. It was sixty or seventy people heckling and singing and laughing all at the same time.

It was something the police had limited powers to manage in a domestic environment, it being a council responsibility, as they explained to Ant over the phone once again – and he couldn't have been the only one to appeal to them this time. They promised to attend, however, if a lull in higher priority call-outs allowed ('attend'? As if they planned to grab a drink and join the fun!).

'You must be aware that this couple have had multiple complaints made against them?' he cried over the hellish, brutal pulse of the music. 'We think they've just killed a swan, as well!'

But it sounded crazy, like a prank call.

Was it any wonder he did what any other desperate person would do? Gather all the alcohol he could find in the house and drink every last drop of it.

When he woke, all he knew for sure for the first two minutes was that he was alive. Pain had claimed his entire body, circulating in his bloodstream and pooling in his head. His first theory was that he'd been beaten up and dumped in a ditch – by whom? Booth? – but once he'd prised open dry, scratchy eyes and seen his earphones tangled on the pillow, still attached to his iPad, he was confident he was in his own home. He hadn't been assaulted, he'd simply given himself a diabolical hangover.

He tried to recall what had caused him to drink two – okay, maybe three – bottles of wine: that phone call with DC Forrester? It hadn't been *that* bad, had it?

Then he remembered: Darren and Jodie. Who else?

'Are you *finally* awake?' Em was in the room, snapping open the blinds and subjecting his retinas to an onslaught of blinding light, as if they lived on Mercury, not Earth. 'Can you *please* get up! I need you to keep an eye on Sam, if that's not too much trouble?'

Ant tried to lubricate his throat. 'What's up?'

'We've got a clean-up operation going, bagging up all the rubbish from the party. It was windy earlier and it's blown all over the place. It looks disgusting, like there's been a festival or something. Tess is worried one of the pets might eat something poisonous.'

'When did the party finish?' Ant asked.

'About three thirty a.m. You passed out at two.' Her tone reinforced the message already understood that this had been an unforgivable error on his part. He'd fallen short by ninety minutes, failed to see the ordeal through to the bitter end.

'Did Sam sleep?'

'Eventually, yes.'

Like a child who lives next to an airport runway, the poor creature was learning how to sleep through the end of the world.

'It only stopped because the police broke it up,' Em added. 'Otherwise, they'd have gone on all night.'

'Really? The police weren't interested when I phoned.'

'I know, but I remembered what you said about the drugs tip-off and that's what I did. You were right, as well, the drugs squad came straightaway and then they called the uniforms for back-up. A completely different story from usual. I said to them, "Lucky no one was killed this time, eh?" Like they care.'

Ant groaned. 'Drugs? I was saving that!'

Em's eyes flared with irritation. 'Saving it? What for? These people are actively feuding with us, Ant, they're damaging our mental health! How much worse does it have to be?'

Disgusted with him, she departed.

One eye on Sam, Ant dragged himself to the window to see how bad the aftermath was. Tess, Sara and another woman he didn't know were moving about with black bin liners.

Naomi and Ralph were on holiday, due back that day – he was pleased one of their families had been spared this latest atrocity. The drive looked as if a couple of nightclub bins had capsized on it, all lager cans and bottles and cigarette ends, even soaked items of clothing, flattened like roadkill.

He was in the kitchen preparing ingredients for a fry-up when Em returned. His guts were sore with hunger, making him impatient when the ignition for the hob stuttered, needing three tries to light. Sam was at his feet, playing with his mechanical pig.

Her face was thunderous. 'You won't believe the stuff we've found. Broken glass, ends of joints, those popper canisters. Even a syringe! So much for the drugs squad – imagine if Sam or one of the other kids picked something up and put it in their mouth. Tess is going to get onto the police about it.' She grimaced. 'Not that we hold out much hope that last night's crew will exchange notes with the ones investigating *us*. That would be far too sensible.'

As she ranted, Ant threw the chopped mushrooms and tomatoes into the pan. 'They must have a central file they all use?' he said, trying to be helpful, but Em glared, as if he'd missed the point entirely.

'What are you *doing*?'

'Cooking breakfast. Have you had any?'

'Two hours ago, yes. Did you not hear what I said about the syringe?'

'I did hear. Sit down, at least have a coffee.'

'Oh, for God's sake, Ant, this is important!' But at the sight of Sam's alarmed expression, she poured herself a coffee and took a seat at the table.

Ant cracked eggs into the pan, mixing everything together in a grey mush. When he noticed the flame had gone out again, this time it reignited instantly with an alarming whoosh.

'Ant, that's really dangerous!'

'I know. The hob's on the blink. I'll see if I can fix it, but we might need a new one.'

'No, I don't want to buy anything new,' Em said. 'I'm not throwing good money after bad.'

'What are you talking about? Look, forget the party.' He felt very keenly that he needed to diffuse her rage, redirect her energy. 'We can't let it destroy our whole weekend. How about we go out for the day? Drive down to the coast?' He plated the half-cooked food and found some bread, breaking off a piece for Sam. 'Em? What d'you think?'

She raised her gaze, an expression of fresh resolution in her eyes. 'I think we need to move, Ant. We're living next door to a very dangerous individual who obviously wants revenge. Sooner or later, he's going to do something that really harms us. Harms Sam.'

'Because of the party?'

'No, not just the party! Because he's murdered a defenceless animal and broken into one of our houses – not to mention the fact that a woman's been killed! We need to move out,' she repeated.

Mouth full, Ant took his time swallowing. In a way, it was extraordinary that it had taken so long for them to reach this point. 'I thought you said you weren't going to be driven out by him?' he said, finally.

'That was before I realized we were still in danger.'

'The thing is, I don't think we *can* sell. One quick search of the address and Amy's death will come up. Plus he's not exactly hiding the fact that he's a neighbour from hell.'

'We'll rent it out then,' Em said. 'Someone must be desperate enough.'

Ant forked more food into his mouth. The stringy egg white made him gag. 'Desperate people wouldn't be able to afford the rent we need to cover the mortgage. Then we'd have to find the rent for a new place.'

Em spoke in a different voice then, the strain of controlling her emotions making her mean. 'When I say we need to move, I'm not *asking*. Not as far as Sam and I are concerned.'

'What?' Ant paused his wolfing to look at her. 'What are you saying, exactly?'

'I'm saying, if you won't move, we'll do it anyway. We'll go and live with my parents. I noticed a really nice nursery when I was there at the weekend and I bet there's not the same waiting lists as here. There're bound to be schools as good as Lowland Primary. I could get a job in Cheltenham. London is full of lunatics, Ant, we could have this same problem wherever we go!'

He stared, aghast, as his most feared thoughts were spoken back to him. 'Does this mean you want to split up?'

She shook her head, the emphatic motion of it making him dread that the person she needed to convince was herself. 'It means I want those people out of our life. And if you're not willing to do something about them, then *I* will.'

23

Ralph

Alone in the hotel room – the rest of the family were at the beach – Ralph was on and off the phone with his logistics manager, Ben, in London when the notification popped up that he'd missed a call from Eithne Forrester.

Well, she'd have to wait.

Ben had just made the inconvenient last-minute discovery that the building next door to their warehouse had been earmarked – and approved by the police – as the assembly point for a 'substantial' group of LGBT protesters intending to march along the river and into the City. He didn't know what their issue was – something to do with a lack of diversity in careers that allowed you to ride roughshod over regulations and steal from pensioners – but he knew what *his* was: the highly inconvenient prevention of access to three delivery trucks, two of which were already on the road.

'Do you know the Russian proverb, "Don't buy the house, buy the neighbourhood"?' one supplier asked, when Ralph called with alternative plans.

'I'm not sure I know any Russian proverbs,' he said, 'but that sounds like a very good one.' As he spoke, he ran his fingers over his left cheek. The skin still felt tender, though the marks themselves had faded, and he had a rather humbling thought: some things caused bruises that lasted longer than those from punches.

What the hell do you think you're doing?

How could you have been so stupid?

Like a two-bit thug.

The words still burned. They burned because they were true and they burned because they were Naomi's. A line had been crossed between them, a balance of power disrupted. Of course, he understood that his wife's fear of the 'consequences' of his assault on Booth was not related to her own personal safety, let alone his, but their children's. Booth had plenty of targets in the Morgan household besides the one who'd given it its name.

According to Finn, all hell had broken loose on the street in their absence: a dead cygnet, a prowler at Sissy's, and a wild party at number 1 to which the drugs squad had been called (surprise, surprise, there'd been no arrests). He wasn't so egotistical as to imagine he could have *prevented* any of these misdeeds, but Jesus, it was quite a coincidence, wasn't it? While the cat's away, the mouse was staging some sort of coup d'état.

Finished with his work calls, he pulled open the terrace doors. Though July's drought had put paid to the lush green valley of flowers promised by the hotel's website, Ralph quite liked the colours he saw instead: straw and sand and pale lemon, everything tinted yellow and a bit 1970s. For a moment he wished he and his family could stay here forever.

Only when he could put it off no longer did he dial the

number for the police and, as expected, reach the refrigerated tones of DC Forrester.

'You didn't mention a babysitter when we spoke, Mr Morgan, and I'm wondering why.'

Ralph exhaled, already irritated. 'Daisy? What about her? You might be better talking to my wife, she handles all those arrangements.'

A pause. 'Did your wife also walk her home on the evening of the tenth?'

Ah. Okay. *Take the initiative. No point lying.* 'No, it's always my brother or me who walks her home. We wouldn't let a teenage girl go off alone in the middle of the night.'

'Which one of you was it that night?'

'I don't remember off the top of my head, but since you've taken the trouble to phone me on holiday, I'm guessing someone's decided it was me?'

'Exactly. Any particular reason why you lied about this before?'

As an ache started up in his bruised cheek, Ralph felt his temper slipping from him. 'Oh, for God's sake, there's a difference between lying and forgetting, isn't there? Is this really your idea of a murder investigation?'

'Mr Morgan, did you walk past number one that night, on the way to or from Daisy's house on Portsmouth Avenue?'

Ralph sighed. 'Both, yes. That's the most direct route.'

'And, on the way back, did you approach the door of number one?'

'No, and I didn't touch the damn scaffolding either.'

There was a pause, a new tension. 'I hear you got into a fight with Mr Booth before you left last weekend?'

Here we go. 'More of a skirmish, I'd say.'

'A skirmish, right. He's still injured from the scaffolding accident, so I wouldn't have thought he'd be able to put up much of a defence.'

'Well, you'd be wrong there, because he's hard as nails, that man. If anything, I came off worse.' Once more, Ralph stroked his bruised cheek.

'I'll take your word for it, Mr Morgan.'

Mr Morgan. The most infuriating thing about her, about that emotionless delivery, was he couldn't tell if she was being sarcastic. He couldn't tell if she was trying to provoke him.

Adrenaline still roiling after he hung up, he watched from the terrace as Libby made her way up the path from the hotel's private cove. At twelve, she'd been allowed more independence over the long break than previous years. Did Naomi and he need to reassess that? You only had to look at the news on any given day to know how easily a young person could be intercepted and harmed. What if Booth beckoned to her when he saw her in the street . . . ? Kept her prisoner in the house – the house the police had turned back to him without a care?

As soon as they got home, he'd suggest to Naomi they sync their phones and begin tracking their daughter's every move. Creepy in normal circumstances, but these were far from normal.

Naomi had had a call too. She told him after they'd dropped Libby and Charlie at her parents' place in Somerset, where they were staying till the following weekend (he didn't say it often enough: his in-laws were a fucking dream). The A road to London was miraculously clear, which meant he'd be back well in time to go out for a drink with Finn. If it weren't for the police – and Booth – he'd be in a fantastic mood.

'I didn't want to tell you in front of the kids,' she said, and Ralph felt his pulse accelerate.

'Eithne bloody Forrester, was it? Checking my alibi – this business with walking Daisy home?'

'Actually, she wanted to double-check something from the morning of the accident,' Naomi said, squinting at her phone in the passenger seat. Ralph wondered if he should be concerned that the single time they'd had sex on the holiday, she had submitted to it rather than sought it. Not disengaged exactly, but not crazy into it either.

'What did she want to know?' he prompted.

'Who it was who went into the house and woke Jodie up.'

'Really? Who was it? You?'

'No, it was Em. I stayed out front and waited for the emergency services.' Naomi shuddered as she remembered, dropped her phone to her lap and squeezed her upper arms with her fingers.

'You think they suspect Em of something?' Ralph asked.

She glanced up, curious. 'I hadn't thought of that. I thought Jodie, maybe.'

Ralph's eyes widened. Ahead, traffic looked heavier, a string of red tail lights winding east. 'Jodie? Wow.'

'Well, it was peculiar that she stayed in her bedroom, wasn't it? If *you'd* been lying in the rubble of collapsed scaffolding, I think I'd have got out of bed and gone to have a look.'

'Pleased to hear it,' Ralph said. She was finally thawing, he thought. Hallelujah. He wondered if Finn would be up for the Star that evening, instead of the Fox. No need to analyse why. He was like a teenager coming home from holiday and hoping to see the girl he wanted to get off with – except he was in fact a middle-aged man coming home from holiday and hoping to see the neighbour he wanted to kill.

How had it got this surreal?

How had it got this *bleak*?

They went to the Fox – Finn was unusually insistent – and it annoyed Ralph from the moment they arrived and found they couldn't get a table. It was the warm, overripe odour, the tanned, post-holiday faces. People like us, except *they* didn't have a feud going with a psycho a few doors down. No, they had what Ralph had allowed himself to believe he would always have and yet had lost in what seemed like a heartbeat: smugness.

He swatted away Finn's questions about the holiday, redirecting them to the topic of Booth. They'd finally got served and found space at the end of the bar. 'Nay's not convinced this break-in of Sissy's was even Booth. She says it's too devious. Too sinister.'

'She doesn't think killing a bird is sinister?'

'Sure it is, it's just that the other things have been short, violent acts – plus the party, but that was par for the course. Can't believe they haven't had one before, frankly. But with Sissy's, nothing was damaged, not even in a minor way. It's not the same MO.'

'The MO is to screw with us, whatever it takes,' Finn said.

Ralph agreed. He far preferred discussing Booth with his brother than with his wife. 'That's exactly what I told her.

He's not looking to establish some signature style, like a serial killer. He's not that interesting. What does Tess think?'

'I'm a bit worried about her, to be honest,' Finn said. 'She's obsessed with the swans. She was just over at the shop on the estate today having a go at them about letting kids take stale bread to feed them. It's not good for them, she says. Threatened to call the police if they don't stop.'

'Right.' How deluded was she, Ralph thought. If the police didn't care about a wildman wreaking revenge on an entire street, they weren't going to care about a bit of expiry-date Mother's Pride being fed to a mute swan. 'We've had the police on the phone again, have you?' He pulled a pained face as he was jostled backwards by a clutch of new arrivals. 'Picking holes in our "recollection of events". By the way, thanks to you, I'm now a prime suspect.' He'd meant it as throwaway, but it came out with an edge, like he was really pissed off, and Finn's reaction was to glower at him over the top of his pint.

'Why thanks to me?'

'Because they're fixated on the fact that I walked Daisy home that night, presumably messing with the scaffolding on my way back. I didn't even remember that myself and they didn't ask Nay, so it must have been you or Tess who told them.'

'Not me,' Finn said, tone short.

'Well, it must have been Tess, then. Tell her she needs to remember whose side she's on here, will you.'

Finn tensed, predictably defensive. 'What're you talking about, mate? What other side is there?'

But such was Ralph's mood, Finn's resistance only made

him push harder. 'She wants to land us in it after what Naomi said to her that night about not working, is that it?'

'Or maybe they just asked her how the babysitter got home? What the fuck is wrong with you? Aren't holidays supposed to put you in a better mood, not worse? Jesus, no wonder Tess feels suffocated by you two. You're not back five minutes and you're already on her case.'

Ralph felt mist rise. 'Pretty easily suffocated, isn't she? And bloody ungrateful.'

There it was, the thing he knew Finn disliked hearing more than anything: that he and his family should be grateful, that he owed Ralph for his cushy set-up.

'Why should she be grateful, exactly?' Finn glared, his forehead glossy with sweat. 'Because you noticed the house next door to yours was for sale? Because you lent us the deposit, which has now been paid back? You have to have people in your debt, don't you? You have to be the one pulling the strings. That's why you don't like Booth, he doesn't fall into line the way you'd like him to.'

Ralph turned on his brother with the snarl of boyhood fights: 'I don't like Booth because he put my son in hospital. He killed an innocent woman. He's breaking into our houses and gunning down wildlife and he's walked away from all of it scot-free.'

Finn baulked; clearly, he'd forgotten momentarily about Charlie's near-miss, if not Amy's death. 'Before all that. You know what I mean.'

'No, I don't know what you mean and I think you should shut the fuck up.'

Aware of the curious looks their raised voices were

attracting from other drinkers, Ralph reminded himself – no, tormented himself – that this wasn't how people in the Fox behaved. It was how people in the Star behaved, maybe, but not the Fox. He was overcome with shame and rage: he'd been so sure he belonged, he'd taken belonging to an art form, and yet here he was not belonging, after all.

Maybe it was a throwback to their sixteen years of sharing a bedroom, but neither brother was in the habit of storming out of rows. They would wait it out in bitter silence if necessary (especially if they had drinks to finish).

'Sorry,' Ralph said, finally. 'I'm just shattered from the drive. This thing with Daisy won't come to anything.'

'Of course it won't,' Finn agreed readily. 'Shows you're a good citizen, that's all. And they *are* detectives. It's well within their capabilities to discover a babysitter's name and address. And maybe *she* noticed something? Have you thought of that? Something that could help us.'

'Yeah, it's possible.'

At last spying a free table, they ordered new drinks and sat for several minutes checking emails and messages. Then Ralph felt a crawling sensation on his skin, an early-warning impulse that he at first put down to their latest nerve-jangling discussion of Booth. But when he glanced around the bar, he saw he was mistaken. 'I don't fucking believe this.'

'What?'

'At the bar.'

They must have been to the Fox a dozen times since Booth had moved to Lowland Way and they'd never seen him here before. The Star was his patch. But it was him all right. With two mates, both men, younger than him and visibly wound up with Friday night expectation. Of the three, Booth looked the most unkempt and yet also the most at ease. His gaze drifted from Finn to Ralph and settled there.

'You don't think he followed us?' Finn muttered.

'No. He's just come in. Saw us walk past his house, I bet. Mobilized his troops. Not hard to guess where we were going.'

'Why would he want to do that?'

'It's a taunt,' Ralph said. 'A challenge. He wants to show us he can infiltrate our domain. Maybe he's seen us in the Star and doesn't like it.' As Booth turned his back on them to order drinks, Ralph willed the girl behind the bar to register his unsuitability and snub him, but she served him faster than Ralph himself had been served. She *smiled* at him as she pulled his pint.

'You know if you get into anything now, there'll be a hundred witnesses,' Finn said, by way of a warning. 'Plus there's three of them.'

'True.' Ralph turned his chair so he didn't have Booth in his eyeline, but still he couldn't relax. 'What's he doing now?'

'He's waiting for their drinks. Here they are.' Finn looked confused. 'Wait . . . I think he's offering *us* a drink.'

Ralph swung around, his willpower shot, in time for Booth to call across to them, just audible over the Friday-night clamour: 'Hey, Kray boys! I said, can I get you a pint?'

The barmaid looked over, grinning at the reference, awaiting the brothers' requests. What was he going to do, Ralph thought, spike their drinks? Come over and throw them in their faces?

He called back: 'I wouldn't take a pint from you if I was

crawling on my hands and knees in the Sahara.' The remark was loud enough, aggressive enough, to draw a range of responses: hostility from Booth's sidekicks, fearful looks from two women at the next table, bewilderment from the barmaid.

'I think that's a no,' Darren told her. 'Just these then, love. Thanks.'

She took his money, sending a disapproving glance Ralph's way.

What the hell was going on, Ralph seethed, as Booth and his party took their drinks outside, presumably to smoke. Not only was he brazenly invading the Morgans' turf, but he'd marked out lanes and was running rings around them. The feeling of impotence threatened to overwhelm him, as if he might overheat and combust.

'Unbelievable how he's been able to hoodwink everyone into thinking *he's* the good guy,' he fumed. 'There must be *something* we can pin on him, something no one can deny is criminal? How about we bring some paedophilia accusation against him? Or just spread the word in the Star? With any luck, some vigilantes'll come and lynch him.'

Though Finn had an approving gleam in his eye, his response might have been scripted by Naomi: 'The police aren't stupid, they'd see straightaway there's nothing like that going on. Plus we'd be opening ourselves up to charges of harassment, or even perverting the course of justice.'

Ralph nodded. 'You're right. We shouldn't have to fabricate crimes, he's committed enough real ones.' He held his brother's eye. 'I think it's time for a whole new game plan.'

Finn didn't flinch. 'With you all the way, mate,' he said.

24

TESS

'Hello, this is Tessa Morgan from Lowland Way. My husband said you wanted to double-check something from our chat?'

There was a short wait while DC Forrester gathered her notes. It couldn't be that serious, then, Tess thought, if she needed to remind herself of the query. No summons to the station quite yet.

'Yes, I'm just looking at statements from the night of the tenth and I see we've had a report that you were seen in the street with your dog at about twelve thirty.'

'Oh!' Tess was taken aback. 'I think I did take Tuppy out. I completely forgot that.'

'You forgot?'

'Yes, I *did*. Because it wasn't important. When you have a dog, you take him out constantly. You don't remember every individual trip.'

'You have a very large garden, Mrs Morgan, if I'm remembering correctly?'

Tess suppressed a sigh. 'I could have just let him out the

back, yes, but that would have got the dogs next door all excited and then there'd be three of them barking and waking everyone up. So I just took him out the front and walked up to the patch of green on the other side of Portsmouth Avenue.'

'Did you approach number one on this late-night expedition?'

'No.'

'Your husband didn't tell you how to go about loosening the bolts that would compromise the stability of a scaffolding structure?'

'Er, *no*.' Tess felt her heartbeat quicken. 'But how hard can it be, anyway? Anyone can pick up a spanner and turn a screw or nut or whatever it was.'

'But not everyone has experience working on a building site, as your husband did.'

'How do you know that?' Was this really a working hypothesis? Husband and wife co-conspirators? 'That was over twenty years ago!'

'The scaffolding fixtures were older than that. I think you said yourself the materials showed considerable wear and tear.'

Tess paused. She needed to start keeping a better track of what she'd said and what she'd left unsaid. 'I did, yes. They looked ancient.'

'Are you in the habit of picking up after your dog, Mrs Morgan?'

'You've got to be kidding me?' Tess sighed. 'I am, yes. While you're on the phone, can I ask if your colleagues in the drugs squad have followed up my complaint after a party at number one on Saturday? There were definitely illegal substances being used. Surely that's more serious than a malicious complaint about my dogs' toileting habits? No offence, but I think you need to have a little reappraisal of what's worth investigating here.'

She'd sounded more strident than she intended and there was a beat of surprised silence.

'None taken,' DC Forrester said, smoothly.

*

Naomi had posted on the residents' Facebook page:

> Has everyone seen this? This is exactly what we want to avoid, for all our sakes! Please DO NOT SPEAK TO THE PRESS!

The link was to a nasty little piece on the property pages of one of the tabloids:

> **Bargain Basement**
>
> Pick up a bargain in posh Lowland Gardens in South London – if you have the stomach for it!
>
> Lowland Way, one of the suburb's smartest roads, is in meltdown following the recent death of a young woman in a building accident. With the police in and out of residents' houses and its famous Play Out Sunday scheme abandoned, sellers have been forced to slash their prices. This three-bedroomed period cottage has been reduced from £1.2 million to £900,000. It has no basement – but you could always dig one out (planning allowing) to maximize your bargain! With Lowland Estates www.lowlandestates.co.uk.

Already, Sara and Ant had commented.

Sara Boulter: Bloody gutter press. How are they getting this stuff?

Ant Kendall: Very callous and upsetting. How awful for Sissy and the family to read this sort of thing.

Though Tess had avoided the group of late, too distressed to follow the multiple queries and comments on the various 'Missing Cygnet' posts, she had been aware of an insistent and unwarranted desire to redeem herself with Naomi. Her phone call from the detective had changed that and the next time she saw Naomi in the garden, playing with Charlie and the dogs, she went straight out, and asked to have a word.

Naomi set Charlie up with a game involving bouncing a tennis ball perilously close to Tess's kitchen window, before saying, 'If it's about this latest article, Ralph's going to ring Lowland Estates and have a word. It's not in their interests for the street to be known as some sort of property Costco.'

'It's not that, no,' Tess said, determined to stay on message. 'Naomi, did you or Ralph say anything to the police about Finn having experience on building sites?'

Naomi eyed her with interest. 'Of course not. But you can understand why they might find that relevant. He *is* the only one who knows how to work those couplings, or whatever they're called.'

'Yes, him and any of the billion other active users of YouTube who fancied watching a tutorial on the subject.

Come on, anyone can learn anything in five minutes these days, it's completely unfair to implicate Finn.'

Naomi sighed. 'That's true.'

The concession was rare enough for Tess to soften her tone. 'So I hear Ralph is worried he's a suspect, as well?'

'Yes. He thinks the police are trying to play us off against each other.'

'People are definitely starting to point the finger,' Tess agreed. 'The police know I was out with Tuppy that night and I have no idea who told them.'

Naomi glanced up. 'You were out with Tuppy?'

Her surprise *sounded* real enough, but Tess wasn't quite ready to trust her. After their row, mightn't she also have stayed awake stewing? Gone to the window to breathe in some fresh night air? 'I couldn't sleep, so I got up again. He was getting agitated, he needed the loo and I didn't want to let him in the garden in case he got Cleo and Kit excited and woke you all up.'

Naomi looked doubtful.

'We *had* just argued,' Tess reminded her. 'I didn't want to start another row and it was just easier to take him out. I put my jacket on over my pyjamas.'

Looking momentarily askance at the thought of such slovenliness, Naomi recovered herself. 'Hmm, highly suspicious,' she said, sarcastically. 'A woman in her pyjamas taking a dog for a pee.'

This was better, she was on Tess's side again.

'Ant said they're on *his* case, as well, so that's at least three of us,' Tess said.

'And it sounds as if they were a bit sceptical about Sissy's report about the break-in, too. You know, I wouldn't be surprised if they think this is one of those *Murder on the Orient Express* things.'

'What, we all did it?'

'It's a theory, don't you think? First we give each other alibis and then we drop little hints, each directed at someone different, just a few innocuous details, nothing really incriminating. It has the same effect: no clear suspect.'

Tess looked at her. 'Four sets of clips were loosened, the police told Finn. How many people could that possibly involve?'

'Well, a maximum of four, I suppose.'

They laughed together, not old-style laughing, but darker, more guarded. As if in direct response, there came the loud, unpleasant wail of a power tool from Booth's garden.

'How can he operate machinery when he's injured?' Tess said. 'We can't fault his work ethic, can we?'

'You know what we should do? Build up the wall between us and number three,' Naomi said, only half-joking, and Tess followed her to the wall to assess its height. 'There's this special fencing apparently, designed to minimize noise from busy roads. We could do the same at the front. Let's build it as high as the council will allow. Or higher – we'll apply for permission retrospectively.'

'Wall them off?' Tess said. 'Like they're Mexico or West Berlin? That's a bit unfair on Ant and Em.'

Still, it wasn't the craziest idea she'd heard to date.

'*Was* it you who sabotaged the scaffolding?' Naomi asked, with a sudden pounce, and Tess felt the same vicious heart pounding she had when questioned by DC Forrester.

'Are you for real?'

'I think I am, yes.' Naomi moved a step closer. 'And I'd take it to the grave if it *was* you, just so you know. Whatever the intention that night – if there ever *was* one – it wasn't to hurt Amy.'

'No.' As their eyes locked, there was a new flare of tension. 'Was it you?' Tess countered, with a note of daring.

Naomi stepped back again. 'Of course it wasn't. I'm one of the few who *isn't* a suspect.'

'Not yet,' Tess said.

Since that unwelcome visit from Jodie, she was wary of the doorbell ringing. Now, if she wasn't expecting someone, she would go upstairs and check who it was from the bedroom window before returning in a great hurry to take receipt of the parcel or let the British Gas guy in to read the meter.

When the bell went that Tuesday morning, expecting it to be Em Kendall for coffee, she approached the door with a smile. Tess hadn't seen her friend since before the cygnet incident and she wanted to show Em the memorial headstone she'd planted in the corner of the garden.

She drew back the door, smiling.

'Hello!' Standing on the doorstep was a woman in her early thirties with bright eyes and a persuasive smile. 'I'm Savannah McKenzie, I write for the *Evening Standard* and I'm working on a feature on the investigation into Amy Pope's death? I've spoken to the police and I'm really keen to give the neighbours' side of the story as well. I wondered if you had a minute?'

Clever opening gambit, Tess thought. Giving the impression that there was a side to challenge, a case to defend. This woman probably hadn't been given the time of day by the police, let alone any details of a working hypothesis.

'Did you know the victim at all?'

'I didn't, no. Sorry, I can't help you.'

'What about this neighbour whose scaffolding collapsed? I gather he's not the most popular guy on the street?'

Ms McKenzie's tone, impeccably judged to suggest affinity with the cause, gave Tess pause. Might the residents have misjudged the situation with the press? Mistaken an opportunity for a threat? Seeing Em approach the gate, she called out in greeting and the reporter turned to see who it was.

'We've already met.' Em pre-empted her. 'Remember? I have nothing to say to you.'

Her bad-natured tone shocked Tess, though evidently not the journalist, who pressed her card on Tess 'just in case'.

'Good riddance,' Em said to the closed door. 'Press, police, the local council . . . they're all just out for themselves. We're nothing but collateral.' She was evidently in a bitter mood.

After putting the coffee on and finding a rice cake for Sam, Tess led her guests into the garden to show Em the headstone. Tuppy sniffed the recently turned soil with interest.

'The body's actually under there?' Em asked.

'No, the police took the corpse as evidence, poor thing. This is a memorial. I couldn't bear the thought of that beautiful creature just being forgotten.'

'So it was shot?'

'Yes, with an air pellet. Have they got an air rifle, do you know? Booth and Jodie.'

'Not that I've seen,' Em said.

'They could have paid someone who does, I suppose.'

'Or it could have been kids,' Em suggested, 'and they dumped it at random?'

'Kids? Why? Wouldn't they just run off, leave it where it

fell? No, this was someone who wanted to upset me.' It was dismaying that Em didn't support her theory unconditionally. 'There's a Swan Rescue notice up by the pond appealing for witnesses and we've suggested they access local CCTV footage from that night, but I don't think there are any cameras between here and the park. I wish I'd had a security camera above my door,' she added, 'then I'd know for sure.' After Sissy's break-in, Ralph and Naomi had installed a video entryphone system, but Tess was loath to spend funds they didn't have on a property they might soon be leaving.

There was a silence – or what passed for silence these days, with the permanent background noise of Booth's cars and tools and music. Em appeared to be grappling with a private dilemma, before finally speaking in an odd, blurting way: 'Look, I just want you to know, I've deleted it.'

'Deleted what?' Tess prompted. She was finding her friend especially skittish today.

Em averted her gaze. 'The footage on our security app that showed you walking up number one's drive on the night of August the tenth.'

Tess froze. 'What?'

'Just after twelve thirty, I think it was, a few minutes before *she* came back from her cigarette run. But like I say, I got rid of it.'

'What security app?' Tess demanded.

At last, Em met her eye. 'You know we set up a surveillance thing on an old iPhone? That's how Ant got the shot of them taking cash for one of the cars.'

'Oh yes, I remember. I thought that was a one-off?'

'No, Ant had it in the front bedroom window the whole

time. It was a motion-activated thing, went on until the battery died. We checked again recently, just in case we could help the police with anything. Anyway, I just wanted you to know.'

Tess took her time in responding to this. *Help the police with anything* ... There was a trace of something in Em's manner as she uttered this phrase that Tess didn't care for: a demonstration of power, a suggestion that this was not a self-contained piece of information, but a gesture that warranted reciprocation. Otherwise, why bring it up at all? Why not just delete anything that might be regarded as exposing a friend in a less than innocent light and keep what you'd seen to yourself?

Were Em and Ant *still* recording their neighbours' movements? Or was Tess being paranoid, allowing her imagination to invent motives that didn't exist? She took a breath, made a decision. 'Well, thank you, I really appreciate that, but it doesn't matter anyway because the police already know I was out that night. So I'm a person of interest with or without your mystery footage.'

'Oh!' Em looked astonished. Whatever she'd expected Tess to say, it was not that.

'Yes.' Tess chuckled. 'Somewhere in a police incident room, there's a picture of me pinned to a board with notes next to it saying, "Overprotective mum" and "Animal rights nutter".' It struck her that things were not going to be able to be the same between Em and her after this and she was sorry for that. Thank God for her rapprochement with Naomi. To be out of sorts with two female allies at the same time was unthinkable.

'So who else did you see on your secret app?' she asked. 'Who else have you deleted?'

'No one,' Em said. 'Forget it.'

25

Sissy

DC Shah was 'eager' to update her, his message promised, which was possibly the polar opposite of how she felt about being updated.

'Are you aware that one of your recent B&B clients has a criminal conviction, Mrs Watkins?'

'*Ms*,' Sissy said. 'No, I didn't know that.'

'There's no vetting process?'

'Not by me personally. They're all registered members of the website, but I imagine the terms and conditions for hosts will include one about it being at your own risk. Who is it, if I'm allowed to ask?'

'Graham Reddy. He booked for one night on August the second.'

'I remember him.' Thank God she was having one of her clear-thinking days and could decide, right away, that she should not complicate the issue with denials. 'He was the chap from Solihull, I think. Yes, he was very nice.'

'So you got chatting, did you?'

'We did. Just small talk.' Sissy paused. 'Why? You're not thinking he had something to do with the break-in, are you? I think that's very unlikely. If he'd wanted to take something, he could have done it while he was here.'

'Actually, I'm wondering if he said anything to you about the scaffolding at number one. It may have caught his eye.'

'Why?'

'Until a few years ago, he worked for Bettany Construction, a building firm in Birmingham. He'd be qualified to comment on any safety issues.'

'Oh.' Though Sissy felt a convulsion deep inside her, her voice remained steady: 'Not that I remember. I mean, guests do often remark on the building work, but it's not the image I want to stick in their minds, not if they're going to come back.'

'Did Mr Reddy come back?'

'No. What was it for, his conviction?'

Theft. Graham and another man had taken a consignment of boilers from a construction site and tried to sell them on. Presumably this was what had ended his career with the building firm, Sissy thought.

'Did he and Booth meet, that you were aware of?' DC Shah persisted.

'Not in my presence, though obviously I don't know what happens after people leave the house.' She stopped, a sudden smack of grief robbing her of her voice. 'I'm sorry. Look, I very much doubt that this man will be able to shed any light on an event that occurred over a week after he stayed on the street for one night.'

'Do you know if any of your other B&B customers have made contact with Booth?'

'No.' Sissy pressed the heel of her free hand into her eye socket and watched stars dance; she had a headache coming. 'And neither will any in the future, since the business has collapsed – thanks to him.'

'I'm sorry to hear that,' DC Shah said.

'Are you?' More sad than angry, Sissy longed for the call to be over. 'Forgive me if I find that hard to believe.'

The end came sooner than expected, in typically impersonal form:

> Dear Property Owner,
>
> We are writing to advise you that booking for your property has been suspended and your membership of CitytoSuburb temporarily revoked following your failure to meet the required minimum approval rating. Any outstanding bookings must be honoured, but be advised that we will be writing to those customers affected to inform them of the change in status for this property and to give them the option of cancelling without penalty.

A scan of recent reviews confirmed the Booth household's role in her fatal plunge in popularity:

> Dreadful couple across the road gave us dirty looks as we left. Felt quite intimidated. (Two window boxes.)

> Steer clear! I heard someone was killed in the house opposite! (One window box.)

Wasn't Amy's death enough? Why did they need to take her livelihood from her?

Well, she would ask them.

Outside, summer's end was evident in the temperature, the scent, the slide of the sun, and even this felt treacherous. She didn't want the season to turn its back on Amy's death. It was too soon, her young life of too high a value.

As if coming out to greet her, Jodie emerged suddenly from the side return, dressed in grey leggings and denim jacket, with a pull-along suitcase at her heel. Yelling goodbye to Darren over the drone of a power tool, she fell silent at the sight of Sissy on the pavement in front of her.

'You're going on holiday?' Sissy asked, incredulous. First a riotous party, now a holiday: life certainly went on for this pair.

'Yeah,' Jodie said, catching the condemnation and hurling it back. 'Going to the Bahamas, ain't I?'

Sissy had the urge to shove her into the dirt, suitcase and all. 'Well, when you're in the Bahamas, spare a thought for the woman crushed to death on these premises. Or have you already forgotten that? I think you probably have, judging by your party last weekend.'

Jodie dragged her bag on, using her foot to correct it when it snagged on pieces of rubble. Reaching the pavement, she drew up alongside Sissy and faced her with a strangely sympathetic expression: 'Look, Mrs Watkins, I know you've had a tough time, but that don't give you the right to come over and start abusing us, all right?'

'Abusing you?' Sissy couldn't contain her emotions, she could feel them bursting from her. 'Jean would be appalled by your behaviour, do you know that? Absolutely appalled. You can't have cared much about her either to conduct yourselves in this way!'

Jodie stared hard at her, face colouring, before rolling off towards Portsmouth Avenue. 'I think you should maybe go and see your doctor, yeah?' she called over her shoulder.

Sissy stood rooted to the spot, breathing heavily, until she realized she was being observed from the doorway of number 3. 'Oh, Ant. Hello.'

He came to join her, tactfully avoiding reference to the altercation. 'She's going to stay with her sister in Margate,' he said.

Sissy could tell he was undecided about whether he should share more. 'And . . . ?'

'Her niece has just had a baby.'

There it was. She was surprised Ant was on good enough terms with the enemy to have discussed this. Guessing her thoughts, he explained, 'Em overheard her talking on the phone. She's away for the whole week, helping, though given her talent for making my own child's life a misery, it's hard to imagine how helpful she'll be.'

It was unbearable, the idea that this horrible woman was about to enjoy a few days cooing over a newborn, enjoying her expanding family. She must have cried out without knowing, because Ant was looking at her with concern. 'They've destroyed my business,' she blurted. 'I'm going to have to sell up.'

'Oh, Sissy, I'm so sorry. Is there anything I can do?'

Faced with his kindness, she felt her despair spill from her: 'I can't go on living near them anyway. It's not just the noise and the mess or even their vendetta against us, it's how *inhuman* they are. Amy died in front of them and they feel nothing. Nothing.'

'I know,' Ant said. 'Are you really . . . ?'

'Putting my house on the market?' Sissy finished for him. 'Yes.'

The estate agent ('negotiator') arrived the next morning. She was a pleasant, respectful woman, her manner finely pitched to inspire trust. And she didn't keep her distance the way most people did, as if grief were body odour, the result of self-neglect.

'The good news is, I'm confident we can sell,' she said, 'and fairly quickly, too. This is a beautiful house.'

'What's the bad news?' Sissy said.

'With the stagnant market and all the activity across the street, we would need to price realistically. Nothing too ambitious.' She suggested listing number 2, Lowland Way at three hundred thousand pounds less than Sissy might have expected pre-Booth.

'Fine,' Sissy said.

'A lot of people are downsizing from properties like this,' the agent added, and Sissy rolled the word on her tongue in silence. Downsizing. That was what she was doing as a person, too, wasn't it? She'd downsized her identity to the point of no longer wishing to be herself. No longer wishing to *be*.

She wondered, impassively, where she would go. She couldn't impose on Pete. Following a period of compassionate leave, he'd been assigned a London-based client and had established a pared-down work/sleep routine that would not benefit from the addition of Sissy and her sorrow. What would he say about her plan to sell? If the two of them had been less vociferous in her claim to the family home, she'd have moved straight after the divorce, that was the truth of it. She'd never have known Darren Booth and Amy would have had no reason to return to the street. The house was tainted with a guilt of its own.

After the agent left, she went upstairs to lie down, as she frequently did now during the day, dropping on top of the unmade bedding, careless of discomfort. Today, she bypassed her preferred room at the back for the master bedroom, the room she'd come to know as the place her self-torture was at its most punishing. She'd curl up or stretch out, remembering what it had meant to her over the years, all of it behind her now, irretrievable for all eternity. It had been her marital bedroom, where a newborn Pete had been fed and cuddled. Later, where he'd come scampering in with his Christmas stocking. Where she'd slept alone after Colin moved first into the spare room and then into the bedroom of his new partner in Blackheath.

Where she'd tumbled into bed with Graham, who may or may not yet know he had caught the eye of the police.

Were they really planning to interview him on the strength of a coincidence that he had once worked in the construction industry? Surely his vanload of stolen boilers showed nothing more than that a historic mistake had been duly punished. It was a leap from that to attempted murder. She hoped he would be able to prove easily that he was nowhere near Lowland Way on the night of 10 August.

Of course, if she told the police about a particular portion of her conversation with him the night he'd stayed, they'd have him in their interview room faster than they could say Jack Robinson.

He'd been at the window, staring across at number 1. Darren and Jodie had finished their cigarettes and closed the bedroom window, but the light continued to cast a glow over the scaffolding structure, bringing a brutal beauty to it. 'I could always mess him up a bit for you,' he said, his tone so easy she mistook it for joking.

'Don't be silly.' Then, 'What do people mean when they say that? Beat him up?'

'Could mean that, yeah. Could mean a few things. The things you want to do, but can't risk.'

Why? she thought. Did he mean for payment? Fairly sure now that he was at least half-serious, she made light of the offer. 'Would I have to do the same with *your* enemies, like in *Strangers on a Train*?'

'Huh?'

'The book? The Hitchcock film? You kill my nemesis and I kill yours?'

'Let's not get carried away,' he said, smirking. 'But I could fiddle around a bit with his scaffolding, maybe. Yeah, that could work. The scaffolding gives way, he breaks his leg and is out of action for a bit, gives you a breather.' The thought caught and he developed the scenario for her: 'Maybe worse, maybe he has a spinal injury. That sort of accident happens all the time on construction sites.'

Sissy didn't know whether to gasp in horror or in glee. 'Then he has to sell up to pay for his highly specialized medical care,' she said, gamely.

Graham was grinning now. 'Has to learn how to walk again. How to talk.'

'Vigilante justice.' Sissy thought briefly of Ralph and Finn Morgan.

'Exactly,' Graham said. 'Don't tell me you're not tempted?'

He turned, his face close to hers, and the look that passed between them was unexpectedly pure, something close to faith. Permission, perhaps.

Only when the doorbell went did she emerge from the bedroom, something unknowable causing her to respond, which she rarely did if she wasn't expecting her caller. She hoped it would be Naomi, with her brisk, generous humanity, but she remembered it was a weekday and Naomi would be at work.

It was peculiar, but when she opened the door she didn't recognize Em Kendall immediately. Still half-asleep from her nap, she thought at first the woman might be a reporter, for there was a flicker of wildness in her eyes, a glimpse of hunter. Then, as Em's mouth opened to speak, she became herself, albeit a nervier version than Sissy knew.

'Hi, Sissy.'

'Hello,' Sissy said, but that was all, because it was no longer second nature for her to invite a neighbour in. These days, unless ambushed as she'd been that evening when they'd all come in for drinks, she conducted polite exchanges on the doorstep, waiting for the other person to give up and go. She was glad she'd specified that no FOR SALE sign should go up: it would attract visits from all the neighbours. More questions, more concern.

'So how're you holding up?' Em asked.

'Not good,' Sissy said, candidly.

'Ant told me about you selling up.'

'Yes.' Funny how Sissy had not the same instinct to confide in Em that she did Ant. It hardly mattered: he told his wife everything anyway. That was what married people did.

If Colin were here with her now, would it be easier to survive? The answer, as heartbreaking as any other revelation these last weeks, was yes. Even the newly unmasked criminal Graham would be moral support.

'I'm sorry,' Em said. 'I really am.' Her voice had something unexpected in it. People spoke so soothingly to Sissy these days, their hearts bleeding on their sleeves, but Em's words carried a note of self-pity that overrode that.

'Are *you* all right?' she said, curious. 'Where's Sam?'

'With a friend. I wanted to speak to you without being distracted. Can I come in?'

She advanced so determinedly over the threshold that Sissy had no choice but to comply. They came to a halt at the kitchen table, the agent's half-drunk mug of coffee still sitting where it had been left mid-negotiation, and before Sissy could offer her new guest a seat, Em took one, murmuring to herself as she did.

Sissy lowered herself into the seat opposite. 'What's this about, Em? You're worrying me.'

Em held up an iPhone, the screen lighting up as she lifted it to show a paused video, monochrome and murky, night-time footage of some sort, a dark figure visible in the top left-hand corner. The white arrow of the play function sat dead centre, awaiting Em's command. Sissy understood then the ambivalence of that doorstep apology: it was a sorry for what was to come, not what had been.

It was not really a sorry at all.

As Em's fingertip made contact with the arrow and the video began to play, it was immediately obvious that the figure was Sissy.

The timestamp read: 11/08/2018 02:10.

26

Ant

The situation was getting *way* too intense: not only had the police taken it upon themselves to speak to his colleagues, but they were challenging him about the 'reports' they'd collected even as he sat on a crowded train into work. Okay, so most of the other passengers were plugged into their private universes, but he still felt hounded, he still felt humiliated.

He still felt scared.

'In a meeting with your team on the twenty-third of July, you were heard to say that you were conspiring with the neighbours about Mr Booth?' DC Shah asked.

'Well, yes, but I meant in terms of our complaints to the council about his car business and the noise problem. If one of my colleagues was worried I meant something more serious, well, that's their interpretation, but I can assure you there's been nothing criminal.'

A couple of sets of eyes glanced up at this and Ant turned his face to the window, to the rolling spectacle of new apartment blocks along the tracks, shiny balconies decorated with already-dying plants and abandoned bikes. How he wished he lived in one of them, instead of the 'idyllic' suburb of Lowland Gardens.

'And on the twenty-seventh, you sent a text to your wife that said, "Still at Ralph's discussing Booth strategy"?'

'What? How've you got hold of my texts? I don't remember that one at all, but you need to read the whole thread of messages.'

'Your wife responded, "I want no part of this".'

'Yes, she thought we were wasting our time with the council.'

'But you can see why messages like these catch our eye,' DC Shah said.

Ant fell silent. It felt as if everything he said could be disastrously misconstrued. As the train pulled up at the platform in Victoria Station, his stop and the end of the line, he remained in his seat as everyone else scrambled to disembark.

In his ear, DC Shah began again: 'Perhaps if you were to help us on what you were doing outside late at night on the tenth? Why you needed to step under the scaffolding?'

For the first time in his interactions with the detective, there was a mood of negotiation. Alone in the carriage, Ant made his decision. 'Fine. I wasn't completely honest when we spoke before: when I went out that night, there *was* a reason.' He breathed in, aware that the facts could hardly sound more fantastical if he was making it up on the spot. 'I've got this thing, it's called a death whistle, I bought it online. It makes the most horrendous sound, really eerie, makes your skin crawl. I was thinking I would blow it through their letterbox, give them a bit of a fright, but then I saw their window had been left open a bit and I blew it through that instead. It was crazy, they were playing music, I knew they probably couldn't hear it. I remember thinking, I'll come back when the music's stopped. Then they'll hear it.'

There was a pause. No detective could have expected *that*. 'Do you still have this whistle in your possession? And proof of purchase?'

'Yes, both. I'll forward the receipt when I get to work.'

As passengers entered the carriage for the outbound service, Ant stood to leave. He already knew he would not confront any of his colleagues. It wasn't as if they'd lied and they may even have thought they were helping.

'*Did* you go back when the music stopped, Mr Kendall?'

'No, I fell asleep.'

'Sure about that?'

'Yes,' Ant said. 'Absolutely.'

If someone had told him it would be him, of all of them, who retaliated against Booth with horrible violence, he would have thought they'd lost their mind. Especially as, for the first time, there was progress with their official procedures. According to Ralph, Booth had finally heeded the council's warning and applied for a licence to trade from a residential address, and the Trading Standards Department had flagged the application for special debate owing to the number of complaints lodged against him. At Ralph's request, Ant was among those to email the committee and plead against granting the licence. He did not consult Em, who was currently relatively upbeat, a state of affairs unexpected enough for him to choose to leave well alone. Her friendship with Tess seemed to have cooled, but she was spending more time with Sissy and, though he knew better than to share the view, Ant hoped exposure to Sissy's grief would help put Em's own predicament into perspective.

'We can't count on the council. Someone needs to scare the bastard good and proper,' Ralph told Ant. 'Me and Finn are putting our heads together, if you know what I mean.' His adoption of this sort of talk contained a certain swagger; their troubles with Booth had released something in him that came very naturally and far from being warned off by Amy Pope's death, he seemed galvanized by it.

'Should we have another meeting?' Ant suggested.

'Nah,' Ralph said. 'Too many killjoys in the group.'

A text message from Em was what triggered his savagery. It was Sunday and she'd taken Sam to visit her old schoolfriend Gwen, who lived in Oxfordshire in bucolic tranquillity (aka a normal house on a normal street with normal neighbours), leaving Ant to finish a work presentation. Earplugs only half-smothered Metallica headlining next door. The message read:

> Gwen says we need to get a referral to a paediatric hearing specialist ASAP. Sam should be making a lot more sounds by now, must not be hearing properly.

He felt immediate and painful drumming in his chest. Had this opinion come from anyone else, he would have disregarded it, but Gwen was a GP and mother of three. This whole time, he'd clung to the belief that Sam would be all right, that the noise pollution wasn't *quite* bad enough to do permanent physical damage, and yet it might actually be that it *was* bad enough, that time had run out.

Filled with a transformative rage he had never before experienced, he snapped shut his laptop, tore out the earplugs, and went to fetch a long-handled rake from the garden shed. Back out front, he sidestepped along the wall towards Booth's front door, not caring if Booth was standing in front of him or not – in fact, he was not, which was fortunate, though his front door was open, music throbbing. Ant took a single step outward and swung the rake over his head to strike the camera. After two cracks, part of it fell to the ground and he kicked this angrily aside. Without hesitating, he then smashed the implement through Booth's living-room window. As glass shattered, showering the room beyond, a violent whirring started up in his ears, preventing him from processing the full impact of what he'd done. It was as he was attacking the nearest car that Booth came out of the house, a human bullet suspending itself just out of range of the rake's teeth. 'What the *fuck* do you think you're doing?'

The rake still raised, Ant held firm, his demeanour defiant, even proud. 'What the *fuck* does it look like?'

Examining the window, Booth's face flushed with confusion and outrage. Breathing hard, he dislodged a shard of glass from the window frame with his fingers and studied it with exaggerated interest. When he raised his gaze to Ant and spoke again, his tone was low and threatening: 'So you're a hard man all of a sudden, are you? Yeah, right. We all know you're pussy-whipped, mate. But that's your problem. Don't take it out on me.'

Ant stared back, unblinking, high on the empowering

energy of pure rage. 'Consider yourself warned,' he said and he stepped very slowly back inside.

A minute later, he heard Booth in his back garden starting up an electric tool of some sort and for a brief, disorientating time Ant anticipated him hacking down his door, hacking *him* to death. But, checking from the upstairs window at the back, he saw that his neighbour was cutting plywood with a circular saw. Tracking him to the front, Ant watched him measure up the window, presumably to board it up with the ply.

Standing at their gates, Sara Boulter and Sissy gazed across in open despair at the destroyed glass, the fragments that covered their neighbours' drive. Ant supposed they must have seen his little spree – like something out of *A Clockwork Orange*. In the street between them, the cars were parked bumper to bumper, the road and pavements empty of children.

He imagined them thinking, *Is this what's become of Play Out Sunday?*

27

Ralph

No sooner had he wound up an unusually fractious call from a longstanding customer about a product he seriously struggled to care about – the prong of a belt buckle had decided to detach; several people had returned the item – than DC Forrester was on the phone again. Jesus, it was ten o'clock on a Monday morning, she couldn't keep away from him!

'I'm interested in a text you sent to Jodie on the subject of moving the camper van parked outside your house. "Or else you'll regret it"?'

'You've read my texts?' Ralph said, aggrieved. 'On what grounds?'

'It sounds a lot like a threat, Mr Morgan.'

'What, asking you on what grounds you're reading my texts?'

'No, the text itself.'

He sighed. 'Of course it wasn't a threat. It was banter.' Unlike *this*. 'And I thought it was *his* number, not hers. She didn't identify herself when she replied, she let me think it was him. I'd call that entrapment.'

Naturally, DC Forrester did not. 'You were also heard to say that you wanted to burn their house down?'

'Well, ideally someone else would've done it.' Ralph laughed at his own joke, but in the reproachful silence that followed he fancied he could hear it: the idea, the consideration, that he might now be asked to come into the station for a more formal discussion. An interview. He'd looked up police procedure online and that was definitely what came next. A recorded interview. *Please state your full name and address*, or however they started it. Usually before or after the subject had been charged.

'Would you say your wife became unusually angry with Mr Booth when her children's play scheme was suspended?'

'Play Out Sunday?' Ralph was struggling to get his bearings in this conversation. 'She was upset, yes. She's invested a lot personally in making this a great place to live. But "unusually angry"? No.'

As it happened, angry was a fairly accurate description of Naomi at the breakfast table three hours earlier, when she'd stumbled upon the latest media dispatch regarding the siege suffered by the residents of Lowland Way:

Award-Winning Kids' Play Scheme Bites the Dust

The community initiative that won an Urban Spaces Award from City Hall has spectacularly failed following a breakdown in co-operation among the street's residents. 'I'd say we're more famous now for the death of Amy Pope,' confided one disappointed resident who asked not to be named.

Ms Pope died in August in a gruesome scaffolding crush on the street and police, who are treating the investigation as a murder inquiry, have cleared the owner of the scaffolding of any wrongdoing.

'It's very hard to keep street play sessions going week after week, year after year,' said a spokesman for the National Free Play Group, which campaigns nationwide to restore old-style play on children's own doorsteps. 'Without the complete dedication of parents and residents, they can easily bite the dust.'

SOUTH OF THE RIVER ONLINE

'Bloody cheek,' Naomi had raged. 'It's nothing to do with our "dedication". It's to do with a complete madman endangering our children's lives.'

'You're preaching to the converted, babe,' Ralph had agreed, grimly.

'Mr Morgan?'

'Sorry, yes?' He'd forgotten Eithne Forrester in his ear.

'I said, I understand there was conflict between your wife and your sister-in-law on the night of the tenth?'

'Did Tess tell you that?' Whatever Finn insisted to the contrary, she was a liability, that wife of his. Ralph wouldn't be surprised if she was the one 'confiding' in the press. Then he remembered Daisy. The kid wouldn't have had a clue they were suspects here; she might well have mentioned the row. 'There was an exchange of words that night, yes, but nothing important. Jesus, he must be loving this, knowing you're investigating us instead of him? Paid for with our taxes, I might add, because I don't suppose *he* pays any. Let's see someone investigate that, eh, rather than insinuating some nonsense about my wife, who's never done anything but good for this community!'

He was getting emotional and when the detective let him go he stood by the window for some minutes, recovering himself. His eye was caught by a campervan in the street below, the same filthy orange as the rust-bucket monstrosity outside his house, which triggered a fantasy about a hydraulic car crusher flattening each of Booth's vehicles in turn as neighbours applauded rapturously from the kerb. For the thousandth time he asked himself how was it was that some jumped-up arriviste had had the audacity to move into their street and start treating it as his personal car park. To kill a woman and yet get 'cleared of any wrongdoing'.

You couldn't make it up.

The campervan was blocking access to the warehouse, which made him remember the protesters Ben had had to wrangle when Ralph was on holiday. Hundreds of Lesbians Against Bankers, or whatever, assembling right here.

And it was then, when he wasn't even trying, in a moment that felt faintly magical, that he finally had his idea.

He rang Naomi to tell her straightaway, or rather he tried to persuade her to let him tell her.

'I don't want to hear it, Ralph,' she said, and he could sense her mouth tightening around the words, 'especially if it's anything like Ant's solution yesterday. He could have injured a passing child or animal, even blinded them. He was extremely lucky not to be arrested.'

'No, this is properly good,' Ralph insisted. Personally, he had been both thrilled and amazed by Ant's response to his call to arms. *Someone needs to scare the bastard good and proper*, he'd said, but he'd never imagined Ant would be the one to step up. *Nice work re Booth*, he'd texted him, when he'd heard (no doubt, *that* would come back to haunt him). Of course, the problem was Booth had *not* been scared off. When Ralph had left that morning, he was already up and out in his filthy old overalls. Still working on his house, still openly selling his cars, still blaring out his music.

'This is something we should have done in the beginning,' he added.

There was a pause and he knew Naomi was considering whether to allow herself to be curious. Not indulging him and his Booth obsession had become a matter of discipline to her. And yet, that news item about Play Out Sunday had offended her deeply and timing was everything.

'I could always tell you tonight,' he said, reasonably, 'but I'd rather get it underway right now. Are you sure you don't want to hear it?'

He waited. One beat. Two. Three.

'Get what underway?' she said.

28

Sissy

The Daredevils' Soft Play Centre, with its climbing frames and slides and giant ball pool, provoked an instant headache in Sissy. The psychedelia of primary colours under prison-camp searchlights, the ceaseless screech of infants. And the heat! It made her want to tear her skin off. Hard to see how Em found it preferable to her own home, even with Booth's renewed programme of drilling and revving and pounding.

A weekend had passed since Sissy had watched herself on Em's phone screen, captured at ten past two in the early hours of 11 August. Her movements were miniaturized and grainy, but it was indisputably her as she hurried towards the camera – positioned, she had learned, in the Kendalls' upstairs window, Sam's bedroom, and right at the end of its battery life. Then off she veered to the right of the screen, towards Booth's door.

The timestamp showed that she was out of range – under the scaffolding – for one minute and fifty-three seconds, before reappearing. Fast, but not so fast that it could be demonstrated to a jury of her peers to be impossible.

Soon after, the camera had caught up with her again as she crouched by Booth's white van; it recorded the back-hand flick of her arm as she disposed of something under its wheels. She'd thought it safer to leave the spanner and wire cutters in the chaos of his premises than to take them with her and attempt to conceal them in her own house. The footage showed her to be wearing gloves, since thrown out with the rubbish.

'Why are we meeting here?' she asked. She was perched on the edge of a huge pit of coloured balls in which Em had immersed herself, Sam wedged between her legs. His little bare arms smacked at the balls, eyes drunk with joy.

'Because it's too dangerous on Lowland Way,' Em said.

'Dangerous?'

'Too many people listening. Cameras watching.'

Sissy had seen the new video entryphone system installed by Ralph and Naomi, listened to Tess's lament that she couldn't afford such state-of-the-art security. Perhaps Sissy's buyers would get one fitted; they were aware of the reasons for the price reduction and would surely wish to secure themselves. 'At least not Booth's,' she pointed out.

'I know,' Em said. 'Ant really impressed me with that, I have to say.'

Sissy had caught the end of Ant's offensive, when he'd cracked a car window, and been dumbfounded. 'Yes, it didn't seem like him at all.'

'Nothing anyone does seems like them anymore,' Em said.

Never a truer word, Sissy thought, which made it all the

more difficult to concentrate seriously on the declaration Em now made that she had a plan to 'put an end' to the mortal threat of Darren Booth 'once and for all' and that Jodie's having left town provided the window of opportunity she'd been waiting for. She intended to go a step further than Ant's senseless violence by breaking into number 1 in the middle of the night. To create an alibi for herself, she needed Sissy to vouch for her by persuading all three Kendalls to sleep at her house. 'So just get us over to your place on Thursday night. I'll help make it happen, obviously, if Ant resists. Then, when everyone's asleep, I'll go back over.'

'What exactly are you going to do to him, Em?' Sissy asked. She felt as if she were humouring an overimaginative child.

'It's best you don't know,' Em said.

It was like making a film in which her character had been told only her own lines, not anyone else's. Nor even how the plot unfolded, though it was clearly in such a way that made it too much of a risk for the next-door neighbours to sleep in their own beds. Of course, even just guessing made Sissy an accessory to any crime, since she would not be informing the police.

Not if she wanted Em to keep her mouth shut about the video.

'Having fun, Sam-Sam?' Em cooed. 'Can you hear me, angel?'

Sam tipped his head back and laughed up at her. He didn't know there was something wrong with his mum, Sissy judged, but treated her in exactly the way he should: as his star, his centre. What was going on in her head to make her plot like this, or even to believe that Lowland Way was too dangerous a place to have a simple conversation? Admittedly, no eavesdropper, witting or otherwise, would be able to pick out their words over the hellish din of Daredevils, but there was more CCTV here than your average public place. A trained lip-reader could probably help the police decipher this very exchange.

'Before you do whatever it is you're going to do, wouldn't it be best to check in with Ralph and Naomi?' Sissy said.

'What, like you did?' Em replied. 'I'm not interested in checking in with them – or anyone. You're the only person who knows about this.'

There was no need to state the reason. Sissy had had many questions when Em had played the video to her, but the first one had been the only one that really mattered:

'Have you shown this to the police?'

Em had tipped her head: no.

'Why didn't you come to me sooner? Why now?'

'I didn't see it myself until last week. I needed some time to think about it.'

I, not *we*.

'Ant hasn't seen it?' What sort of a couple hid incendiary material from each other in this way? She'd clearly been wrong to think them close.

'No. I cut it before he could see it. I sent it to myself in a WhatsApp message. End-to-end encrypted, like Finn said at the meeting. He would've wanted to go to the police and I thought you'd suffered enough.' Em paused, eyes grave. 'Turns out you've suffered more than any of us realized.'

That was an understatement. What Sissy knew now, what she knew in the rawest way, a way that shocked her several times daily like ice-cold liquid injected into bone, was that the only thing worse than a loved one dying was a loved one dying by your hand.

'Why are you showing *me* then?' she asked Em, a catch of grief in her voice. 'Why not destroy it?'

But she knew the answer, she'd known it immediately: she had not thought to spare Em and now Em would not spare her.

'You know I only meant him to fall,' Sissy said, 'maybe break an arm or leg. I just wanted time off from him, that's all.'

'But how could you do that, Sissy, knowing we were next door? Knowing we could have been standing right there when the thing collapsed?' Em's voice rose to a cry: 'Sam could have been under it in his buggy. If Booth's not there, I often push it slightly underneath it when I come out the door.'

'If Booth wasn't there, it wouldn't have collapsed. It was his weight that caused it.'

'You can't say that for sure. With all those bricks and sacks of sand, it could've given way even without him walking on it.'

'I wasn't thinking,' Sissy said. 'I wasn't myself.'

But she *had* been thinking, hadn't she? Just one end, she'd been advised, and that would be the direction in which the boards would collapse. She'd chosen the end at Booth's front door, which would have made it relatively safe for anyone on the Kendalls' side. And yet, had she chosen the Kendalls' side, Amy might have survived and the Kendalls would have been unaffected, since they were safely inside.

She felt a bolt of hatred towards Em. *Haven't I been punished enough for my mistake?*

But Em was nodding as if she'd read Sissy's mind, self-consciously reasonable once more. 'Well, we can't change that now. What's important is what happens next. And this time it needs to be done with no one in the house next door. I'm not taking any chances.'

Sissy paled. *This time.* 'Are we really having this conversation?'

'Yes,' Em said. 'We really are.'

How had she allowed the criminal spirit to take possession of her? Had it been present in her her whole life, but never invoked? Why had she entered into that exchange on the doorstep with Graham? An exchange that, by the time she'd visited her friend Anthea in Wiltshire and noticed the hardware store near Salisbury train station (the old, unreconstructed kind without cameras), had grown into a set of instructions, a commission.

'What exactly would you need to do?' she'd asked him, as they looked together towards Booth's scaffolding. 'If you wanted it to fall?'

'You'd need to loosen the bolts that hold the couplings together,' Graham said. 'I'd just do the set in the middle and the set at one end. Four altogether.'

'What are couplings?' Sissy asked.

'You see where the poles join, under the boards? Those metal bracket things are called bolted couplings. You'd just use a spanner to loosen them and the next time he walked on the boards, it'd come crashing down. It's just the lower platform so he's not going to die.'

'The very next time?'

'Yeah, unless he's Twinkletoes. Hang on, it's not alarmed, is it? I can see a wire, so I think it might be.'

'There we go then,' Sissy said, with exaggerated dismay, but Graham was undeterred.

'Probably fake, but you'd just cut that before you touched anything,' he said. 'To be on the safe side.'

'Cut it with what?'

He grinned. 'What d'you think, nail scissors? No, wire cutters.'

'Right.' She paused. 'What kind of spanner?'

'Just a standard one. You've probably got one in your garden shed. If not, pick one up at a hardware store. Maybe not a chain, a smaller one, where they probably won't have cameras. And pay with cash. Seriously, it's simple. And don't worry, I won't tell a soul.'

'Really?'

'Yeah, really. Some people just deserve what they get.'

Funny, but she trusted him. It was a covenant peculiar to strangers, perhaps, or near-strangers, as they were.

In any case, it was his word against hers, if it ever came to it. What Em had was evidence sufficient to persuade the most ardent Sissy supporter that she'd killed Amy – including Pete. And he would never understand, never forgive.

Returning, drained and depressed, from her outing with Em, Sissy played voicemails from two missed calls.

The first was from the police, who, after Pete and Naomi, Sissy now counted as her most dedicated correspondents. She returned the call, hoping to get voicemail, dismayed to have it picked up on the first ring.

'It's just a small thing, Ms Watkins,' DC Forrester said.

She'd remembered the 'Ms'. A meticulous mind such as hers was a wonderful thing when applied in one's favour.

'We've read a text message to you from Ralph Morgan? I'll repeat it to you: "I believe we have a common cause".'

That was it? They called *this* fighting crime? 'When was this?' Sissy asked, politely. 'Something to do with Play Out Sunday?'

'It was sent at eleven twenty-one on Saturday the fourteenth of July.'

'Oh.' Was it only Ralph's texts they'd accessed or hers too? But her indignation was born of muscle memory. She no longer cared. 'That particular common cause was getting the council to stop Booth destroying our street, but we've had many over the years.'

'You like to work together when you have a problem?'

'I suppose so, yes.'

'Would you say Ralph Morgan is well off?'

The change of direction took her aback. 'He's comfortably off, yes. He owns his house and a warehouse in Bermondsey. That's probably worth a few million these days.'

When the call had ended, Sissy stood for a minute in the garden, regulating her breathing, and the sounds from Portsmouth Avenue made her nostalgic, took her back to a time when all she'd had to grumble about was the screech of traffic braking at the lights on the other side of her wall. The sirens of emergency vehicles racing to the hospital or to the Rushmoor Estate, bypassing Lowland Way, where nothing frightening ever happened.

The second voicemail required no response from her, but was, in its own way, more upsetting than the first.

'This is a message from Arrowby Legal. We understand that you or a loved one has recently been involved in an accident. If you would like advice on how to claim for personal injury compensation, please phone one of our qualified advisors on this number . . .'

'There is no compensation,' Sissy murmured, feeling a crumpling sensation in her legs and managing to keep herself upright by sheer force of will. 'There won't ever be.'

29

TESS

She was beginning to think she was being picked on by the police.

No, that was irrational. She was just feeling fragile because Dex had started school.

'Yes, that is true,' she said down the phone to DC Shah. 'I *did* scream "I hate you" at him.'

'Why?'

'Because he'd just killed Amy Pope, a lovely young woman with her whole life ahead of her, and he was completely remorseless!'

'I see. Returning to the walk you took with your dog in the early hours . . .'

'That again?' She exhaled, worn down. 'Fine, yes, I hold my hand up to that one. I put the dog shit on their doorstep the night before the scaffolding collapsed. I'm not proud, it was stupid and petty. Actually, from what I've been told since, it must have been when Jodie was out getting cigarettes. I was lucky she didn't come back and catch me.'

'And yet she came to your house to remonstrate about it, didn't she?'

'Yes. That's how I know she was the one who killed the cygnet. It was right after that. She knew how much I cared about them. Can I ask *you* something? If I were to record her confessing to it, would you take me seriously? It wouldn't be a crime, would it, to record her on my phone?'

'It could certainly be considered a breach of her privacy,' DC Shah said. 'It's some time since the incident with the bird, isn't it?'

'Yes. But some of us aren't so knee-jerk as others. We wait for the initial anger to subside before making a plan.'

'Who would you consider knee-jerk?' DC Shah asked.

Kicking herself, she made no answer.

'Is it correct that you plan to move, Mrs Morgan?'

'Who told you that? Okay, well, yes and no. I wanted to, because of schools, you know? But then we had all these problems with Booth and we thought there was no point, we wouldn't be able to sell. I mean, I know Sissy's selling, she has no choice, but I heard her house has been seriously undervalued. If I were her, I'd be really disappointed.'

'So the value of your house is a major concern for you?'

'Not major, but a concern, yes. Certainly not a motive to do away with a bad neighbour, if that's what you're thinking. People don't kill over house prices, do they?'

'I'd say it's a question worth asking,' he responded.

Well, she'd walked straight into that one.

She was up in Dex's bedroom, about to ease shut his sash window in anticipation of Booth's night music, when she heard Finn and Ralph on the terrace below. Quite unbidden, the memory of meeting Ralph for the first time surged to the surface. The brothers had been in their twenties and yet she'd thought right away of the Artful Dodger. Which made Finn Oliver Twist, the one who got caught. This evening, her fingers gripping the window frame as if tethering the house to its moorings, she felt memory transform into premonition.

'Have you done it?' Finn asked.

'I certainly have,' Ralph said.

'I can't believe it. When will it happen?'

'Sooner rather than later, I hope.'

'Nay okay about it?'

'Took a bit of persuading, I'm not going to lie.'

Tess stiffened. Whatever this was, Naomi knew about it. Only she, of the four adults, was not included. Incredible. Inexcusable.

'Amazing to think it could all soon be over,' Finn said.

'Amazing to think we could have done this right at the start,' Ralph said. 'Saved ourselves all this crap.'

'Let's go over it tonight,' Finn said. 'There's stuff I need to ask you.'

Another night at the Fox. It wouldn't have surprised Tess if they asked her to babysit so they could take Naomi with them.

When Finn came back in, she was waiting for him, resentment burning. '*How* will it all be over?' she demanded, then, the thought striking, 'Is this about the wall? I thought that was Naomi's idea, not Ralph's?'

Finn rearranged his face from guilt to innocence. 'What wall? This is news, tell me!'

But Tess knew a deflection when she heard one. 'What then? What's going on?'

He gave her an infuriatingly secret smile. 'Something good. Really good. Don't look at me like that, I promised Ralph I wouldn't say anything. It needs to be kept completely confidential or it might not happen.'

In other words, Ralph thought she was a blabbermouth. He'd spotted another opportunity to subtly downgrade her.

'But Naomi knows?'

'She has to.' He paused, a flicker of irritation crossing his eyes. 'This isn't a competition, Tess.'

Tess bristled. 'If you really think it's competitive for a wife to ask her husband for information about his behaviour that someone else's wife already knows, then I don't think there's any point.'

'Any point what?' Finn said and his tone was not fearful or conciliatory, as she might have expected, but challenging. His eyes held hers as if *she* were the one with something to answer to. 'And what "behaviour"? You make it sound like I'm a child.'

'Keeping secrets with your brother? Sounds pretty childish to me.' Tess felt a great heaviness, then, not so much of defeat as of loss. All of a sudden, her happy, robust marriage felt like an irrevocable tragedy. 'I can't go on, Finn. I can't go on with you two plotting. How do you think it makes me feel knowing you'll help him, but you won't help me?'

Finn threw up his hands. 'Help you do what? You haven't asked me to do anything!'

'I'm asking you now. I want to get a confession from Jodie about the cygnet and you could come with me, intimidate her a bit. It's something the police will definitely be able to prosecute. I've spoken to them about it.' She didn't mention the breach of privacy caution.

Finn sighed deeply. 'Oh, that.'

'Yes, that. It was just a bird to you, wasn't it? Its life doesn't matter. Well, it matters to me and I'm doing it tomorrow, with or without anyone else's support. I'll go round in the morning after I've dropped the kids at school.'

Finn's gaze was stern. 'Don't go into that house, Tess. It's not safe.'

'Why? There's no scaffolding to kill me. Amy Pope already took one for the team, remember?'

There was a shocked silence. As they stared at each other, each as revolted as the other, it struck Tess that it was a miracle they hadn't reached this point before now, so immense had been the stress; the *grief*.

'Don't go,' Finn repeated.

'I'll go exactly where I please.' Tess turned to leave. 'You've got your plan, I've got mine. Let's see whose works best.'

30

Sissy

Was it really surprising her instincts were so savage now, so uncivilized? Guilt was fingers at your throat, it choked you of your breath. Your aim was survival and survival alone; honour was a luxury now. She would collude in any crime – *commit* any – so long as it stopped Pete from finding out about the first.

In the grand scheme of things, Em had asked little of her. On Thursday night, at eleven o'clock, dressed in pyjamas and her dressing gown, she left the house and hurried across the road to number 3. The night air, though temperate, felt pleasurably icy on her burning skin, the young fox that dashed from her path and cast her a fearful look a closer ally than the humans she was about to encounter.

There was the usual pulse of music from Booth's house, perhaps a notch quieter in Jodie's absence. Sissy had lost her ability to judge. Balanced against the wall, below the new window, was the ply used to board it after Ant's vandalism.

Reaching the Kendalls' door, she rapped the knocker loudly, calling their names in an urgent voice.

Ant opened up, alarmed, innocent. 'Sissy! Are you all right?' He was ill, too, his voice thickened with a cold, hand clutching a shredded tissue.

'Oh, you're in,' she cried. 'I'm so glad!'

'What is it?'

'I think . . . I thought there was someone trying to break into my house again.'

'Oh, God, how awful. Come in, let's get straight onto the police!'

She had no need to fake her agitation at this suggestion. 'No, please. He's gone now, whoever he was . . .'

Ant's head inclined to his right, wordlessly communicating that Booth was currently at home. 'I'll come and have a look, just in case,' he said, and he reached for something behind the door. A garden rake, his weapon of choice.

There was no trace of an intruder in her house, of course, but as they toured the rooms Sissy could tell Ant was noticing the eeriness of the atmosphere. Rooms were not just dark, but had the stale odour of neglect, a mood of abandonment that was almost Gothic. *No wonder she finds it creepy here*, he was probably thinking. *No wonder she thinks she hears footsteps*. He kept sneezing, apologizing for having a cold, but Sissy thought it might be the dust that was irritating him and she felt ashamed, as well as anxious.

'I don't want to be alone here tonight,' she told him, truthfully.

'Would you like to stay at ours for the night?' Ant suggested. 'We can make up the sofa bed in the spare room. It's next to the centre wall, but the music's not that bad tonight. He hasn't been staying up so late on his own.'

'Are you sure? Let's check with Em that's okay.'

Em was waiting for them. Sam was up, silent and disorientated. She'd woken him, Sissy realized. As Ant fussed about the sofa bed not passing muster, Em now made the counter-proposal that the two women had prearranged: 'Why don't we come over and stay with you, Sissy? I wouldn't mind escaping the music for once.'

'Oh, would you?' Sissy exclaimed. 'That would be *wonderful*.'

'I'll go on my own,' Ant told Em. 'There's no need to move Sam.'

'He won't mind,' Em said. 'We'll take the travel cot. It's *much* quieter at your place, isn't it, Sissy?'

'You can hardly hear the music at all at the back,' Sissy agreed. 'And it would make me feel better if I wasn't separating you.'

'Bring what you need for work in the morning,' Em instructed Ant. How would she have swung this, Sissy wondered, had Booth been out or already in bed asleep? She was a very good actress. It helped that Ant's default position seemed to be abject co-operation.

Sissy went ahead and began making up a guest bed. She hoped Em's scheme might somehow be aborted but, soon after, the doorbell rang and she had no choice but to proceed. Seeing the three of them on her doorstep with everything they needed for Sam was like watching a family of refugees crossing the border, displaced, enveloped by an aura of disaster.

While she made tea, Ant settled Sam upstairs. Was he the primary carer? That would be of benefit if Em got in trouble with the police.

Seated at the kitchen table, Em looked exhilarated, her eyes darting about the room before alighting on Sissy. 'Well done,' she told her. 'You did really well.'

'Look, Em, *I'll* do it,' Sissy said, abruptly. She hadn't known she was going to make the offer until she did, but her thoughts were suddenly clear and logical.

'Do what?' Em frowned, not understanding.

'Whatever you're planning tonight, I'll do it for you. I'm the one who's already caused a death.' She couldn't say 'killed someone'; the distinction meant something to her. 'You said you were going to break in, but you've got keys, haven't you? How did you get them?'

Em hesitated, then, aware of Ant's footsteps overhead, answered in a low, rapid flow: 'It was the day of the accident, when I went in to find Jodie. They were in the kitchen door, just hanging there, so I took them.'

Sissy gaped. While Amy had been dying, this self-absorbed woman had been scheming.

'It was opportunistic,' Em said, 'a split second thing, an impulse. I just had a feeling I might be able to use them in the future. And now I can.'

Overhead, pipes groaned, a fan thrummed. Ant was in the bathroom. Sissy could hear him coughing, blowing his nose.

'Surely Jodie would have noticed they were missing and changed the locks?'

'No, the house was open the whole weekend, police going in and out, Health and Safety, endless personnel. I knew they'd accept it in the mayhem of it all, maybe not even notice. And they'd have other sets, anyway, wouldn't they?'

'Clever,' Sissy said, thinking, *Crazy*. Em didn't even know if the locks had been changed. Her keys might be useless. 'So what's the plan for tonight? Quickly, tell me before Ant comes back down.'

At last, it came out. Once satisfied that Booth had gone to bed, Em was going to let herself into his house and bury a lit cigarette down the side of the sofa, where it would smoulder and catch fire. At the very least, there'd be bad enough damage for Booth to have to move out. 'Tess said the sofa's really old. Nylon and foam, totally flammable.'

So it was arson. Sissy tried not to show how appalled she was. 'Fires can get out of control a lot more quickly than you expect.' Hence the family's decamping, she supposed. If the sofa ignited, both numbers 1 and 3 could be incinerated.

'We're insured,' Em said.

'He definitely hasn't replaced the security camera?'

'No. I checked earlier. There isn't one at the back either.'

'What about an alarm?'

'I don't think so.'

This was amateur hour. Not only could Sissy not allow this deranged creature to go ahead with her plan tonight, or any other night, but she could not, as she'd claimed, do it for her. Her brain worked quickly, constructing an alternative narrative. She'd leave the house and keep herself out of sight for a few minutes, then come back and tell Em she'd done it. When the house failed to go up in flames, it could be put down to the cigarette end burning out before it caught, and Sissy would have a window in which to decide what to do next. Speak to Ant, certainly.

'Where are the keys?'

Em passed them to her, along with a pack of cigarettes. 'I

think that's his brand.' (She *thought*?) 'Remember, you'll have to wait till the music stops, then give him a few minutes to fall asleep. Do you want to take a knife or something in case he hears a noise and comes down?'

'A knife?' Breaking in while armed with a deadly weapon: that alone would carry a prison sentence, even before the arson. Thank God Em had agreed to let her act for her.

Thank God she was in a position to put a stop to this. 'I'll take my chances,' she said. 'The video clip, Em. Before I go, I need to see you delete it. I've already done what you asked me to originally.'

She watched, breathless, as Em turned on her screen, located the file, and hit the 'Delete Video' button.

'A deal's a deal,' Em said, with what seemed like genuine integrity.

Really, it was impossible to tell if she was sane or insane.

It was two in the morning when Sissy left her house for the second time and slipped across the street. For a disorientating moment, she thought she was having a flashback, some sort of PTSD episode, but this was real, this was right now. This state of being, this fragment of time, was entirely unconnected to her and yet wholly her own.

In case Em was watching from the window, she intended to get as close to Booth's door as was practical before dipping behind a car or van. She didn't like the hot, tempting feeling of his keys in her hand and decided to slip them in her pocket, but her fingers were numb with nerves and, just as she reached the bottom of the drive, she let go of them and they dropped to the ground with a musical clatter. Crouching to find them in the dark, she became aware of Tuppy barking in Finn and Tess's house, faint at first, but growing gruffer, closer. If she didn't move quickly, he'd wake the whole Morgan clan and she'd have one of them peering over the wall. Oh, God, was that the sound of a door closing? 'If anyone sees you crossing, just say you've gone to get a toy for Sam for me,' Em had said. 'Say his giraffe, he normally sleeps with that.' Sissy rehearsed the lie as she continued to fumble for the keys. There, she had them again!

Even before she straightened, before she heard the shuffle of footsteps, the rough rubbing sound of clothing not her own, she knew she wasn't alone. Em must have had second thoughts, decided she couldn't trust Sissy, after all.

'Em?'

As a hand landed on her shoulder, she heard herself shriek.

31

Tess

Smartphones had made sleuths of them all, Tess thought, double-checking that hers was fully powered and ready for the imminent sting. *Jodie*, she would say, *I know it was you who killed the cygnet. There's a webcam in the park and it caught the whole thing from start to finish.*

There was no webcam and most likely Jodie would call her bluff, but she would extend the interrogation for as long as it took to provoke the admission of guilt. Then she'd be straight on the phone to the police.

At least she hadn't seen Finn that morning to hear any more warnings, or any cryptic denials of his and Ralph's conspiracies. She'd already fallen asleep when he came home from the pub and then, in the morning, he'd slept while she got the kids ready for school. When she'd returned from drop-off, he'd left for work, the steam still warm from his shower. Ships passing, which suited her just fine. If they weren't going to be a team, sharing information, forgoing secret-keeping, then they might as well be ships.

The Kendalls' house was silent. She'd seen little of Em since her talk of deleting evidence against Tess from an old iPhone; a mutual withdrawal. They used to text regularly, trade complaints, but there'd been no contact all week. Another compromised relationship thanks to *them*.

She tiptoed up the Kendalls' side of the drive and arrived at the door of number 1 feeling jumpy and nervous. Though Jodie was known to be a late riser, she was usually in evidence by this time, and Booth would normally have been up and working since eight. But there was no sign of either having started their day. On the wall above the door was the bracket for the vandalized security camera; its destruction, like the window, had been Ant's doing, if Sissy was to be believed. The window had been replaced, its installation managed without disturbing the neighbours, thanks to the use of a professional.

The audio function was prepped on her phone and she hit 'Record', before knocking sharply on the door. No response. She moved to the window. There was a broad gap between the curtains and she peered in. As her eyes adjusted to the contrast between exterior and interior light, her gaze came to rest on a figure outstretched on the sofa: Booth, clothed and sleeping, obviously having not made it up to bed the night before. He was on his back, his right arm raised over his face, exactly the same position he'd lain in that time she'd sneaked up the stairs. She remembered the feeling she'd had as she'd watched the rise and fall of his chest: *I could kill him*. It had just been some primal reflex, of course, she'd had no weapon. But if she had, or if she'd smothered him perhaps and somehow got away with it, what might she have spared them all?

What might she have spared herself?

Determined to wake him and raise Jodie, to confront the bird killer exactly as she planned and prove Finn wrong, she returned to the door and crouched at the letterbox, ready to yell their names.

She sprang back at once, letting the flap bang shut. Gas. She'd smelled gas.

Back at the window, she hammered on the glass. 'Darren! Darren! Wake up!'

But there was no reaction, not a twitch. She could not see his chest moving.

She fumbled with her phone, turned off the recording function and dialled 999. 'I'm at One Lowland Way in Lowland Gardens and there's a really strong smell of gas. There's at least one person in there, I can see him through the window, and I think there's a woman upstairs too. Should I break a window?' Ridiculous, but she thought what a shame it would be to have to smash a brand new window.

Absolutely not, she was told. It might not be safe. 'Is there anyone at home next door?'

'I'll check.' She tried the Kendalls' doorbell, called Em's name through the letterbox. 'There's no reply, but no smell of gas either.' Ant would be at work, she reasoned, while Em might be away at her parents' again. Tess had lost track.

The Fire Service would be there any moment, she was advised, and she needed to get herself out of the immediate vicinity in case of a blast. From her own front garden, she tried Em's phone, but went straight through to voicemail. The same for Ant. Naomi didn't answer, but texted, *In a meeting, can't speak*, which meant both that she was safe and that she couldn't, for once, issue Tess with instructions. At last, someone answered: Ralph, who confirmed that he was also at work and the kids safely at school. He gave her Jodie's number, which she phoned next, only to be diverted to voicemail.

Remembering Sissy, she sprinted across to number 2.

'Tess, what's wrong?' Sissy, in a drab grey robe, looked terrible, with semi-circles of dark shadow under exhausted eyes.

'Don't leave the house, Sissy, there's a risk of an explosion across the road. Stay in here, preferably at the back.'

'What do you mean, an explosion? Where?'

'At number one. There's a gas leak and they'll need to evacuate us while they find the source. Booth's inside. He's not conscious.'

What little colour there was in Sissy's cheeks drained from them. 'Not conscious? Is he . . . Is he alive?'

'I don't know. I couldn't tell if he was breathing or not. I can't get hold of Em, I assume she's out of town with Sam, but—'

'Em's here,' Sissy said. 'They stayed overnight. I asked them to.'

'Ant as well? You've seen him this morning?'

'Yes, he went to work an hour ago.' At the sound of a siren on Portsmouth Avenue, Sissy looked thunderstruck, as if she hadn't understood what Tess had been saying until then. 'You smelled the gas from your house, did you, Tess?'

'No, I was at their door and I saw him through the window. I'm pretty sure Jodie must be in there, as well. I've phoned her number, but there's no reply.'

'Jodie's away. She's staying with her sister this week, helping with a new baby.'

'Oh!' If Tess had known this, she wouldn't have gone

anywhere near number 1 and the fire brigade might not have been warned for hours yet. 'The police will need to tell her not to come back for now.'

What else would the police need to tell her? From Sissy's open door, they watched as a fire engine turned into the street. Within seconds, a police car had arrived.

'What's going on? Is that the police?' It was Em, pale and birdlike, at the bottom of the stairs, Sam crawling at her feet.

'I'd better go out and speak to them,' Tess told Sissy. 'Can you explain what's happened, Sissy? And keep Sam away from windows, just in case of a blast.'

'Okay,' Sissy agreed.

'Oh, and could you phone the others?' Tess added. 'They might want to come back home.'

'Why?' Em was demanding, as Tess departed. 'Why do they need to come home?'

'You tell me,' Sissy said, which was odd, because how could Em know? But Tess didn't have time to think about it as she marched across to number 1 to make herself known.

He was dead.

Darren Booth was dead.

The paramedics told the police and the police told Tess. It was an incontrovertible fact that he was dead.

Along with the other neighbours, she, Sissy and Em gathered at the police cordon to watch the body being removed. By then, the whole of their end of the street had been evacuated, the crowd thickening with gawkers and partially obscuring their view. But there was no mistaking the lifeless form being stretchered to the open ambulance. The workers were in special full-body suits, as if in need of protection from some terrible contagion.

Finn, Ralph, Naomi and Ant arrived just in time to catch a glimpse of him.

'I'll go and find out what's going on,' Naomi said, craning over the cordon to identify a leader.

'No need,' Tess said. 'They've got my number and they said they'd let me know as soon as it's safe to go back in.'

'Tess discovered the body,' Sissy explained to Naomi. 'Without her, there might have been an explosion. A lot more serious damage.'

Ralph, for one, looked pretty pleased with the damage as it stood. 'This is unbelievable,' he said. 'Is Jodie in there, as well?'

'She's out of town,' Tess said. 'The police have contacted her and she's on her way back to London.'

Ant began questioning Em: 'You didn't take Sam back to the house this morning, did you?'

'Of course not,' Em said.

'Thank God we weren't at home last night.' His voice was that of a hundred-year-old man, one who'd spent most of his century dodging disaster. Tess knew how he felt. She was aware of Tuppy pushing at her shins. All three Morgan dogs were out here with them, winding their leads around legs, unsettled by the evacuation. Tess wondered if they could smell the residual gas. She wondered if they could smell the *corpse*.

'What do you mean, not at home?' Ralph said, his interest aroused by the Kendalls' exchange. 'Where were you?'

'We stayed at Sissy's last night. As non-paying guests,' Em

clarified, almost playfully. Tess had not seen her in this great a mood in months.

'Why?'

It was Sissy who answered, sending a cool glance Em's way. 'I thought I heard someone downstairs, so I asked them to stay. It was probably just my imagination.'

Naomi was more interested in Tess's role in affairs. 'What were you doing at number one this morning? I don't understand.'

'I'd rather not say.' Tess paused. She felt a provocative energy coursing through her, a strange disinhibition. 'Maybe you're not the only one with something to hide, Naomi,' she added, boldly.

'Tess,' Finn warned, but she ignored him. A man may have died, but she had not forgotten her husband's betrayal. This morning, she was closer to Sissy and the Kendalls than she was to any of the Morgans.

'What does that mean?' Naomi demanded. 'What have I got to hide?'

'Oh, for God's sake, Naomi, I'm not a fool.'

'Come on, girls,' Ralph said, and you could almost read his thoughts: *Stop bitching. We've won. Nothing else matters.*

'"Girls"?' Naomi echoed, displeased.

Of all things, *that* bothered her?

The ambulance doors crunched shut and, by Tess's side, Sissy began, very quietly, to cry. Then came the abrupt diesel throb of the engine and the vehicle rolled away.

'We might not be allowed back in for hours,' Em said. 'Shall we go and get a coffee somewhere?'

'Let's take the dogs for a long walk,' Ralph suggested to

his brother. He found Em irritating, Tess knew, and would not want to sit in a café with her.

'I'll come with you,' Naomi said to Ralph. As the trio removed themselves and checked leads and harnesses, it seemed to Tess that they subtly discouraged others from joining them.

'Maybe you ought to stay,' Finn told her, in case she had any such thoughts. 'The police might want to contact you.'

Tess gave him an unimpressed look. Only Tuppy, not liking the separation, pulled back towards her. 'Good boy,' she said, then, turning to Sissy and the Kendalls, 'It's fine for me to leave if I've got my phone. Let's go.'

From the brasserie on the high street, she posted on the residents' Facebook page:

> Be aware that there has been a gas leak at number 1 and the Portsmouth Avenue end of the street has been evacuated. I've been told it will just be for a short while and I'll post when I have more information.

'How long before the police do the rounds again?' Sissy said, her eyes on Em. Though she'd stopped crying, her hand was shaking as she stirred her coffee, metal clunking on china.

'They said they've got all they need for now,' Tess assured her. 'I got the impression they're linking it with his DIY, which makes sense.'

'I didn't know you could die from household gas like that,' Sissy said.

'Well, obviously you can,' Em said.

There was a curious sense of cross purposes between the two of them, Tess thought, an edge of wariness to Sissy's shock that rubbed against the undisguised relish of Em's response.

Ant had gone to the library, pleading work email, but Tess sensed he'd lacked the stomach for a lengthy debrief.

'I seem to remember my central heating man saying gas isn't toxic anymore,' Sissy went on. 'Not like in the old days.'

'The fire people told me what happens is it displaces the oxygen in the room and you suffocate,' Tess said. In spite of her horror at the awful, creeping death she now imagined, she acknowledged to herself that she was enjoying being the emergency service's contact, the one who knew the extra details.

'It must have been a very big leak for that to have happened,' Sissy said.

'Maybe he'd disconnected the boiler or cooker and not shut off the supply properly, so it pumped out in large quantities? Anyway, there'll be a post mortem, so they'll soon know. Poor Jodie. I mean, I'm no fan, but to lose your partner like that, it's terrible.'

'Terrible,' Em said, and though it was Tess's word she repeated, it was Sissy she spoke to.

There was definitely something not quite right between them.

Tess checked the time and fished in her bag for her purse. Forty-five minutes before the school day finished. 'I need to think how to brief the kids on this latest disaster. Does anyone want to walk up to the school with me, get some air?'

'I'm all right here,' Em said, gesturing to Sam, content on her lap with breadsticks and juice. 'We'll wait for Ant.'

'I'll come,' Sissy said. 'That might be what I need.'

But she seemed reluctant to part from Em, addressing her in a low, urgent voice while Tess went to the counter to pay. Distracted while choosing cookies for the kids – *Your neighbour has died of asphixiation by gas, but I chose you triple choc chip!* – Tess returned to find that they appeared to have settled their little difference. 'Nothing to worry about,' Em was telling Sissy. 'It's all good.'

Tess's eyes widened. If she meant Booth's death, then, *well*. Even by their standards, it was a little heartless.

32

Ralph

Man Found Dead After Gas Leak in South London Home

A fifty-seven-year-old man has died following a suspected gas leak in a house in the South London suburb of Lowland Gardens. A neighbour called the emergency services after smelling gas at approximately 10 a.m. yesterday morning and fire fighters entered the house after evacuating residents from neighbouring properties. The road was closed for several hours while the body was recovered.

The event is the second tragedy at the property in the last month, following the death of twenty-nine-year-old Amy Pope on 11 August. A murder investigation is ongoing.

The man's death is being treated as unexplained, said a Met Police spokesman, adding that an official post-mortem investigation will provide more information.

'I became concerned for his welfare when I went to the front door and smelled gas,' said Mrs Tessa Morgan, who raised the alarm. 'After that, the street was cleared very quickly. Luckily, the children were all at school and most of the neighbours at work.' Mrs Morgan added that the deceased was known to be a home improvements fanatic who had been working on his kitchen, though she was not aware of his holding any professional qualifications.

It is thought that millions are at risk of death or injury from gas leaks in the UK, according to the Gas Safe Register, which launched its 'Don't Cut Corners' campaign earlier this year in a bid to raise awareness. One in six homes inspected in the last five years was found to have dangerous gas appliances installed, it claims.

LONDON EVENING STANDARD

'Well, at least she can't come sniffing around about this one,' Ralph said to Naomi, the Friday evening after Booth's death, when they'd both read the piece, and he caught the flicker of revulsion on her face.

He knew what she was thinking. *This one*. As if life were cheap. Amy's life.

'You know what I mean,' he added. September sun blazed through the glass roof of their kitchen as if it were still high summer, but it was an illusion: outside, the air temperature had dropped, a sudden, brutal plunge.

'By "she", I assume you're talking about DC Forrester?' she said, her caustic tone more familiar these days than he would have liked.

'The very same. She's my number one bugbear. My *bête noire*.'

'She's a detective, Ralph, she's hardly likely to be your bestie.'

'Fair point. But you've got to admit it's a relief, knowing it's all over. And she *is* a bit of a bitch.'

With a glance to the door and the TV den beyond, presumably to check that Libby and Charlie were still as absorbed in their double-screening as they had been ten minutes ago, Naomi appeared to be deciding whether to have this out now or to leave it till later when the kids were in bed. As she pinched her upper lip between index finger and thumb, Ralph thought he might be the only person in the word who knew this signalled nerves.

She dropped her hand and began: 'Don't take this the wrong way . . .'

Ralph hated it when people said that. It always meant they were about to say something insulting – and by showing you were insulted, you'd already taken it the wrong way. A classic catch-22. 'What?'

'I don't know if it's new or maybe I just haven't noticed it before, but you are very, very critical of women.' She hastened to modify this, correctly understanding that by 'women', Ralph thought chiefly of her: 'Not me, I'm not saying that. Maybe that's been the red herring.'

Ralph laid his palms flat on the marble worktop. It was pleasurably cool. 'What are you talking about? What red herring?'

She studied him as if with corrected vision, eyes wide and horrified, a thoroughly unnerving experience for him. 'I mean women like Tess and Em and this detective. You haven't had a half-nice thing to say about any of them. I find it very . . . dismaying.'

He'd thought she was going to say 'disrespectful', which was bad enough, but 'dismaying'? That was the word teachers and other trained community figures used when they meant fucking annoying.

'I'm not saying I don't have my ups and downs with people, but this . . .' Her arms outspread, Naomi turned her palms upwards, as if to indicate the immeasurable scale of Ralph's problem.

He sighed. He was not an idiot, he was aware of the political movement sweeping media and society. Women speaking out against men, seizing power. But this was not to do with that. This was a moment of revelation deeply personal to Naomi. It related to domestic life, to their household's standing on the street, in the family.

'Look, babe, if you're saying I'm some sort of misogynist, trawling Lowland Way for female neighbours to hate, then I have to object. There's only one person I hate around here and that's Darren Booth. *Hated*.'

Naomi tilted her head as if watching another penny drop. 'You've never bothered with Jodie, have you? It's like she hasn't been worth your attention. Even when you were told you'd been texting with her, not him, you just dismissed her.'

No time like the present to rectify that, Ralph thought. When the post mortem was done and the funeral over with, Jodie would be the one to decide what to do about the house and the business and the cars. He looked at his wife, careful to strike a balance between defence and attack. 'Let me get this straight. You're allowed to criticize other women, but I'm not. Does it work the other way around with men?'

'We're both allowed to criticize whoever we like, just not to dismiss or disdain someone on the basis of their gender.'

Dismiss, disdain, dismay. All the 'dis' words. He recognized a no-win marital argument when he was in one and he was on his knees here, his hands and feet roped together behind him. He'd been wrong to speak about women and he'd been wrong to *not* speak about them. He was just wrong. 'I'm sorry if it's looked that way, but it's not true. I do have respect for the women you mention, as it goes. Maybe not Jodie so much, but Eithne F, for sure.'

'Why do you say her name like that?' Naomi pounced on this new crime. 'I don't even know DC Shah's first name.'

'Jason. Third-generation Indian, I'm guessing. What? I'm good with names. You know that. It's my thing.'

But Naomi was making no concessions. 'I think it would be better if you were good with women. You have a daughter. More importantly, you have a son.'

Ralph stared at her. There was no doubting her severity, that formidable ink-black gaze, but was this really what she was worried about? As far as he was concerned, they no longer had a care in the world.

'Stop now,' he said, at last. 'You've made your point, but stop now.'

Naomi just nodded and Ralph wondered if there was actually something else troubling her, this little rant an outlet for emotions so unwieldy she did not know how to express them. Men, of course, would know not to try.

This must be what hell was like. Not fire and brimstone, but the glimpse of clear seas before the armada came over the horizon. Light at the end of the tunnel before it collapsed and buried you alive.

Okay, not the best analogy.

The point was, Eithne – DC – Forrester was back. She *had* come sniffing around. First thing on Monday morning. She had a sharp new haircut and the air of someone whose workload had just doubled. She wanted to know what Ralph had been doing on the night of the gas leak.

'Why?' he demanded. 'The papers said it was to do with his putting in a new kitchen? He disconnected an appliance, didn't know what he was doing. Is that not right?'

'We have new evidence to suggest there might be an alternative reason for the leak.'

'Anything you feel like sharing?'

Of course not. 'We'll have more information soon.' She twisted in her seat, as if her clothing were bothering her. 'Someone close to you seems to think you've been plotting something very recently involving Darren Booth.'

'Someone thinks something,' Ralph repeated. 'Right.' It could only be Tess. Dear darling Tess, as he was expected to speak of her. 'You're quoting my sister-in-law, I assume? The hero of the hour. Well, take it from me, she's just annoyed she wasn't in on it.'

'How about you tell me what "it" is?' DC Forrester suggested.

Ironically, given Naomi's criticism, he'd never felt *less* dismissive of this woman, the female register of her voice, the tiny light of compassion in her eyes that he'd not noticed before, as if every question were a chance, not a challenge.

'Fine,' he said. 'It's nothing illegal and she would have been the first to hear the news if she'd just held her horses. A few days before Booth died, I took out a loan to buy his house. The plan was to sell it on to a buyer I'd choose, someone a bit more suitable. I asked a local estate agent to approach him with an offer, a pretty decent offer, considering the state the place is in. Through a subsidiary of my company, so he wouldn't know it was me. I'd just had an answer from the agent the evening before the gas leak. I couldn't tell Tess because it needed to be anonymous. She's at home all day, talking to the neighbours in the street, over the wall, and he might have overheard her and turned me down on principle. By the way, I wasn't avoiding your original question, I'm happy to answer it: I was out with Finn on Thursday night. We went to our local, the Fox, on the high street. Like I say, we had something to discuss.'

The detective nodded as she made notes, adjusting her glasses on her nose when they slipped. 'What time did you get back home?'

'Pretty late, maybe twelve thirty. I'd had a bit of a skinful, I honestly can't remember.'

'Did either of you call in at number one?'

She made it sound so plausible, like they dropped in all the time for a nightcap and a quick listen to Anthrax's greatest hits. 'Call in? Why would we go anywhere near there? We were finished with Booth. Totally done. We just wanted to buy him out and forget he ever darkened our door.'

There was no comeback to that and he knew then that she had nothing to incriminate him. Perhaps this was no more than a new point of entry into the Amy investigation. The same old questions from a different angle. How tedious police work must be, how much stone had to be worked to get the tiniest drop of blood.

'Any idea when they'll get rid of all his vehicles?' he asked. 'Is that down to Jodie?'

'It will depend if they're registered to the deceased or to other people,' DC Forrester said, 'but it's reasonable to start your enquiries with her, yes.' She almost floored him then by smiling. 'Can I ask what the estate agent said? You said he called with an answer.'

He realized she was embarrassed because the information could have no bearing on her inquiries, she was simply curious, and he smirked back at her. 'He said yes. Booth accepted the offer. After everything we've been through, he said yes.'

Ralph had made it clear to the agent that his offer for the house still stood should Jodie want to continue with the sale, but the agent had said the death of one half of a couple usually meant delays, if not reversals of previous decisions. And yet, without Booth, why would Jodie stay? Without him, without the car business, the size and location of the premises was irrelevant. It had never been a home, not in the way the other residents knew a home to be.

At a rare advantage, Ralph held the detective's eye. 'So you see, there's really no reason for me to have snuck into his house on the way home from the pub and tampered with his gas pipes.'

DC Forrester was serious again, borderline offended. 'I'm not sure that's what I suggested, Mr Morgan.'

'Really,' Ralph said, flattening the question. He'd learned, by now, how to have the last word with her.

33

Tess

Fine. It was inevitable that the detectives investigating Amy's death would be looking for links, she reasoned. There was no such thing as a coincidence, after all (except when it *was* a coincidence). Police were now as much of a presence on Lowland Way as postal and delivery services. The rubbish and recycling lorries or the van that drew up twice a week to dispatch cleaners for the Boulters.

'I understand you were very helpful to our colleagues,' DC Shah told her, and she pulled the good-citizen face she had perfected in her numerous encounters with neighbours keen to know details of the gas incident. Somehow, her actions had been elevated to the foiling of a blast that might have taken out the whole street. She was the heroic saviour of multiple souls.

'*And* you've been speaking to the press,' he added.

'So have you,' Tess pointed out. Tuppy had settled next to the detective's legs, a sign of the times if ever there was one: he thought DC Shah was a regular member of the household now, probably expecting to welcome him back for Christmas. 'So I gather from my brother-in-law that you think it might not have been a straightforward gas leak?'

'Word travels fast.'

'We're next-door neighbours, remember. Have you had the post-mortem results?'

'Not yet. But we do know that one of the rings on the gas hob had been left on and the flame either not ignited in the first place or somehow blown out.'

Well, they hadn't told Ralph *that*. It was surely a positive sign that they'd told her, she thought. She would WhatsApp the group to warn anyone yet to be interviewed. 'You've come to the right place, then,' she said, 'because the only time I've ever been in their house I found one of the gas rings left unattended. Which suggests it might have been a regular occurrence. I got the impression they lit their cigarettes from the flame, so he might have turned it on for that reason and been distracted.'

'It's a possibility. Except Booth kept a lighter inside his cigarette pack.'

'A working lighter?'

'Yes.'

Tess suppressed a sigh. This was the problem with law enforcement: no sense of poetic justice. She remembered what Sissy said about the relative harmlessness of household gas. 'Would a hob being left on be enough to kill someone? It wasn't like he was in a confined space.'

'As I say, we'll know that very soon.' DC Shah chewed the end of his pen, a new habit or at least one that had not caught her eye before. 'For now, we're trying to get a picture of all the neighbours' movements last Thursday night.'

'Right. Well, mine were very boring. I was in with the kids and Finn went out to the pub with Ralph.' Her tone was unattractively waspish and she had a sudden picture of herself as a neglected suburban housewife, bursting into tears without quite knowing why, treating tradesmen as therapists. She needed to be careful not to get emotional here.

'What time did your husband leave and return?'

'Seven thirtyish. He was back late. I don't know what time exactly, but he was there in the morning, lying next to me and I'm pretty sure it wasn't an imposter.'

Her sarcasm drew no response. 'And in the morning you went to Mr Booth's house to speak to Jodie. I understand you keep spare keys for some of the neighbours? In case of emergency.'

'That's right. For Ralph and Naomi, Sissy and the Kendalls. Sissy and I are usually the ones neighbours ask, because we're based at home.'

'How about the spare key for number one, who kept that?'

'You'd have to ask Jodie, but it's certainly not me. We hated each other.' Tess felt her rage swell. 'This woman killed a defenceless animal and dumped it on my path, remember? That's why I was there!'

She could see what DC Shah was thinking, *It's the defenceless human I'm interested in here*, but Booth had never been defenceless, had he? Expecting a mild rebuke for her outburst, she was surprised by his next comment: 'We've been passed some information about the cygnet and it looks very much as if it wasn't your neighbours who left it at your door.'

'What?' Tess flushed in disbelief. 'You mean, it wasn't her? It wasn't them? Who, then?'

He leafed back a page or two in his pad. 'It was a Mrs Becky Wallace. She responded to the Swan Rescue notice appealing for witnesses and came forward with information. She found the bird in the park just before the gates closed. She believes it had become separated from its parents and was the victim of a group of boys with an air rifle. They've been warned before about using it. She's helping us ID the individuals involved.'

Tess pressed her fingers into her hot cheeks. 'Oh! I can't believe that! That's very upsetting. I don't know her, do you have a photo of her?'

He did not. 'She gave her profession as child minder. She's local, goes to the park once or twice a day.'

'I think I might know who you mean. She's got quite a few kids. I saw her in the shop next to the Star, as well, when I went in to complain about them selling stale bread to feed to the birds. So she found the poor thing, did she? Why did she bring it to me?'

'She said she'd noticed you were active in the swans' welfare and she knew where you lived. She thought you would know what to do with it. She didn't know about Swan Rescue until she saw the appeal after the event.'

'Why didn't she ring my doorbell and ask me face to face?'

'Perhaps she didn't feel confident enough to do that. These houses look quite grand to most people, Mrs Morgan.'

Again, Tess felt the pain of imminent tears. 'Oh, that makes me so sad. For her to see me that way. To bring the cygnet, but be too shy to ring the bell. That makes me so sad.'

'It's been an upsetting time,' DC Shah agreed.

*

She contacted Daisy to babysit and booked a table at the Fox.

Finn was a little discombobulated by proceedings, she could tell. He was probably thinking, *This is where I come with Ralph*, and out of sheer bloody-mindedness she tried to avoid what Ralph would order from the menu – something demonstrably male, a pie maybe.

'I'll have the mackerel and beetroot salad,' she said.

'Oh, that's what Ralph always goes for,' Finn said.

'Really? I'm surprised. He must be worried about middle-aged spread.'

'Or Naomi is. I'll have the beef.'

Extraordinary though it was, Ralph had apologized to Tess for excluding her from his plans to buy number 1. He'd seen her as a risk to his anonymity, he explained, too likely to confide in Em in earshot of the enemy. 'I shouldn't have come between you and Finn,' he said. 'You have my word I won't do it again.'

Wonders would never cease, but then he was in excellent spirits now that Booth had been removed (dead or alive, it was only the removal that counted to Ralph).

Finn had apologized too, of course. Had he not, they would now be discussing divorce.

'So what's this about?' Finn paused. 'Hang on, is the fact that I even have to ask the problem? We don't go out enough on our own?'

Tess smiled. 'You're becoming quite fluent in passive aggressive, I see. I do want to talk, though.' She took a few fortifying gulps of her Sauvignon Blanc. 'About moving.'

'Okay.' Finn rolled a piece of bread between finger and thumb, creating a marble-sized dough ball. 'Actually, I have a proposal for you on that. A deal.'

He was quite serious. Once, a proposal had involved champagne and diamonds, but this was what marriage was by this stage. Deals and negotiations. Because people tended to agree less as they advanced, not more. They came to trust their own judgement over others', to feel they'd earned the right to what *they* wanted, not what someone else did.

'I'm happy to put the house on the market whenever you think will work,' Finn said. 'Bearing in mind there's a murder inquiry going on on the street.'

'Two – if they really do think someone broke into number one and turned on the gas.'

'That won't come to anything,' Finn said, placing the dough ball back in the basket, as if one of them might want to eat it. 'He must have done it himself. Passed out in a drunken stupor without smelling it. Ralph thinks they're only questioning us in the hope of scaring out information about Amy and the scaffolding. Now we're off our guard a bit.'

'I wouldn't be surprised. If it weren't for the fact that they haven't actually solved the case, I'd say these detectives are pretty clever.' Tess topped up their wine, icy water from the bottle running down her wrist. 'What's the other bit of the deal?' she asked.

'I leave my job and go and work for Ralph.'

Unable to tell whether she'd been expecting this and, if so, when it was that she'd stopped fearing it, she offered a noncommittal 'Hmm'.

Finn continued, 'Before you say it, I won't do that until we've had an offer on our place and decided where we want to go. Otherwise . . .'

Otherwise, the moment he was working with Ralph, Ralph

would be working on getting him to reconsider the move. She imagined their desks set side by side, their satisfied faces turning as one when some underling brought in their bean-to-cup coffees.

'The day we complete on the sale,' she said, 'you can resign. No sooner. And I'm going to be working as well, once we've got the kids settled in new schools.'

Obviously relieved by the ease of the negotiation, Finn struggled to conceal his elation. 'Maybe we can find something for you at the business?'

Tess raised her dripping wine glass to her husband. 'Let's not get carried away here,' she said.

34

Ant

Though he said so himself, Ant was doing an excellent job of acting as if a police visit to his home at eight in the evening was nothing outlandish, or at least nothing to provoke any urgent desire to abscond. It helped that he'd already downed two large glasses of red by the time the doorbell went. Since Em had left – again – it was his habit to pick up wine on the way home from work, usually from the Tesco Metro by the station and never more than two bottles. 'If it's in the house, I'll drink it,' he'd told his colleagues just that day and they'd sympathized, as if they too had a dependency issue. 'Only way to cope,' they agreed.

DC Shah explained that he'd called by twice earlier, without success, and was trying one last time on his way home.

Not an arrest then, Ant stopped himself from joking. He was third in this new round of police inquiries, as he understood it, after Ralph and Tess, who reported that Naomi and Finn hadn't yet made the cut. But Em would, surely. The Kendalls were the Booths' nearest neighbours and their actions on Thursday night had been irregular by anyone's standards. Perhaps police had also travelled down to Gloucestershire this evening and he and Em were being interviewed simultaneously so they couldn't tip each other off.

'I heard a gas ring was left on and you want to know where we all were on Thursday night?' he said, on the front foot.

It was the first time in all his conversations with the police that he had rehearsed what he was going to say. He and Em had gone over it while walking through the park on the late afternoon of Booth's death, Sam strapped into the racing-green push-along car they'd just bought from the toy shop next to the brasserie (did that look suspect? Too callous? Buying toys within hours of a neighbour suffocating to death?). Though they'd interacted quite naturally with their son, they must have looked like spies when they addressed each other, speaking sideways while staring at the path ahead.

'I suggest we say nothing beyond going over to Sissy's,' Em said. 'We got there, we settled Sam, we went to bed. End of story. If anyone says they saw one of us in the street later, we were nipping back to fetch Sam's giraffe. I've told Sissy the same.'

She was confident she could dictate to Sissy what she should and shouldn't say to the police, but Ant was warier. Sissy was not the woman they'd known six months ago, decent to a fault, shatterproof. She was vulnerable now, if not already broken.

'Let's go back a bit, if that's all right,' DC Shah said. They were sitting in the living room, mugs of tea on the coffee table – black, because in Em's absence Ant had run out of milk. He had half-seriously offered wine, but of course been refused, and he had left his own glass in the kitchen. His reunion with it couldn't come soon enough.

'We're interested in a text Ralph Morgan sent you on the Monday before Darren Booth's death. "Nice work re Booth"? What did he mean by that?'

Ant blinked. 'Oh, okay. Well, it was because I'd smashed a window next door.' Did that sound too cavalier? He altered his tone. 'You probably know about that from Jodie. I shouldn't have done it, I'm very sorry.'

The notebook was open, the pen sliding left to right. In an idle moment, Ant had googled 'police supplies' and found the model. Investigator's Notebook, it was called, though civilians were allowed to order it. 'You're saying you're responsible for damage to Mr Booth's property?'

'Yes, and no doubt you'll want to prosecute me for it, but before you do, let me ask you this: is what I did really worse than damaging the health of a young child?' The alcohol was causing his tongue to outpace his brain. 'D'you want to know what my wife and I are doing next week? Taking our son to a Paediatric Audiovestibular Clinic. Know what that is? It's a clinic that treats kids with hearing problems. The day I smashed the window, she'd just sent me a text saying we needed to get a referral. I'd been so restrained till then and I just lost it. I took out his camera and a car windscreen, as well. I would have done more if he hadn't come out.'

DC Shah raised his gaze from his notes. 'No complaint has been made about the incident, but that doesn't mean we can't choose to investigate it.' He tilted his head, thoughtfully, as if assessing whether to do so there and then.

Ant nodded, feeling wretched. 'That's good of Jodie not

to report it.' *And* Booth: there'd been four days between the attack and his death.

'We understand that you and your family slept at Ms Watkins' home on the night of Thursday the sixth?'

Ant reached for his tea, to buy himself a few seconds, but immediately wondered if this were a known sign of incipient dishonesty and put it down again without taking a sip. 'That's right, she came over late, maybe about eleven? She was in a bit of a state because she'd had an intruder a couple of weeks earlier and she thought she'd heard a disturbance. It was obvious she couldn't be in the house alone, so we suggested we stay with her.'

'Had you ever done that before?'

'No, but as I say she'd only recently had the break-in and so hadn't been nervous about being on her own before. She used to have B&B guests a lot, too, but that's all changed. I think she's lonely.'

If there was any sense that Ant was leading the subject in a different direction, DC Shah was having none of it. 'You and your wife had been under a lot of strain following a noisy party, I believe. You didn't call on your neighbours earlier in the evening, did you?'

'No. Definitely not. And it's neigh*bour*, not neigh*bours*. Jodie wasn't home, only Booth.' He picked up his tea more confidently now and drank, feeling the hot liquid surge through his gullet.

'It's quite a coincidence that you weren't there on the night of a life-threatening gas leak,' DC Shah remarked.

'You could say that,' Ant agreed. 'Personally, I'd call it a stroke of luck. A rare stroke of luck. I'd say it was about time the cards fell in our favour. You know they've done this before? Left flames unattended, that sort of thing. Anyway, Tess said the firemen told her we would most likely have been fine at our place if we'd been sleeping there – so long as the gas wasn't ignited.'

'Did you go back to your own home in the morning for any reason?'

'No, I'd taken my work clothes and laptop with me, so I went straight to work. I get the overland train into Victoria, if you want to check. Then my wife phoned me later in the morning, said they'd all been evacuated.'

'What was your reaction to that news?' The detective laid his pen on the open pad in an unnerving gesture, as if he wanted to listen to Ant's answer with particular attention.

'Well, once I was sure she and my son were fine, I was sad,' Ant said, and the wine exaggerated his words, made a child's story of them. 'I didn't like Booth, but it's still horrible. I also thought it could have been worse.'

'How so?'

'It could have been both of them. But like I said, Jodie was away.'

'Yes, you did say that,' DC Shah said.

Em was staying with her parents. It was only time apart, she had said, at the close of that walk in the park, with Sam squealing away in his little green car. Nothing as formal as a separation and as much for Ant's benefit as hers.

Ant thought time apart and separation amounted to the same thing.

'I'm worried about myself, the way I spoke to you last

night,' she said. 'The way I spoke to Sissy. That whole ridiculous plan. What if she *had* gone in? Not smelled the gas and lit a cigarette like I told her to? She'd have blown them both up!'

'She would have smelled it,' Ant said. 'And so would Booth if he hadn't been drunk as a skunk. He was a danger to himself, first with the scaffolding and then with the gas.' He paused. 'How long will you be away this time?'

'I don't know,' Em said.

He tried to ignore the last-ditch desperation that had seized him, and yet, he *had* to ask: 'Are we . . . are we all right, though?'

'Oh, Ant.' Her expression was a blend of pity and determination. The pity was for him, the determination for her and perhaps for Sam, too. They were inseparable, mother and son, as once husband and wife had been. 'How can I say for sure we are? How can you? The best I can say is I hope so. I hope so.'

He'd never heard the word 'hope' sound so hopeless.

'We'll see you for the hospital appointment,' she reminded him. 'We'll be back next week for that.'

Yes, he'd see them again at the hospital and for any subsequent consultations. He'd talk to Em then, think of a way to rebuild the family Booth had destroyed.

Ironically, it was only when they hugged that he truly felt it, her withdrawal from him. He felt the ghosts of all the bodies left in Booth's wake, not just Amy's, but the ones still living too.

35

SISSY

She presented herself at the police station in sound mind – or as sound as it had been since she'd caused the death of her son's lover and delivered herself to the twin tyrants of guilt and Em Kendall.

'Say nothing,' Em had instructed her the day Booth's body was found. 'If we all say nothing, we'll shut it down.'

'Whatever I say, I won't implicate you in any way,' Sissy told her. 'You have my word.'

Which was not quite the same as saying nothing. Instead, with the news that his death had been caused by gas from an unlit hob, her brain had seized on an opportunity. A punishment fit for her crime, a karmic solution to her wickedness. A selling of her soul at a price she was confident she could bear.

'I've come to confess to killing someone,' she said to the front counter staff. Not a dramatic announcement like a time waster might make, but not an uncommon one, either, judging by the lack of alarm with which it was received.

She was taken to a room that was not like the interview

rooms she'd seen on TV, but simply a private space, a small conference room, perhaps, glazed on two sides. She was allowed to choose her seat – she opted to sit with her back to the strip-lit honeycomb of police workers visible through the glass – and offered a hot drink. There was a wait for the detectives to become available; she couldn't have said how much time passed before DC Forrester arrived, but the growl in her stomach told her she'd missed a meal.

The detective had, of course, her regulation blue book and black biro with her. The date was already at the top of the page, with Sissy's initials. 'Ms Watkins, you've come here to tell us—'

'That I did it,' Sissy interrupted. 'I turned on the gas at number one.'

DC Forrester's eyes widened only very slightly, as if the surprise were minuscule. 'That's quite a revelation. How did you enter the premises?'

'I had a key.'

'And how did you come by this key?'

'Booth gave me a spare, right at the beginning, before we all fell out.' A lie, but just about plausible. Jodie would dispute it, of course.

'So you had a key and you let yourself in. Through which door?'

'The front door.'

'What time?'

'It was about two in the morning.' Almost exactly the same time of night she'd committed her crime against Amy four weeks earlier. 'He'd passed out on the sofa, so he didn't see me.'

'Which gas ring did you turn on?'

'I beg your pardon?'

'There are several rings on the hob. Which one was it?'

'The front one.'

'Left or right?'

Sissy swallowed. 'Right.'

During this exchange, the detective's expression was analytical, almost scholarly, with a pause after each of Sissy's answers as if waiting for a simultaneous translation to catch up. 'Why would you do such a thing?'

'You wouldn't understand,' Sissy said, truthfully.

'I see. Well, I know it's been a very upsetting few weeks for you, so tell me how you feel. Help me imagine what was going through your mind that night.'

Sissy looked at her, unexpectedly keen to oblige, the words ready to be spoken. 'Imagine a girl you love, who's as good as family, is taken from you. You are sinking and sinking down a narrow pipe, you can just about breathe, but any time you try to move, you only slip further down. You come home and your front door won't open because the chain is on. Someone has broken in and he's still in there as you're rattling the door and phoning for help. It's him. Then every night after that you can't sleep because the slightest noise makes you think it's him. You have your eyes closed and you imagine opening them and he'll be there, standing over you, deciding whether to kill you.'

DC Forrester seemed mesmerized by this speech. She rotated her shoulders, forwards, then backwards, as if to release herself from its spell. 'That sounds very frightening.'

'It *was* frightening. I wanted to stop it. I couldn't take any more.'

The detective looked worried. 'I'm not sure I understand completely, though. You were selling your house, you had planned a way out. You only needed to wait a few more months and you'd be free of him, so why would you put yourself at risk by invading his house? You must have known there was a very good chance he'd wake and defend himself.'

'I didn't care,' Sissy said, then, to clarify, 'I didn't care about me.'

DC Forrester pressed her lips into a tight line. 'Why do I feel you're not being honest with me today, Sissy?'

Sissy gave her a pleading look. 'I *am* being honest, that's why I'm here. To put an end to the uncertainty, to let everyone else go back to normal.'

'That's very honourable.' But there was a new edge of impatience to DC Forrester's compassion and she stood suddenly, knocking her hip against the table. 'Think back to that night, Sissy, minute by minute. Then we'll go over it again. Take as long as you need. I'll get us another cup of tea.'

Sissy's chin dropped. She didn't want to think back, but the detective was leaving the room, closing the door, a therapist allowing her client to collect herself after a treatment. Or before one.

First, there was that unfamiliarity you felt in the dead of night, as if the street did not belong to you. As if being unseen meant not existing.

She remembered dropping the keys on the drive and her sudden spinning at the touch of a hand on her shoulder. Her scream, primal in the quiet of the night, and then Ant in front of her, his face urgent with concern.

'What are you doing, Sissy? What has Em asked you to do?'

Sissy faced him in the gloom, trying to steady herself. 'I wasn't going to do it, I was just going to pretend I'd done it.'

'Done what?'

As if ridding herself of a snake squeezing her chest, she told him Em's plan. Somehow, with her phrasing, her whispers amplified by the cold silence, it sounded less ridiculous, less juvenile. It sounded like malice aforethought.

'Where the hell did she get the keys?' Ant asked. His breath was thick and laboured; thanks to his cold, he must have been breathing through his mouth.

'She says she found them on the day of Amy's death.'

'Give them to me and go back. If she gives you a hard time, tell her I forced you to hand them over.'

He'd snatched them from her then with some force, to make it easier for her. 'Go back.'

She obeyed. Her ears boomed as she crossed, her footsteps inaudible. It was too much to expect that Em had retired to bed; she was waiting at the bottom of the stairs, her face in the half-light devilish, unforgiving.

'Why are you back so soon?' she hissed. 'Where did Ant go?'

'He followed me,' Sissy said. 'I had to come back.'

'Why?'

'How could I do it when he was right there?'

'Oh, for God's sake,' Em cried, 'why did you say you'd do it when you weren't going to! I'll go myself.'

'Ant's got the keys,' Sissy admitted.

'You gave them to *him*?' Em's fury was causing a tremor in her shoulders. 'This is not what we agreed!'

Sissy watched her tear out of the door. She thought about

chasing after her, but remembered Sam. She was alone with him in the house, she had to stay. Neither Ant nor Em had keys to Sissy's house, so she left the door on the latch before retreating to her room (the irony of leaving the house unsecured, given they were nominally here to help her feel *more* secure, was the least of her concerns). She felt weak and worthless for landing Ant with the job of talking Em down from her ill-conceived mission, but he *was* her husband. He might succeed where Sissy had failed.

Except they did not return together. She thought they did, at first: she heard the front door open and close, footsteps on the carpeted stair, the neighbouring bedroom door easing open and shut, and she allowed herself to sleep. Then, some time later, she woke to the same sequence: the front door opening and closing. Footsteps on the carpeted stair, this set so careful she scarcely caught them. The guest-room door easing open. A baby's whimper, an adult's murmur.

She had no doubt that Ant had lost to Em. He'd given up the keys and come back alone. Em had gone ahead with her plan and planted the burning cigarette. Unable now to sleep, Sissy kept vigil at the front window. The moment she saw smoke, she'd phone 999.

But there was no smoke, only the gently rising light over the rooftops.

After breakfast, when Tess had arrived with her extraordinary news, Sissy could only guess that Em had adapted her crime with shocking success. All day, she'd looked at her and thought, *What did you do?*

Em had at least had the wherewithal to declare the thing a miraculous coincidence. 'I can't believe he's dead,' she said, *kept* saying, and even when left alone with Sissy, she had kept up this version of events, a method acting so powerful that it seemed to Sissy she believed it herself. Her only reference to what had passed in the early hours was when she coached Sissy on her subsequent handling of any police inquiries. 'We all went to bed at the same time. No one left the house again. Unless someone insists they saw you and then you say you were getting Sam's toy giraffe for me. But only then.'

'All right,' Sissy said.

What did you do? she thought.

DC Forrester was back in the room with fresh cups of tea, picking up the interview with ease, a dropped stitch retrieved.

'Tell me the truth, Sissy, yes or no: did you go into number one that night?'

'No,' Sissy whispered.

'Why would you claim you committed a crime when you didn't?'

Sissy did not answer.

'Were you protecting someone else?' How coaxing the detective's tone was now, almost sweet. 'Did you see or hear Em Kendall go out that night?'

'No,' Sissy said. But, to her consternation, emotion was overtaking caution, her voice gaining a hectic new energy: 'You have to understand she's been driven mad by this situation. She's got a baby who can't sleep, who she's desperately worried about. If she's done anything wrong, she doesn't deserve to be punished. I . . . I'm older.'

I have reason to atone.

The detective put her mug to her lips, her expression

accommodating, even kind. But she was thinking, no doubt, how frustrating it was to explain to witnesses that culpability was not transferable. You couldn't take the blame for the guilty party because your remaining years were fewer than theirs – or worth less. 'Sissy, were you aware of any of your neighbours searching the internet for information about deaths caused by domestic gas leaks?'

'No,' Sissy said. 'Definitely not.' Surely Em had not searched online on one of her own devices?

She had gone, once more, to stay with her parents, Ant had reported, failing to conceal how dejected he was. But now Sissy wondered if Em might in fact have taken Sam and run. Run from the police. And that maybe Ant had intuited this.

She understood that she had made a terrible mistake coming here and speaking as she had. Not only had she implicated the very person she'd hoped to keep from harm, but she'd also placed herself in peril. If DC Forrester had enough evidence to charge Em, then Em would have no choice but to try to make a deal, to offer something in return. A plea bargain. She'd deleted the clip of Sissy and the scaffolding from her phone, but not from her memory.

'The reason I had to keep you waiting earlier was we were viewing the results of Mr Booth's post mortem,' DC Forrester said, with a sudden, almost airy change of direction. She paused, as if deciding how much intelligence to gift Sissy in return for the little she'd confided. 'We've already let his next of kin know, so I think I can now tell you as well that his death wasn't caused by the effects of gas.'

Sissy, feeling her heart catch and her throat close, could only gape.

'He died of a condition called Sudden Unexplained Death Alcohol Misuse.'

'I don't know what that means,' Sissy said. She'd never heard of it.

'I'll let you look it up at home,' DC Forrester said, 'but as I understand it, the heart suffers an electrical fault that causes it to lose rhythm, triggered by long-term binge-drinking. It's only recently been named. SUDAM, it's known as, in case you want to let your WhatsApp group know.'

Their gazes met. How did she know about that? A lucky guess? More likely an educated one.

'Of course, this doesn't mean we aren't continuing to pursue the person who turned on the gas and *tried* to kill Mr Booth.'

Sissy felt her pulse quicken. 'You mean, it could still be seen as attempted murder?'

DC Forrester nodded. 'You look exhausted. Let me see if someone's free to take you home.' Then, as she got to her feet, 'And just to put your mind at rest, Sissy, the investigation you're most concerned about is still very much top of our agenda.'

Sissy stared at her, not following.

'Amy,' DC Forrester said, delicately.

Sissy rose, her heart a withered fruit in her chest. 'Amy. Of course.'

36

Tess

They were a little late for school, which meant they missed their customary detour through the park. The rigours of the school day were new to Dex, not least the necessity of getting dressed for it. Though he was returned to her with his jumper on inside out or with one his socks bearing another child's nametag, it was not encouraged that pupils arrive in this condition.

Tess checked on the cygnets on her way home, instead. There were still five, which in this precarious life was quite an achievement. She wondered who would leave first, their family or hers? If only departure were as easy for humans, just a few practice flights on the water and then one day the real thing. Lift off. You spied your new home from on high, made your descent and trusted in a happy integration.

They wouldn't make their own getaway quite yet, but wait until it was clearer what Jodie intended to do with number 1. She was still in contact with the police – Tess had seen DC Forrester visit her only yesterday – but everyone agreed that the removal of the cars was an excellent sign. Realistically, they would let Dex finish a full year at Lowland Primary, before moving the following summer and managing Isla's senior school applications from their new address, which would need a decent commuter link to London Bridge, the nearest mainline station to Ralph's business and Finn's new office.

Her gaze came to rest on a woman with a double buggy, a third child spraying the water with grain. She checked her FitBit – still half an hour before school pick up – and strode over.

'Hello, I hope you don't mind my asking, but are you Becky Wallace? The one who found the dead cygnet?'

Briefly stricken, the woman recovered quickly. 'I didn't know what to do. I had a box in the bottom of the buggy and I put it there. I didn't want them to . . .' Who she meant by 'them' and what she feared their doing was left unsaid.

Tess smiled. 'I'm glad you did. If it had been left for long, the rats and crows would have got to it. It was brave of you, though. You could have been attacked by the parent swans. Are these three yours?'

'Sean is. I just mind the twins.'

'My boy's about your age,' Tess told Sean. 'He's just started school this term. When do you start? Next year?'

'No,' the boy said, regarding Tess with deep suspicion.

'Yes,' his mum corrected him.

'Then you should meet Dex and he can tell you all about it. Have you heard of Play Out Sunday on Lowland Way? It's when we close the road and everyone can play in the street. We took a break over the summer, but we're starting up again this Sunday. You should come along.' Tess returned her attention to Becky. 'Would you like a quick coffee from the hut, my treat? We could ask the girls if they'd put up a permanent notice with the Swan Rescue number?'

She felt like Naomi, sweeping the woman along with an irresistible stream of offers and ideas, but the little boy was her counterweight, unseduced, whining at his mum to take him directly to the zip wire, and she stood uncertainly between them.

'Or maybe some other time,' Tess said, with an easy air. In her pocket, her phone buzzed and she checked the screen: a new WhatsApp message from Sissy. *I spoke to the police yesterday . . .*

For goodness' sake, would it never end?

She was about to move on, when Becky Wallace surprised her. 'No, now's good,' she said, smiling. 'Sean can hang on. A coffee would be really nice.'

37

Sissy

Pete was with her when the police came a final time. It was the Monday morning after her ill-conceived visit to the station and he had taken a day off work to help her make a start with the packing. The sale price had only just been agreed and the solicitors instructed, but it would take weeks to empty a 3,000-square-foot house of over thirty years' worth of possessions.

She remembered when she and Colin had arrived on the street, when she'd been pregnant with Pete. Jean had brought over a cherry cake for them, warm from the oven. Sissy still remembered the springy sweetness of it in her mouth, the pickled sourness of the fruit. They'd thought Jean ancient at fifty-five, a potential babysitter with no life of her own. 'It's not exactly party town, is it?' Colin had said. Lowland Way had felt more ordinary then. The mania for renovating houses had not yet taken hold of society and houses still had values that felt fair and affordable, nothing like the fabulous prices of today. Once everyone was paid off, she'd be fine. Fine or in prison, one of the two.

She had, at least, disposed of the cigarettes Em had given her, which she'd found, to her horror, in the pocket of the jacket she'd worn to the police station. Was that why Em had used gas instead of fire? Finding herself without her murder weapon, she'd had to improvise?

Pete arrived on the Sunday in good time for lunch. Roast lamb, the first proper meal Sissy had cooked since Amy died. It was his suggestion, not hers, that he should help pack. She would never have subjected him to such an emotional wringer, but his therapist had said it might be a positive part of his bid to move forwards, a dry run for the process of packing Amy's things, still untouched in their flat.

'It's all experimental now,' he told her, as they worked. 'It's all provisional,' and she didn't disagree.

All afternoon and into the night, they filled the boxes, one for every bin liner of discarded items. Sissy thought Pete's therapist very clever when she caught glimpses of the man he would be in a year's time. His spirit had been paralysed, but not destroyed. He would recover, he would renew.

'Is that the post?' he said, in the morning, when the doorbell rang. It was a little before 8 a.m. and, inspired by those thoughts of Jean, Sissy had made cherry muffins for breakfast.

'Or a reporter,' she said, dismally. 'I'll get rid of them.'

But, on the doorstep, she found DC Forrester. She had a small stain of white in the corner of her mouth that Sissy supposed was toothpaste. A male colleague Sissy hadn't met before waited on the path behind her.

'This is my colleague, DC Nardini,' the detective said, with the lack of preamble of a close friend. 'With your permission,

I'd like him to search the room upstairs at the front. Would that be all right?'

Pete strode forwards to stand abreast of Sissy. 'What's going on? What exactly are you looking for?'

'I'll explain while he works, if that's okay?' Scrupulously awaiting Sissy's nod, DC Forrester released her colleague up the stairs and accepted Sissy's offer of coffee and muffins.

This must be it, Sissy thought. The other detective was searching for clothing, fibres to match those found on the scaffolding. Or on the tools she'd used, perhaps. It was remarkable how unafraid she felt, sitting at the kitchen table with Pete by her side. As it was, DC Forrester disarmed her by complimenting her on her baking, before smilingly detonating her bomb: 'We can now tell you that it *was* Darren Booth who broke into your house on August the twenty-third.'

Sissy's heart pumped with brutal force. 'I knew it was him! I told the officers who came and they went to speak to him, but they insisted he had nothing to do with it.'

'It's likely they were looking for evidence of theft, but Darren Booth entered your house with the purpose of *leaving* something, not removing it. He was installing a camera.'

'What? You mean . . .' Sissy stumbled, horrified. 'He was watching me?'

'Not you. He was watching his own house. From what we can judge from the material we have, the camera is in one of your first-floor windows.'

'The material you have?' Sissy repeated, over the continued smacking of her own heartbeat.

'Stored on one of his phones,' DC Forrester said. 'Our

downloaders have now been able to collect all the video – he set it up so he could look at it remotely.'

'How could someone do that?' Sissy's technological skills were rudimentary; she knew only enough to check that her bills were correct and to supply the internet password to her customers. 'Wouldn't he need my internet details?'

The detective nodded. 'We've been able to discover that he used the password he found on a sticker on your router.'

Pete took over the explanation: 'You know when you access the internet, Mum, different networks are listed? They're the networks in range, neighbours' providers. With the password in his possession, this guy would have been able to access yours whenever he liked.'

'Thank you,' said DC Forrester, who'd finished her muffin, including the crumbs.

She'd 'been able to discover' what she had from Jodie, Sissy presumed. 'Did Jodie tell you why he felt the need to do this? He already had a camera of his own to protect his premises.'

'His aim was to improve his security following the scaffolding collapse. He wanted to record any further attempts on his life. He expected his own camera to be a target for vandalism and he was proved right. As you may know, it was disabled by one of the neighbours the weekend before his death.'

'Yes.' Sissy felt nausea choke her airways. One thought dominated all others: whether or not the camera was found, the police now had video of the night Booth died.

DC Forrester awaited her gaze, speaking again only when she had it. 'It looks as though you *did* leave your house a second time that night.'

'What night? Mum?' Pete didn't understand and she wished with all her heart he was not present for where this discussion might lead them. She had the unearthly sensation of having been hypnotised, which she knew could not be right. It was important to order her thoughts, plan the course ahead, with all its possible obstacles.

'Yes. I went across to the Kendalls – or, at least, I got halfway. Em asked me to get Sam's toy, a giraffe he sleeps with. They've been having a lot of problems with his sleeping.'

'I know all about that,' DC Forrester said, with a small smile.

'You have a baby?'

'She's three now. But she was a terrible sleeper the first year.'

Was she saying this to humanize herself, to lull Sissy into a false sense of security? Unsure, Sissy stayed silent and so DC Forrester resumed her questioning: 'Why did Em not get the toy herself? Or ask her husband to go?'

'I suppose because I was still up. I offered. But Ant came after me and he went to get it and I came back home.'

Exactly as it would be on the video.

'You dropped something, I think?'

Sissy thought back, thankful that her heart was drumming less violently now. 'Yes, that's right. Just Em's keys. I gave them to Ant.' Would the police be able to lip-read her conversation with him? Surely not, the video was hardly likely to be MI5 levels of clarity.

There was a call from the top of the stairs – 'Eithne!' – and DC Forrester led the little group to the master bedroom, where Sissy and Pete were allowed to see the small, flat camera found attached to the back of the chest of drawers and now being bagged as evidence.

'It's a shame it wasn't set up for the night before Amy died,' Pete remarked.

'Not every crime is so conveniently recorded,' DC Forrester told him.

Oh, Em, Sissy thought.

She and Pete stayed in the room after the detectives left, he at the window and she in the armchair by the bed, exhausted by the combination of raid and reprieve. The bedclothes were crumpled, the pillows flattened. When Pete had said he was going to stay the night, Sissy had wondered if he'd choose the bedroom in which Amy had slept her last sleep, but instead he'd suggested this one. Seeing him at the window, she understood now that he'd chosen it in order to be able to study the scene of Amy's death. To imagine it and then to extinguish what he'd imagined.

'They're heading across the road now,' he reported. 'The woman who was just here and the guy I've met before. DC Shah. He must have been waiting in the car.'

'Really? I didn't think Em was home.' She hadn't bolted then – the idea seemed preposterous now. More likely the police had demanded she return, threatened her with an arrest at her parents' house, in front of their community. Should Sissy warn her on WhatsApp? Where was her phone? In the kitchen, charging. She'd told the group about Booth's post-mortem results the morning after she'd learned of them herself, but this was different. This could be construed as tipping off the guilty party, conspiring to evade capture or something of that kind.

'Oh my God, they've got their cuffs out!' Pete exclaimed, and Sissy rose to her feet as if having been read her rights herself. She would be next, that much was certain, for she and Em were joined, their two fates sealed or spared as one. She felt not fear now, but sorrow, the most tremendous sorrow. For Em, for Sam, for all of them.

'Poor Em, this is terrible. Really terrible.'

'No, it's not her they've got,' Pete said. 'It's a man.'

'Let me see!' But by the time Sissy got to the window, Ant Kendall was already in the back of the squad car, head bowed low as if in prayer, as the vehicle pulled away.

38

Ant

—Anthony Kendall, Three Lowland Way, Lowland Gardens. Yes, I understand this interview is being taped.

—What do I know about natural gas? That's your first question? I know it didn't kill Darren Booth, even though that's what the papers said.

—No, I don't mean I thought it could *kill, I mean I assumed from the press that it did kill him, but I learned from a neighbour that it was in fact this binge-drinking syndrome. Well, I can vouch for the heavy drinking, if that helps?*

—I did google 'gas hobs', yes. Ours was broken and I wanted to find out how to fix it and if it was dangerous to carry on using it.

—If you say so, yes, I was online for forty minutes – there was a lot to find out.

—No, I decided I'd call a gas engineer. I didn't

want to risk doing anything myself, not with a baby in the house.

—No, I haven't made that call yet. I haven't got around to it.

—What? I told you why I smashed his camera, I was upset about Sam's hearing problems. It was nothing to do with this.

—No, I wasn't trying to disable it in advance. I didn't even plan what I was going to hit, I just saw red and started smashing things. It was a one-off.

—What the hell . . . ? That video image is of me, yes. Oh my God. Where did this come from? Who took this?

—Yes, that's me. Oh, God.

—I'm crossing the road from my neighbour Sissy Watkins' house towards my own and I'm putting a hand on her shoulder.

—The date and time reads the seventh of September, two oh nine.

—I was asking her what she was doing and she said she was fetching Sam's toy giraffe for Em. I said I'd go in and get it and she should go back. Which she did.

—I wouldn't call it a long discussion, no.

—I'm taking the keys to my house, that's all. The ones Em had given Sissy. I went into the house and I went upstairs to get the giraffe.

—No, I didn't come straight out. It's on your video, I guess. I sat in the living room, I don't know, just thinking.

—Not particularly unusual, no. We're up a lot in the night, because of noise issues from next door.

—Yes, that's my wife. She's crossing the road and knocking at the window. I went to the door and let her in.

—The time is two twenty a.m.

—We talked for a few minutes, yes. She just wanted to know why I'd followed Sissy over. She said Sam was asleep.

—That's her returning to Sissy's place. Look, before we go any further, can I just state clearly that neither Sissy nor Em knew what I was going to do next. They didn't know anything. I mean, I didn't know myself!

—Yes, that's me. I'm approaching the door of number one. The time is two forty-six a.m.

—I'd had the keys since the day of the scaffolding collapse. I saw them on the ground and I grabbed them.

—No, no one else knew I had them.

—No, I swear I didn't have a plan. I don't know what I was thinking. I was just tempted to go in and look around. I suppose I wasn't feeling normal feelings, like I should have been scared, shouldn't I? He's done aggressive things to us in the past and I could have been attacked if he heard me. All I can say is it was like it wasn't me. It was like I was watching myself do it, a weird, out-of-body feeling.

—I closed the door behind me and waited in the hallway. I couldn't hear anything and I assumed he

was upstairs in bed. I knew Jodie was out of town and was going to be away all week. I crept a few steps towards the living-room door and I got the shock of my life because he was right there! Asleep *on the sofa.*

—No, not snoring or making any noise, just lying there, his right arm over his face. You *don't think... You don't think he might already have been dead?*

—Well, I just stood there, completely frozen, thinking he would wake up and see me, but then I saw there were cans everywhere, he'd obviously drunk a hell of a lot and was out for the count.

—I knew I had to leave, that I shouldn't be there. I tried to leave, but I couldn't get the front door open again, it had some funny mechanism that I couldn't work out in the dark and I didn't want to risk putting a light on. I had no choice but to sneak past him through the living room to the kitchen and use the back door.

—There was no smell of gas, no, not that I remember, but I had a bad cold, so I might not have smelled it. Em and Sissy will tell you that, or the people I work with.

—I didn't look at the hob, no, so I couldn't have seen if one of the knobs was turned.

—I opened the back door and when I closed it behind me it locked automatically. I dropped the keys by the fence and kicked a bit of soil over them. Then I came around the side of the house – there's a gate with a bolt and it was easy to open.

—Yes, that's me. The time is two fifty a.m. I was

on the premises for four minutes. Wait, you'd have fingerprints on the knob, wouldn't you, if I'd turned it on? And you don't, do you? Other than this video, what's your evidence?

—Of course, I see it looks bad that I went into his house in the middle of the night. But he went into Sissy's, didn't he? No one arrested him for that. People do weird, illegal things, but that's not the same as trying to kill someone.

—No, I wasn't thinking that he'd be dead by morning, why would I? I didn't touch the gas! You have to believe me, when I heard the news, I was as shocked as everyone else. Anyway, if the gas didn't kill him, what does it matter? I don't know why I'm here, why we need to discuss this.

—Fine. Yes, I went back to Sissy's house and went to bed. Em had left the door on the latch. She and Sam were both asleep and they were still asleep when I got up and went to work. Talk to my colleagues – ask them if they think a murderer came into work that morning!

—No, that's not right. I was the last person to see him alive, that might be true, but I didn't do anything to harm him, I swear.

—I disagree with that. You're putting two and two together and making five. D'you know what? All along you've been looking for some kind of clever plot, but maybe the reality is that they were the bad guys, not us? They've been the bad guys all along.

—No, no comment from now on. This is

harassment. What's the process from here? I'd like to talk privately with my solicitor. I'd like to phone my wife. When will I be allowed to see my son?

Recorded interview with Mr Anthony Morgan, 3 Lowland Way, by DC Shah and DC Forrester at Milkwood Lane Police Station, 17 September 2018.

They'd come for him at eight thirty, when he was about to leave for the train, reached the police station at about the time he would have been halfway to Victoria, watching an episode of something on his phone or reading the morning briefing on the *Guardian* website. He was taken through the back yard and through a metal gate and then booked into custody. It happened as if to someone else, in front of his eyes, and only later was he able to remember all the component pieces: he'd been searched and had his possessions removed, except for his wedding ring; given the opportunity to see a nurse (he'd said no, he was fit and well, though hungover, and the custody sergeant had chuckled at that); asked if he had his own solicitor or if one should be provided from the duty scheme (he'd been grateful to accept the latter); he'd had photographs, fingerprints and DNA taken.

It must have taken almost five hours in all.

Then the interview, with his assigned solicitor by his side, a woman called Harriet who he hadn't known existed until today but who now appeared to be the only person on deck to have noticed him in the water, drowning.

*

After the interview, he was taken to a cell while the detectives sought to persuade the CPS that they should go ahead and charge him. The cell had a narrow bench with a mattress, a high frosted window far from reach, a metallic toilet bowl. The temperature was okay, the atmosphere actually less bleak than he might have expected, but he felt naked and helpless without his phone. Extraordinary to think that this morning he'd planned to go to work, that the clothes he wore had been selected for a day at White Willow Foods & Drinks, not prison.

They were going for the attempted murder charge, Harriet said, which was 'a bit of a stretch' even by police standards.

'They've got the wrong man,' Ant told her. It was funny how people reached for clichés when finding themselves in terrible jeopardy. Perhaps it was a survival thing, the limitation of vocabulary, to preserve brainpower for life-or-death thinking.

Harriet had been able to view the post-mortem results and confirm that there were not harmful amounts of gas from the hob in Booth's lung tissue or bloodstream.

'So if Booth definitely died of this alcohol-related thing, why are they bothering with the gas?' Ant asked.

'Attempted murder involves the intention to kill, even if the attempt fails,' she explained. 'The police will have to prove you believed the gas could kill and that you intended it to kill him. They'll also be trying to find a medical expert who says the gas might have been a contributory factor. The slightest possibility, if it's credible, is bad news for us.'

The problem Ant had – well, there were several problems, but the chief ones appeared to be: the video of his break-in, recorded by a camera hidden in Sissy's bedroom; his Google search about the workings of gas hobs; and his (witnessed) destruction of the Booths' security camera, the only one of which he and the other neighbours had actually been aware.

But there was reasonable doubt, Harriet said. There was Tess's testimony about the unattended gas ring and multiple other accounts of the deceased's carelessness. Crucially, Em and Sissy would confirm Ant's having had a heavy cold, which meant the gas could already have been flowing when he entered the house.

'They've got a case, but it's not the strongest I've seen,' she concluded.

'They've got the wrong man,' Ant repeated.

'Who's the right man, do you think?' Harriet asked, but he could tell she didn't really expect an answer.

39

Ralph

He'd been circling the streets of the Rushmoor Estate for so long he worried he might get picked up for kerb crawling. Not that there were any prostitutes here, it was pretty decent in that respect, as far as he knew. Drugs, yes. Those spoons lying around, they hadn't been used for stirring sugar into cups of Earl Grey, oh no. And that couple, trailing along the pavement towards the shop by the Star, pupils massive, they were totally clean, right.

Cars – some of them pretty pricey models – were parked bumper to bumper; there was nowhere to pull over if he wanted to.

The previous morning on Lowland Way, Jodie had been out front directing two guys in boiler suits as they systematically removed the last of Booth's cars from the street. Evidently, she was offloading them as a job lot to some other salesman, or else she was selling them for scrap. The camper van would have to be dealt with separately, she'd told Tess, its battery now dead, surprise, surprise. She seemed to regard

Tess, discoverer of her husband's body, as the only neighbour above suspicion. Even so, Tess had not raised with her the subject of Darren's post mortem (they weren't getting on *that* well) and the extraordinary new information regarding his cause of death had originated from Sissy.

At last, Ralph spotted the girl he'd come looking for. She was with her baby and a couple of mates, plus a bunch of pre-schoolers, at a miserable little square with swings and a climbing frame. Quite apart from the fact that it was after seven and kids this age should be heading to bed by now, what were they doing here when they could have walked ten minutes to a beautiful park with a landscaped kids' zone and hundreds of trees?

He pulled over in the 'No Parking' zone by the gate and unwound the window. 'Hey, you in the silver jacket? Can I have a word?'

The group ignored him.

He turned off the engine, unbuckled his seatbelt and opened the door. Never in all his previous drives through the estate had he actually left the car. On foot, he'd never come as deep as this, only as far as the Star, sprinting distance from Lowland Gardens. The sky was cold, the air close and granular: it was like entering the atmosphere of a different planet after the sealed neutrality of his BMW.

Locking the car, he strolled over to the group and stood in front of the girl in the silver jacket. The others cast sidelong glances at their friend, who stuck her chin out and glared up at him. 'You probably don't even remember me,' he said. 'We ran into each other a couple of streets over, back in July.' He'd remembered her from their fight as diabolical, but she was actually quite sweet-looking. Smooth-skinned and comically skinny, just a kid really.

'Oh yeah. He's the one who almost ran me over,' she told her friends.

'I should have slowed down, I admit, but you shouldn't have been walking in the middle of the road like that. It's not in the best interests of your kid, is it?'

She screwed up her face as if he'd addressed her in Cantonese.

'Also, it's not good to show that kind of anger in front of your kid.' He gestured to the buggy, as if she might have forgotten which child was hers. 'You don't want to pass aggressive behaviour down to the next gen, do you?'

The group snickered at 'next gen'. He felt as ancient and ridiculous as he knew they perceived him to be.

'What d'you want?' the girl asked him, and her friends looked at him in voiceless echo. What do you want? *What do you want?*

What *did* he want? It was like being asked the meaning of life.

Becoming aware of peripheral characters approaching like zombies, perhaps sensing the only working brain in range, he held the girl's gaze. 'I just wanted to say I'm sorry.' He offered her a business card, unsure whether she and her mates even knew information could come in printed form. 'If you ever need anything, maybe work experience or a job, phone me. I'd like to help.'

The friends cackled with derision. 'Phone him, Leesha, he'd like to help!'

'He wants to get in your knickers, Leesh, what's your new boyfriend gonna say about that?'

The girl reared, angry. 'Don't say my name, you idiots!'

'Shut up.'

'You shut up.'

Unexpectedly, she brushed off her crowd and looked at Ralph as if they were the only two present. Was it too much to hope for a moment of connection in this, his first ever attempt at community outreach beyond his own street? Something profound that would have a lasting effect on both of them? It seemed to him she was wavering, until she smirked at her mates and aimed a kick in his direction. 'Fuck off, perv.'

But she took the card. Slipped it in her pocket, eyes averted.

Ralph grinned and made for his car, now the object of attention of a trio of teens. 'Off!' he barked in his best parental tones and they abused him in return with a vocabulary he might once have understood but now did not.

He was just pulling into Lowland Way when Naomi phoned, her voice coming through the speakers and filling the leather-and-chrome interior with its low, buttery tones: 'I've just got back from work and heard the most incredible news from Tess. Ant Kendall has been charged with attempted murder!'

Ralph's right foot made involuntary contact with the brake pedal, causing him to lurch forwards. 'Are you serious? Booth's or Amy's?'

'Booth's.'

Of course. The attempt on Amy had succeeded.

'I think they've given up on Amy,' Naomi said. 'Not that I would say that to Sissy, but it's been over a month now. Unless someone confesses, I don't see what more they can do.'

Ralph was inclined to agree. 'Ant, though? Poor bastard,

that can't be right.' In a summer of shocks, none astounded him more than this. 'Listen, I'm just pulling up, babe, so I'll see you in a second.'

In spite of the awful news, the agonized discussions that awaited him, both with Naomi and the other neighbours, his mouth curved into a smile as he spied the empty space outside his house. At last, the camper van was gone and he was able to park the BMW by his own gate, back where it belonged.

40

Ant

He had been charged. He had been charged and remanded in custody until a later, unspecified date when his trial would take place. Though the facility in which he was held was modern and well run, his future resembled the abyss itself: lightless and unknowable.

He had at last been allowed to phone Em and she'd promised to leave Sam with her parents and dash back to London. 'Just keep on telling the truth,' she urged. 'You didn't do anything.'

Ant imagined a courtroom, with Em and Sissy and the Morgans sitting in a line, watching him. Not a single one of them was religious, but they would pray for him and talk together about keeping the faith. They would agree it was a blessing that Sam was too young to understand what was happening to his father. He'll be found not guilty, they'd tell Em, but even if the worst happens, Sam's got you and that will be enough.

Ant agreed with this fictitious platitude. No matter how

many times the police interviewed him, no matter how skilful the prosecuting barrister, he would never implicate Em. Sam needed his mother and that was all there was to it.

Gradually, however, as one blank day blurred into the next, the irony of his predicament sharpened and it was this, not his many deprivations, that tempted him to beat his fists against the cell door as he'd heard other inmates do. If the gas had killed Booth, either through suffocation or by deadly blast, the risk might have been worth it. But it had not and now he might be sentenced for intention alone.

Even if he didn't know himself what his intention had been.

The night shadows of their living room had been heartbreakingly familiar from countless nights up with Sam, the light from the streetlamp on the corner of Portsmouth Avenue making a monster of the high-backed armchair in the corner, the shade at the foot of the curtains like black pools of blood. Em's angry face at the window did not belong to his wife but to some vengeful spirit who had taken possession of her.

He opened the door and her fury preceded her, chasing him into the depths of the hallway, cornering him.

'I know Sissy told you. I know she gave you the keys. I want them back. You might have stopped her, but you're not stopping me.'

He'd stared at her, uncomprehending. 'Why is Sissy helping you? I know you must have set it up that she would come over and persuade us to sleep there? Why would she go along with something so dangerous?'

Em paused and there was an illusion of thoughtfulness before she spewed her words: 'Why'd you think? Because she's not a fucking coward like you! No one's asking *you* to do anything, Ant, just give me the keys and go.'

'No.'

'Give me them or tomorrow I find a solicitor and start divorce proceedings.'

Though Ant felt heat rising to his face, he was not scared of her. She was unidentifiable as herself, but she was still Em, the mother of his son. She was a good mother. 'I'm not giving you the keys, Em. Go back over, forget this nonsense.'

'Fine. Then we're no longer married.'

'That's ridiculous!'

Though her eyes glowed as if bewitched, her words were cruelly human: 'You have a choice. Give me the keys and stay married, or stand here and do nothing and in the morning Sam and I will be gone. For good. Your choice.'

'I'm not giving you the keys,' Ant said.

'That's it then. That's it.' She kicked out then, making contact with the wall, and then her small clenched fist smashed into his shoulder. It took all his strength to battle her furious body towards the door.

When she'd gone, he sat for some minutes, breathing heavily, Booth's keys clutched in his aching fingers, Em's words tormenting him:

No one's asking you *to do anything.*

Fucking coward.

All at once, nothing was the same, nothing felt real. Wild thoughts flared, rogue impulses that caused his thigh muscles to spasm. He answered Em soundlessly, angrily, his lips moving:

I am not a coward.

Didn't I smash up his place?

Maybe I should have smashed him?

Propelled by instinct, not purpose, he left number 3 and approached number 1. The night was so still he started at a sound from Portsmouth Avenue – the belch of the night bus – but paused for only a moment, confident that no neigbour would appear around the corner. Any resident of Lowland Way out so late would be shuttled home in a taxi or their own private car.

Turning the key and stepping inside made him feel so powerful – to be defying Em and challenging Booth in one act! About to prowl around downstairs while the enemy lay feet away in a room above, alone and vulnerable.

But then he saw him: Booth, right there, dead to the world on his sofa island in a sea of cans and junk food wrappers. He waited, completely still, as if underwater, lung function suspended. Only when he was confident Booth wasn't about to wake did he allow himself to inhale. He thought about Em's plan. It was obvious it would have failed. Different if Booth had been upstairs in bed, but not here, where the smoke and heat would have been so close – and that was if a burning cigarette ignited the sofa fabric in the first place.

He turned back to the front door, intending to leave, but he couldn't work the lock and felt his body flood with a fresh tide of adrenaline. Was he trapped?

Don't panic, he thought. He'd leave by the kitchen door.

It was as he crept, soft-footed, past Booth's sleeping body and through to the kitchen that the memory had come to him, as if by divine revelation: Tess telling him how she'd found the flame unattended. *It could have blown out and gassed the pair of them*, she'd said. Just like his own defective model next door. He drew to a halt. There was a roll of kitchen towel on its side and he took a square from it. Then, covering his fingers with it, he turned the knob for the front left-hand ring. Let the gas flow. He didn't know how long it would go on for, he didn't know if it had some sort of safety catch and would cut out automatically after a certain time if left unlit. It was the same hob Jean had used for years, so there were probably no safety features.

He imagined Booth waking in the morning and reaching for his cigarettes. When the lighter sparked, it would ignite the gas in the room and Booth would be no more.

He liked that phrase: *be no more*. It had a sense of the abstract, a serenity.

He kept the kitchen roll in his fist. He would shred it and flush it down the loo. There'd be no evidence.

Back at Sissy's, in their bedroom at the back, Em was asleep, her face turned to the wall. Whatever demon had possessed her had now left her to her rest.

Sam whimpered and Ant put a soothing hand on his tummy. 'Shh, back to sleep.'

The whimpering faded and for once, in Ant's world, there was silence.

The prison staff were very fair about access to solicitors and the space in which his meetings with Harriet took place was private and well ventilated. When she talked him through the process that lay ahead, describing the highly regarded team who would do battle on his behalf, Ant found he could visualize himself as a hero of the trial – a victim, no less! Not guilty and back in his house on Lowland Way as if nothing had happened. Drinking his wine, checking his phone, being subjected to the music from next door.

How long between now and then? Would Jodie still be in residence? He hoped she would be. After his companions in prison, she'd be a welcome neighbour, a consoling presence on the other side of the wall.

He often thought about the night before his arrest. He'd returned home from the off-licence and opened a bottle of Cab Sav the moment he closed the door behind him, the glass angled in readiness, not a second to lose. The glug-glug of the liquid was comforting, but the evening ahead felt enormous and unfillable. Booth was gone, but so was Em. So was Sam.

He couldn't be bothered to search the TV channels for something to hold his ragged attention, but when he heard Jodie turn hers on next door, he listened to the dialogue as if to a radio drama, straining to hear whenever voices were lowered. It was a soap, something to do with a falling out between bride and bridesmaid. He struggled to make the first bottle of wine last longer than an hour.

When he became aware of Jodie opening her front door and leaving the house, he found himself doing the same. She was standing by her living-room window, smoking, the drive and garden vacant now of all cars but Darren's white van and an old Toyota. The evening air was pleasingly sharp.

Ant called out to her: 'I realize I haven't offered you my condolences. How are you?'

Her eye contact was grudging. 'How d'you *think* I am?'

He stepped closer. 'You've been through a hell of a lot. If there's anything I can do . . .' He gave an open-armed shrug, as if his helpfulness had no bounds, and smiled. He had an image of her offering him a cigarette and them smoking together, speechless and exhausted, survivors of the apocalypse returned to civilization.

But when he met her eye, she was looking at him with abject scorn. 'No point being all friendly *now*,' she said.

41

Jodie

—No, you've got the wrong end of the stick. The house was Darren's, not mine. We're not married or nothing. It made me laugh when the neighbours called me Mrs Booth. That's how miserable they are, never even bothered to find out my name!

—One hundred per cent sure. He only owned it for a few months, anyway, I've got no claim. No such thing as common law rights in the UK, apparently. The only thing in my name is the car I drove here in. And you know what else? He didn't have no will. The solicitor said he should get one sorted after he inherited the house, but he hadn't got round to it.

—He did have a brother, but he died years ago. It'll be his nephew who gets it. Liam, he's called. Lives on the Rushmoor Estate, not far from us. From me. He's Darren's next of kin. I spoke to him yesterday, asked him if he knew Darren had accepted an offer on the place but he says the lawyer reckons he's better

off tax-wise if he lives in it for a bit. Tax-wise! Like he's ever paid a penny of tax in his life! You probably know him, actually, he's had a couple of run-ins with the law. Did six months inside a few years ago. Assault, it was. You don't want to get on the wrong side of Liam, that's all I'll say. His new girlfriend gives as good as she gets, mind you. She's a character, is Leesha, got a serious gob on her. Got a baby as well, I don't know how Liam'll cope with that.

—Why am I laughing? I'm laughing because I just thought: if the people on this street didn't like us, they definitely won't like them. They won't like them at all.

MS JODIE RAYNOR, 1 LOWLAND WAY, INTERVIEWED BY DC SHAH AND DC FORRESTER AT MILKWOOD LANE POLICE STATION, 19 SEPTEMBER 2018.

She would have liked to have seen Ant Kendall for herself before she left the police station. Looked him in the eye and asked him why in hell's name he should want to steal their key and let himself into their house. Attempt to kill an innocent man, a next-door neighbour! What kind of a psycho had that level of hate in them? But he'd been moved to a remand facility, DC Shah said, somewhere down near Woolwich.

'Thank you for coming in,' he said to her, as they exited the interview room. 'I can assure you you're under no suspicion whatsoever and we're here to support you.'

That was a laugh – he couldn't get rid of her fast enough once he knew she wasn't inheriting anything and had no motive to harm Darren. It had taken a while for her to realize they were interviewing her about the scaffolding – apparently they hadn't been able to pin *that* on Ant Kendall. A right cheek to act like it might have been her!

'So you'll keep going with this?' she asked him, as he escorted her through the corridors to the reception area. 'With what happened to the girl? The family'll want closure, yeah?' She cared for Sissy Watkins' sake, if no one else's. Much as she found the woman annoying, Jodie respected her grief. Weren't they in the same boat now? Sissy had as much of a right to know who'd hurt *her* loved one as Jodie did hers.

She had not seen Amy Pope alive, only dead (it sounded weird to say it like that: *only* dead). Darren had been the last person to see her alive and now he was gone, as well.

'We'll keep going until we find the person responsible,' DC Shah said. 'I'm about to talk to another potential witness now, in fact.'

Just before reception there was a windowless waiting area and he pulled up there to say something to another member of staff. Jodie's eye was caught by a seated male figure, whose body language expressed exactly the same reluctance and mistrust of his surroundings that Jodie felt. Now she thought about it, his face was half-familiar. She couldn't place him, but in the split second of eye contact between them, she got the feeling he recognized her too.

'Are you DC Shah?' he said, his attention switching to the detective. His voice was not familiar, a Midlands accent. 'I told you on the phone, this is a total waste of time. I've got nothing to say.'

'I'll be with you in two minutes,' DC Shah said, and ushered Jodie on.

'Who was that?' she asked, but of course he wouldn't tell her. He was only interested in asking the questions, not answering them.

It was only as she buckled into the old Toyota – the last of their cars, even the camper van Darren had loved so much had gone now – that it came to her. She'd seen him once on Lowland Way.

Darren had been smoking out of their bedroom window one night, about a week before the scaffolding collapsed. 'Jodes, come and see this!' He was drunk, a bit unsteady, leaning right out the window and snickering. 'I told you she needed a good shag, didn't I?'

'Who?'

'Sissy Spacek. 'Cross the road.'

Jodie joined him, had a cigarette herself while she was at it. It took away the horrible smell of scaffolding, which she made a point of never touching in case she caught something. Upstairs at number 2, there was an old guy at the bedroom window. Naked, by the looks of it. 'What're you on about? He'll just be one of her guests. She probably sleeps at the back,' she told Darren.

'No, no, she's in there as well. I just saw her. You wait.'

He was right, the guy was turning and talking to someone in the room, and suddenly Sissy popped up right by his side, smiling. It was funny seeing her in a couple like that.

'I think it's nice,' she said. 'Everyone gets a bit lonely sometimes, don't they?'

And Darren had put his arm around her then, kept it there while they finished their cigarettes.

Sitting there, in the Toyota, she felt tears coming, as they always did when she thought about Darren and all his contradictions. He'd say something mean like that thing about Sissy needing a shag, and then he'd *do* something nice. Blinking, she turned the ignition on and thought again of the face of the man she'd seen at the station. Yes, Sissy's friend. It was definitely him. It beat Jodie why he should have been summoned here to be questioned about Darren's scaffolding, but whatever he'd done, whatever he'd seen, she had a feeling DC Shah would get it out of him.

With a greater sense of resolution than she'd felt in some time, she indicated right and set off for Lowland Way.

Acknowledgements

Firstly, I would like to thank Jo Dickinson of Simon & Schuster and Danielle Perez of Berkley, to whom this book is dedicated. Your contributions have been transformative and are immensely appreciated, even – maybe especially – when they involved urging me to 'lose fifteen thousand words from the middle'.

The teams at Simon & Schuster and Berkley are both magnificent and I hope I'm not missing anyone out when I thank, at Berkley: Fareeda Bullert, Loren Jaggers, Jenn Snyder, Ivan Held, Christine Ball, Jeanne Marie Hudson, Craig Burke and Claire Zion; and at S&S: Sara-Jade Virtue, Jess Barratt, Hayley McMullan, Laura Hough, Dom Brendon, Joe Roche, Maddie Allan, Gill Richardson, Emma Capron, Alice Rodgers, Susan Opie, Saxon Bullock.

Thank you to designers Katie Anderson (US) and Pip Watkins (UK) for their exceptional covers.

My grateful thanks also and as ever to Sheila Crowley, Deborah Schneider, Luke Speed, Abbie Greaves, Ciara Finan,

Sophia Macaskill, Claire Nozieres, Katie McGowan, Callum Mollison and Alice Lutyens – what a team!

I am indebted to Lisa Cutts for her police expertise – and generosity in sharing it. Any mistakes are of course my own and would certainly not be found in Lisa's own brilliant novels.

There is an army of retailers, journalists, librarians and fellow authors on both sides of the Atlantic who have championed my work over the last year or two and who continue to do so. Thank you from the bottom of my heart, everyone! Without you I would be my only reader.

I raise a glass once more to my family and chums, including Nips, Greta, Mats 'n' Jo.

Finally, my apologies to Metallica, Motörhead et al. While I would be happy to have your music booming through my walls from the house next door, I have worked on the assumption that there are those in our more tranquil communities who would not.

If you enjoyed *Those People* you will love

our house

Turn the page for an extract from
Louise Candlish's *Sunday Times* bestseller

1

Friday, 13 January 2017

London, 12.30 p.m.

She must be mistaken, but it looks exactly as if someone is moving into her house.

The van is parked halfway down Trinity Avenue, its square mouth agape, a large piece of furniture sliding down the ribbed metal tongue. Fi watches, squinting into the buttery sunlight – rare for the time of year, a gift – as the object is borne shoulder-high by two men through the gate and down the path.

My gate. My path.

No, that's illogical: of course it can't be her house. It must be the Reeces', two down from hers; they put their place on the market in the autumn and no one is quite sure if a sale has gone through. The houses on this side of Trinity Avenue are all built the same – red-brick double-fronted Edwardians in pairs, their owners united in a preference for front doors painted black – and everyone agrees it's easy to miscount.

Once, when Bram came stumbling home from one of his 'quick' drinks at the Two Brewers, he went to the wrong door and she heard through the open bedroom window the scrambling and huffing as her inebriated husband failed to fit his key into the lock of number 87, Merle and Adrian's place. His persistence was staggering, his dogged belief that if he only kept on trying the key *would* work.

'But they all look the same,' he'd protested in the morning.

'The houses, yes, but even a drunk couldn't miss the magnolia,' Fi had told him, laughing. (This was back when she was still amused by his inebriety and not filled with sadness – or disdain, depending on her mood.)

Her step falters: the magnolia. It's a landmark, their tree, a celebrated sight when in blossom and beautiful even when bare, as it is now, the outer twigs etched into the sky with an artist's flair. And it is definitely in the front garden of the house with the van outside.

Think. It must be a delivery, something for Bram that he hasn't mentioned to her. Not every detail gets communicated; they both accept that their new system isn't flawless. Hurrying again, using her fingers as a sun visor, she's near enough to be able to read the lettering on the side of the vehicle: PRESTIGE HOME REMOVALS. It *is* a house move, then. Friends of Bram must be dropping something off en route to somewhere. If she were able to choose, it would be an old piano for the boys (*please, Lord, not a drum kit*).

But wait, the deliverymen have reappeared and now more items are being transported from van to house: a dining chair; a large round metallic tray; a box labelled FRAGILE; a small, slim wardrobe the size of a coffin. *Whose things are these?* A rush of anger fires her blood as she reaches the only possible conclusion: Bram has invited someone to stay. Some dispossessed drinking pal, no doubt, with nowhere else to go. ('Stay as long as you like, mate, we've got bags of room.') When the hell was he going to tell her? Well, there's no way a stranger is sharing their home, however temporarily, however charitable Bram's intentions. The kids come first: isn't that the point?

Lately, she worries they've forgotten the point.

She's almost there. As she passes number 87, she's aware of Merle at the first-floor window, face cast in a frown, arm raised for Fi's attention. Fi makes only the briefest of acknowledgements as she strides through her own gate and onto the tiled path.

'Excuse me? What's going on here?' But in the clamour no one seems to hear. Louder now, sharper: 'What are you doing with all this stuff? Where's Bram?'

A woman she doesn't know comes out of the house and stands on the doorstep, smiling. 'Hello, can I help?'

She gasps as if at an apparition. *This* is Bram's friend in need? Familiar by type rather than feature, she is one of Fi's own – though younger, in her thirties – blonde and brisk and cheerful, the sort to roll up her sleeves and take charge. The sort, as history testifies, to constrain a free spirit like Bram. 'I hope so, yes. I'm Fi, Bram's wife. What's going on here? Are you . . . are you a friend of his?'

The woman steps closer, purposeful, polite. 'Sorry, whose wife?'

'Bram's. I mean ex-wife, really.' The correction earns a curious look, followed by the suggestion that the two of them move off the path and out of the way of 'the guys'. As a huge bubble-wrapped canvas glides by, Fi allows herself to be steered under the ribs of the magnolia. 'What on earth has he agreed to here?' she demands. 'Whatever it is, I know nothing about it.'

'I'm not sure what you mean.' There is a faint puckering of the woman's forehead as she studies Fi. Her eyes are golden-brown and honest. 'Are you a neighbour?'

'No, of course not.' Fi is becoming impatient. 'I live here.'

The puckering deepens. 'I don't think so. We're just moving in. My husband will be here soon with the second van. We're the Vaughans?' She says it as though Fi might have heard of them, even offers her hand for a formal shake. 'I'm Lucy.'

Gaping, Fi struggles to trust her ears, the false messages they are transmitting to her brain. 'Look, I'm the owner of this house and I think I would know if I'd arranged to rent it out.'

The rose-pink of confusion creeps over Lucy Vaughan's face. She lowers her hand. 'We're not *renting* it. We've *bought* it.'

'Don't be ridiculous!'

'I'm not!' The other woman glances at her watch. 'Officially, we became the new owners at twelve o'clock, but the agent let us pick up the keys just before that.'

'What are you talking about? What agent? No agent has keys to my house!' Fi's face spasms with conflicting emotions: fear, frustration, anger, even a dark, grudging amusement, because this *must* be a joke, albeit on an epic scale. What else *can* it be? 'Is this some sort of prank?' She searches over the woman's shoulder for cameras, for a phone recording her bewilderment in the name of entertainment, but finds none – only a series of large boxes sailing past. 'Because I'm not finding it very funny. You need to get these people to stop.'

'I have no intention of getting them to stop,' Lucy Vaughan says, crisp and decisive, just like Fi usually is, when she hasn't been blindsided by something like *this*. Her mouth turns in vexation before opening in sudden wonder. 'Wait a minute, Fi, did you say? Is that Fiona?'

'Yes. Fiona Lawson.'

'Then you must be—' Lucy pauses, notices the querying glances from the movers, lowers her voice. 'I think you'd better come inside.'

And Fi finds herself being ushered through her own door, into her own house, like a guest. She steps into the broad, high-ceilinged hallway and stops short, dumbstruck. This isn't *her* hall. The dimensions are correct, yes, the silver-blue paint scheme remains the same and the staircase has not moved, but the space has been stripped, plundered of every last item that belongs in it: the console table and antique monks bench, the heap of shoes and bags, the pictures on the walls. And her beloved rosewood mirror, inherited from her grandmother, gone! She reaches to touch the wall where it should be, as if expecting to find it sunk into the plaster.

'What have you done with all our things?' she demands of Lucy. Panic makes her strident and a passing mover casts her a correcting sort of look, as if *she* is the threatening one.

'*I* haven't done anything,' Lucy says. '*You* moved your stuff out. Yesterday, I'm assuming.'

'I did nothing of the sort. I need to look upstairs,' Fi says, shouldering past her.

'Well . . .' Lucy begins, but it isn't a request. Fi isn't seeking permission to inspect her own home.

Having climbed the stairs two at a time, she pauses on the upstairs landing, hand still gripping the mahogany curve of the banister rail as if she expects the building to pitch and roll beneath her. She needs to prove to herself she is in the right house, that she hasn't lost her mind. Good, all doors appear to lead to where they should: two bathrooms at the middle front and rear, two bedrooms on the left and two on the right. Even as she lets go of the banister and enters each room in turn, she still expects to see her family's possessions where they should be, where they've always been.

But there is nothing. Everything they own has vanished, not a stick of furniture left, only indentations in the carpet where twenty-four hours ago the legs of beds and bookcases and wardrobes stood. A bright green stain on the carpet in one of the boys' rooms from a ball of slime that broke open during a fight one birthday. In the corner of the kids' shower stands a tube of gel, the kind with tea tree oil – she remembers buying it at Sainsbury's. Behind the bath taps her fingers find the recently cracked tile (cause of breakage never established) and she presses until it hurts, checking she is still flesh and bone, nerve endings intact.

Everywhere, there is the sharp lemon smell of cleaning fluids.

Returning downstairs, she doesn't know if the ache has its source inside her or in the walls of her stripped house.

At her approach, Lucy disbands a conference with two of the movers and Fi senses she has rejected their offer of help – to deal with *her*, the intruder. 'Mrs Lawson? Fiona?'

'This is unbelievable,' Fi says, repeating the word, the only one that will do. Disbelief is all that's stopping her from hyperventilating, tipping into hysteria. 'I don't understand this. Please can you explain what the hell is going on here?'

'That's what I've been trying to do. Maybe if you see the evidence,' Lucy suggests. 'Come into the kitchen – we're blocking the way here.'

The kitchen too is bare, but for a table and chairs Fi has never seen before, and an open box of tea things on the worktop. Lucy is thoughtful enough to push the door to so as not to offend her visitor's eyes with the sight of the continuing invasion beyond.

Visitor.

'Look at these emails,' Lucy says, offering Fi her phone. 'They're from our solicitor, Emma Gilchrist at Bennett, Stafford and Co.'

Fi takes the phone and orders her eyes to focus. The first email is from seven days ago and appears to confirm the exchange of contracts on 91 Trinity Avenue, Alder Rise, between David and Lucy Vaughan and Abraham and Fiona Lawson. The second is from this morning and announces the completion of the sale.

'You called him Bram, didn't you?' Lucy says. 'That's why it took me a minute to realize. Bram's short for Abraham, of course.' She has a real letter to hand too, an opening statement of account from British Gas, addressed to the Vaughans at Trinity Avenue. 'We set up all the utility bills to be paperless, but for some reason they sent this by post.'

Fi returns the phone to her. 'All of this means nothing. They could be fakes. Phishing or something.'

'Phishing?'

'Yes, we had a whole talk about neighbourhood crime a few months ago at Merle's house and the officer told us all about it. Fake emails and invoices look very convincing now. Even the experts can be taken in.'

Lucy gives an exasperated half smile. 'They're real, I promise you. It's all real. The funds will have been transferred to your account by now.'

'What funds?'

'The money we paid for this house! I'm sorry, but I can't go on repeating this, Mrs Lawson.'

'I'm not asking you to,' Fi snaps. 'I'm *telling* you you must have made a mistake. I'm *telling* you it's not possible for you to have bought a house that was never for sale.'

'But it *was* for sale, of course it was. Otherwise, we could never have bought it.'

Fi stares at Lucy, utterly disorientated. What she is saying, what she is *doing*, is complete lunacy and yet she doesn't *look* like a madwoman. No, Lucy looks like a woman convinced that the person *she* is talking to is the deranged one.

'Maybe you ought to phone your husband,' Lucy says, finally.

Geneva, 1.30 p.m.

He lies on the bed in his hotel room, arms and legs twitching. The mattress is a good one, designed to absorb sleeplessness, passion, deepest nightmare, but it fails to ease agitation like his. Not even the two antidepressants he's taken have subdued him. Perhaps it's the planes making him crazy, the pitiless way they grind in and out, one after another, groaning under their own weight. More likely it's the terror of what he's done, the dawning understanding of all that he's sacrificed.

Because it's real now. The Swiss clock has struck. One thirty here, twelve thirty in London. He is now in body what he has been in his mind for weeks: a fugitive, a man cast adrift by his own hand. He realizes that he's been hoping there'll be, in some bleak way, relief, but now the time has come there is something bleaker: none. Only the same sickening brew of emotions he's felt since leaving the house early this morning, somehow both grimly fatalistic and wired for survival.

Oh, God. Oh, Fi. Does she know yet? Someone will have seen, surely? Someone will have phoned her with the news. She might even be on her way to the house already.

He shuffles upright, his back against the headboard, and tries to find a focus in the room. The armchair is red leatherette, the desk black veneer. A return to a 1980s aesthetic, more unsettling than it has any right to be. He swings his legs over the side of the bed. The flooring is warm on bare feet; vinyl or something else man-made. Fi would know what the material is, she has a passion for interiors.

The thought causes a spasm of pain, a new breathlessness. He rises, seeking air – the room, on the fifth floor, is ablaze with central heating – but behind the complicated curtain arrangement the windows are sealed. Cars, white and black and silver, streak along the carriageways between hotel and airport building and, beyond, the mountains divide and shelter, their white peaks tinged peppermint blue. Trapped, he turns once more to face the room, thinking, unexpectedly, of his father. His fingers reach for the armchair, grip the seat-back. He does not remember the name of this hotel, which he chose for its nearness to the airport, but knows that it is as soulless a place as he deserves.

Because he's sold his soul, that's what he's done. He's sold his soul.

But not so long ago that he's forgotten how it feels to have one.

2

March 2017

Welcome to the website of The Victim, the acclaimed crime podcast and winner of a National Documentary Podcast Listeners' Award. Each episode tells the true story of a crime directly in the words of the victim. The Victim is not an investigation, but a privileged insight into an innocent person's suffering. From stalking to identity theft, domestic abuse to property fraud, the experience of each victim is a terrifying journey that you are invited to share – and a cautionary tale for our times.

Brand new episode 'Fi's Story' is available now! Listen here on the website or on one of multiple podcast apps. And don't forget to tweet your theories as you listen using #VictimFi

Caution: contains strong language

Season Two, Episode Three: 'Fi's Story' > 00:00:00

My name is Fiona Lawson and I'm forty-two years old. I can't tell you where I live, only where I *used* to, because six weeks ago my husband sold our home without my knowledge or consent. I know I should say 'allege', that I should say it before everything, so how about this: I 'allege' that what I say in this interview is the truth. I mean, legal contracts don't lie, do they? And his signature has been authenticated by the experts. Yes, the finer details of the crime are still to be revealed – including the identity of his accomplice – but as you can appreciate I'm still coming to terms with the central fact that I no longer have a home.

I no longer have a home!

Of course, once you've heard my story you'll think I have no one to blame but myself – just like your audience will. I know how it works. They'll all be on Twitter saying how clueless I am. And I get it. I listened to the whole of Season One and I did exactly that myself. There's a thin line between a victim and a fool.

'This could have happened to anyone, Mrs Lawson,' the police officer told me the day I found out, but she was just being kind because I was crying and she could see a cup of tea wasn't going to cut it. (Morphine, maybe.)

No, this could only happen to someone like me, someone too idealistic, too forgiving. Someone who'd deluded herself into thinking she could reform nature itself. Make a weak man strong. Yes, that old chestnut.

Why am I taking part in this series? Anyone who knows me will tell you I'm a very private person, so why open myself to mockery or pity or worse? Well, partly because I want to warn people that this really can happen. Property fraud is on the rise: there are stories in the press every day, the police and legal profession are playing catch-up with technology. Homeowners need to be vigilant: there's no limit to what professional criminals will try – or, for that matter, amateur ones.

Also, this is an ongoing investigation and my story might nudge a memory, might encourage someone who has relevant information to get in touch with the police. Sometimes you don't know what's relevant until you hear the proper context, that's why the police don't mind my doing this – well, they haven't asked me *not* to, let's put it that way. As you probably know, I can't be compelled to testify against Bram in a trial, thanks to spousal privilege (that's a laugh). We're still married, though I've considered us exes since the day I threw him out. Of course, I could *choose* to testify, but we'll cross that bridge when we come to it, my solicitor says.

To be honest, I get the feeling she thinks there won't ever be any prosecution. I get the feeling she thinks he's got a new identity by now, a new home, a new life – all bought with his new fortune.

She says it's ever-expanding, the lengths to which people will go to cheat one another.

Even husband and wife.

Speaking of which, you said this has a good chance of being heard by him, that it might be the factor that prompts him to get in touch? Well, let me tell you right now, let me tell *him* – and I don't care what the police think:

Don't even think about coming back, Bram. I swear, if you do, I'll kill you.

#VictimFi

@rachelb72 Where's the husband then? Has he done a runner?

@patharrisonuk @rachelb72 He must have disappeared with the cash. Wonder how much the house was worth?

@Tilly-McGovern @rachelb72 @patharrisonuk Her HUSBAND did this? Wow. The world is a dark place.

Bram Lawson, excerpted from a Word document emailed from Lyon, France, March 2017

Let me remove any doubt straight away and tell you that this is a suicide note. By the time you read this, I'll have done it. Break the news gently, please. I may be a monster, but I'm still a father and there are two boys who'll be sorry to lose me, who'll have reason to remember me more kindly.

Maybe even their mother too, a one-in-a-million woman whose life must be a nightmare now, thanks to me.

And who, may I say for the record, I have never stopped loving.

3

'Fi's Story' > 00:03:10

Ruinous though the situation is, catastrophic even, it is also quite fitting that it's ended the way it has, because it has always been about the house. Our marriage, our family, our *life*: they only seemed to make proper sense at home. Take us out of it – even on one of the smart holidays we used to treat ourselves to when the kids were very young and we very sleep-deprived – and the glue would ooze away. The house sheltered us and protected us, but it also defined us. It kept us current long after our expiry date.

Plus, let's be frank, this is London, and in recent years the house had earned more in capital growth than either Bram or I made from our salaries. It was the family's primary breadwinner, our benign master. Friends and neighbours felt the same, as if our human power had been taken from us and invested in bricks and mortar. Spare cash was sunk not in pension funds or private education or marriage-salvaging weekends in Paris, but in the house. You know you'll get it back, we told each other. It's a no-brainer.

That reminds me of something I'd forgotten till now. That day, that terrible day when I came home and discovered the Vaughans in my house, Merle asked them outright what I hadn't yet thought to ask: *How much did you pay for it?*

And even though my marriage, my family, my *life* had been annihilated, I still paused my sobbing to listen to the answer:

'Two million,' Lucy Vaughan said, in a broken whisper.

And I thought, *It was worth more.*

We were worth more.

*

We bought it for a quarter of that – still a substantial enough sum at the time to have caused us sleepless nights. But once I'd set eyes on 91 Trinity Avenue, I couldn't consider being an insomniac anywhere else. It was the bourgeois confidence of its red-brick exterior, with its pale stone details and chalky white paintwork, wisteria curling onto the wrought-iron Juliet balcony above the door. Impressive but approachable, solid but romantic. Not to mention neighbours with the same sensibilities as ours. One after another, we'd rooted out this delightful spot, sacrificed a tube stop for that languidness you get in the suburbs, that sweetness, the air dusted with sugar like Turkish delight.

Inside was a different story. When I think now of all the improvements we made over the years, the energy the house absorbed (the cash!), I can't believe we took it on in the first place. There were, in no particular order: the remodelled kitchen, the refreshed bathrooms, the reimagined gardens (rear and front), the refurbished downstairs cloakroom, the repaired sash windows, the restored timber flooring. Then, when the 're-' verbs had run out, there was a slew of new: new French doors from kitchen to garden, new kitchen cupboards and worktop, new fitted wardrobes in the boys' bedrooms, new glazed partition in the dining area, new railings and gate for the front, new playhouse and slide out back . . . On it went, a constant programme of renewal, Bram and I (well, mostly I) like the directors of a charitable body carving up its annual budget, all free time spent canvassing for price quotes, booking and supervising labour, searching on- and offline for fittings and fixtures and the implements needed to fit and fix them, curating colours and textures. And the tragic fact is never, ever did I stand back and say 'It's done!' The idea of the perfect house eluded me like a rake in an old romance novel.

Of course, if I had my time again I probably wouldn't touch a thing. I'd concentrate on the humans. I'd re-purpose them before they destroyed themselves.

#VictimFi

@ash_buckley Wow, unbelievable how cheap property was back then.

@loumacintyre78 @ash_buckley Cheap? 500K? Not in Preston. There is life outside London, you know!

@richieschambers Reimagined gardens? Curating colours? Is this woman for real?

*

The previous owners were an older couple, just the kind I imagined we would become. Moderately successful in their teaching careers (they'd bought the place when you didn't need corporate careers like ours or, later, banking ones like the Vaughans', to afford a decent family home) and confident of the job they'd done raising their kids, they'd wanted to release equity, release themselves. They planned to travel and I imagined them as born-again nomads making a desert crossing under the stars.

'It must be very hard to say goodbye to a house like that,' I said to Bram as we drove back to our flat after a visit to measure up for curtains that had ended with a bottle or two of wine. He would have been breaking the speed limit, possibly the drink-driving one too, but it didn't bother me then, before the boys, when there were only our own lives at risk. 'I thought there was something a bit melancholy about them,' I added.

'Melancholy? They're crying all the way to the bank,' Bram said.

Bram, Word document

So how did I get to this point? The point of terminal despair? Believe me, it would have been better for all concerned if I'd reached it a lot sooner. Even the short version is a long story (okay, so this is a bit more than a 'note' – it's a full-scale confession).

Before I start, let me ask this: Was it actually the house itself that was doomed? Did she simply take down all who sailed in her?

The old couple we bought it from were splitting up, you see. The estate agent let that slip when he and I nipped into the Two Brewers for a drink on the way back from a visit with our builder. ('Fancy trying out your new local?' he asked, and I don't suppose I needed any second invitation.)

'Not the sort of information you share with prospective buyers,' he admitted. 'No one likes to think they're moving into a house that's witnessed marital breakdown.'

'Hmm.' I gripped the glass, raised it to my lips, as I would at that bar thousands of times to come. The pale ale was more than acceptable and the place had an old-school feel to it, hadn't yet gone the gastro route of most of the boozers in the area.

'You'd be surprised how common divorce is with these empty nesters,' he went on. 'Pack the youngest off to university and then suddenly you and the wife have time to notice you hate each other and have done for years.'

'Really?' I was surprised. 'I thought it was only our parents' generation who stuck it out for the sake of the children.'

'Not the case. Not in areas like this, people like this. It's more traditional than you'd think.'

'Well, it's only divorce, I suppose. Could be worse. Could be body parts found in the drains.'

'I definitely wouldn't have told you *that*,' he said, laughing.

I didn't say anything about it to Fi. She had some romantic notion of this past-it pair collecting their final-salary pensions and riding camels across the desert like Lawrence of Arabia. Flying hot air balloons over Vesuvius, that kind of crap. Like they hadn't already had forty years of teachers' holidays to travel the world.

We'd seen at least a couple of dozen houses by then and the last thing I needed was her changing her mind about the first one to pass muster on the grounds that 'melancholy' was some kind of airborne disease. Like smallpox or TB.

'Fi's Story' > 00:07:40

Was I aware of the house's escalating value? Of course I was. We were all on Rightmove constantly. But I *never* would have sold it. The opposite: I had hopes of keeping it in the Lawson family, of finding some tax-efficient way for the boys to raise *their* kids there, my grandchildren's heads resting on the same pillows, under the same windows, as my sons' did then.

'How will that work?' my friend Merle asked. She lives a couple of doors down from my place (my *old* place, it's still hard to say it). 'I mean, what're the chances their wives will want to share a house with each other?'

It went without saying that the women of the future would be making the decisions. Trinity Avenue, Alder Rise, was a matriarchy.

'I haven't thought about the official negotiations,' I said. 'Can't you just allow me my little castle in the air?'

'That's all it is, I'm afraid, Fi.' Merle pulled that small secret smile of hers that made you feel so *chosen*, as if she bestowed it only on the very special. Of the women in my circle she was the least concerned with her appearance – petite and nimble-bodied, dark-eyed, occasionally dishevelled – and that made her, inevitably, one of the most attractive. 'You know as well as I do that we'll all have to sell up sooner or later to fund our nursing homes. Our dementia care.'

Half the women on the street thought they had dementia, but they were really just overloaded or, at most, suffering generalized anxiety. That was what had caused Merle, Alison, Kirsty and me to gravitate towards one another: we didn't 'do' neurosis. We kept calm and carried on (we hated that phrase).

When I hear myself now, it's laughable: didn't 'do' neurosis? What about the kind caused by marital breakdown, betrayal, fraud? Who did I think I was?

You've probably already decided that. I know everyone will be judging me – believe me, I'm judging myself. But what's the point of me doing this if I'm not going to present myself honestly, warts and all?

#VictimFi

@PeteYIngram Hmm. IMO losing your posh house isn't on a par with being the victim of violent crime.

@IsabelRickey101 @PeteYIngram Wtf? She's homeless!

@PeteYIngram @IsabelRickey101 She's not on the street, though, is she? She's still got a job.

*

What do I do for a living? I work four days a week as an account manager for a large homewares retailer – recently I've been involved in our new line of ethically sourced rugs, as well as some beautiful pieces by Italian glassmakers inspired by spirals.

It's a great company, with a really holistic and forward-thinking ethos: can you believe they suggested my reduced hours to fit better with my parenting? And this is retail? They'd signed up for an EU initiative to support working mothers and I was in the right place at the right time. Well, you know what they say when that happens: never leave.

It's true, I could probably earn more working for one of the big cut-throat conglomerates, but I've always valued work–life balance over salary. Some of us don't want our throats cut, do we? It's a cliché, I know, but I love working with the kind of handmade products that really make a house a home.

Yes, even now I no longer have one of my own.

Bram, Word document

I worked for the best part of ten years for a Croydon-based orthopaedic supplies manufacturer as one of their regional sales managers for the South East. I was on the road a lot, especially in the early years. I sold all kinds of braces – for knees, elbows, you name it – and neck pillows and abdominal binders, but really they could have been anything. Paperclips, dogfood, solar panels, tyres.

It was meaningless then and it's meaningless now.